A Prince Among Men

Chris Coffman

ODYSSEUS PRESS

Published by Odysseus Press
Springtown, Pennsylvania

A Prince Among Men
Copyright 2021 Christopher Coffman

ISBN: 978-1-7367391-9-8

Cover design: by Virtually Possible Design
Photo on front cover: Eugene Tan
Photo on back cover: Tony Sernack

Printed in the United States of America

Publisher's Cataloging-in-Publication data
Name: Coffman, Christopher W., author.
Title: A prince among men / Chris Coffman.
Description: Springtown, PA: Odysseus Press, 2021.
Identifiers: LCCN: (Pending) | ISBN: 978-1-7367391-9-8 (paperback) | 978-1-7367391-8-2 (Kindle)
Subjects: LCSH Financial crises--Fiction. | Bankers–Fiction. | Banks and banking, International–Fiction. | Family–Fiction. | Sydney (Australia)–Fiction. | Thrillers (Fiction) | Love stories. | BISAC FICTION / Thrillers / General | FICTION / Romance / Suspense Classification:
LCC (Pending) | DDC 813.6--dc23

Author's Note

A Prince Among Men is a work of fiction. The characters, conversations, and events in the novel are the products of my imagination, and no resemblance to the actual conduct of real-life persons, or to actual events, is intended.

Although, for the sake of verisimilitude, the characters participate in situations that may be analogous to situations in which public figures may have been involved, I have imagined those situations without the knowledge or cooperation of any public figure or living person; all the interactions between my characters are completely invented and are wholly my creation.

No aspect of this novel is intended to be understood as a description of real events or to reflect negatively upon any public figures or persons living or dead, or to suggest anybody in real life has ever acted in any way as depicted in this story.

***

To contact the author, email to: coffman@alameda.net.au

In memory of
my beloved Onkel

Christof Wilhelm Bald

Epigraphs

Again, the devil took him to a very high mountain and showed him all the kingdoms of the world and their glory ...'
   Mark 4:8

'In omnibus requiem quaesivi. Si notre condition était véritablement heureuse, il ne faudrait pas nous divertir d'y penser (If our condition were truly happy, we wouldn't need to distract ourselves from thinking about it.)'
   Blaise Pascal, *Pensées* 165

'Jeder sittliche Ausdruck gehört nur dem oberen Teil des Körpers an (A refined gesture is socially acceptable only if it originates from the upper part of body).'
   Johann Wolfgang von Goethe, *Über Leonardo da Vincis Abendmahl zu Mailand*

'Supra-human intelligence expressed itself from the beginning through three mediums— humans, animals, and plants, in each of which life pulses with a different rhythm. Chance came to be utilized as the fourth medium: the very absence of an immediate meaning in the random permits a deeper meaning to be expressed.'
   I Ching: The Book of Changes, Eighth Wing

Contents

Chapter 1

Countless tendrils of water reached out for his body. The withdrawing wave extracted him from the shelf beneath the cliff and pounded him against the rocks as he tumbled back towards the ocean. Max Ring skidded for twenty or thirty metres, tossing helplessly in the tumult of water and stone as he gasped for air – and then more whitewater spun him back towards the base of the cliff. This wasn't that different from falling off a big wave with his sharp, heavy surfboard spinning somewhere close to his body. Years of surfing taught him to stay soft and relaxed while tumbling head over heels in a wave pulling him in all directions.

A sudden deluge of foam broke over him, heavy with water, and twisted his neck. His head snapped against the rocks and he blacked out, but the water was so cold he revived after a millisecond. Stay loose and soft to avoid being cut and pierced – or be knocked unconscious and drown. Be soft, one drop in the water, a drop of water against the rocks.

He heard the roar of another wave and saw a huge dim wall of white foam in the darkness speeding towards him. Yield and be invincible. If Max's body were a rock against the rocks, an edge against the edges, the hammering waves would beat him upon the anvil of the cliff and kill him.

The wave flooded over him, and tonnes of water lifted and smashed him against the boulders. Max surrendered, trying to breathe at every opportunity, willing himself to be as pliable as the water slamming him against the cliff.

He had to calm down. He had to figure this out.

Here I am.

The surge lifted him so high he almost washed up onto a rocky shelf at the base of the cliff, but as he slipped along, bouncing and scraping his agonised body against the rocks, Max realised he was too tired to climb out.

Chapter 2

Max exhaled lightly as he walked along the sandstone paving stones surrounding his swimming pool. It was a perfect winter day in Sydney, and even though it was the shortest day of the year sunlight scattered in all directions, seeming to illuminate everything. Eucalyptus leaves shone like coins against the blue sky, framed by the mansion's stately roofline and the curves of its porch colonnade, his family's world during the lockdowns. It already felt like a century ago.

'Max?'

He'd seen his wife's frown the moment she opened the French doors and walked into the garden looking for him, so he walked in the opposite direction pretending he didn't know she was there until she caught up with him.

'Good morning, beautiful,' he said, turning.

Ilona pursed her lips, her eyebrows drawn together. 'Max, the girls are very upset this morning. If Mort says anything about what happened this weekend –'

He breathed in her scent of jasmine and rose, sandalwood and musk.

'Do we know what happened?'

'Our girls didn't do anything wrong, that's the main point.' Ilona's mahogany-coloured hair swayed just below her jaw. 'I'm not so sure about Trixie Norton. No wonder nobody likes that girl.'

Max and Ilona turned back to the house and walked across Bermuda grass groomed as meticulously as a Brazilian. Lounge chairs Ilona had delivered at the beginning of the lockdowns were arranged on the lawn, their steel and white mesh shining, like diamonds on a jeweller's tray. They had been a good investment, despite costing the price of a small car. The family had spent a lot of time on them for a year and a half.

'So when does work start?' Max asked.

'A week Tuesday,' she said. Max and Ilona were about to spend two million on renovations, completely gutting their house. Planning it had been Ilona's main solace during the lockdown.

'We'll have our own Taj Mahal,' said Max. He'd agreed to each stage of the growing budget as Ilona seemed to go crazier and crazier with Max and their two daughters all living on top of each other; it was the price of peace. He'd had the opposite reaction: he'd loved getting to know his daughters, really for the first time he'd realised, and he'd grown fond of their house just the way it was.

'It'll hardly be the Taj Mahal,' Ilona said. For two years she'd envied Alexandra Norton, Trixie's mum, for finishing her renovations in early 2020. 'The Nortons – that's what they built—and just in time.'

'You realise nobody ever lived in the Taj Mahal, don't you? The Maharaja built it as a sepulchre for his dead wife. Maybe the Nortons should have waited a few decades.'

'You can't help yourself, can you, Max?' Ilona's face was slightly flushed under her almost-transparent make-up. 'Sam and Billie are beside themselves with stress this morning and you make jokes.'

Max blinked. The truth was, he almost never got angry anymore. Perhaps the most important lesson of those two years was it just wasn't worth it. 'I don't know how I do billion dollar deals when you won't explain what happened on a weekend sleepover. Maybe I can offer helpful advice.'

'I don't need your advice, Max – I need your support!'

As soon as vaccines became available, Ilona had done a masterful job expanding the girls' lives again beyond the screens of their computers and phones, inviting over a continual stream of fully vaccinated friends, always ensuring the events included just under the legal limit of participants.

'Darling, you always have my total support, you know that. It's just that for all the girls' lives I left home early in the morning and came home late. I never saw this place in full daylight. And then we all spend two years together and by the end of the first school term since everything went back to normal I feel like I'm watching my girls growing up at arms' length again.'

'Max, this isn't about you – it's about the girls!'

'I provided ample room for us, a small paradise really, in which we could quarantine,' Max indicated the expanse of their home and its walled garden with his arm. 'I do everything I can for you, Samantha and Elizabeth. Why do you think I put up with Mortimer Norton?'

Ilona's eyes appraised him coldly.

'Oh, Max,' she said condescendingly. 'You love having *the most powerful man in New South Wales* as your partner. Be honest with yourself, Max – for once.'

It was one of their oldest shared jokes, and the only one she still used.

'You know what I would love? I'd love to know what Sam and Billie are thinking and feeling,' Max said quietly as he exhaled softly. 'I'd love for them to know what I think and feel, too. I'm their father. That's what I would love, Ilona!'

She stared at him silently, defiantly. It was a stand-off.

Max sighed, turned his palms skyward, and opened his arms. After a moment studying his face, Ilona stepped into his embrace, and they came together like two pieces of sandstone, shaped differently but fitted. It was one of the little things, years ago, that fooled him into thinking they were perfect for each other.

She was a great mother, their daughters were the luckiest girls in Sydney. Max gently kissed Ilona, just where her jaw and cheek converged next to the curtain of fragrant hair. His eyes looked at the house and garden shining in the sunlight. It had been their oasis, their desert island. Now it was going to become Ilona's Taj Mahal. A sepulchre, whether she acknowledged it or not. A tomb for bones and rotting bodies like the Nortons' palatial compound. Why do ugly people so often live in beautiful houses?

'I'll go kiss Sam and Billie and say goodbye,' he murmured.

'Good, darling.' She patted his arms briskly through his suitcoat as she stepped back, disengaging from his embrace. 'And please – no jokes.'

He dimly heard mockingbirds singing in the trees as he walked towards the kitchen while Ilona stayed back to inspect what the gardener had been doing to plant a new bank of peonies.

They'd bought the place several years before Corona, and with the renos it would be worth a bomb. Max stepped through the French doors into the kitchen with a feeling of quiet satisfaction. People are less likely to fuck with you when you live in a twenty million dollar house.

'Good morning, my darling daughters!'

Sam and Billie, already wearing their wide-brimmed straw hats, were scraping the remains of breakfast into the rubbish bin, careful to avoid splattering their school uniforms.

It was so good to see them back in their uniforms. Under the hats they wore their hair in different school-approved styles: Billie had long braids plaited with ribbons in school colours which she had flipped over her shoulders before she leaned over the rubbish, and Sam's hair was drawn back and held by a school-coloured scrunchie in a sloppy bun at the base of her neck. For two years he'd watched them anxiously, both before and after the lockdown, looking for signs of the withdrawal and depression affecting so many school kids.

But Ilona's epic social efforts seemed to have worked wonders. Still, since going back with no masks and everything normal again, they seemed to disappear into their school uniforms. He hadn't realised until the lockdowns how much time even the short commute from Belluvue Hill to the CBD had cost him with his daughters.

The eyes of Sam, their twelve year old, were red. Billie was sneaking glances at Max, assessing him with the same expression Ilona did. He wanted to ask what was wrong, but instead, as they paused like statues, he silently removed their school hats and pressed a kiss onto the top of each head and replaced their hats. It was difficult to know when to prompt the girls, and apart from Ilona's fierce warnings he didn't want to intrude. Perhaps this morning was just another passing drama.

'Have a great day, Sammie! Have a great day, Billie! I love you!' he called to their vanishing, lilac-and-red plaid uniformed backs, feeling futility open like a vacuum.

Max tried to catch their eyes once more, but they flicked away, and his heart ached as he watched them gather their notebooks, murmur their goodbyes, and hurry out the kitchen.

He walked reflectively across the house. He and Ilona barely survived the lockdown, but he and the girls had thrived together—sharing their lives every day had been one of the best experiences of his life—until they went back to school. Now everything had changed back, and he didn't even know why the culminating social event of the semester, the sleepover with Trixie Norton, had gone wrong.

A moment later, the voices of Ilona, Sam and Billie swelled like a small, frightened flock of birds. He stopped and listened, but he knew it would only exasperate Ilona if he reappeared. She always had the girls totally under control.

Max stepped into the garage letting the door close behind him, and felt the space between his shoulder blades loosen like a flower opening. This immaculate interior space was the border territory of his world.

Immediately in front of him the shining surfaces of a black Porsche 911 S convertible gleamed like a dark mirror, Ilona's midnight blue SUV parked next to it. A fluid shadow of him shimmered in the black steel of his Porsche.

Max strolled calmly around the Porsche, admiring its curves shaped for the truth of speed. His reflection moved across dimensions more elemental than the domestic surfaces upon which he felt so helpless and exposed. The Porsche's gleaming chassis incorporated him into its voluptuousness as he walked past the décolletage of its headlamps, assimilating him to its mind-blowing power.

Max flexed his thumb against the key and both doors unlocked with a wet click. He got in and closed his door solid as an airlock. The seat was still damp from his short drive from Bondi Beach after surfing just before dawn.

Max hit speed dial on the Porsche's console. 'Mort, how ya going?'

'Maxie. Good. ZettaData closed down again last night. It's now at 5 cents.'

Ilona's joke in the garden referred to his first meeting with Mort, back when the Rings had just returned from London. One of Max's most trusted friends suggested he meet Mortimer Norton.

As Max had sat in Mort's fairly non-descript office suddenly Mort had his secretary call the Premier of New South Wales, and once he was on the line Mort hit speaker and demanded, 'Barry – who's the most powerful man in this state?' His immediate answer, 'You are, Mort!'

Max touched the ignition and the engine roared to life, its energy nuzzling up and down his spine. As he backed out of the garage, the convertible's canopy opened and folded back like a private jet's undercarriage retracting after take-off.

It had seemed impressive at the time, years before Corona, but now it was the Premier who could shut down life in the entire state anytime she or he felt it was necessary, and it was Mort who had been reduced to sitting on Zoom calls and trying to wheel and deal to be the first to get the vaccines and the booster. Half way through the lockdowns Mort still needed his daughter Trixie to help him get through a Zoom call.

Fresh morning air flowed across the open top as he eased down the driveway and backed the Porsche into the street. Max thumbed the steering wheel's Tiptronic button and caressed the car into first gear. 'Couldn't have come at a worse time,' he said.

Every Kairos is a chronos, but not every chronos is a kairos.

'Why?'

Max eased down the street, the tachometer flitting just above zero, the engine rumbling portentously as he constrained its power to the limitations of posh, tranquil Bellevue Hill. He felt irritated, limited. 'Because it means it's crazy to invest in ZettaData.'

'Since when don't we buy low and sell high? Why wouldn't we invest one or two bars in order to make a hundred bars?' grunted Mort. A bar – a million dollars.

'Yeah, of course – if that's what it takes to make the hundred bars.' Max pressed hard on the accelerator.

Kairos.

Abruptly, the Porsche streaked down the quiet street, unleashing an alarming roar from the metallic pinions that sounded like a nightmare from Ezekiel crying out to the neighbourhood for a reckoning. 'But the whole thing feels clunky.'

'Got any better ideas?' demanded Mort.

That was rich: it was Max who had made them a hundred million by investing aggressively, scooping Australian and US stocks during the worst of the fears and riding them all the way back up while Mort kept insisting that mega-death was right around the corner.

'Mort – I don't see the point of getting tangled up with a company that might go bankrupt any day.'

The acceleration pushed Max back in his seat, old-school iridescent CDs flying around him into the back seat as the car reached 120 kilometres per hour. He was totally free – briefly. Max braked and immediately the Porsche baulked like a bird shot out of the air.

'I want to get Luke Terry's balls in my hands and squeeze them – hard,' said Mort. He didn't seem so tough anymore after two years cowering behind the walls of his Vaucluse compound, letting his wife Alexandra sanitise the groceries because he was too fearful to touch them.

He was in no mood to justify himself to Mort just because they were all back in the office, and Mort's idea had nothing to do with the way Max had made a killing for them during the pandemic. Buying low only works when you can sell high later. Not much chance of that with ZettaData.

'We should run – not walk – from ZettaData,' Max said, keeping his voice calm. 'Anything could happen.'

Max reached the intersection that ends Arthur Street, and to his right a Range Rover was gliding down Bellevue Road, fifty metres up the hill and closing fast.

'That's exactly why I think we should go to ZettaData's AGM this morning,' growled Mort. The Annual General Meeting of ZettaData's shareholders.

Max took a sharp left turn onto Bellevue in the moment between two heart beats, syncopated with the churning pistons of the Porsche's Flat 6.

Kairos.

Annoyed as he was, hurtling down Bellevue Hill Max permitted himself a small smile at the reflection in the rearview mirror of the Range Rover bouncing along, now a hundred metres back. He'd gone the better part of two years without this kind of fun.

Max eased the Porsche to a stop behind an Aston Martin waiting at the red light on New South Head Road.

'Ok – fine,' said Max. 'I'll go – but only for the first half hour.'

He killed the line and pressed another speed dial button. He never said goodbye.

'Yes?' said Ilona's harassed voice.

'Hi Hon,' said Max. 'Mort either doesn't know what happened this weekend, or doesn't care. He didn't say a word about it.'

'Thanks for that, darling,' Ilona said. 'I appreciate it.'

'Love you,' Max said, and killed the line.

One thing was for sure: he'd never dreamed he'd be glad to see morning traffic again—but he was. Max sat at the red light watching cars driven by his friends and enemies, both former and future, streaming past as they poured out of Bellevue Hill, Rose Bay, Point Piper, Vaucluse and Watson's Bay, soon to be joined by cars from Woollahra, Double Bay, Darling Point and Paddington. Thousands of nearly racetrack-ready high-performance cars, mechanical proxies for masculinity and status, gleamed in the morning sun, millions of horsepower rolling along the harbour shore at the pace of a tired nag. The cars streamed out of Sydney's east, where money is spent, towards the Central Business District of Sydney – where money is made.

The light blinked green and Max squeezed his 911 into the cavalcade heading west into the CBD. On Max's left, the blue Audi TT belonged to a guy he'd been mates with at Cranbrook. The heavy, grizzled driver of the black SL 55 just ahead was Graeme Newton, owner of a big structured finance house, his days as an accountant long behind him. From the look of his jowls through the window, he'd not only survived the Corona, but there was more of him now than before.

Max touched the console and made his next call. 'How's the ZettaData capital raising going?' His close friend Richard Wander's firm was running the deal.

'Why do you care?' asked Wander. 'Has Norton & Ring just restructured itself as a charitable institution to give away all your Corona profits?'

'The hell with that,' Max said pleasantly. 'You know I believe in the law of conflict and the survival of the fittest – i.e. *moi*.'

'Stay out of this deal, Max.'

Max was surprised. 'Why?' Surely Wander wanted to attract investors.

'Just stay out of it.'

'Has it already gone belly up?'

'No, it hasn't.'

Wander was one of the few people in the markets Max trusted, but Max was realistic about him. Wander pursued his own interests as if governed by the laws of physics, by a force like magnetism or gravity – totally objective and unaffected by human considerations. Even though he was still only in his late thirties, by acting on his bleak worldview Wander had already amassed a substantial fortune.

'Anything else?' Max asked.

'Nuh.'

Max doubted that, but it was clearly all Wander wanted to say.

Max saw Scott Crossman's gold Lexus fifty metres ahead driving up the hill towards Edgecliff. Crossman was the lead banker to ZettaData. Max cut off Wander and dialled Crossman's number.

'Max! How are you going?'

'Mort and I are coming to ZettaData's AGM this morning.'

'That's great news!'

'Thanks. Anything we should know?'

'Are you and Mort just browsing?'

'Probably. Don't know yet.'

'I know you guys drive hard bargains—'

'That's flattering, Steve . . .'

'But if you have any interest in the company after the AGM, let me know.'

'Thanks, mate.'

'I can deliver the support of the bank group.'

'Appreciate it,' said Max and killed the line.

He watched as a Range Rover eased behind Crossman and hid his Lexus, wondering who Steve was calling now to report his conversation with Max Ring.

Sure beat doing business on Zoom calls.

Interesting. The M & A advisor Wander was saying no, and the lead banker was saying yes – please!

Too bad he and Wander had gone separate ways and started separate firms. Max was truly sick of Mort, but they were yoked together for at least one more deal: closing Norton & Ring's investment in the McConnochie Tunnel Consortium. It was a game changer, especially for Max.

Max crested the hill at Edgecliff and saw the weathered ZettaData billboard, erected back when the company was worth five billion dollars on the ASX. It flashed scenes of sand blowing along Australian beaches and galaxies sprawling towards infinity, while scrolling ten-metre high blue numbers indicated the continual increase in the amount of data the company controlled – these days reminding most drivers the market value of ZettaData was hurtling downwards almost as fast.

Many of the cars around Max bore number plates that ended in a double zero – as if all these investment bankers, barristers, business executives and property developers had secret service licences, and hadn't spent the lockdown in fear of their lives, sitting in their underwear on Zoom calls still trying to make more money than good conscience or sanity could justify.

Lords of the Jungle. Licensed to Kill Her Majesty's enemies.

Right.

Max recalled the *Bhagavad-Gita* where Krishna tells Arjuna his enemies were already dead and so Arjuna is only the instrument of karma: "Therefore O Arjuna, rise up and fight them, confident of success." Everybody on the road was about to start busily competing against each other for wealth to bring home to their families, but they were like those shining blue zeroes on the ZettaData billboard – nothings in themselves but representing the vast resources of the Australian financial system and economy. A zero raises the power of the number one to the power of ten, six zeroes turn the number one into a million, and twenty-one zeroes turn the number one into a Zetta. They brought their emptiness every morning to a financial order that possessed the power to create something from nothing.

Zero – the nothing that is. The secret exponential power of emptiness.

Max pressed one more speed dial button. Another development since life had returned to normal after Covid, his first affair since getting married almost fifteen years before.

'Hey babe,' he said.

'Hi,' said Claudia's sleepy voice, throaty and hollow in a way that was something else entirely from the snarl of his Porsche.

'Watcha doing?'

'Sleeping.'

'I thought I might pop by tomorrow,' Max said. He'd last been with her the week before.

'Sure, darling,' she said.

'See you soon,' he said.

They'd met at an Eden Street Theatre fundraising event when Max walked over and intervened in order to rescue Claudia from the newest director. Max had just sponsored Mort onto the Eden Street Theatre Company Board, a tried-and-true fundraising tactic for the company – and just in time for the premiere of the hottest play in Australia, the Covid drama *TransGod*.

Shortly after his appointment, Mort wrote a low six figure cheque, then wrangled his daughter Peggy a job as Assistant Stage Manager for the new production – and in his first theatre event began hitting on the cast.

It was the first time Max and Claudia met, and to her surprise and relief, after easing her away from Mort, Max turned out to be a well-informed theatre connoisseur. He extracted her from the Surry Hills dump where she was living with four roommates and installed her in an investment apartment he owned in the CBD, where she joined the countless women saving other women's marriages post-Corona.

Shining water glittered through the big plane trees on his right. The masts rising from the hundreds of sailboats moored at Rushcutters Bay cluttered the sky like lances from a host of knights in the entourage of a prince. Directly ahead the office towers of the CBD shimmered and after the brief chat with Claudia, Max felt aroused and fully alive. Max was startled to realise he had reached the bottom of the hill that rises towards Hyde Park.

Sparagmos. An ugly word for an ugly concept: rending, tearing apart, mangling. In ancient Greece *sparagmos* was the word used to describe tearing a person limb from limb. Max had read the book for the play *TransGod* and realised it was a wildly ambitious mash-up of the Euripidean tragedy *Bacchantes, Oedipus Rex* by Sophocles, and the great Tennessee Williams play about evolution *Suddenly Last Summer*. At the climax the unvaccinated character President Orange is torn apart by masked activists he allowed to be infected with the Corona. Euripides and Tennessee Williams wrote their endings so the final atrocity happens off-stage but the payback in *TransGod* culminates in a sensational on-stage finale with a realistic simulation of *sparagmos* and *omophagia*, eating raw flesh. It wasn't easy to rock millennials—but that's why it was so profitable.

Nietzsche's joke about evolution could be the post-script on the pandemic: "Survival of the fittest? Gentlemen, look around you!" Max glanced at the soft, flabby drivers surrounding him on all sides in nearly motionless traffic, fully vaxxed and boosted but for the most part still pale and overweight after the lockdowns, sitting again in their racing machines like oysters inside their shells, and after fearfully obeying the law for so long, illegally holding their mobile phones as their dangerously distracting phone calls rose like incense in the morning air.

Ahead was a diesel Peugeot, over ten years old, chugging up the hill. The Peugeot would just make the last of the green light at College Street, but the fucker was going to leave Max sitting at the red light as it limped through.

Fuck that. Max felt a wild yearning to throw off all the limitations and frustrations that had been building for years.

Kairos.

He flung his body back into the embrace of the bucket seat and accelerated. The Porsche convulsed up William Street, burst in an inky blur through the dazzling morning sunlight into the College Street intersection, and cut right and across the rear bumper of the Peugeot as Max stamped on the accelerator just as the traffic light turned red.

He was through the intersection while the feet of pedestrians were still suspended centimetres above the street on their first step into the crosswalk.

Hovering in his mind was a dim image, a downed driver thrown from his car lying directly in Max's path, helpless. A weird fantasy that had troubled him long before Corona. But it was a lovely sunny morning, on his left the trees of Hyde Park spun by in a blur, and on his right the sandstone of St Mary's Cathedral shone in the winter sunlight with a golden glow.

Not every chronos is a kairos.

Max listened to the soothing murmur of the Porsche engine. There was no longer mega-death hovering invisibly in the air, no downed driver in the street, no intersection with fate – it was just another day in the CBD.

Chapter 3

'The return of their self-esteem?'

Every cell in Peggy Norton's body felt alive, quivering with the same intensity she used to feel when she starved herself.

'Yes, Peggy – their self-esteem!' said Alexandra Norton vehemently. Only Mortimer called his oldest daughter Margaret. 'I want to see my daughters flourish, in fact, if that means testing boundaries a bit, I say "good on them"!'

Peggy glared at Alexandra. She would not allow the voice stifled along with her appetite for all those years to be silenced again. 'So you consider what happened during the sleepover the return of Trixie's self-esteem?'

Alexandra looked indulgently at her, and Peggy felt herself blushing. Peggy was no longer frail and hollow-cheeked as she had been before going to London. She had recovered her model's physique and looks, but Alexandra's inspecting gaze reminded Peggy she was completely outclassed by Alexandra's radiant good looks. Alexandra was one of the few who seemed to have truly thrived during lockdown. 'Peggy, darling, as long as Trixie is happy and full of life, I'll support her choices.'

Alexandra was the daughter of an Earl. This morning she looked wonderful as always: her gabardine slacks perfectly outlined the lower half of her splendid figure, the soft drapes of her silk blouse discreetly concealed her upper body and she sported that rarest of English attributes, excellent teeth.

'But is Trixie really full of life? Do happy girls do what Trixie did?'

'I don't know, darling. Trixie isn't saying why she did it, and I haven't spoken to Ilona Ring about it yet.' Alexandra's heavy, blonde hair gleamed almost brighter than the gold necklace swinging with the casual rhythm of her breasts; she seemed to flow when she moved. As always, she exuded supreme self-confidence.

'You know I love my little sisters. I'm just worried Trixie may be acting out, not being high-spirited. You know what's going on with so many girls their age,' Peggy said carefully. Peggy thought she recognised in Trixie's actions a familiar desire from her own adolescence.

'Acting out?' Alexandra regarded her mockingly, then shook her head. 'Margaret, darling, just because you're a bit of hippie doesn't mean there's anything wrong with other women's grooming choices.'

A few months back, Alexandra and Ilona Ring took their older daughters to their favourite salon in Double Bay, whose beleaguered owners had just managed to re-open have narrowly escaped bankruptcy during the lockdown, to have their bikini lines waxed. The girls were only twelve – there was hardly anything to wax – and the pain!

Peggy couldn't help wondering whether the girls had interpreted the salon outing to mean their mothers considered the first signs of womanhood something to be ashamed of. 'I don't want Trixie walking the same road I did.'

'I appreciate that, Peggy, darling,' Alexandra said softly.

Peggy knew the main source of the eating disorder which had blighted her adolescence and most of her twenties was her relationship with her father, and now that he was Alexandra's husband and father of their two young daughters she was ultra-alert for anything that reminded her of her past.

'I think we just need to see what happens,' said Alexandra briskly, changing tone. Peggy knew Alexandra and Ilona had simply introduced their daughters to a taste of what they themselves endured regularly to maintain full Brazilians.

Peggy raised her eyebrows and shook her head. She hoped she wasn't seeing in Trixie's actions what she herself had felt: the urge to attack, to escape – the rejection of authority she despised by a kind of self-sacrificial purging, even if it had meant making herself the victim. She was especially concerned about what almost seemed to be Trixie's desire for disgrace.

The odds against finding the way back from that road could be long.

Alexandra put her hand on Peggy's arm soothingly. 'Besides,' she said in her most persuasive tone, 'if I thought something truly amiss had happened with my darling Trixie and the Ring girls, I'd shoot Max Ring!'

Peggy laughed weakly. Alexandra had run their palatial compound like a hospital during the lockdown, maintaining a standard of pristine hygiene, mindful that Mort was well into one of the most at-risk age groups and he was overweight and a former smoker.

'I mean it,' Alexandra said. 'I have my father's service revolver, you know, in the night stand next to our bed.' She pointed upwards in the direction of the master bedroom suite.

'Alexandra!' Peggy exclaimed. 'You can't own a pistol in Australia. It's against the law – you could go to prison.'

Alexandra looked at Peggy, arching her eyebrows in exasperation. 'Oh, as if you're the one to talk darling—Miss Quarantine Runner! You could have been Covid Peggy—responsible for infecting thousands of Sydneysiders!'

Her brother Hugh had died during the lockdowns in a motorcycle crash just below Byron Bay Lighthouse when he had illegally left their mum's house. Almost immediately, her father filed a lawsuit to bring Hugh's body from the morgue in Byron to Sydney. The moment Peggy found out, she hitched a ride with a truckie who was a good mate and permitted as an essential service to keep transporting goods between Sydney and Byron.

'Oh, as if—' said Peggy. 'Regardless of what you said about Vitamin C and D and zinc, I was perfectly healthy then, and I'm perfectly healthy now.'

Peggy had appeared unannounced outside the gates of the Norton compound in Vaucluse.

'Of course you were, darling,' Alexandra said soothingly.

She so wanted to reconcile her parents that she'd agreed to Alexandra's insistence that she self-quarantine in the gatekeeper's cottage for fourteen days when she came down from Byron, even though she tested negative on arrival and was double vaxed and boosted. She admired how fiercely protective Alexandra was of her father.

'I don't know how you meet the people you know darling,' Alexandra shook her head. 'Probably the less said about that, the better.'

Peggy knew she was joking – just.

Alexandra was now a grande dame of the Eastern Suburbs, but Peggy knew that as a young woman Alexandra rode a motorcycle to Dakar, repaired Range Rovers in the savannah of southern Africa, cleaned out the clogged sluices of her stepfather's barns in Derbyshire, and cut the glands out of deer carcasses as she and her father dressed his kills in the Scottish Highlands. She got things done.

'Well, anyway, you shouldn't have a pistol, it's a serious crime here in Australia.'

'The lawbreaker lecturing me about breaking laws!'

'My duties to my loved ones comes before the laws of any premier or any parliament!'

'Of course they do, darling,' said Alexandra. 'Mortie and I feel the same way, that's why he organised the shipment of those Pfizer vaccines.'

Peggy felt herself flushing to the roots of her hairline. Her father somehow had managed to get his hands on the first vaccines before they were generally available in Australia, had offered one to her and Hugh, but not to Tori. So she and Hugh refused to accept. Their father's action had increasingly preyed on Hugh's mind, and Peggy often wondered if it may have been the last straw.

Alexandra seemed to have forgotten, or perhaps never knew about it. In any case, she seemed to misunderstand why Peggy suddenly looked so upset.

'People like us can be locked down, but we don't go to prison. Let's be frank, darling – we just don't. It's the way it is. I don't support it, but it's reality.'

Peggy grimaced with disapproval and tried to calm herself.

Alexandra tossed her head. 'And you and I are just going to have to agree to disagree about the weekend. I'm focused on the fact the girls seem to have bullied Selena Wood-bridge, and I'd hate for that to somehow cause an incident at Nightingale School. This morning will be the test.'

'To see if it's blown over?'

'To see if what's blown over?' asked Mort, appearing at the bottom of the staircase. He was a powerful, compact figure with the deceptive stillness and sudden reflexes of an old cat.

'Oh nothing, darling,' Alexandra said, smiling, her hand floating around Mort's neck and shoulders as she drew him to her for a kiss on the cheek. He was resplendent in the clothes Alexandra had chosen for him, one of many changes in the father Peggy knew growing up.

Alexandra had achieved an amazing transformation in her husband. Peggy was the first to acknowledge her father often seemed to be a new man. Otherwise she would never have agreed to continue living in the cottage on the edge of their Vaucluse property.

'Peggy and I were just talking about this morning being the first day of the new term. Trixie's feeling a little stressed.'

'Mmmm,' he murmured. Mort looked at Alexandra, his expression sympathetic. 'Poor Tinkerbell, what's the matter – is she ok?'

'Oh yes, of course she is, darling,' said Alexandra. She tossed her thick blonde hair. Peggy watched him relax.

Her father was looking at Alexandra as if he could eat her. Their bond was a mystery, and to Peggy, however she tried to be accepting, a repellent one.

Alexandra once told her why she adored Peggy's father, despite his rough manners and the working-class Australian accent he had picked up after emigrating from Europe. Alexandra said when they met, Mort immediately reminded her of her own father, who beneath his upper-class English accent, his vast, mortgaged properties, and his patina of refinement was at heart a cheeky old rogue.

'It's just a little mix-up with another girl. It happened this weekend during that sleep-over at the Rings, and Trixie's just worried about seeing Selena this morning.'

Mort's forehead drew together into the familiar network of lines. 'The Rings?' he growled.

Alexandra smiled indulgently at her husband, nibbled his earlobe, and blew a gentle puff of breath into his ear. He flinched with a shy smile and kissed her.

'Yes, darling,' Alexandra said.

Peggy smiled bitterly. She had more on her mind this morning than Trixie's predicament, even though compassion for her little half-sister had distracted Peggy, until now, from the constriction in her chest that had been twisting and tightening since the night before, when Peggy's mum called her in tears.

'Poor little darling,' her father said. 'Where is Tinkerbell? I'll go give her a hug.'

Surprising and a little nauseating as it was, Peggy had to admire how Alexandra had re-directed her father's attention. But this was the same man driving her mum into bankruptcy – and Peggy knew it was exactly what he intended to do. Her mum had just received another twenty thousand dollar invoice from her lawyers – the third month in a row – the cost of defending herself against Mort's lawyers.

'Hugh's body is still in a metal cabinet!' Peggy hadn't felt the rage coming until she was actually shouting at her father.

His face was suddenly alert. Alexandra turned to Peggy with a warning expression.

'Don't start, Margaret,' he said in a low voice.

'Then *when*? How long are you going to keep him there?'

Mort blamed his ex-wife Tori for their only son's death, a bitter irony to Peggy. The thought of Hugh's body lying in the morgue as lawsuits escalated between her parents felt like a curse on them all.

'Your mother's gotten to you.'

She could see her father sizing her up, taking in the healthy glow of her cheeks, the newly-returned curves of her figure. For years, her hunger had trumped his terrifying and overwhelming power. Becoming small and fragile had been the ultimate weapon, lethal as it almost became. His bewilderment, exasperation and anger as she wasted away was the first authentic and reliable proof he had ever revealed that he loved her. Now that she was healthy again, she felt disarmed.

'Mum has gotten to me? You're suing *her*. *You're* destroying her financial security and she's going to lose her farm if you don't stop. *You've* placed an injunction on Hugh's body, so we can't remove it from that awful morgue, have his body cremated and scatter his ashes in the waves the way he would have wanted – and it's *Mum* who has gotten to me?'

'I'm doing what's best for our family,' he said, putting his arm around Alexandra. Punishing Tori wasn't his sole motivation. He was constructing a new Norton family crypt in Old South Head Cemetery, right next to the enormous Logan family crypt. He had formed the idea on a trip to England when he and Alexandra visited her family's burial plot on the Blasingame family estate in Berkshire.

'Oh, Dad – drop that lawsuit against mum!'

'Don't ever try to tell me what to do,' he said. Above his white shirt collar her father's face darkened.

She glared at her father, incandescent with anger. 'Give us Hugh's body – now!'

He was probably capable of attacking her again.

'Fuck off.'

She had to believe he loved her, even without the protection of her hunger, no matter how terribly he acted. She had to.

She stepped up to him and grabbed his shoulders. 'Daddy – please!'

'I'm warning you Peggy,' he said, pulling her fingers off with his incredible strength. He pushed her away. 'I'm this close to tossing you out—and I mean out of the shack. You can just fuck off.'

'Oh, Mortie, darling,' Alexandra said soothingly. 'You don't know what you're saying.' She looked at Peggy. 'He doesn't mean it, darling. You're family. The girls and I are so happy you came back to us.' She patted Mort's arm. 'And your father is, too. You have such tempers, you two!'

'I'm not afraid of you,' Peggy said hotly to her father.

Her father observed her silently, his eyes smouldering the way she remembered so well. 'Get out,' Mort said slowly.

'You're being so hateful, Daddy.'

When she was growing up her hunger had been a weapon as subtle and decisive as any martial art, allowing her to control the father she couldn't tame, much less heal. But hunger had also stolen her energy, leaving her detached, merely a family observer, invulnerable behind its force field, unable to save her mother or her brother – and now she was ready to fight.

'The girls will be down in a second. Keep your voices down.'

'I have to go back upstairs to my office and make some phone calls, anyway,' Mort said sullenly.

'Shhh!' Alexandra hissed. She glanced nervously towards the far entrance of the kitchen. A sudden clatter of school shoes signalled Trixie and Anastasia hurrying down the hall, no doubt shooed by their nanny.

Trixie burst from the suite of rooms anchored by the kitchen, wearing the lilac- and-red plaid on a dun background of her Nightingale School uniform and sporting an exasperated frown.

'Good morning, Princess,' said Mort with a loving tone that pierced Peggy. At least her sisters hadn't had to make themselves sick to hear him speak that way – yet.

Trixie shrugged her book bag to the floor with a crash, totally accustomed to the luxury of the family kitchen, as neither Peggy –and probably her father – ever would be. Trixie knew exactly where to push the wooden panelling to make one of the three concealed refrigerators swing open. Peggy had watched her father reduced to pounding with his fist on the cabinetry, trying to find that spot.

Anastasia bolted in next. 'Good morning, sweetie,' Mort said, his face creasing into a smile. 'You wear that frown all the time and it'll grow on your face, honey,' he told Trixie.

Peggy watched him hover awkwardly around the girls as they rummaged through the refrigerator, their backs to him. He glanced once or twice at Alexandra, hoping for some kind of signal what to do.

Alexandra walked over to Peggy and put her arms around her, nuzzling her ear and murmuring, 'It will be all right, darling, once he cools down.'

Peggy smiled, and reached up with one hand to let it rest affectionately on Alexandra's shoulder.

Alexandra's sympathy reminded Peggy mildly of the wonder and relief Peggy experienced when her body restarted after she recovered from bulimia. It was a joyful redemption that continued to give her strength. The various ticks and gag reflexes subsided, and as her tissues were replenished she felt the gushing return of her energy – even the reappearance of the monthly life force that had vanished for years like a river going underground beneath the desert outback. Yes, she was even glad to be bleeding again.

To triumph over her father when she was not much older than her half-sisters, she had found the courage to die. To succeed against him now, she would have to practice the courage to live.

Chapter 4

Mortimer Norton looked out his office window on the top floor of his Vaucluse mansion, surrounded by eight walled acres of manicured garden along the Sydney harbourfront. Across the water to the west rose the office towers of downtown Sydney, incandescent in a golden torrent of morning light.

The Norton family had a great lockdown, thanks to Alexandra who'd convinced him to buy the spread and completed the renos just before Corona. Even on a bad day in the markets he was worth a quarter billion, and every fucking dollar was a part of him, like a cell in his body. He didn't mind giving Alexandra credit for their luxurious internal exile during Covid, but his blood pressure went up at the thought of Max Ring trying to take credit for the killing they'd made at the same time.

Max was a nobody when he returned from London to Sydney. It's no good having ideas if nobody will take your call, and he was the one who made that happen. At least he got two-thirds of the profits and Ring got one-third.

His wealth gave him his ability to create events and shape them the way he wanted, to make the world work in a certain way because he willed it. Max Ring didn't have that right, and never would. The way Ring took credit for the hundred bars they'd made during Corona was a kind of stealing, and he would no more let somebody steal a thousand dollars from him than think of letting somebody slice a piece of skin off his finger. He wasn't going to put up with Ring stealing the credit, either.

Mort's gaze found the top floor of the tallest tower in the CBD, an ugly mountain casting deep shadows over the best parts of downtown Sydney. The headquarters of the Australian Natural Gas Company, ANG. ANG rhymed with 'Fang', and rightly so.

His eyes narrowed. Behind those windows, perhaps in a meeting, or possibly taking a call while he enjoyed his coffee, was ANG's Managing Director, Luke Terry. Terry was hell-bent on costing him one hundred million dollars. One hundred fucking bars, as much as the Corona windfall.

For all he knew, Terry might be looking right back at him. Now that Terry was back in his office, Mort knew his waterside mansion was visible and unavoidable, like a dog's balls, right in the middle of Terry's spectacular view. For decades their interests had repeatedly collided, not because he and Terry were different, but because they were so essentially alike. Early in their careers they had even played crucial roles helping one another.

While Mort rose from penniless immigrant to great wealth and influence over almost everyone in Sydney who mattered, Luke Terry rose from being the crazy-brave street brawler Mort first met to the tribune of the New South Wales union movement. Terry's powerful intellect and strategic vision had garnered for him the role of managing director of the largest government-owned company in Australia, and perhaps a gurney to be the country's next prime minister.

After decades of grudging co-existence, since everything became fully normal again Luke Terry had made it clear to everyone who mattered, from the premier down, that the tunnel deal wasn't going to earn Mortimer Norton a brass razoo. Maybe the newly obvious power of government during Corona had given Terry a rush of blood to the head.

McConnochie Engineering was the construction company sure to win the right to build Sydney's last great tunnel – a vast subterranean structure that would direct millions of cars around Sydney's perimeter and connect all the existing tunnels into one network. Billions of dollars were at stake. Greenlighting the project was a huge signal by both Federal and State government—even bigger and more consequential than ending the lockdowns, sending children back to school, and ending all the mask mandates and other restrictions—of confidence in Sydney and in Australia's future. The economy would come roaring back bigger than before Corona, and with it would return Sydney traffic. And so it was proving to be.

The tunnel project was the largest deal of the twenty-first century so far in Australia. Terry's decision to blackball him was probably a taste of things to come after the next election. Mort couldn't let Terry get away with it.

Norton dialled a number.

'Leonard Roebling,' a voice answered.

'So how are we going to bankrupt ZettaData?' Mortimer asked.

The ANG building seemed to smoulder in the morning light.

'I've been through all the data. The simplest, lowest risk option is to get the banks to pull the plug,' Roebling said. 'That won't be hard – they're very nervous.'

Mort could hear the fatigue in Roebling's voice. He'd been at the office all night analysing options for ZettaData's destruction. 'Yeah, yeah,' Mort said, disappointed Roebling's recommendation was so obvious. 'But the banks might do that themselves anyway. I want to make sure Luke Terry knows I'm the one who crushed his investment – and I want it to blow up this week!'

'You could get GenCorp, their largest customer, to pull their contracts,' Roebling suggested.

'Yeah, I'm seeing my mate Louie for a coffee this morning; he's on GenCorp's board. The problem is, management like what they're getting from ZettaData: apparently the data is great. GenCorp won't pull the contract,' said Mort. 'I liked your last option.'

'It's the riskiest,' said Roebling.

Sunlight flooded his home office. Every imperfection in the glass of the floor-to-ceiling windows, every fingernail of dried salt on their surfaces, even the least filament of fabric rising from sofa or carpet, sparkled in exquisite detail like jewellery under x-ray. Mort hated the light and turned away from the windows. He paced, his arms crossed.

'There's no going back if we do it,' said Roebling.

'That's fine with me,' said Mort. 'I want a king hit on Luke Terry.'

'Well, that's what it will be. But it's messy. It'll take down all the small shareholders, too.'

'Any issues with the Corps Act?' He couldn't bloody ask Max.

'Not if you stick to the script,' said Roebling.

'Ok. I'll rehearse it with you when I get to the office,' said Mort. He paused. 'Now listen, Max agreed to go to the AGM this morning and I want him publicly mixed up in this from the start. Don't say a word to him. Got it?'

'No worries, Mort,' Roebling said. A small sigh exhaled from the speaker, seemed to hang in the air, and was gone.

Roebling was tired, but so what. Mort pushed a button and ended the call.

He hadn't slept well himself. The police rescue helicopters had been at it again last night, flying overhead on their way to The Gap. Just on the other side of the walled mansions, gardens, and quiet winding streets of Vaucluse rises the escarpment that forms Sydney Harbour, its ancient shale and sandstone directly exposed to the ceaseless hammering of the South Pacific. The Gap is a stone cauldron hundreds of metres high, slippery with the ocean spray that has eaten into the battered ocean-facing cliffs like bone cancer. The cruel rocks at its base are washed by great swells that rush across them and explode against the cliffs.

The Gap is a favourite place to commit suicide. It's easy to walk from Vaucluse and Watson's Bay through the quiet park surrounding The Gap and jump off the cliff. The night before, two helicopters had circled for hours above the Norton mansion. The police don't launch them while a person is still on the cliff, because the slightest surprise makes them jump.

Mort's brow knitted. There must have been a problem pulling out the body. God damn whoever it was. He'd hardly slept. Selfish fuck. The world was better without him.

Mort started down the staircase. Life evolves, it never stands still. In a year or two, he might be worth four or five hundred million, maybe more – or a new prime minister might be trying to drive them out of Australia. Look how badly things went wrong with Hugh. Fuck. Who needed a son like him anyway? Fucking Max Ring was just like him.

Mort looked at his watch. He had to get to the ZettaData AGM.

By splattering on the rocks of The Gap, that fucking jumper – whoever he or she had been – left him with hardly any sleep this morning. At the start of a day as big as this one was going to be.

Chapter 5

Ilona Ring perched on the seat of her Lexus as she glided under the palm trees lining the driveway of Nightingale School for Girls. Even behind the wheel she kept her posture perfect. Her mother was short and wiry and dynamic, still aggressive in her sixties, and most importantly *erect* – while her tall, lanky father had bobbed in the eddies of life, a high school teacher with a useless family pedigree, slumped shoulders, and a drooped head. She grew tall like her father but hoped to be like her mother. Winner, loser: posture signalled the difference.

'Mummy,' said Billie from the back seat. 'Why was Daddy so red in the face when he left this morning – was he mad again?'

'Darling, your father is a very important man, with lots of responsibilities,' Ilona said. 'He was very stressed this morning about work.'

'Ok,' said Billie, resigned.

It was a small lie, but it made her feel anxious. When she suddenly felt anxious, Ilona often heard the words of the Nightingale School song scrolling through her mind: 'Parth-en-ope, we sing to thee, Of knowledge, hope and chast-i-ty ...'

The tune was as catchy as a breakfast cereal jingle: Tra-dee-la dee la-dee-dee.

They had come to a standstill in the queue to discharge the girls at the school gates. Behind her sunglasses Ilona's eyes glanced in the rearview mirror and scrutinised the curve of her cheekbone. In the last year, she had decided to follow Catherine Deneuve's advice that, after a certain age, a woman has to decide between preserving the looks of her face or her body. To avoid the gaunt look that started to creep into many women's faces around forty, Ilona had allowed extra kilos to cling to her body. Alexandra had suggested collagen and botox injections but Ilona was still squeamish, and besides a bit of the fat had gone to her breasts, which was nice. But she had to accept the slight thickening of her waistline, and the blurring of the lines of her upper thighs, as a fair exchange for naturally preserving the glow of health in her face. What she hadn't expected was the flood of unruly emotions that emerged once her hunger vanished.

The brake lights in front flared red, and Ilona eased to a stop where the driveway curved along the façade of the main school building. Right now a tide of emotions, like little hungry fish, were swirling inside her and nibbling away: a dread of public confrontation between Selena and Sammie at the school gates, a mummy lion sense of indignant protectiveness towards her daughters – but also a pang of shame for bungling her responsibility for their daughters, and *in loco parentis*, for Trixie Norton, on Saturday night.

'Parthenope, we sing to thee ...'

Ilona carefully set the parking brake, turning to her daughters with a bright smile. 'All right, my darlings – hats, book bags, tennis rackets – quick sticks! Have a wonderful day – love you!'

'Bye mummy! Love you!' sang Billie, while Sam slouched under her backpack, thrust herself off the seat, and slipped down through the open side door like a luge rider. The girls released themselves in a sudden flurry of hats, jackets, school uniforms, bags, and rackets and flopping art projects. Sam was a very young swan, Billie still a cygnet.

The car was suddenly a void. Ilona felt abandoned, exactly as she had felt this morning waking up in an empty bed, while Max was already surfing at Bondi. She'd gone from feeling suffocated by his presence during the lockdowns to feeling abandoned as soon as the beaches re-opened. Sometimes she felt lonelier in her marriage than when she was living by herself.

A Mercedes station wagon pulled away from the curb where it had been hidden from Ilona's view. Oh my God – it was the Woodbridge family car!

She could see young Selena Woodbridge standing facing her girls like a stone statue. Oh no.

Ilona eased her Lexus ahead in order to keep them in sight a bit longer. Selena was saying something with great emotion. Sam and Billie stopped. It was hard to see from the Lexus, but their hats were moving back and forth towards each other. Their bodies, burdened by heavy backpacks, were staccato and jerky.

Ilona caught her breath, gripping the steering wheel so tightly her rings hurt her fingers. Oh, why did it have to happen here?

Selena, her face contorted and glazed in tears, turned and ran clumsily towards the main gate.

Nightingale School was a simple, elegant universe at a manageable scale which included everything essential to life in Sydney, and excluded everything unseen, imponderable, or objectionable: poverty, sickness, reminders of failure or death. Only the awesome power of Corona had managed to disrupt, temporarily, the illusion that Nightingale was not only a more perfect version of their world, but its essence.

Selena was hustling into the throng of girls passing through the gate when Miss Whidbey, Headmistress of Nightingale School, spotted her. Ilona watched as Miss Whidbey's iron grey head nodded towards Selena. Stricken, Ilona watched the possibility of failure appear abruptly in the very place it couldn't possibly exist.

A car horn sounded briefly, politely, behind Ilona's Lexus. Ilona watched Miss Whidbey stoop over Selena, draw herself to full height and scan the crowd of girls, no doubt looking for her girls.

Ilona's chest clenched. She hadn't been able to admit her real fear to herself until forced to – which was now. It was, and wasn't, about Selena receiving nasty Snapchat messages, and what Sam and Trixie had done to themselves - which was awkward enough.

What really bothered her was the strange Instagram post Billie showed her this morning on her IPhone. What was the image – and could it possibly be connected to the sleepover?

Nightingale girls weren't allowed to turn on their mobiles during school hours. Ilona would have no way of knowing about Miss Whidbey's interrogation of Sam and Billie – or its consequences – until three that afternoon. Unless the school contacted her.

Out of her sense of isolation appeared the first icy feelings of panic. She couldn't ring Max – she hadn't really told him anything about what happened Saturday evening, and now was no time to tell him. Earlier this morning, it had taken every ounce of self-control to hide from him the loneliness she had been feeling. If she revealed any vulnerability to him, he would immediately challenge her control of their family, and she would have to start over. She had worked too long and hard to take that risk.

'Magda ... Wexroth,' pronounced Ilona distinctly towards the microphone of her car phone. She hummed to herself unconsciously while listening to the dial sounds. Ilona and Magda had grown up together in Erskineville, where Ilona's father taught at the local high school. He never understood why almost nobody cared he was directly descended from the Reverend George Erskine who founded Erskineville in 1830. But Magda's family were impressed.

'Hello, darling,' said Magda's warm voice. 'How did you go?'

Of course Magda knew all about the bullying and Sam's side of what she and Trixie had done to themselves. Ilona and Magda had discussed it for almost two hours on Sunday afternoon, but Ilona had yet to share about the Instagram post Billie showed her before breakfast.

'I'm telling myself it's going to be ok,' Ilona breathed.

'What happened?' Magda's voice was taut with concern.

Ilona nosed the Lexus into the line of cars slowly moving out to New South Head Road. 'Selena ran right up to the headmistress. I don't know what she will say about Sammie and Trixie. Miss Whidbey is known to make examples of girls.'

'As if!' Magda snorted.

Magda was right, Ilona knew. Miss Whidbey wouldn't dare discipline Trixie Norton. Mort had just been elected to the school board, and was close friends with the chairman, Justice Rosebery, who served on the High Court. Mort was also close to Kent Logan, whose family had donated the money for many buildings on the campus. Max wasn't as well connected – but Mort and Max were partners, after all. The Ring girls were hard targets, too.

It was good Magda was thinking clearly. 'I ... hope so,' Ilona said hesitantly.

'Are you worried about her parents making a fuss?'

Ilona considered for a moment. 'The Woodbridges can't easily cause trouble.' They were *only doctors*. Ilona caught herself – how had she ended up being so haughty?

But she couldn't quite bring herself to tell Magda about the Instagram image. Maybe it was nothing – she didn't want Magda to think she was going mad. 'It's just ... it's just that I feel so alone in this –'

'Of course you do, you poor darling. Max needs a good smack! He is so out of touch and completely self-absorbed! I'd be surprised if he remembers how many daughters he has! You are practically raising those sweet girls all by yourself, you poor thing. They're so lucky to have you as mum, especially with a father like Max.'

'You know how I put my foot down with Max during Covid,' Ilona said. She had done exactly what Magda encouraged her to do – assert herself and demand respect. 'I got crazy upset!'

If she really let herself feel these things the pain would be unbearable.

'Of course you did, Sweets – it's so sad,' said Magda.

'I push and prod him – anything to get a reaction! I don't think he feels anything. I'm not sure I even matter to him.'

'You're the best thing in his life, honey.'

'I so hope you're right,' said Ilona. 'Max doesn't seem to have any feelings – he's just turned himself into a machine to make money. I do everything I can to protect the girls.'

'Don't worry about the girls, it will all be fine.'

Magda had always been her rock, even when she'd been cooped up in her tiny apartment during Covid. Now Ilona was finding herself also leaning more and more on her relationship with Sammie and Billie – and Alexandra Norton. Alexandra was so experienced, so capable, so confident – and she had one of the worst husbands of them all!

Magda kept talking but Ilona tuned her out as she steered through the heavy morning traffic in Double Bay. Magda wasn't married. She'd been pressuring her long-term boyfriend for the last couple years, but Ilona sensed he had listened to what Magda said about the Rings and come to his own conclusions about the wisdom of proposing.

The revelations about the sleepover began Sunday night and continued through breakfast this morning – what would Alexandra's response be? In forty-eight hours, out of a clear blue sky, she suddenly felt on the verge of being completely discredited and having the most important relationships in her life at risk: daughters, husband, and Alexandra.

And now that damn Instagram. Oh god!

The image could be anything you wanted to project onto it: cleavage, bum cleavage, a close-up of lips, outlines of boulders at North Bondi, scoops of gelato from Messina, the crease in the side of a peach floating out of a blurred perimeter. Anything, really. Whatever it was originally, the image had been filtered into enhanced contrast and dramatic Pucci lime-green and tangerine orange tints. The caption was Sl33ping BeauTie ... juvenile and harmless – apparently.

What was it, Ilona wondered?

' . . . it's all a storm in a teacup,' Magda summarised briskly. 'What else do you have on this week?'

Another call was coming through on Ilona's phone.

'Magda, darling, I have to go –' Ilona said breathlessly.

It was Alexandra Norton ringing

Chapter 6

'Hey.' Max greeted Matina as the lift doors opened and he stepped into the reception area of Norton & Ring.

'Good morning, Max,' she said. Her dark, very bright eyes followed him from the reception desk with its bold grey steel letters spelling out 'Norton & Ring'. He and Mort had taken over the lease of a struggling English merchant bank, one of several whose eighteenth and nineteenth century glory had faded, and hammered their own names on spikes into the dark wood of the reception desk.

'Is Mort in yet?'

'What do you think?'

It wasn't long before Max regretted his decision to establish Norton & Ring.

Max had just returned from London when he and Mort agreed to their partnership, and he was finding it more difficult than he expected to find a suitable role mid-career in the small world of Sydney. So he'd reluctantly agreed to a one-third / two-third's partnership in Mort's favour.

'He'd better get here soon—he wants us to go to an AGM at eleven o'clock.'

'Mort will do what he always does.'

'What he wants,' said Max.

Matina's eyes gleamed. Was there something malicious glinting in her fathomless eyes this morning?

When Max quickly established his worth to the partnership, culminating five years later in the fortune he'd made for them during Covid while Mort was sitting in his underwear learning how to use Google to find the latest vaccine developments and spending the rest of his time badgering ministers and bureaucrats to accelerate their anti-Covid policies.

Max smelled toast and heard the hum of the coffee grinder. 'See ya,' he said to Matina and instead of going directly to his office, he walked through the board room and into the firm's kitchen.

'G'day,' said Max. Two analysts, Leonard Roebling and Alyssa Hauptraum, stood in the middle of a phalanx of food appliances. 'Is there any reason Mort is interested in ZettaData besides the fact Luke Terry is a shareholder?'

Roebling was waiting for his toast. The commercial-grade kitchen was used frequently for client functions, but its true purpose was to encourage staff to arrive before breakfast and work until long after dinner. He looked at Max, face faintly flushed and eyes bright, then cast his gaze downward. 'I don't know what Mort's thinking, Max.'

Two large companies owned most of ZettaData, SpecTel and ANG. SpecTel was bankrupt and based in America, and Luke Terry was Managing Director of ANG, which happened to be the largest government-owned company in Australia.

'Your research should be showing Mort what to think,' Max said crossly. 'What do you think of the company?'

'Covid helped ZettaData a lot, but the company has too much debt.'

'Why is the stock trading at five cents? It's down ninety-nine percent from its high.'

Roebling shrugged. 'They're just going cashflow positive now, three years behind schedule. The government doesn't have any money left to bail them out, and the Americans just got taken over themselves by a big hedge fund.'

'Which one?'

Alyssa Hauptraum looked at Max with her voyeur's stare. 'Nebula.'

She had spent so much of her young life looking at screens brimming with financial information and social media posts, especially during the lockdowns, that she didn't seem to register when a real human was looking back at her.

'Brilliant,' said Max. Nebula was owned by Todd Edgell, the most successful hedge fund investor in the world during Covid, and still on a hot streak.

'And of course ZettaData still has public investors, so we have to be super-careful about the Corps Act,' said Max. 'Not that Mort cares—but I do.'

The extremely complicated provisions of the *Corporations Act 2001* – called 'the Corps Act' so that it sounded like 'the Corpse Act' – requires scrupulous compliance by financiers.

Roebling and Hauptraum regarded Max expressionlessly.

'Who's got the float?'

The float is the number of company shares actually available for trading on the Australian stock exchange, and since between them Todd Edgell and Luke Terry controlled seventy percent of the shares there wasn't much float.

'Instos are out. Only small investors are left.'

Institutional investors, who Max could count on to be rational, had abandoned Zetta-Data. The remaining investors were tens of thousands of small shareholders holding a few shares each that were now five cents: close to worthless. It was a financial, legal and public relations nightmare just waiting to happen.

'What do you lot reckon ZettaData is worth?'

'As a going concern?' asked Roebling. His toast popped up.

'Oh, is it that bad?" exclaimed Max, annoyed. Roebling was stalling, for some reason. 'Mort's thinking we might tip a couple bars into it. What do you think, Alyssa?'

'Their crypto strategy might work,' said Alyssa in her German accent, carefully cutting an apple and a banana into muesli moistened with organic skim milk. She, Roebling and the rest of the team had greedily taken the bait, feeding on all the delicacies Max and Mort made available to lure them back to the office after Covid.

'What crypto strategy?'

'The company is executing a pivot from their Big Data and cloud storage business,' she said, pronouncing every word with precision. 'They have a new crypto coin ready to launch.'

'Don't tell me,' Max said. 'The "Zetta".'

Alyssa nodded.

'So let me summarise Mort's investment thesis,' said Max. 'Mort wants to invest in a company that is going bankrupt so he can intimidate or embarrass Luke Terry—who may be Australia's next prime minister. He's also running the risk of starting a fight with Todd Edgell, who last time I checked was managing four hundred billion dollars. Finally, the rest of the ZettaData shareholders are mums and dads, widows and orphans, who have already lost most of the money, and so it's not only a PR nightmare but we're walking a tightrope across the Corps Act.

'Have I got that right?'

'I wouldn't argue with that,' Roebling said, scraping Vegemite into tiny crevices of bread.

Alyssa didn't blink.

'Oh—I forgot!—but they're about to launch a crypto currency, so if we don't get sued by Luke Terry, crushed by Todd Edgell, lose our equity when the banks pull the plug, or screw up accidentally and get investigated by ASIC, we might make a profit! Am I missing anything else?' asked Max.

Roebling looked up and gave Max a wide smile. 'That's it, boss,' he said.

'I wouldn't put the Zetta into our Base Case,' said Alyssa, smiling thinly.

Max looked from Roebling to Hauptraum.

'Don't waste any more time on ZettaData,' said Max.

'Sure thing, Max,' said Roebling with his eerie smile.

Max looked from Roebling's unsightly teeth to Hauptraum's cold stare. Something odd was going on. He was temporarily distracted by the aroma of Roebling's decaf organic fair trade latte with soy milk intermingling with the delicate steam from Alyssa's cup of aged Pu-Erh tea.

Max walked to his office. It cost a fortune to nourish the delicate physiologies of predators.

He entered his office and stared at the Mignano print hanging on the wall. Max couldn't remember a single deal when Mort had been a nice guy. Mort had often come close to wrecking Norton & Ring deals by insulting people.

In the beginning, Max asked himself almost daily how he could get out of the partnership. But he realised he was stuck for five years so Max decided to make the best of it, and after a few months started telling himself it wasn't all that bad. Once they'd done the first couple of deals Max started to feel he could raise Mort's game, transform him into a more professional financier, and possibly a better human being – and told himself Mort recognised it, too.

The Mignano print was a symbol of Max's independence. It had been left on the wall by the Poms when they took over the lease. It was a hideous thing, an arbitrary splotch of greens, yellows, purples and light blues depicting Sydney Harbour.

Max hated the print; the only reason he kept it was because Mort wanted it. Max wasn't quite willing to do anything for Mort. He swivelled in his chair and stared at it.

Max turned away from it.

Mort's was the corner office just past Max's. He'd claimed it along with his two-thirds of the profits. Their partnership agreement expired during Covid, and they'd mutually agreed to keep acting like it was in force until they had time to re-negotiate. At minimum, Max was going to demand fifty percent, not one third, of the profits he'd made for the firm during Covid. In truth, a fair deal would be switching the one third / two thirds arrangement in his favour. He'd been considering approaching Richard Wander about the possibility of joining him as a partner.

Max dialled Mort's mobile. It was switched off.

It was still half an hour before the ZettaData AGM. The annual shareholders meeting was being held in the Royal Court Hotel, only a ten-minute walk away. AGMs are completely choreographed and scripted; nothing ever actually happens at them—but sometimes a director or two could be found wandering through the crowd of shareholders before the meeting started. Maybe he'd leave now, arrive a few minutes early, and have a look around.

Soon Max was descending the elegant, wide steps of the old hotel towards the ballroom where the meeting would take place. The worn carpet of the stairs was worked in garish orange and red figures, which must have seemed like a good idea in the 1990s, when the carpet was last laid over the civilised old bones of the hotel. The choice of venue was convincing evidence of ZettaData's financial distress.

As he neared the bottom of the staircase Max heard the thrum of the meeting, and when he reached the foyer he walked straight into thick clusters of people mingling without fear like in the old days, his eyes glancing rapidly in all directions seeking other players: directors, company management, financial investors, consultants, and advisers.

The ordinary-looking people whom Max took to be shareholders were mostly middle-aged or elderly and they had dressed up a bit, like respectable couples standing in a church foyer on Sunday morning. Covid hadn't seemed to cull much of ZettaData's shareholder register even though they were in the most vulnerable cohort. Succumbing to the virus might have been the easy way out.

Standing only a few metres to Max's left was Luke Terry, talking in a disengaged manner to several men. Max was a little surprised to see him mingling with the crowd because as a ZettaData Director Terry represented the government, not ordinary shareholders. He had no obligation to consort with this vast flock of lost sheep, especially because ZettaData was Terry's Achilles heel. After a spectacular career, with the stock price at five cents Terry didn't look so smart now.

Terry, whose expression was simultaneously disapproving and amused as he listened to the men standing with him, glanced up and noticed Max. Having never met Mort's enemy, the prudent thing was to walk away since Terry hadn't yet placed him. But Max had never known anybody else who dared to openly defy Mortimer Norton, and he was curious. He walked over.

'Hello, Luke,' said Max, offering his hand. 'Max Ring.'

Terry wasn't one of the residual elbow—bumpers. He took Max's hand, looking quizzical. Terry clearly still didn't know why he recognised him.

'Norton & Ring,' said Max.

Terry released Max's hand. 'So you're the other cunt.'

'That must sound better when you're sitting in your underwear on a Zoom call,' said Max.

Terry looked him up and down. 'What are you doing here? Better not be business.'

'I'm glad you asked,' said Max. 'We might, in fact, have something to discuss.'

'Not likely.'

A young man approached Terry, murmured something, and tilted his head in the direction of the ballroom. Terry glared at Max as he listened, then turned away without a word and disappeared into the throng.

Max didn't need an explanation; it was probably time the chairman wanted all directors to take their places up on stage. He smiled to himself as he strolled unseeingly through the crowd, brushing past shoulders fitted in tweed and worsted wool and inhaling long-established fragrances like Old Spice and Chanel N° 5.

Max agreed with what he'd read in the Tennessee Williams play about evolution and how natural selection eliminates irrelevant forms of life. Sebastian Venable and his mother make a voyage to the Galapagos Islands to witness an annual spawning of sea turtles. When the baby turtles hatch from their eggs they scuttle across the beach trying to reach safety in the ocean. The sky is black with flocks of circling birds, who dive in an orgy of *sparagmos* and *omphagia*, attacking the baby turtles and eating them alive. Sebastian himself, the unproductive poet who channels his creativity into a sterile life of self-indulgence, is killed the same way by the end of the play – and for the same reason. He doesn't create or produce anything, so he's irrelevant. Just like the small shareholders surrounding him.

'Pardon me?'

The voice, a woman's, was pleasant to the ear. Friend or foe? Max glanced warily to his left. A middle-aged woman stood next to him, with an elegant old purse pressed between her elbow and hip. In her other hand she held the AGM agenda and shareholders pamphlet with its list of resolutions. A common shareholder.

Max glanced around, looking for other investment bankers, or perhaps a member of the management team, so he could make a quick apology and escape a waste time with a small investor.

'I hope you don't mind me approaching you, but I saw you speaking just now to Mr Terry,' she said. 'I recognised Mr Terry from the website and I know he represents the government.'

Max smiled non-committally.

'Will the government save ZettaData?'

'I don't know.'

'Oh yes, you do,' she said, surprising Max.

'Ok,' said Max. For some reason he decided to tell the truth. 'I'm afraid not. Covid's over, and government has turned off the spigots.'

'It's such a pity, the company is so close to being self-funding,' she said, looking at him with intelligent blue eyes under thick greying blonde hair combed back from her high forehead. 'I estimate ZettaData only needs another ten or perhaps fifteen million in shareholder funding, before it reaches profitability.'

Max studied her closely. He had come to the same conclusion after a quick look at Roebling's analysis. Did she somehow know about the imminent launch of the Zetta, too? Surely not. She didn't strike him as an insider.

'If only the government, or that new hedge fund – you're not a very joyful person, are you?' she asked, suddenly reversing her own line of thinking mid-sentence.

'I beg your pardon?'

Max felt her scrutiny. A swarm of unseen tailors and shirtmakers and weavers and cobblers from Italy, France, England and Australia had ensured he looked elegant as she looked him up and down, so he patiently accepted her inspection with quiet confidence.

'Those wonderful clothes are only a substitute for joy,' she said.

'I have no idea what you're talking about,' replied Max.

'I have two sons, and the eldest is a barrister,' she said, looking him in the eyes with her own delicately lidded ones. 'You remind me so much of my son's bosses – brilliant, interesting, making loads of money – and desperately unhappy.'

Max didn't know what to say. She seemed warm and concerned, not critical and contemptuous, and it completely threw him.

'I'm Susan Casner,' she said, extending a hand adorned with gold rings. One was a wedding ring hazy with scratches that looked twice as old as she did, the other an engagement ring with a large, luminous diamond. She must be double vaxxed and boosted or at her age she had no business shaking stranger's hands, even now.

Max shook her hand reluctantly. 'Max Ring.'

Susan's grip was strong and dry, and he somehow sensed through her arm how firmly she stood on those confident, well-upholstered hips.

Susan had probably lost most of her investment in ZettaData, whatever it was: five thousand, maybe even ten thousand dollars. At the current stock price, she'd have less than a thousand left of her investment. Even under this stress, and despite her own problems, she was aware of him – and kind. She was everything his mother had not been.

'Look, Mrs Casner –'

'Call me Susan. May I call you Max?'

'Of course,' said Max, resigned. ZettaData would soon vanish. It had taken on Amazon, Apple, Google and the other overseas Big Data companies, and had competed amazingly well, but took longer than planned to reach profitability. Neither strategic investor could give it more funding, so it was being left to wither and die. For Susan and the rest of the small shareholders, it was over. They didn't have money to invest, so they didn't matter. Whatever happened to ZettaData, they would be left to the natural selection of the markets.

'I've carefully read these resolutions, Max, and it's just a waste of time using this AGM to vote on them. The same thinking that got the company into this mess is never going to get us out! We need to discuss fresh ideas this morning – what do you think?'

A turtle asking advice from a raptor.

'Look, Susan, I like you, so I'm going to be completely frank,' Max said. 'AGMs are completely stage-managed, choreographed in advance down to the finest detail, like a ballet. Nothing ever happens at an AGM.'

'You might be wrong this morning, Max!'

'Perhaps, Susan. I certainly hate to think of you wasting your time, so I hope you're right. Did you travel far this morning?'

'Oh no, I just took the train in from Pymble.'

'Right.' Pymble was a lovely suburb on the North Shore full of nice people. Max nodded, his glance darting over her shoulder in all directions, seeking a plausible excuse for an immediate exit. 'Such a pleasure to meet you.'

Max started to turn away.

'Max,' she said, reaching out to hold his arm. She had tremendous presence.

'Yes?'

'I can tell you haven't figured out how to make money from ZettaData, because you don't seem to care what happens,' she said. 'But there's more to life than making money – there are other reasons to act.'

'Perhaps.' He wasn't going to let Mort, Susan, or anybody else talk him into supporting a stupid idea. 'But making money is what *I* do.'

'Do you know anyone who can help?'

Her eyes were clear and resolved. She seemed to have emerged from a world of human regard and civility of which he'd only heard rumours. He wouldn't dream of introducing her to Mort.

'No, I'm sorry.' He smiled briefly, a parting gesture.

'Well, goodbye Max.'

There was a reproach in her tone Max found mysteriously difficult to dismiss, and for the first time he began to notice individuals around him in the group of doomed investors, not just their general age, race and social class. He studied the faces around them. It was a subdued crowd, even by the standards of corporate AGMs. Many of them reverently held their voting papers and that morning's edition of the *Australian Business Digest*. They'd never been told the fundamental axiom of investing: information is worth what it costs.

The bell began sounding in the ballroom, indicating it was time to take seats. He hadn't seen Mort.

The Norton & Ring team had probably arrived and already taken a seat somewhere in the ballroom while Max was distracted by Susan. Max allowed the disconsolate masses to sweep him through the doors, until he found himself standing at the back of the darkening ballroom. Life was about survival. He had himself, Ilona and the girls to look after. They were his responsibility. Nobody else.

Max looked out across countless rows of shareholders, an audience shrouded in fear, sitting in a kind of visible darkness, to the stage where the Board of ZettaData squirmed under bright lights. Besides the money, there was only one other reason to do deals: to expunge the bottomless pit of self-loathing inside himself.

Chapter 7

'Perhaps our daughters just want to look like us,' said Alexandra. 'That's not such a bad thing.'

'I'm sure you're right,' Ilona said, eyeing Alexandra.

The truth was, Alexandra's daughters would be lucky to look like her when they grew up. Her English beauty, figure and long legs were, like Ilona's looks, entirely God-given. But Mort was the father of Alexandra's children, and it was still too early to tell how badly that might work out.

'There was only a little fleece to remove. Trixie hardly looks any different than she did a few months ago,' said Alexandra, grandly extending her fingers and allowing them to be gently submerged in the fingerbowl by Jo's assistant, Vanessa. 'It would have only taken a few seconds to whack away.'

Ilona placed her left hand in a bowl as Jo began to eliminate traces of cuticle from her right. It was like comfort food, her hand in the warm water, but her heart was heavy with a sense of failure. Sam's puberty seemed to have arrived so quickly, before she had time to resolve her own feelings; it was strange, but true.

'Of course,' said Ilona, trying to emulate Alexandra's nonchalant tone. 'It was nothing.'

In truth, she couldn't be matter-of-fact like Alexandra – or her own mother. Her mother, still working for the Family Planning Association in the UK as she had in Australia, briefed Ilona early and often about sex and all the related considerations in the most pragmatic way. Accordingly what Ilona learned was the activity was embarrassing, dirty and dangerous – and if she participated, she would likely become pregnant, infected, or dead.

Since meeting Alexandra, Ilona had been drawn to her bold, unapologetically practical approach to life because it seemed to breathe a completely different spirit, even though Alexandra shared the same unblinking pragmatism as her mother. Their relationship warmed into a friendship during the lockdowns, when Ilona eagerly took Alexandra's lead as they defended their families against the virus. Alexandra set the standard and Ilona imitated every measure, coordinating many times a day on FaceTime, which Alexandra preferred to Zoom. As their teamwork deepened, Alexandra had an allocation of the rubbing alcohol Mort had been able to requisition delivered to the Rings. Ilona's triumph was to find a recipe for the best possible disinfectant that involved steeping lemon peels in vinegar for three weeks. She and Alexandra applied it to every surface of their homes and any delivery that arrived.

This morning's session was only a mani-pedi, but it was Jo's where Alexandra and Ilona came for full Brazilians performed by Jo's employee Vanessa, who was Brazilian herself. Jo's was a Double Bay spa on a quiet side street which had somehow survived the lockdowns and continued servicing the most demanding clientele in the Eastern Suburbs. Behind an elegant door only a few steps away was another bespoke practice, also redolent of fresh flowers, mists of aromatherapy, and antiseptic, where many of Jo's clients obtained equally discreet abortions. Ilona had no idea how Jo had survived, but she always was too relaxed and at peace to get around to asking.

'I just don't understand why Trixie keeps denying knowing how it happened,' mused Alexandra. 'What's the big deal?'

Ilona shook her head. She couldn't speculate about Sam and Billie the way Alexandra seemed to understand her daughters Trixie and Anastasia so intuitively. Ilona's mind just went blank. Despite half-a-dozen lovers, a fifteen year marriage, and two childbirths, Ilona still felt uncertain, somehow a little damaged, certainly not a mature, complete and confident woman – like Alexandra.

'I don't know,' said Ilona, feeling the heavy burden of the other disclosure she had yet to make. She had done everything possible to make the sleepover a success: horseriding at Centennial Park stables, where Sam took lessons but Trixie not only took lessons, but had her own horse stabled. Then the Rings went to dinner at a teppanyaki restaurant in Double Bay, even though Max loathed the place, because he hated having scrambled eggs Japanese-style thrown on his head and clothes for the amusement of shrieking children. They returned home to Bellevue Hill for a Netflix movie and hot chocolate.

Everything had seemed fine by nine forty-five that Saturday night, except Ilona was exhausted and Max was in a bad mood, because he could still smell the eggs in his hair, but was too tired to take a shower. They were in the TV room drinking a glass of Pinot Noir and idly watching test rugby, when the phone rang. It was Selena's mother calling to complain about the bullying – the first crack that was growing to be as big as the Grand Canyon.

'I need to show you something,' Ilona said, her tongue thick and unresponsive.

She took a deep breath, wriggling her fingers and sending drops of water flying, and reached down in her purse to pull out her phone. She quickly called up Instagram and showed Alexandra the image of the Pucci planet, oddly familiar and yet oddly alien. 'Look at this, darling,' she said.

'Why, that's a pussy!' Alexandra took the phone with her fingertips in a distant yet familiar way. 'Hmmm,' she said, inspecting the screen, and showing it to Jo and then Vanessa. 'Am I right?'

They studied the image with their expert eyes and nodded. 'Sleeping Beauty – 357 likes! – the account is N1ghtyN1te,' said Alexandra. She tilted the screen to Ilona.

Jo looked up at them both as she held Ilona's left hand in a firm, competent but affectionate grip. 'It's a crazy age, especially for girls – drinking, drugs, lipstick parties ... it could have been worse.'

'The problem,' Alexandra remarked, 'is that at least 357 people have now been treated to the sight of a pussy that probably belongs to one of our daughters.'

Ilona shivered. 'There were only twenty-three likes when I saw it this morning!' Even then, this image hadn't just existed in some obscure corner of the Internet. She should have acted more quickly. Jo ran a polishing block across each fingernail of Ilona's left hand, applying its flat surface to the arc of nail. It was no longer soothing.

'Who is this?' Alexandra demanded. 'Trixie? Or Sam?'

Ilona shook her head weakly, terrified of Alexandra abandoning her, or turning on her. But she had to be truthful. 'I don't know. Maybe even Selena Woodbridge? Who are the likes?'

'My god!' exclaimed Alexandra, 'surely they didn't upload it themselves? Who did this? Whoever this pussy belongs to is going to be famous – she's already famous!'

The likes were girls from Sam, Trixie and Selena's year at Nightingale along with hundreds of others, including boys, many of whom she or Alexandra knew, and many they did not.

'Right!' said Alexandra. 'Well, the first thing we need to do is contact Instagram and get this account taken down – immediately!'

'I'll do it!' said Ilona, taking back her phone.

She glanced at Alexandra. How would sour, vain Trixie Norton react to being exposed publicly on Instagram? Oh, and her own dear Sam, already on her way to being Head Girl of Nightingale one day – would this destroy her self-confidence?

Alexandra clicked on the Instagram account and continued to report her findings. It was newly established that weekend, with a blurry photo of the moon, there was only the one post, and 497 followers. She turned in her chair and put her hand on Ilona's forearm. 'The girls may want to look like us,' she said fiercely, 'but it's even more important we show them how to *be* like us!'

'Yes, of course!' said Ilona loyally, but in her heart, she knew she really wanted someone to lift from her shoulders the burden of being herself. It wasn't going to be Max, or her mother, who had always acted as if her daughter's body was a marginal district in an electoral map, or Magda, who had run out of ideas, and may never have any good ones. Alexandra, thank god, had enough boldness and confidence for all of them: herself, Ilona and their four daughters.

As if reading her thoughts, Alexandra said reassuringly, 'Don't worry darling – we'll get the girls through this!'

'Yes, of course,' whispered Ilona, tapping as quickly as possible at her phone.

'We have to keep an eye out for any sign of body dysmorphia,' exclaimed Alexandra. 'The best defence is that we continue being healthy, confident models for our girls!'

'Oh my god, my worst nightmare is for Sam to develop an eating disorder,' said Ilona. Her phone rang. 'It's Nightingale!'

Alexandra locked eyes.

'Hello?' Ilona said.

'Yes, good morning, Mrs Ring, this is Mrs Whitehead in Miss Whidbey's office.'

'Good morning, Mrs Whitehead,' Ilona weakly. 'Are the girls okay?'

'Miss Whidbey would like to speak with you about exactly that issue,' said Mrs Whitehead. 'Would you have some time to come in for a chat tomorrow morning?'

'Why, yes, certainly,' said Ilona.

When arrangements were made, Ilona hung up and looked at Alexandra. Alexandra's phone rang. 'It's the school,' Alexandra said grimly. 'We'll go in together, darling.'

Chapter 8

M ax worked his way down the aisle to where Mort was sitting, surrounded by journalists and professionals from the big accounting firms, law firms, management consultants, and investment banks who had various interests, either in ZettaData's current situation, or in its fate. They were attending the AGM like expensive medical specialists at the bedside of a dying patient with Covid, hermetically sealed inside PPE and scrupulously attentive as long as their fees were paid and ZettaData's woes still sold newspapers.

Elegant and sleek, even as their patient went from bad to worse, they nodded and murmured greetings to Max as he squeezed past their knees to get to the seat beside Mort.

Luther V. Telford IV, the chairman of ZettaData, a patrician middle-aged man with silvery hair combed back in an elegant wave, was standing at the dais with the projection of a bar chart behind him. '... doubled revenues by delivering innovative information solutions ...' His heavy Texas accent boomed through the ballroom.

Max looked at Mort, who was listening to the chairman with narrowed eyes.

Telford droned on about vast new data centres, the colossal pipes that funnelled bandwidth into and out of those centres, the mind-boggling amounts of information continuously collected and subjected to unique algorithms to reveal to customers the hidden inner workings of economy and society.

He leaned over to Mort. 'It's doomed,' he murmured.

Mort gave Max a long, appraising glance and shrugged.

'We're not putting a cent into it,' Max said quietly.

Projected onto the vast screen above and behind the chairman, red and blue bars, enormous and fat and seemingly bursting with energy, marched in a steep upward angle to the right – a good performance for a doomed company. But none of it made any difference; time had run out.

'It is my pleasure to introduce your Chief Executive Officer, Donald Ormsby!' The big, robust figure of the CEO charged up to the dais. Reluctant applause rustled through the ballroom. The remaining directors, one of whom was a woman, sat at the table blinking disconsolately in the glare. Max saw Luke Terry sitting in the middle of the other directors with a sour expression on his face.

'Good morning!' Ormsby surveyed the room with a big smile on his face. 'Mr. Chairman, fellow directors, fellow shareholders – ladies and gentlemen - I'm delighted to see such a big turnout this morning to hear about the bright future of your company ...' His loud syllables flowed like a bass guitar line over the PA system, as he detailed the company's admirable yet irrelevant recent achievements.

'Your company achieved revenues of almost $100 million this year, and as you know we won all those customers under the most difficult circumstances possible.'

Ormsby spoke into the numb silence of the ballroom, and as he listened Max realised he wasn't just a CEO going through a perfunctory post-mortem of a company that had foundered on his watch.

Ormsby's bear-like face broke out in a grin. 'We've had billions of dollars' worth of bad publicity – but here in Australia, your company is strong and growing ...'

Ormsby was refusing to accept the death of his company. Max could feel how much he wanted life to flow through him and back into the families that packed the ballroom. But what was the investment opportunity?

Ormsby finished his presentation and returned to his seat, and Telford intoned, 'Ladies and gentlemen, now that the formal portion of our presentation is over, are there any questions from the floor? Yes, sir.' Telford nodded to a man with neatly cut grey hair holding up one of the little blue shareholder passes, who was wearing a tweed coat, regimental tie and inexpensive reading glasses.

'Thank you, Chairman,' said the man decorously. 'I would like to direct this question to the Chief Executive, Mr Ormsby.'

The shareholder had an intricate and apparently irrelevant query about the existing Big Data business. Ormsby leaned into his microphone to deliver his reply. 'Thank you for your question, sir.' He crossed his arms, and with quiet intensity, unspooled a detailed explanation that addressed the question from every perspective imaginable: technological, engineering, commercial, accounting, and legal.

Max glanced at Roebling and Hauptraum, who were gazing raptly at Ormsby like reptiles monitoring their next meal. Once reptiles appeared on Earth, Max wondered idly, why did natural selection continue operating until mammals evolved too? Reptiles are such efficient killing machines.

He looked up on stage at Luke Terry, looking sardonically but indifferently into the lights. Who needs fur, warm blood, and a pre-frontal cortex? The directors on either side of Terry seemed to be quailing at the thought of a question being addressed to them. It was a traumatised board.

'Yes, ma'am.' Telford recognised a woman holding up one of the little blue shareholder passes who sat three rows ahead of Max.

'I would like to know, Chairman, how you and your fellow directors can sleep at night knowing small shareholders like me have been all but wiped out!'

It was the voice of the woman he had just met in the foyer filling the ballroom. He could see her holding the portable microphone with both hands. Susan Casner.

Telford acknowledged the woman with a respectful nod. 'I'm not sure any of us are sleeping all that well,' he drawled. 'I know it helps me to know we've been doing our best.'

'Well, why aren't you doing something different?' demanded Susan. Her voice had risen without losing its calm, articulate quality.

Fair enough, thought Max.

'Ma'am, we've been very open about disclosing our cash flow constraints,' said Chairman Telford. 'We're just taking things step by step.'

Max thought how he had been stalking through the foyer before the AGM not even noticing the hundreds of small shareholders until Susan Casner introduced herself.

'But what is your *vision*, Mr Chairman? Without vision a company perishes!'

Max admired Susan's slightly old-fashioned bravery and forcefulness. She was trying to save her investment, and she didn't have the least idea how to go about it. Still she had powerful qualities.

'Ma'm, it's all very clear if you read your shareholder information –'

'Chairman, we both know that so-called information is worthless. It dissects the past in great detail but says nothing about the present or the future. I thought I was making a long-term investment in a company run by honest people. And yet my money is almost gone as surely as if you were car thieves. I'm sorry if that hurts, but it's true.'

Even angry – and probably a bit desperate – she was expressing herself graciously to the chairman, showing empathy for his feelings. In their conversation out in the foyer, Susan had treated him with similar regard: like an honest man, one with power and resources to save a company.

Max realised he had unconsciously enjoyed being respected, looked up to and trusted, by this stranger. He certainly had never experienced the same open trust from Mort, the Norton & Ring team, or, for that matter, from Ilona.

The problem for Susan Casner was that she, and all the other small shareholders, were like that Peugeot that got in his way on William Street this morning. They weren't designed for this kind of traffic.

The loudspeakers filled the ballroom with the sound of Chairman Telford clearing his throat. 'We're doing our best, ma'am.' An usher reached for the microphone and she started to resist, then relinquished it and sat down with resignation.

Mort jostled Max, and to Max's amazement got to his feet and waved to be recognised.

Telford, squinting into the lights, flung his hand out over the podium, finger pointing towards Norton, and said, 'Yes, sir.'

'Thanks, Chairman,' Mort grunted. Max looked up as Mort rolled on the balls of his feet like a boxer, circulating his bulk with surprising grace. 'I wanted to ask a question of ZettaData's auditors, if I may.'

'Yes sir, our auditors are right here,' said Telford. 'What is your question, please?'

Max sat back in shock. Not only was Mort not keeping a low profile, he was asking a question – one directed to the auditors. Was he crazy? Putting a question to the auditors sounded like he was going for the jugular. He had no idea what Mort was doing.

A narrow-faced, bald man in a crisp pink shirt, elegant suit, and fashionably square eyeglass frames fixed his gaze on Norton like a tennis player awaiting a serve.

'Can you please confirm there are no commercial contracts between ZettaData and any directors – especially not with Luke Terry?'

Max's face reddened. The question was a direct attack on the integrity of the company and its entire board, particularly – and very publicly – Luke Terry.

Max instantly knew Mort hadn't devised the question himself – it must have been Roebling's or Hauptraum's idea. It manipulated provisions of the Corps Act and AGM protocols to raise a potentially fatal question in the minds of shareholders at this fragile time in the company's history: a contract between ZettaData and one of its directors would appear to be corrupt, no matter how justified it might be. Max also recognised in an instant how brilliant the question was: because it was so unlikely that a contract existed, the auditors probably hadn't even checked.

There would be no way to refute the question during the AGM.

Mort wasn't planning to invest in ZettaData – he meant to trigger a collapse in confidence—starting by attacking Luke Terry's reputation—that would start a wave of selling that would force ZettaData into bankruptcy that day.

Tense silence filled the cavernous ballroom and then the auditor cleared his throat. 'I can't confirm that, no,' he said bleakly.

Just as Max expected.

Murmurs immediately started and rapidly grew louder. The disconsolate thrum of the crowd in the foyer before the AGM had a threatening quality to it now. Mort had scored a direct hit. There was a savageness in the sounds all around them starting to come from such civilised people.

How could the shareholders be calmed down? Even if the auditors confirmed the next day that Mort's question was baseless, it would be too late. The rising anger in the ballroom was happening in real time. In another minute shareholders would pull out their phones and start dumping their shares in panic or disgust, triggering a trading halt by the ASX and requiring the bank group to step in and take control of ZettaData. The collapse would annihilate the investments of ANG, the American shareholder, and all the small shareholders, including Susan Casner.

Terry knitted his brow as he looked into the glare, trying to focus on Norton. Max saw a faint, mocking smile appear on Terry's lips. 'There's no contract between me and this company,' Terry spat into the microphone.

Mort looked around the ballroom. 'Thanks, mate – but if you don't mind – ZettaData shareholders are entitled to hear the truth, whatever it may be, from the auditors themselves.'

A rumble of support for Norton coursed around the room. Mort's question could very well be ZettaData's *coup de grâce,* given its precarious financial situation and the fragile sentiment of its customers, banks, and the remaining shareholders – all of whom were demoralised amateurs, no matter how intelligent. It was despicable but clever – Mort had only asked a seemingly innocent question – no violation of the Corps Act. It was probably Roebling who'd come up with it.

Terry glared at Mort, now on notice Mort would stop at nothing until Terry dropped his objections to Norton & Ring's investment in the McConnochie Consortium. Mort was willing to wipe out thousands of small shareholders, and ANG and SpecTel's position, just to send Terry a message to back off.

Max wanted no part of it.

Max could see the sweat glistening on Telford's forehead; his glasses almost misted over. He knew what it felt like: the shock, the uncertainty, the awareness of sudden, outrageous injustice – and the way it produced paralysis.

There was no doubt in Max's mind why Mort had said what he did: Mort enjoyed destroying people. He couldn't let Mort get away with it.

Here I am.

Max stood up, grabbing the microphone from Mort, who gave him an angry and puzzled grimace. 'Good morning, Chairman, I'm Max Ring, the other partner in Norton & Ring along with Mortimer Norton, who has just spoken ... I know, I know,' he said smiling, putting up his free hand to quell the shocked reactions from the audience 'my partner has such a fierce commitment to the truth he sometimes lets it get away with him – he hasn't had time to explain that the reason for his question is because at Norton & Ring we are just completing our due diligence on ZettaData. We're very interested in putting an investment proposal to the board.'

'What?' hissed Mort.

'Yes, that's right, ladies and gentlemen,' said Max. His voice reverberated around the ballroom.

'Give me that,' said Mort, reaching for the microphone.

Max knocked back Mort's arm, which felt like a bar of iron. He realised he'd never touched Mort before. 'Ladies and gentlemen, we'll be communicating directly with the board later this week and sincerely hope they consider our vision for the bright future of ZettaData. Thank you for your attention.'

Max handed back the microphone with a smile to one of the attendants as shareholders on all sides turned around and looked at him with hopeful expressions. A faint buzzing of excitement floated through the ballroom.

Mort glared furiously at Max. Max smiled at him. Mort's bellow rose in the darkness through the growing murmurs. 'The auditor – until the auditor states –' he shouted, but even his deep, powerful voice was hushed in the vast space by the surging sibilance that filled the ballroom like the sound of a great foamy wave rushing up the beach.

'If there are no other questions I hereby bring this Annual General Meeting of the Shareholders of ZettaData Limited to a close.'

The chairman banged his gavel, the AGM was over. Max glanced in the direction of Mrs Casner. It was dark, but he could see she had reacted to his bold announcement.

Mort slowly turned. 'You'll be sorry you opened your gob this morning,' he said looking fixedly at Max.

Max casually buttoned his suit coat. 'I did it for our own good, Mort. Since when did you start running Norton & Ring?'

Max would put together some half-hearted offer the board wouldn't want to accept, just to follow up on his pronouncement; he had to be careful not to violate the Corps Act by creating a false market, of course. It was worth the risk. He couldn't do much to help ZettaData, but at least he had stopped Mort from destroying it that day.

Max looked at Roebling and Hauptraum, realising he'd never be able to trust them again. He was going to clean them out of Norton & Ring.

Max started to walk down the row of seats past the professionals who were suddenly uneasy, bereft of their previous aplomb. They had brought nothing that might avert the death throes of ZettaData.

It was Susan Casner who had tried to offer a new and fresh choice. Max wanted to believe in Susan's call for a vision, and he was attracted to her civility and regard for others, but she didn't know how to pursue her quest.

Max made his way into the clogged main aisle and Richard Wander eased up beside him. 'You and Mort were the life of the party today.'

Wander looked displeased, but it was his default expression. 'I'd like to walk through what you plan to present,' Wander said.

'No worries,' said Max. He had no idea yet what a proposal might look like, but it didn't matter as long as he prevented all-out war from breaking out between Norton & Ring and Luke Terry and kept ZettaData from going to the receiver that day. Perhaps it wasn't too late to find a reasonable compromise on all sides. 'Don't get too excited – they are going to struggle to swallow anything I put to them. I just didn't want Mort turning the lights out this morning.'

Wander nodded calmly.

Max started to walk up the centre aisle towards the doors. He was surprised Wander wasn't more upset about Mort almost wrecking his capital raising. There were still knots of shareholders talking among themselves, and as Max passed they smiled and nodded.

Susan Casner fell in next to him. 'Until I heard you speak just now I had given up hope.'

Max smiled, but he didn't want her to misunderstand the predicament of ZettaData. 'Hope isn't a good idea,' he said.

'I feel better knowing you're involved, Max.'

Max stopped and looked into her kind brown eyes, feeling her integrity. He let the moment linger, basking in her trust. She believed in his power like nobody else did in his life. To be truly powerful would be to be strong enough, rich enough, secure enough to consider the welfare of others, and look out for them. Forget survival, Max thought to himself, it was the obsession of the weak.

'Thank you, Max, for what you said today,' she continued, reaching out and touching the back of his hand.

'Look, Susan ...'

'Yes?'

On the eve of battle, Krishna told Arjuna his enemies were already dead and Arjuna was only an instrument of karma. All his career Max had taken Krishna's justification to heart, but what if it were perfectly possible to be an instrument of karma not just for killing but for healing and for engendering new life?

What if Susan Casner's investment in ZettaData had already been restored to its original value – and was profitable – and Max simply had to find a way to act?

'The Corps Act isn't going to let me say anything more to you, Susan. I'm sorry, but you'll just have to wait and see what the company announces publicly. It'll be up to them. Don't get your hopes up.'

'Of course, Max,' she said, smiling gratefully. 'I understand. Thank you, anyway.'

Rise and fight, O Arjuna, confident of success.

There were certain things he could do.

Magnanimity is the quality of a king.

Chapter 9

Peggy walked down Hall Street sipping a Green Room with extra cacao and plant protein – her lunch – peacefully enjoying the feeling of drugged contentment. She didn't feel a trace of sadness as she sipped her smoothie, none of the regret at letting herself down that for years had tainted eating. She felt *engagé* and fully alive, rejoicing in the fact she had relinquished hunger and its false sense of meaning. She rounded the corner into the noise and grime of Campbell Parade, and literally bumped into Charlie.

She knew the hard weight of that body all too well.

'Oh, hi!' she said, as they both stepped back.

The surprise on Charlie's face quickly changed as his sad brown eyes studied her gravely. 'Hi.'

He was wearing work shorts, a tank top, and boots with heavy socks, all covered with powdered cement. A little crease across his forehead indicated the pressure of a helmet strap. His left hand was bandaged.

It had been almost two years. Was the happiness she had been feeling a moment ago a delusion, and a dangerous one? Was her edge gone, along with her hunger – was that why she had no anticipation of Charlie's presence?

'Do you live around here now?' asked Charlie. Though he was far bigger than her, he seemed to float before her like a tethered cloud. Had she drifted insensibly into him because he was no longer dangerous, or because she had relinquished that jittery protective, hungry state when every cell in her body was activated and alert for the next threat? She couldn't tell.

'No, no,' she said, instinctively wary. 'I live at my dad's in Vaucluse. I just came here to get a smoothie.' She tilted the drink towards him.

'Oh,' he said. His unhurried gaze seemed to pass across her as inevitably as the shadow of a tree darkens the ground under a rising sun.

'Do you live here now?'

'Yeah, I was on the dole and living with me mum during the 'Rona, but as soon as everything re-opened I got work here in Sydney as a builder's apprentice. I stay at the backpackers place up the hill.' His beautiful eyes met hers, asking for nothing. 'I'm sorry about Hugh.'

'Thanks.'

Charlie and her brother were friends once – before they got in the fight that left them both more dead than alive. Hugh was the one able to walk away, just barely, after he left Charlie in the dirt, not that different from the way Charlie had left her. It was no coincidence. Hugh fought Charlie over what he did to her.

'Well, nice to see you,' she said. The past few seconds were enough reunion time with Charlie – more than enough. He'd done it tough during the lockdowns, like so many friends of hers from Byron and Sydney who had to show up to make their living: yoga teachers, chefs, fitness coaches, owners of health food stores and small boutiques. On impulse she put out her hand.

His hand, the same hand that had beaten Hugh and done worse to her, enveloped hers – soft, strong, dry. It felt nice, her hand in his hand; she didn't feel her heart beat faster, and her breathing was normal.

'Ok, Peg, see you,' he said softly. 'I'm going to get something to eat at Maccas.'

It was almost as if his effect on her was limited to her wrist. Only her hand felt Charlie. Not the rest of her, not her heart. She was safe, at last. Charlie was another form of hunger, and his power had vanished along with the hunger.

When they lived in Byron, McDonald's had been his favourite food. The one here in Bondi was just a few metres away on Campbell Parade.

'I'm headed that way,' she said. Peggy had never thought she would be able to feel so deeply and still cope, and now she knew she could.

'I just had a roll and coffee before work,' he said as they crossed Hall Street.

He walked beside her, nodding to the buskers and beggars he already knew. This was the sweet, childlike Charlie who could look at dried sand from Clarkes Beach gleaming on his skin, and see the shimmering galaxies concealed above the blue sky.

'I didn't expect to be invited,' he said. 'But none of me mates were, either. I wondered about that. They were Hugh's mates, too.'

'Invited to what?'

'The funeral.'

'There hasn't been a funeral, bro, not yet.'

Charlie looked at her with alarm. She shook her head. It was just too hard to explain. Charlie was Koori, and because of his people's traditions and beliefs, the heritage of 40 000 years in Australia, he would find it shocking even with the limited funerals permitted during the lockdowns, a violation of the natural order of the universe, that Hugh's body still lay unburied and unmourned in the Byron Bay morgue.

Charlie said nothing, but Peggy could see the situation was even more distressing for him than it was for her. It was weird, after all that had happened between the three of them, but it was true.

As they arrived at Maccas she permitted herself to put a hand on his shoulder, feeling the energy flowing from him like a slow ocean swell on a gusty afternoon. This time she felt the current rise through her hand, course along her arm and down her spine. There was a living dynamic between them, but she felt no need to control it or recoil.

Charlie ordered the McDonald's meal and she watched as he ate the dreadful stuff. She thought of the smear of grease she used to smell on her own lips when she relaxed her austere standards and permitted herself to eat, and listened to his desultory talk, his way of observing the world and accepting it as he found it. He had work a couple of days a week in construction, and thought he might pick up another day working in a warehouse. He might get his forklift licence, might move back to Byron. He didn't know.

For now he had moved to Bondi.

They sat on stools next to each other and when he finished and began collapsing all the paper together in his big hands she hitched her bag on her shoulder and swivelled. Their legs touched. A strange warmth overcame her. It cleared and she was herself again. She was more powerful than she could have ever imagined, and now she could accept the unknown.

Suddenly the anger awakened and was entrancingly incandescent – a suppressed but fiercely alive desire for reckoning. 'How could you hurt me?' she said. 'What's wrong with you?'

His face softened. 'I'm so sorry, Peggo, I love you.'

'I don't know how I survived you.'

He had beaten, choked her.

He looked at her, his eyes full of the pain of self-loathing and a love that was rejected but still alive. She held his eyes, willing herself to overpower him.

His eyes glistened. Then tears ran down his cheeks.

Charlie rubbed his palms together, and as he moved his powerful hands against each other, the white bandage tore. She saw that motor grease still streaked his hand, and an angry red burn mottled his gleaming cacao skin. Two of his fingers were bleeding under the nails, filaments of dark purple across the pink skin.

'You're hurt.' She didn't mean to say the words; she didn't want to feel concerned. Where was detachment? It was hunger's gift, and had vanished along with it.

'It's ok. It's nothing,' Charlie said almost to himself.

'What happened?'

'Tried to adjust a diesel engine and my hand brushed the manifold.'

'Let me see.' Peggy grasped his wrist, and with a mixture of revulsion and fascination clinically she examined the broken, bloodied nails and the puffy red shreds of skin. She recognised within herself stirrings of compassion, the new mode of intensity that appeared once the effects of malnourishment had disappeared. 'It's burned, too.'

'The manifold was red hot.'

'What?' Peggy looked up sharply. 'You're lucky this is only a second degree burn – it could have been worse.'

Blackened, charred flesh.

'You still have great reflexes. Did you clean it and get it treated or just bandage it?'

He shrugged, still crying quietly.

The afternoon sun glinted in his black hair even through the dark glass of the Maccas window. He wept for what he done to her, she knew, not for his hand. He moved slowly, hesitantly on the stool, tears trickling down his cheeks, his other hand against his face, trying to cover it.

By the time she and Charlie were dating she looked almost normal and she was strong enough to surf. She was still struggling with hunger, and had no illusions she was healed. He had been tender to her many times, loving and gentle. Charlie introduced her to his simple, elemental way of being alive, to being honest about what she wanted. She had been conceited about her standards and too full of self-loathing to claim what she hungered for, and it was Charlie who, with his matter-of-fact confidence that seemed rooted in eternity, opened her to a spacious humility to permit acknowledging, simply and honestly, her own desires and right to be sated.

She had nothing to fear now, while aware of being unable to discern the source of her conviction. It was only a few steps away to Juanita's building. A dear friend, she had made her penthouse available to Peggy any time she wanted, whether Juanita was there or not.

Often Peggy would go over after the beach and shower off the sand and sun crème, or take a nap in one of the recliners on Juanita's verandah high above Bondi Beach.

'Come on, let's go,' she said quietly. Did her sense of security arise from perceptions blunted by nourishment, or newly heightened capacities for insight that resulted from the release of fear? 'Let's take care of that hand.'

They left McDonald's and in less than a minute reached Juanita's building. She led him through the foyer, where she got the key that was always available to her from the concierge. 'Is she in?' Peggy asked.

The concierge shrugged. 'Not sure, I just came on my shift. Sorry.' He eyed Charlie coolly and professionally, aloof from Bondi's reflexive tolerance, taking in Charlie's work clothes, covered in cement powder and still damp with sweat.

He handed Peggy the key, apparently having concluded she was conducting the big man up to the penthouse to do repairs. Peggy thanked him and led Charlie to the lifts. As they went up, Charlie stood with a rounded back, his shoulders pulled forward and his chest seemingly small. His hands dangled.

Her father hadn't treated her mother much differently than Charlie treated her. She recognised the connection between Charlie and her father, as different as they were – and was eager to confirm Charlie had evolved. Her father certainly hadn't.

She was increasingly experiencing her father as a vortex that had slowly and irresistibly drawn her back to Sydney, into his life, into the theatre company where he and his partner served as directors on the board. She was determined to fight for her own identity, and that included her and her mother's rights to mourn Hugh's body fittingly and lovingly. Despite everything, she felt stronger than her father in some secret way yet to be revealed, which meant she could be stronger than Charlie.

Charlie had been so wounding, and was wounded in so many ways. When he first flew into a rage Peggy experienced a shock of recognition. Not because she succumbed to rages herself, or because of her father's, but in his rage Charlie had confronted her with something that had appeared many years before the hunger it had possibly summoned.

The lift opened into Juanita's penthouse, and Peggy called out, but there was no answer. 'It's not my place – it belongs to a friend,' she explained, just to make sure there was no misunderstanding. She switched on the air conditioning, lights, and the TV. Juanita furnished her apartment in white furniture. The traffic on Bondi Beach, seven floors below, was silent.

Peggy walked to the kitchen and felt a sudden stab of anxiety in her stomach at the sight of the glass-doored cabinet stocked with a dozen bottles of liquor and liqueurs, including half a bottle of Bundaberg rum. Grog was Charlie's downfall.

Juanita kept the rum for her tradies, the men who were always working on the constant construction and renovations transforming a sleepy beach community into glamorous, world-class Bondi. Plenty of them were healthy, handsome and strong, and they did jobs for Juanita, too: she liked sleeping with them. Juanita didn't drink beer, nor did Peggy, and she and her friend often laughed about the Victoria Bitter Juanita kept chilled in her refrigerator, alongside the organic, vegan and bio-dynamic food Juanita curated for her own nourishment.

Charlie took no interest in the well-stocked bar. Peggy relaxed. 'Now then,' she said, walking into the bathroom, 'let's see what we have here. Come on.'

Peggy turned on the taps of the generous, Italian-designed sink and held Charlie's hand in hers beneath the warm flowing water. She cleansed away all the oil and dirt, delicately running her fingers around and through his injured fingers and circling his hand and wrist. She smelled his skin and hair, the cement dust, and the faintly outdoors, sunny smell of his singlet. Her movements acquired a certain deliberateness as Peggy lifted his hand from the water and dried it. She took a face cloth and loosely wrapped it around his clean hand and led him back into the living room. Still holding his hand in hers, she sat with him on the white sofa positioned to take in the view of North Bondi glowing in the afternoon sun.

'Can I get you a glass of water?' she asked casually, aware Charlie knew as well as she did there was plenty of grog.

'Sure, thanks,' Charlie said.

Peggy opened the cabinet where Juanita kept her glassware, took two tumblers and filled them from the filtered water tap in the kitchen, her back to Charlie. All the while the cabinet full of coloured bottles seemed to glisten, and she could almost feel on her skin the rich glow from the bottle of Bundy. She felt the ultra-clarity of hunger.

'Here you go,' she said, handing Charlie his glass of water and taking a sip from her own to set the example. They sat together on Juanita's sofa.

'You know North Bondi is really East Bondi, and South Bondi is really West Bondi,' she said, conscious her chatter sounded almost like a children's rhyme. 'That's why the sun sets behind South Bondi – because it's really west, not south, and the sunlight falls on North Bondi – because it's really east of the beach. You know?' The real meaning of her words was hidden in the plain sight of their very randomness – and she was shocked to realise it.

Charlie permitted himself one look and then stared fixedly at his knees, resisting, to his credit. 'They could always re-name it.'

Peggy felt his hand tremble faintly but steadily. She felt the tremor through his body, from his hand to where their knees were in contact. He glanced at her again, afraid of meeting her eyes, saw they were lowered and staring intently at his lips.

'How are you feeling?' she asked.

They kissed. Immediately familiar.

Peggy explored the well-loved terrain of Charlie's lips and teeth and tongue. She was again aware of a presence within herself, elusive and yet sovereign, proud and warlike, a consciousness she could discern most clearly when she was with him, hovering as in an obscure mirror, as present as Charlie.

Warmth spread within her as she rested her forearms on his strong shoulders. She wasn't prepared for this, but she hadn't bled for almost a month so she was safe. She let her hands move from the back of his neck down the muscles of his arms until she was gripping the backs of his hands.

All the while Charlie sat almost motionless, following her but without any momentum of his own in the almost imperceptible dance. She sensed Charlie felt out of control as she made decisions for both of them, but their relationship formed some unknowable combination of the best and worse of themselves – so the situation was out of her control, too. Charlie was suppressing his own latent power, but she wanted it. It was time for her to commit. She wanted the avalanche.

She intertwined with him. He moved to envelope her but she pushed out of his embrace and he lay back on the sofa, and she smiled, recognising his desire for her. She pressed herself against him, feeling his muscles and imagining, as they touched, what he could feel of her lithe body. She looked into his eyes, asking him silently, Do you want me? It would be good to see how well he could still read her.

'Yeah, babe,' he said audibly. It could have been meaningless, or a cliché – or he could be answering her. She didn't care. Peggy kissed him again.

Now his hands were moulded around her hips and she was sitting on him with her legs on either side of his legs, his face in her hands as they kissed. She was aware of the presence, aware she might yet extinguish it – or it might extinguish her.

'Baby, let's chill. I'm thirsty.'

'Huh? Of course, get a drink.' Peggy looked around in a kind of stupor for one of their glasses of water.

'No, I mean, just a nip.'

'No, honey.'

'Just a nip, baby...'

'Honey, no.'

This was not what she wanted. But Peggy felt herself rising, as Charlie stood up, still embracing her, and laid her tenderly on the sofa. He walked to the kitchen towards the cabinet glowing with liquor.

She could jump up, right now, and easily escape. The hallway to the front door was to the left and she had plenty of time to slip past and get to the lift. She could go to the front desk and, if necessary, call the cops. If Charlie suddenly snapped she could get out.

He took one tiny sip before deliberately screwing the top back onto the bottle. He smiled at her as if to say, *See? I was just thirsty.* Was she flattering herself that she could manage him? She'd been wrong many times.

He walked back to the sofa with the bottle, placing it on the floor.

Peggy smiled, feeling uncertain. 'Let's put it out of the way,' she said, picking it up and putting it a step away on the glass coffee table.

Charlie smiled and shrugged. 'Sure.'

He was beautiful when he was good, perhaps because she knew what he struggled to overcome. Peggy sat back on his lap, put her arm around his neck, and began kissing him. The rum on his lips was faintly spicy and she felt its heat in her mouth like the stirring of a warm breeze – but she knew how dangerous the storm stirred by that breeze could be.

Hovering over him she lowered her lips towards his. Ever so slowly she started to move away as she watched the tense breathing in his belly and chest.

'Hey honey,' she murmured, stroking his cheek and inhaling the smell of his skin.

'I've missed you, babe,' he said. 'I love you, hey.'

'Mmmm,' she said, licking his neck and under his jaw.

They were in each other's arms and she gripped his hips with her knees, surging against his taut belly, feeling his desire for her hard and hot. Their breathing was in synch, all the consent needed.

Charlie embraced her with one powerful arm, and holding her tight stood up and reached for the bottle of Bundy. He sat back down again and released his arm as he grasped the bottle of rum in both hands to open it.

'No, honey,' Peggy said, slipping from his knees to the floor and releasing him from his trousers. She had brought into their relationship, along with her hunger, a hair-trigger gag reflex. It conferred, like the fragility and proximity to death that tamed her father, a decisive instrument of control over Charlie. Except when Charlie, like her father, responded with violence – and unlike her father, Charlie directed it implacably and brutally onto Peggy herself.

She was going to flaunt her return to health and bestow what he had almost never been able to have – and when he had it experienced this once – would never have again.

But she also wanted something that only Charlie could confer. Their encounter had given Peggy the chance to continue a quest to seek within herself the capacity for heroic self-expression she sensed had somehow been tragically deflected early in her life. The resulting estrangement had produced a sense of herself as a victim and was responsible, she felt, for the mania for control that introduced the hunger that dominated more than ten years of her life – and almost extinguished it.

Only in Charlie's presence could she possibly reclaim her capacity for heroic action and self-expression. Her courage had lingered only in the vestiges of martyrdom and near-suicide, and now she yearned to exercise her will, to act on her own choices. She knew her quest required accepting the risk of violence.

At first Charlie was shocked, and then wondering and grateful, and when she looked up, he was regarding her with awed wonder. Charlie gripped her head. She felt anxiety rising. Rather than succumb to panic she deflected the reflex down within herself and like a wave that is invisible in the open ocean it pulsed through her until at last Charlie cried out. After a long while he moved and kneeled behind her on the rug, caressing her, kissing her all over. She smelled the rum on his breath and realised he had continued drinking.

'Babe, babe, babe . . . ' he said softly, smiling at her.

She looked into Charlie's eyes and they were bleary, emotional, obscurely distraught. Did he sense their reunion was also a farewell?

Charlie slowly sat up and then moved suddenly and decisively, and she was on her hands and knees with Bondi spread before and below, while at their level great white clouds boiled up from the ocean.

'Oh god I love you,' Charlie said as he entered her. 'I always loved you.'

Peggy lifted her eyes and looked out at Bondi. Waves rolled in serenely as if summoned by their ritual rhythm. The skin between her throat and breasts glowed, a path of fire tracing along her body like sunlight on the ocean.

Then it all went wrong. There was something she couldn't define, something elusive about his rhythm as it quickened – just as she should have been assuming control he was moving to dominate her. The body doesn't forget. She refused to disassociate from what might happen. Peggy rejected the retreat into numbness that hunger had once conferred, she was totally, raptly aware of what was happening to her body as power between them shifted.

His rhythm quickened. He heaved, his thrust despairing and yet somehow exultant, and he released a primitive cry. The pathetic broken boy she cared for and had wanted to love again was being replaced by a violent man she remembered all too well. She felt his arm snake over her back and his fingers gripped her neck and throat, pressing against the arteries under her jaw. His old trick.

He was going to put to the test her capacity to endure and suffer, as he had done before. The last time, they were in the hills outside Byron and afterwards he dumped her by the roadside. Peggy was weak and battered, dehydrated and in pain, and she had to walk barefoot several kilometres before a passing car picked her up and drove her to hospital.

She refused to say what had happened to her, or who did it, because she knew if Charlie were arrested for what he had done to her, he would have been found hanging in his cell, a 'suicide.' Hugh knew what happened, and he and Charlie almost killed each other, yet another cycle of violence that resolved nothing.

'Don't,' Peggy said, twisting away and disengaging, but not able to untangle his fingers from her throat. Her awareness was suddenly overflowing with the presence, now fully radiant in the splendour of her confrontation with Charlie, integrated within herself and available in all its clarity to confront Charlie – or any contenders who considered themselves entitled to exercise power over her.

She moved and he lunged with her. She threw herself into a roll against the rug and again he followed, trying to wrench her back into his arms. She could breathe again. As he tried to crush her into his arms he tensed and inadvertently opened a space between their bodies, enough for Peggy to move. She flung her arm out and closed her fingers on the neck of the Bundaberg bottle, whipping herself around and slamming the bottle fast on the side of his skull. She heard the rum splash inside the bottle and saw it spurt out of the open top all over her hand and arm.

Charlie's grip went slack and he collapsed.

Peggy stood up. She no longer had any sensation of the presence but knew the warrior was within her now; every cell of her body was newly vibrant with the truth of life and hope. The siege with which hunger invested her mind and body for ten long years had been raised. The bottle she gripped in her fingers was intact, but her nostrils filled with the smell of rum splashed everywhere – on herself, on Charlie's head and shoulders, and all over the floor.

Blood trickled from Charlie's head just above his ear. He was breathing; she hadn't killed him.

Peggy gingerly put out her foot to the side of his chest and pressed down hard, stepping on him and rocking his whole body. He didn't stir.

'Hey,' Peggy said. She kicked him several times in the ribs and he groaned and slowly moved to avoid her blows.

Peggy gathered up Charlie's clothes, walked briskly to the door of the lift, locked it open, dumped them in the lift, and walked back to the living room.

'Get out.'

He opened his eyes. His retinas were normal, not the pinpoints that would have indicated a concussion, but he was confused.

Peggy showed him her mobile, letting it float above his eyes. 'Get out now, or I'll call the cops.'

He slowly heaved himself up on his hands and knees and crawled in the direction she pointed. Yes, it was love – but like her hunger, it no longer belonged in her life.

Peggy followed him warily, and when Charlie was in the lift she pressed the button for the lobby and stepped back as the doors closed. She walked back into the shining light pouring through the windows. The flat was a mess, but she'd be able to tidy it up.

Her father was next.

Chapter 10

'I don't care about the difference between 'complex' and 'complicated'!' Ilona said with exasperation. 'I want to know what happened between you and Mort. And don't tell me the situation is complex – or complicated.'

'. . . or I'll kill you,' she said, as if to herself.

She didn't give two hoots for Max's theories, she wanted to understand why he chose that very morning to start the row with Mort – as if she weren't already stressed enough.

Max looked at her with a knitted brow and paused, his fingers fragrant with the rosemary leaves he had been picking from the little potted bush in the kitchen window which she grew for her recipes. He looked a bit worried, she noted with satisfaction.

'I first started thinking about the difference between complexity and complications when you were pregnant with Sam,' he said softly. 'Is this enough?'

She nodded, trying to hold back tears of anger and frustration, and he pushed the bowl full of leaves to her.

'Complexity is simultaneous differentiation and integration: when you conceived Sam, within a day your fertlised egg was differentiating by rapidly dividing into cells that became her brain, spinal cord, liver, and lungs, and within a month her heart was beating. But those cells were not just parts: they were also integrating into our baby Samantha. That's complexity.'

Oh god.

Ilona frowned, watching him reach for the bundle of fresh thyme she needed for the roasted potatoes as well. As usual, Max was oblivious to her feelings, to how exposed she felt because he had picked a fight with his partner on just this day, of all days.

'Now complications have the appearance of differentiation, but it's all fake, because those details don't have different purposes, like forming hearts and livers and lungs and eyes, they all have the same purpose, for example the complicated provisions of a software license that give a software company all the rights and a software user no rights.'

Ilona nodded impatiently, fury rising, as she watched Max strip herbal sprigs from their fragile spindles on the thyme stalk, waiting for the right moment to interrupt. Of course she wanted him to stand up to Mort – but not by throwing a public temper tantrum – and not before she and Alexandra had met and sorted out the Instagram mess with the headmistress.

'Complexity is everywhere in nature. But mostly we don't notice because on top of nature is another level of reality – the complications invented by humans. Sam's childbirth was a complex, natural event but it was also shaped, in practical ways, by complications including the fact you were giving birth in Portland Hospital, we had a certain kind of medical insurance, your medical care was subject to the specific legal framework of the UK, and so on. Those complications affected the way we experienced the complexity of nature when you gave birth to Sammie. Thank God we didn't live in America!'

She felt her blood pressure rising and began vigorously chopping the freshly plucked rosemary leaves on the board, restrained now only by reverence for the memories of her pregnancy. He'd better not start on his theories about Covid. She'd spent two years listening to him sneering at government policies and official statistics, especially from America.

'Pregnancy and childbirth are natural and they're complex,' Max continued, 'but medical insurance, regulations and hospital protocols are human inventions and they're complicated, but not complex. Do you see difference?'

'By the way, is this enough thyme?'

Ilona glanced at the bowl in Max's hand, nodded, and looked at him fiercely. 'Dammit Max, you didn't start a row with Mort about pregnancy and childbirth –'

'Well, in a way I did –'

'That's absurd,' Ilona said, exasperated. 'Give me that bowl.'

She set the thyme to the side as she continued chopping the rosemary leaves. She hadn't told him about the appointment with Miss Whidbey, but he also hadn't noticed anything different about her mood. As usual, Max was absorbed in his theories, and indulging himself instead of paying attention to her. Making a hundred million in the stock markets during Corona had made Max absolutely insufferable, as if he knew everything about everything.

'The Corps Act is a masterpiece of complications. It expressly forbids any mergers or acquisitions of public companies, but then it specifies a vast number of complicated rules that govern the merger of public companies under very specific, very complicated circumstances. It's as if the medical industry could have physically prevented you from the complexity of giving birth until you could prove you had memorised the complications of our health insurance policy.'

Max was oblivious to her mood, incapable of empathy as usual – but at last he seemed to be getting to the point.

'Dammit Max, what's your point?'

'So, I asked myself this morning, why are these people sitting around me at this AGM so completely fucked?'

'And it's because of all the complications in ZettaData's financial situation. The business itself is complex, but its financials are full of completely unnecessary complications. I mean, these shareholders are smart people – lots of them are probably scientists and engineers. But think about it – why aren't the Eastern Suburbs and the Lower North Shore full of scientists and engineers anymore? Remember when doctors were usually the wealthiest people in a community?'

She tried to stifle the brew of rage and despair welling up inside her.

'Instead, these days the most expensive parts of town are full of lawyers, investment bankers, accountants and business people, and not coincidentally we're all masters of complications—not complexity. Because today it's not complexities that make you rich, it's complications!'

'What I realised this morning is that Mort and I have been exploiting the complications created by the Corps Act, ASX Listing Rules, and so on, to make our millions. There's no real differentiation in the Corps Act, it's designed so that a few people like me who understand it can make money from everybody else. I don't have any insight into the complexity of nature – but I am expert at understanding complicated, totally artificial financial systems, and I'm also really good at designing complicated deals myself to make loads of money.'

He had finished stripping the thyme from the stalks and was just staring at the shallow dish full of herbs. This was where he was going to bring up his killing in the stock market; Ilona braced herself.

'I'm not sure I want to do that anymore.'

Max's mobile trilled. He extracted it from a pocket with his rosemary and thyme-scented fingers. 'It's Mort,' he said dismissively. 'Fuck him.'

'Take it, Max.'

He looked at her, surprised. 'But we're making dinner, hon.'

'*Take it*, Max!' she said, chopping down so hard through the rosemary leaves that her knife blade struck the cutting board with a bang. Max looked at her with surprise.

'Yeah,' said Max into the phone. 'Yeah ... right ... umhmm ... nuh, not yet,' he continued, walking to the refrigerator and removing eggs, butter, a shallot, and a lemon.

So obsequious – 'Yeah, Mort', 'Right, Mort' ... *anything you say, Mort ... three bags' full, Mort*. No doubt Max was scrambling to kiss Mort's arse after the temper tantrum he threw this morning.

Complexity. Complications. Ridiculous!

'Yeah – see you then,' said Max into the phone, and put it back in his pocket.

'Well?'

'I didn't think you'd want me to take the call,' Max said. 'You're always on at me about how I do everything Mort wants.'

She brushed aside his comment. 'What *did* Mort want – is he ok?'

Finally, she'd forced Max to get to the point! She was worried, too, about what Mort might have heard from Alexandra about the appointment at Nightingale, and the reasons for it.

Max shrugged. 'He seems ok. His plan this morning was unbelieveably fucked up. He was going to cut Luke Terry's balls off in public, right at the AGM – and simultaneously Mort would probably have fucked over 20 000 shareholders. Not that he cared,' he said. 'So I stopped him.'

Ilona didn't care, either. 'Is he upset with you?'

Max shrugged. 'Yeah, he was pretty dark this morning. No surprise. He just said he's got another plan. He must have realised how stupid his first idea was. It wasn't a crime, but it sure as hell would have been a big mistake. I'm so sick of that guy ... honey, are you through with the knife and cutting board?'

Ilona nodded, pushing them across the marble towards Max. Cut his balls off. She had never become used to the way Max talked about his work – it was so crude and awful.

'What's Mort's plan?'

Just when she and Alexandra were getting on so well, were such allies in this crisis, Ilona had begun feeling hopeful their husbands would get along, too.

'He says he knows how to rip Terry's face off,' said Max. 'He'll explain tomorrow at the office – doesn't want to say anything over the phone.' Max concentrated on finely chopping tarragon leaves.

'Well, try not make things worse, Max.'

'We're heading for a bust-up,' Max said. 'The only question is when – but we both have every incentive to lock away the McConnochie deal first.'

She had no illusions about how hard it was to make the kind of money Max earned. She could only imagine the awful things Max did – probably simultaneously boring and heartless – to make his millions in the financial markets. She imagined the money Max made to be bloodstained and covered with hair and bits of teeth and bone. Revolting--but she certainly didn't like the idea of him quitting, either. Because of vague feelings about two scarcely discernible, much less distinguishable, abstractions? Complexities and complications. How absurd!

'Alexandra and I are getting on so well, Max ...' She wanted to put it out there, watching as Max poured white wine vinegar into a saucepan and sprinkled chopped tarragon leaves and ground black pepper onto the mixture as it heated. '.... and the girls are such good friends, too.'

'Don't worry, I've got my eyes on the prize,' he said. 'I'm not going to do anything until McConnochie is a lock.'

Ilona glanced down and found herself slapping hard with the brush as she basted the potatoes with olive oil infused with salt, pepper, rosemary and thyme. Oil splattered everywhere. She looked up and watched as Max whisked in egg yolks and then butter to the pan simmering on top of the double boiler. He worried her sick.

'Will the McConnochie deal really change anything for us?' Ilona asked. The McConnochies' youngest daughter Jennifer was two years ahead of Sam at Nightingale. 'So many of your deals fall over.'

'You remember McConnochie can't lose, right?' Max murmured, adding a dash of lemon juice to the Bearnaise.

'Why?'

'Because it's fixed, darling.'

Could it be true?

'Really, Max?'

'Yep.'

'Months ago the state government announced a competitive, public bidding process to select the winning tunnel contractor! It's been all over the papers for weeks – even the lifestyle sections!'

'Yeah, I know,' said Max. 'The bidding for WholeSydney, which is what the new connecting tunnel is going to be called, will take a year, and cost each of the four bidders millions of dollars in fees for engineering consultants, transportation market consultants, investment bankers, lawyers, accountants, tax experts and public relations consultants.'

'I don't understand, darling,' said Ilona with a frown. 'It sounds super-competitive.'

'That's how it's meant to sound. But the other three companies already each built one of the three existing tunnels,' said Max. 'It's McConnochie Engineering's turn to build a tunnel. They had to wait a couple decades, but they get the biggest one of all. Simple as that.'

'You mean the whole bidding process is a sham?'

Max nodded.

'Is that legal?' She knew the answer.

'It may as well be when the government is on your side,' Max shrugged. 'Haven't you figured out by now that government can do anything it wants?'

'Surely you're being too cynical, Max—or optimistic, I don't know which. He's not the only big engineering company in Australia.'

Martin McConnochie certainly didn't seem impressive enough to fix something; he struck her as kind of weak and a little out to lunch. But Bianca McConnochie did intimidate Ilona, although so far she had treated her graciously at Nightingale events.

'Honey, it's exactly what I was just talking about,' Max exclaimed, unpleasantly triumphant. 'The Tunnel deal is just the opposite version of the AGM this morning. Because you know the secret, hon? Complications are designed to rig the game. It's deliberate. Do you think I made all that money during Corona by believing what the CDC and NIH were saying in America?

'The average person has no chance who believes the information that's available, no matter how smart they are. This morning, for the first time, I didn't feel good about it.'

What he did supported his family. He had some nerve talking about quitting. Max just did what he wanted to do, unaware – or uncaring – about the effect of his actions on her life and the girls' lives – like the way he was making that fat-filled Sauce Bearnaise for the steak he insisted on eating, even though she and the girls were so dedicated to healthful, mostly vegan, meals. His selfish attitude towards meals had contributed to making the lockdowns a special hell for her. Besides, Max's casual slander of Martin McConnochie might circulate through their over-lapping worlds and get back to Bianca. That was the last thing she needed. Max seemed to have a knack for introducing unpleasant surprises into her life.

She and Max had met in the Royal Enclosure at Royal Ascot, moments after Max's girlfriend – a beautiful, burned-out Italian aristocrat desperate to marry and have children had picked a fight and abandoned him. Max was handsome, self-confident and – despite the curious and disapproving glances directed his way after his girlfriend slapped him and then dramatically exited between the tables, seemed amused rather than mortified by his predicament, completely unimpressed by the surrounding royal pomp and circumstance. Ilona's date was a bitter, alcoholic American banker who had abruptly passed out after his fifteenth pink gin, and when Max offered her a lift back to London in the limousine he had hired, and then kissed her in the backseat, Ilona found herself spontaneously responding.

'*Voilà*! Perfect Sauce Bearnaise!' Max said with a theatrical flourish, unaware how tone deaf he sounded. He looked at her, and Ilona could see he had caught her displeased expression. 'The mother sauce is Hollandaise, darling – would that we all had such a good mother!' he said, registering her expression and immediately trying to placate her. 'Of course *you're* the best mother, honey. The girls are so lucky to have you as their mother.'

'Mmhhmm,' Ilona said, refusing to yield. Max was theatrical himself but utterly lacked dramatic skill. She was convinced he enjoyed being a director of the Eden Street Theatre more than being partner at Norton & Ring. He'd better keep his day job. 'When are you ready, darling?' she said, bringing him back to the practical. 'I'll need to call the girls to set the table.'

'I'll go out and grill the steak,' Max said. 'I'll be back in just under ten minutes. But trust me – the McConnochie deal will change everything for us.'

'Ok.' Ilona dropped marinated tofu into the hot skillet and moodily watched the chunks sizzle.

Their first weekend together had been unforgettable, they almost never got out of bed, just ordered in takeaway – Ilona had never had sex like that and was shocked by what she and Max were capable of – and by how fulfilling it felt to subdue and satisfy a big, strong man, leaving him exhausted and utterly depleted.

They continued to date and as part of their growing intimacy Max confessed to all his previous lovers. While he tried to be reassuring, Ilona was shocked by the number of women and the significance these relationships represented.

She had been terribly betrayed, she realised. That wonderful first weekend felt like a trick, a mockery of the romantic and unique connection Ilona thought she and Max had established.

Ilona pulled out the pieces of tofu, placing them to cool on paper towels, and then walked over to the back stairs leading from the kitchen. 'Girls! Time to set the table!'

When the girls appeared they seemed to be in ok moods as they bustled around getting plates, glasses and cutlery and setting the table. Neither had said much about their conversation at the gate with Miss Whidbey, but they hadn't seemed particularly fazed by it, either. Hopefully it wasn't just the calm before the storm.

'You know I'd just love to find the way to really let him have it,' Max said, not realising the girls were already there, as he walked back into the kitchen with his steak resting on its plate under aluminium foil.

Without further discussion they all sat down at the dining room table and silently watched as Ilona served out all the food except Max's steak and Sauce Bearnaise.

'So, how was school today?' Max asked, cutting tentatively into his steak.

Ilona watched with distaste the look of satisfaction appearing on Max's face.

'Dad? Why do you want to let Mort have it?' Sam asked, and shoved a forkful of steamed carrots into her mouth.

'What?' said Max with surprise. 'Who said I wanted that?'

'You said you want to let him have it,' said Billie. 'You obviously meant Mort.'

Max ladled more Sauce Bearnaise on his steak, stalling. He looked up. 'Would someone please pass me the salt and pepper?' he asked innocently.

'Dad – has something gone wrong with the McConnochie deal?' Sam asked.

'What?' said Max, putting down his knife and fork. He looked from Sam to Ilona.

'Yeah, daddy, don't let Mort Norton keep it all for himself!' chimed in Billie.

Max turned to Ilona in disbelief.

'I haven't said a word!' Ilona said, shaking her head.

'How did you hear about the McConnochie deal?' Max asked.

'That's all Trixie talked about during the sleepover,' said Sam.

Ilona watched the girls exchange significant looks and she gazed at them sternly, willing them to look at her so she could signal they were verging on dangerous territory and she would hold them responsible if their father twigged.

'Yeah,' said Billie. 'And Trixie said Mort's your boss. Is that right, daddy?'

Ilona watched Max flush.

It was true her husband was the minority partner. It was an expensive and humiliating mistake to accept only one third of the equity in the partnership, given how much money Max made for Norton & Ring—of which Mort had received two-thirds. Ilona never let him forget it, but she thought only the four of them knew—she and Max, Alexandra and Mort. Obviously the knowledge, in distorted terms, was all over the playground of Nightingale School.

' – and she said it's her dad's tunnel,' said Sam.

Ilona could see Max forcing himself to smile. 'That's ridiculous, sweetie, Trixie's exaggerating the truth to make herself seem important,' he answered calmly. 'Her father wouldn't have said that because it's not true. It's a huge tunnel and we're only going to be investing in a very small piece of it – probably about five percent. The five percent will be owned by our firm, which means the Nortons and our family will each own a very small piece of the tunnel.' He signalled the table with his finger. 'All of us.'

'She said the firm is his. His name's first. All your customers are his friends.'

Max reddened further. 'Mort and I are partners,' he said, slowly and deliberately. 'We're –' he choked a little. 'Friends.'

'Yeah, right, daddy!' sang Billie.

'Come on, Dad, everybody says Mort is bad,' said Sam. 'Other parents are afraid of him.'

Max sat back. 'Now sweetie, that's ridiculous! Where do you get this stuff? Do you think Richard Wander is afraid of Mortie? Justice Rosebery? Martin McConnochie? Kent Logan?'

'Martin McConnochie is,' said Sam firmly. 'That's why he's giving Mort a piece of the tunnel.'

Ilona broke in. 'That's such awful gossip – don't believe it, darlings. These private schools are hotbeds of slander – and unfortunately Nightingale, so superior in every other way, is no exception when it comes to harming perfectly innocent people with terrible lies. All imaginary! People are jealous, darlings, you have to understand that. They try to drag down those better than them, the only way they can – with their awful lies. It's just disgraceful!'

Ilona looked at her daughters severely.

'You know what a wonderful person Alexandra is,' she scolded. 'How could she be married to Mort if he was a bad man? Do you think Alexandra is afraid of Mort?' Ilona's laugh trilled. 'I can assure you she is not!'

Max cut away at his steak with a troubled expression.

The Sauce Bearnaise on his steak added insult to injury, and Ilona glanced away, trying to stifle her resentment at Max for being so casual about what he ate. *Sure, a bit more*

Bearnaise, why not? Of course – I'll take that last cutlet! Everything she ate was always so calibrated, chosen so thoughtfully, scientifically, so responsibly – and anticipated for so long, and with such longing – before it ever touched her lips.

'You know, Sam and Billie, what you've said about Mort and me isn't entirely –'

'Darling,' she broke in firmly. 'I think it's time to move on. Really, darling.'

Max's gaze rested on her. He seemed to be considering what she said, and at the same time processing other voices, other memories, possibly other rules and codes. Tangled in his own damned complications.

'Ok,' he said, at last. He took a spoonful of Bearnaise and offered it to the girls, his eyebrows raised hopefully. 'Would you like some, Sam ... Billie? It would taste so yummy with your steamed green beans and carrots ...'

To her quiet but immense satisfaction, the girls shook their heads, loyal to her.

The remainder of the dinner was eaten quietly. Max didn't even ask about their classes or homework, which was highly unusual.

Even after the demoralising revelations of Max's past, Ilona was still competitive enough to snatch him away from that Italian countess, convincing herself she had forgiven Max – a self-delusion that didn't even survive their honeymoon.

Max had such a knack for making things worse. If Max hadn't looked at her so crossly the night of the sleepover when she got off the phone with Selena's mum and he asked her what happened, her courage might not have failed and she might have told him.

Couldn't he see how distraught she had been to hear that their daughters had allegedly been bullying the Woodbridge girl? She just hadn't been able to bear the thought of listening to another one of his lectures. Her heart had been in her mouth already, feeling so guilty about what had just happened under their roof, on her watch. Maybe if she and Max had been able to work together that evening, everything would have turned out fine – it probably wasn't until after that call that the shaving and the Instagram post happened.

The more she thought about it, the more she realised Max was the cause of the Instagram disaster—it was actually all his fault. Max just had to be so over-bearing that evening, so petty, about the damned scrambled eggs in his hair.

And yet again it was she who had to deal with the consequences – in this case the meeting with Miss Whidbey.

She felt alone, abandoned, enduring her own personal lockdown, an exile in her own life. Ilona had never imagined emptiness could feel so unbearably palpable, that loneliness could seem as physically suffocating as being crushed by a crowd. Not until she married Max, that is.

Chapter 11

When he saw the sun rise above Ben Buckler, Max knew he had one last wave. Then he would drive home, jump in the shower and get ready for work. He'd been surfing for forty-five minutes in shadows, but now the dazzling light looked molten on the heaving waves, and suddenly the foam seemed illuminated from within.

If he returned home early enough Sam and Billie would probably still be asleep, and he loved being able to gently awaken them. What they said last night still bothered him. What would they be thinking when they sleepily looked at him? It was a moment he usually loved.

Several dozen surfers bobbed on their boards around him. He could hear Spanish, Portuguese, and German. The usual Bondi mix of European backpackers, Australian uni students, and plenty of locals. Surfers in the line-up had a wide range of skills, from experts to beginners – dangerous to themselves and others. Typical Bondi surf traffic, as bad in its way as New South Head Road would be on the way into the CBD. It had been a bad couple years, with the lockdowns and the really wet, cold El Niño summer that followed. Bondi was back in all its glory.

Max imagined Sam and Billie sleeping. He couldn't refute what they said, certainly not as emphatically as Ilona, because it was mostly true.

Max smiled at Manon, who had just paddled up and was sitting on her board next to him.

'Ça va?'

Manon smiled at him through her wet cinnamon curls. 'Oui. Ça va?'

Max nodded with a smile. She was a French backpacker who worked as a waitress in a Bondi café. He inhaled deeply. Manon had learned snowboarding in Chamonix, but mountains don't move, and waves not only move, they appear and then disappear forever. The wave you've surfed will never appear again, and what you learned on it has to be adapted to the next: unlike a mountain slope, you never surf the same wave twice. It's hard to get enough experience to be a good surfer.

Max looked out at the horizon, where there was no indication of an approaching wave. A breeze nuzzled his shoulders.

Sunlight outlined Manon with a golden thread, her thighs brown and glistening on either side of the surfboard, water lapping against her half-submerged legs. A thin band of red stretched tightly across her hips. Max tore his eyes away and looked again at the horizon.

She had the usual beginner's problem: not knowing where to catch the approaching wave, and so was usually beaten to the right spot. Competition for Bondi waves was just as ruthless as in the financial markets – and outsiders had similar odds of success.

He couldn't let Sam and Billie think about him the way they had last night. He was their father. But he had to continue working with Mort long enough to secure a place for Norton & Ring in the McConnochie Tunnel Consortium. There was too much money involved to screw that one up. Fuck-you money.

As he looked out to sea, Max felt uneasy. An amorphous blob appeared on the Cartesian line of the horizon, the first sign of the next wave, but he wasn't interested, his practiced eye told him it would be too small for him.

'There's one for you,' Max said in a low voice to Manon, pointing with his chin to the almost imperceptible ripple along the horizon. He didn't want the other surfers to hear him, and sound carries easily across water. They were alert to Max's every move, hoping to catch waves by imitating what he did. They knew how good he was.

'Here's what we'll do,' said Max quietly. 'I'm going to take off and start paddling to the right. The pocket will appear to the left.'

A pocket is the point where the wave first becomes possible to surf. Depending on how it breaks, sections on either side often become surfable too, but the surfer in the pocket is first and has right of way on the wave. At the moment of lift off, a surfer's board points straight ahead, but immediately after standing a surfer cuts to the left or right along the wave, and other surfers yield to avoid collisions. Max had noticed Manon floundered in the ocean, unable to anticipate where the pocket would appear.

'Don't worry about me or anybody else. I'm going to draw them away. Count to five, and then slowly start paddling towards the beach. When you've gone about twenty metres take a few strokes to the left and the pocket should be right there. Keep looking over your shoulder – paddle hard – and go for it!'

Manon looked at Max questioningly with her beautiful eyes. He flashed her an encouraging smile. They exchanged nods and Max took off, making a flurry of big splashes to attract as much attention as possible. It was the same kind of strategy he used in the markets when positioning Norton & Ring for a deal.

Max drew off most of the pack, with a couple dozen surfers eagerly paddling after him, hoping to ride a section of the same wave even though they knew he would ride the best part. Max decoyed them thirty metres away from the sweet spot and then looked around.

He was rewarded by the sight of Manon up on her board, her lovely red and orange bikini bottom swinging above the spray coming up through her tanned legs as she disappeared down the face of the wave.

'*Allez, allez, allez!*' he called, his last glimpse of Manon's tangled cinnamon curls flying in the breeze.

Max contentedly paddled back to wait for his last wave. All around him in the backwash Max heard the hissing and popping of spray, and then the rumble from the close out of the wave he'd helped Manon catch. Life could be simple.

The last big wave had been about fifteen minutes before so another big set was due any time now. Archie, a local in his early sixties, eased up close to Max, and despite all the beauty surrounding them, Max suddenly felt like he was back at Norton & Ring. Archie had been surfing Bondi since he was a boy, could move fast on that big board with his powerful chest and shoulders, and had expert timing. Max had seen him wield his board like a war galley in the ancient Greek navy to ram other surfers off the wave. The Mort Norton of Bondi.

'That was a neat trick you just pulled, mate,' said Archie, sitting up on his board as water streamed off him. His gut was even bigger than his powerful shoulders, and he looked like a pink walrus. Archie was leader of the pack who made it a point of pride to snatch waves from newbies like Manon. 'I watched the whole thing as I paddled up.'

Max smiled briefly and nodded.

Max suddenly felt dread in his stomach; a powerful urge to pull the nose of his surfboard around and start paddling towards the beach. The dread appeared for no reason – as it often did these days. It had nothing to do with Archie. Was it his intuition warning him? The ocean, once glassy and buoyant, began to seem enigmatic and menacing.

Max could remember a time, long ago, when he trusted his intuition, and counted on his emotions generally as reliable guides to what he should or should not do. Perhaps after forcing himself to act against his deepest feelings – marrying Ilona even though she didn't seem to love him, and he wasn't sure if he loved her; agreeing to return to Sydney with the girls; becoming partners with Mortimer Norton and accepting a minority stake – he had wrecked his intuition and it went haywire, broadcasting random attacks of dread for no reason.

The problem now was that both his good and bad decisions seemed hopelessly entangled with one another. Starting many years ago, he'd begun to notice a particularly strong sense of dread almost overcoming him just before something wonderful happened – the births of his daughters, confirmation a big deal had closed. His personal lesson from Covid was to be not afraid, to stay objective and rational and trust his intuition. But despite his renewed confidence, somewhere something deep inside himself seemed damaged, and continued sending wild, random signals into his consciousness.

Max forced himself to remain sitting calmly on the board. For example, what might he miss if he gave in to the fear he was feeling right now? Even though it was an almost physical tug drawing him out of the water and back to the beach, he had a mysterious awareness, detectable behind the powerful dread in the foreground, that a fateful synchrony depended on his mastering this fear and staying for the next wave.

A couple minutes later Max and Archie simultaneously spotted a blobby swelling of water forty or fifty metres long as it emerged out of the chop in the ocean, steadily rose and extended its clarifying curve across the horizon. A big wave. Archie grinned sheepishly, reared up his longboard and began paddling to the left to intersect with the approaching wave.

Instantly Max was on his belly, paddling with deep, confident strokes in a wide arc around Archie who looked over his shoulder in the foamy chop and gave Max a half-smile, half-grimace.

There was a general sound of splashing and jets of spray exploded upwards on all sides as the best surfers paddled after Max and Archie in an attempt to get a section of the same wave, while the majority paddled away from the break zone as they realised how big the wave was going to be. It would crush newbies.

Max and Archie competed stroke for stroke towards a seemingly empty patch of water in the flux of the ocean. Max was stronger but Archie's big board moved faster through the water than Max's short board.

They arrived together at a spot where the water swirled shapelessly and looked over their shoulders. Soon a perfect wall of water appeared behind them and loomed three metres above their heads, a shining vessel of light, supple and voluptuous. Already trailing thin plumes of white foam unravelling on the sea breeze, the wave reflected sunlight like the blade of a sword.

A split second between Max and Archie would decide who claimed this wave. The sea in front was suddenly smooth, its level dropping as water was drawn beneath them into the wave looming behind. Both paddled furiously, apparently frozen in place as currents flowed under them, sucking them up and onto the wave as the tails of their boards lifted. They rose skyward – heads low, feet high – on the steepening slope of the wave, its roar loud in their ears as its mighty pulse pushed them forward.

Archie was about a metre in front, ready to wield his big board like a club. Max surged forward and his board caught the lip where the wave first folds over into a tender spiral and opens like a woman's body to the surfer: the pocket, the secret structure where a man fits perfectly.

Kairos.

Max sprang to his feet right behind where Archie's feet kicked. Max's board surged out of the pocket the way he picked off the Range Rover careening down Bellevue Road yesterday morning, laughing as he plummeted down the wave. Swinging his arms in a great arc, Max cut to the right and hurtled along the face, staying high on the wave and exulting in the speed, air and light.

Max relaxed and stayed just ahead of the flux and chaotic avalanching foam, surrendering completely into his expanded senses, all other dilemmas left behind as Max maneouvered without thinking. Sea foam streamed off the wave in the shore breeze like the horsehair plumes of Greek warriors charging into battle. For the first time in a long while, as he danced exultantly along the curves of the wave on his way to the beach, Max was filled with the joy of being alive.

Chapter 12

'Are you worried Charlie might come looking for you here?' asked Juanita.

Peggy wasn't worried about Charlie. She was done with worries. She felt a new sense of power and self-confidence, an acceptance of her identity. The lies of hunger, the sensation of self that was defined by thoughts, was a delusion of meaning. She fought her way to the truth.

'His mum called me last night,' she said. 'He told her some version of what happened. She told me he was really sorry. He's leaving this morning for Byron and going back to live with her.'

'Really? He's gone?'

'If he isn't, I can handle him.'

They walked south along the Bondi water line, waves washing over the tops of their feet, on the way to practice yoga against the sun-warmed rocks of South Bondi.

Juanita looked at her searchingly without a word.

'I know,' said Peggy. 'Why did I put myself in the very same situation again?'

'I'm not blaming you, darling.'

Peggy put her arm around Juanita's shoulders as they walked. The beach often felt colder at sunrise. For most of their walk Peggy had regretted not bringing a jumper, but with the sun well above Ben Buckler the light was now flooding everywhere, carrying a delicate, satisfying warmth.

'I wonder whether what happened to Ryan, and Charlie, is the new normal for me,' said Peggy.

Ryan was fifty-five and Peggy had been seeing him for a few months, a ruggedly handsome widower with a lucrative city accounting partnership and two teenagers. Two weeks ago Ryan broke his pelvis in a motorcycle accident.

Juanita laughed.

Juanita was the founder and publisher of a free weekly magazine, *The Waverley Tribune*. It thrived on cascades of revenue generated by lavish, full colour, full-page advertisements for the mansions of Sydney. Real estate porn displayed to inflame the imaginations of the wealthiest women in Sydney and prompt them to encourage their husbands to rise to the occasion. The royal road to social glory in Sydney was *The Waverley Tribune's* society column, featuring the owners of those houses and their friends at play.

'When I was a girl, my father would sometimes do a trick at dinner he learned growing up in Europe,' Peggy said. 'He'd wet his forefinger and move it around the lip of his wine glass in circles until a clear musical tone came from the glass.'

Juanita nodded. 'I remember him doing that.'

'What used to bother me was his expression,' Peggy said. 'He'd be looking expectantly around the table, watching everybody, and to me it was so obvious he was manipulating us, especially the guests, who would be so amazed. He had us exactly where he wanted us.

'All I wanted to do was figure out how I could sing at exactly the right pitch to make his wine glass shatter. I wanted to surprise him the way he surprised everybody else.'

'Sometimes I think you're crazy,' said Juanita affectionately.

'I'm not crazy.' Peggy shook her head looking at the water. The nearly-spent waves nuzzled her feet, and the water was warmer than the air. 'Not any more.'

In the distance, a choice wave had just appeared at the south break, where the swell is biggest. A surfer with a wide chest and shoulders outlined in his black wetsuit against the white sea foam, muscled up on the rising wave and leaped to his feet right in the pocket, dropping past a longboarder. The surfer glided adeptly to the right, staying high on the wave as he carved across its glistening surface with a relaxed, rapid rhythm.

'Look at that guy,' Peggy said, nodding towards the ocean.

He surfed with unusual grace, dancing lightly along the complex curves and planes of the wave. A male surfer typically cuts aggressively back and forth through the sections, heedless of natural shapes as he carves his path across the face with arbitrary power. But not this guy, who surfed gracefully in harmony with the wave. The way a woman would.

Juanita's eyes followed Peggy's gaze. 'He's not bad, is he? Probably some tradie having a bit of fun before the day starts.'

Peggy smiled at Juanita. She liked her tradies.

Just when it looked like the surfer was going to rocket up the face of the wave burst through the curling lip and dive off the board to land on the back of the wave, he leaned deeply and flung his arms around in a pinwheel, exploding through the lip curling above him then carved a deep foaming line back down the wave and threw a rooster tail of spray as he raced just in front of the wave while it collapsed into chaos.

Peggy and Juanita walked in silence along the beach watching the surfer as he skimmed through the whitewater towards the beach.

As the surfer approached the beach he leaped up and ran out of the water, racing the shorey that reared up behind him.

'That's Max Ring!' said Juanita. 'Max!'

The surfer turned his head and smiled.

'Don't tell him who I am,' Peggy said in a low voice. She had never seen him in person, only the photo on the Norton & Ring website and photos with his glamorous wife in the social pages of *The Waverley Tribune*.

Max stripped off the top half of his wetsuit and walked towards them with his board. He was a strong older guy and moved easily. Not what she expected from her father's partner.

'Hey, Juanita!'

His thick black curls were cut a little too short to express themselves. His eyes scrutinised Peggy impersonally as he walked up and then smiled at Juanita, his smile framed by a solid jaw set in a high box of cheekbones.

'Hello, darling,' Juanita said, her arm lightly encircling his shoulders. She kissed him softly close to his mouth, and Peggy noticed her press her breast firmly against his naked ribs.

'I'm wet,' Max said, his face relaxing into a boyish smile.

'It doesn't matter, darling.'

Peggy had always thought the black and white photographs on the Norton & Ring website were meant to portray traditional respectability. Her father looked like a European film producer from the 1950s, and his partner looked determined, his mouth clamped shut in a tight line, his eyes blank and uncompromising. The boring partner. Seeing him in the flesh, she wondered what he and her father had in common.

'This is Peggy, my friend from Byron ... Max.'

His eyes fixed her frankly, observant but neutral, as if assessing a menu in an expensive restaurant. 'Love Byron,' he said. 'Where?'

'My mum has a farm off Skinner's Shoot Road.'

'Nice,' he said. His eyes rested on her, blankly, but absorbing every detail of her.

Now she understood: a predator.

She wasn't going to back down: their eyes held each other until Peggy had the sensation they were touching. It was Max who glanced away, and his gaze rested on the rolled yoga mats the two women were carrying. 'Going to practice against the cliff?' he asked casually.

'It's time for our Surya Namaskar,' said Juanita.

'Sun salute,' Max nodded. There was something hard about him, and he seemed to know it. His boyish smiled reappeared, a glaze of charm over unyielding rock. 'It's nice and warm there after sunrise. Maybe I should try it.'

His eyes returned to Peggy, the moment of charm dissipating as he assessed her.

'I didn't know you did yoga, darling,' said Juanita.

'Well, I'm just a beginner,' he smiled, making much more of an effort for Juanita. 'But I take classes once or twice a week at Avalokiteshvarashala.'

'Really? I go there myself,' said Peggy, smiling at how well Max pronounced the daunting name of Bondi's best yoga studio.

'When?' he asked.

'Wednesday afternoon at three.'

'Ah – I go Tuesdays and sometimes Thursday mornings at six.'

She sensed a filament of interest cast over her. He buried the tip of his board in the sand and rested a hand on the tail.

'Hey Juanita, when was the last time you featured somebody from Pymble in your social pages?'

Peggy and Juanita looked at each other.

'Oh – I don't know!' said Juanita. 'It's probably been a while.'

'A long while?'

'Yes, probably,' said Juanita.

'There must be plenty of expensive houses.'

'Yes, we do get ads for houses in Pymble from time to time.'

'Pymble's so peaceful,' said Peggy. 'All those big trees.'

'What about your social pages?' Max asked. 'Any events in Pymble?'

'Oh, not really,' replied Juanita.

Max nodded sagely, glancing out at the waves.

'Why do you ask?'

'Oh, no particular reason,' Max said. 'I met someone from Pymble yesterday. I was quite impressed.'

'Was it a charity event?'

Max laughed. 'No – more like a feeding frenzy. One I brought to an abrupt halt before lots of little turtles got devoured.'

Peggy blushed, recognising the reference to the play she was working on. Max was looking out at the waves and didn't notice.

'Maybe that's it,' said Juanita, looking as confused as Peggy felt. The turtle reference was definitely obscure, and Max seemed to feel no obligation to explain. 'Respectable, successful, good people – but perhaps they're not hungry enough in Pymble. I don't know.'

'I haven't been hungry for a long time,' Max said. 'But that's not the point. A man can live for weeks without food. Hunger is a motivation for people who don't really care.'

Peggy smiled, ruefully this time, hearing the way he under-rated the terrible power of hunger. But it was true hunger doesn't force you to eat. It forces you into a blind ascent towards a metaphysical delusion high above eating, or caring, and finally breathing and life itself.

He looked at them, rapt in some inner vision. 'I'm thirsty. All my life I've been thirsty. Thirst torments you every second. It can kill you in a day.'

He gave her a chill.

'Thirst makes you hallucinate about water if you can't get it. Thirst can make you drink the blood of the other guy in the lifeboat.'

'Ah, the inner secrets of Norton & Ring,' said Juanita lightly.

Peggy suddenly understood the strange flickering in Max's eyes between warmth and coldness. It was self-protection.

'You can't satisfy thirst like that, Max,' said Peggy. 'You can't ignore it, or make it go away.'

Juanita shot Peggy a warning glance.

'That's true,' said Max.

'Your problem is you can't get enough of something you don't need,' said Peggy. 'You just want what everybody else wants. They don't know why they want it, either.'

'What?'

'I don't think you know what you really need.' Even in just a few minutes, she recognised the same desperate attempt to prove he was worthy of being loved she had felt for so long.

'Maybe that's right. What do I need?'

'Well – as a first step – you need to become like water.'

'What?'

'You're a surfer – you know the power of water.'

'But I'm a surfer, not a wave.'

'Nothing is softer and more yielding than water, and yet nothing can resist it. You can put your fist through water without damaging it, and yet water carries the biggest ship effortlessly,' she said. 'Gracefully.'

Max nodded. 'I get that, I think. That's how I think about waves, yielding but powerful.'

Peggy smiled and reached out to touch his arm. 'So we all need to become living water ourselves.'

He looked at Peggy contemplatively. 'I like it.'

He leaned forward and gave Juanita and Peggy each a kiss on the cheek. 'Maybe I'll see you in yoga class,' he said to Peggy. Then knees high, his surf board under his arm, he charged off across the sand.

Juanita looked at Peggy with an eyebrow raised. 'Living water. Sometimes you're so cosmic, darling.'

Peggy smiled. 'I can tell Max is one of those guys who knows how to make women feel good about themselves. But he doesn't give himself; he can't.'

'Sounds like you when you were sick,' said Juanita. 'You were *so* self-obsessed, darling.'

'I know,' Peggy nodded. She turned and watched Max thread his way through the crowd on the beach and disappear.

Juanita smiled. 'You realise Max just wants to root you, don't you darling?'

Chapter 13

'Are the latest CVs in the Dropbox?' Max asked Matina as he passed the front desk. Every week dozens of CVs flooded in to Norton & Ring. He was going to sack Roebling and Hauptraum, two of their five analysts, so it was time to go through the hopefuls accumulated in the file.

'Yes, Max.'

It was the second morning in a row he thought he saw a malicious gleam in her eyes. He almost stopped, but there was lots to do to clean up the mess from yesterday's AGM.

Unlike Mort, who liked the cave-like atmosphere of a darkened office, Max always kept the office blinds open. His view to the east included the breathtaking line of sight across Sydney Harbour, taking in Rose Bay, Vaucluse, and the curious notch where the slope of Vaucluse seems to disappear before re-emerging in the hump of Watson's Bay, The Gap. Once in a while he turned from his work and looked out the window, contemplating the great beauty produced by the ancient catastrophe that flooded the valley.

'Hey Mort,' Max called towards Mort's office as he stepped through the door of his own office.

There it was – as always – the first thing Max saw every morning: the Mignano print.

But it isn't what riveted Max's attention: to his surprise, Mort was sitting in one of the chairs at the table in Max's office. Behind Max's desk was a powerful looking young man with a square-shaped skull and a sweet face. Perhaps a Pacific Islander. He was wearing a t shirt printed with the word 'SECURITY.' Next to him stood a man wearing a suit and a nervous expression.

'What's up?' asked Max. Had there been a burglary? Another leak in the air conditioning system?

The nervous man in the suit was holding a sheaf of papers.

'This is it, Max,' said Mort. 'You're out.'

Mort was smiling.

'What do you mean "I'm out"?'

The sounds that came out of Mort's mouth only gradually assumed form as English words in Max's mind.

The muscular young man didn't move, but the nervous man in the suit shifted his weight on his feet, ineptly, like someone unaccustomed to exercise.

'Why are these guys behind my desk?' Max asked. He was pleased to hear his voice sounding as languid as it usually did.

'They're your transition team,' said Mort.

'My what?'

'Nige, give my soon-to-be-former partner the papers that dissolve the partnership,' said Mort. 'By the way, I'm still going to call the firm Norton & Ring; I like the name.'

Max looked out the window and across the harbour to The Gap, visible from the CBD only by the tall conifers that mark it like crosses at Golgotha. He'd known it since he was a boy – a hidden, negative space. The Gap was the fatal fissure in the Vaucluse cliffs where they crumbled a million years ago, along with the cliffs between what is now North and South Head, flooding the primeval valley and drowning every being living there.

Max regarded the nervous man, whose face hardened and lost its expression of anxiety, his eyes suddenly alert and glittering as he stepped forward. In two fingers of his left hand he offered his business card, which Max accepted and read.

Nigel McKee. Mort had called him 'Nige' – he always chewed off the end of names like Nigel. He was a partner in the law firm Norton & Ring regularly worked with. Not a name partner – Max had never heard of him.

'You're partners with Allan?' Max asked in wonder. 'I'm a client.'

'Actually, Norton & Ring is our client,' McKee said, his nod out of synch with what he said. He should have shaken his head.

'Nigel, give him the fucking papers,' said Mort loudly. 'Jimmy here will help you pack whatever you can personally carry out of your office, Max. You've got twenty minutes to sign the papers, pack up, and leave the premises. I'm terminating for cause.'

Max kept his hands at his side. His first emotion took him by surprise. Wild, exhilarating glee welled up from deep inside, from a place he didn't know. He stifled a delighted laugh. Krishna had also told Arjuna it is better to fail at your own *dharma* than succeed at another's *dharma*. For the past five years, he'd been succeeding at Mort's *dharma*.

'Mort, do you have any idea what you're doing?' Max grinned.

'Sign the papers and fuck off,' Mort grimaced. 'Give him the pen, Nige! Jimmy, tell him to get out of here!'

'Are you mad? What the fuck is going on, Mort?'

'You're fucked,' said Mort.

'Yesterday you tried to start a bear run on ZettaData's stock in front of the board at their own AGM – and this morning you've organised this?' Max demanded. 'You're barking mad.'

Mort sat very still at Max's table. 'You're bloody lucky I don't rip you a new arsehole before I turf you out of here, after what you did yesterday,' said Mort. 'Sign the fucking papers, and get out. Nige, I said, "Give him the fucking pen!"'

'Give me the papers,' Max said to McKee.

Max took the papers from the lawyer's hand. 'Presumably John oversaw the drafting of this Deed.'

John was the main partner in McKee's law firm, a man with a bleak view of human nature who persisted in acting on the basis of a private code mostly consistent with traditional ethics. He was a desperately unhappy man, but Max trusted him.

'Absolutely,' McKee said in a strange, dusty way.

Max smiled. 'He knows this is total bullshit,' he commented as he scanned it.

He rapidly read the Deed: he was being terminated for cause, being offered a lump sum payment of ... $3 million – Ridiculous!

... and two further payments of $1 million each – even more ludicrous!

Max recalled with a twinge of conscience how many times he'd listened to Mort threaten a person in meetings. Mort's threats were preposterous: ridiculous, illegal. Max would wonder why victims of his tirades lacked the presence of mind to realise Mort couldn't possibly do what he was threatening to do – and why they lacked the courage to call him on it. How many times had he listened, wondering why they didn't call Mort's bluff, feeling a total lack of respect for them – yet never acknowledging the ugliness of Mort's actions? It had been so obvious to Max their predicaments weren't real, that Mort's threats were just a bully's ugly joke, so he had done nothing. But they weren't a joke to Mort's victims.

Max shook himself slightly and continued reading.

' ... any further payment shall be subject to his performance of the termination provisions ...' He and Mort would be signing mutual indemnities, holding one another harmless, and Max – but not Mort – would be signing a three year non-competition agreement and consenting not to solicit the employees of Norton & Ring.

The inevitable, coming from Mort – these nasty clauses were popping up like fish-hooks, insults added to injury.

Mort was trying to steal tens of millions from Max and force him out of the Sydney financial markets completely. The document was a variation on Mort's attempted dirge for ZettaData, another occasion Mort was using intimidation and manipulation. The proposed Termination Deed was a fractal pattern, the merest discernable form of a shape replicated on a vast scale in all Mort's deals, in his career, in his life, and the universe he formed around himself.

Max's mind was now functioning smoothly in rapidly ascending gears, roaring along well within its performance envelope, navigating the treacherous road and anticipating what lay ahead. The ancients considered *kairos* a basic law of the universe: the moment when an arrow could be released to hit its target, when a shuttle could make its way through the warp and woof of threads on a loom. It was the opportune moment, suddenly opened like a path or a tube through the flow of ordinary time, *chronos*, that tallied the chaos of reality. *Kairos* was the opening in traffic for the driver in his Porsche, the pocket in a wave unfolding into a tube that might drown an ordinary man but powered the surfer to glory and joy.

This document hadn't just been thrown together. It was obviously carefully prepared long before yesterday's AGM. The provisions were carefully tailored to his and Mort's partnership agreement and the exact current financial circumstances of the firm. It would have taken days – weeks – to draft and finalise.

Max looked up at Mort. 'This is about McConnochie, isn't it? You've been preparing to do this for a long time, haven't you? You want the full hundred bars all to yourself, don't you? Fifty bars isn't enough for you. Greedy pig!'

'Fifty? You mean sixty-seven!'

'Oh no Mort – we split fifty-fifty – or I'll walk anyway.'

'Is that right, Max?' Mort said at last. 'You know the truth? You're a ten per-center, mate. I never should have agreed to give you one point more. If you were a real partner I might have been right to give you twenty percent. But one third – all these years? Just because you went on a hot streak during Covid—when the people I've talked to said you were taking more risk than you admitted—you suddenly think you're a star. As far as I'm concerned, you owe me about thirty-three bars I've overpaid you over the last five years. And I'm going to take it out of what you made during Covid. Now sign – and get out.'

Max's exhilaration was transforming into a sense of meaning. It was no longer just a feeling, it had a name: freedom. His relationship to Mortimer Norton, and everything he represented, had just magically evaporated. That night he would be able to look his daughters in the eye.

He was cleansed, liberated. He savoured the deep breath flowing through his nostrils and into his lungs.

'I'm surprised you're so sentimental about our *nom de guerre*, Mort. Very gratifying.' Normally Mort didn't understand sophisticated allusions but he spoke about seven European languages, apparently all badly but functionally. He would know what *nom de guerre* meant.

'Don't be a dickhead, Max,' said Mort. 'This offer is only available for the next ten minutes. You leave this office without signing, you get nothing.'

Max glanced around his office: the personal photographs framed in silver on the credenza behind him, the dozens of plexiglass tombstones on the low wooden filing cabinets on either side of the door that signified both the deals he'd done at Norton & Ring and the graveyard he was escaping.

The Mignano print.

On his desk was a small cardboard box. Mort clearly intended Max to make what he thought would be an agonising choice between his personal effects and the Mignano print. He wouldn't be able to carry both.

'In the first place,' said Max calmly, 'I'm not about to sign this piece of shit. It's a web of lies not worth the paper it's printed on. Secondly, I need a trolley and the help of Jimmy here to assist me with taking a few items I'll need over the next few weeks' – he smiled at Mort – 'before I return.'

Mort grinned. 'Maxie, let me give you a little friendly advice. My mate Mick, Chief Justice Roseberg to you, will eventually get this case after you've spent a bar on lawyers getting it to the Supreme Court.' Mort stood up. 'Sign and get out.'

A million dollars was probably right. Divorces are expensive – because they're worth what they cost. Max tossed the papers on his desk and headed towards the Mignano print.

Mort stood up and blocked him.

'Get out of my way, Mort – that's my print.'

Max couldn't see Mort's eyes even though they were only inches away, only a shiny darkness between his heavy lids and the pouches underneath.

'Deck him, Jimmy,' Mort grunted.

Max reached for Mort's throat with his left hand, shifting his weight smoothly as if he were on a surfboard, his hand coming up under Mort's line of sight.

Mort instantly reacted and knocked Max's rising forearm aside. Max dropped his hand to Mort's chest and leaned with all his weight, his palm directly on Mort's sternum, shoving him hard. Mort twisted to shed as much of the pressure as possible, but still staggered backwards and fell into the chair.

Max was astonished by Mort's agility and quickness – the reactions of an experienced fighter – but there was no time to lose, and he reached for the print. Then Jimmy enveloped Max with his bulk and threw him against the wall.

Max was jammed against the wall, one hand still on the side of the print's frame. 'Nigel – this is common assault,' he said, through gritted teeth. 'I have a lease on this office, the print is my personal property, and I've been attacked. As a lawyer you're an officer of the court and will perjure yourself if you say anything different.'

'My client is within his rights to remedy the breach in the agreement,' said McKee, almost panting out of nervousness.

Mort was breathing heavily, too. 'You ever touch me again and I'll take off the body parts that touched me, dickhead. Get him out of here, Jimmy.'

Max's hand was wrenched from the print and he was spun around to the door. Jimmy was all over him, enveloping Max and carrying him towards the door as if he were being swept along by cement discharged from a truck. Despite Max's struggling, Jimmy forced him to the door of the office and shoved him into the corridor.

'I hope this feels good while it lasts, Mort,' said Max, leaning against the opposite wall, straining to breathe. 'Because I'm going to get an injunction and an AVO. I'll think about criminal charges while I'm at it.'

An Apprehended Violence Order would have been handy before he walked in.

Max glanced to his right. Matina, Roebling and Hauptraum were watching from the end of the corridor. They could have warned him but didn't. Matina's eyes were blank now, while Roebling looked at him in glum triumph. Hauptraum, as usual, didn't even seem to register Max.

What really hurt, more than Jimmy's sharp grip on his biceps as he was hustled down the hall, was acknowledging to himself that he had been complicit in all those occasions when Mort was a bully. How could he blame the team for gloating? They were following not only Mort's example, but his, in aligning with oppressor against victim. No doubt they were thrilled by the unexpected fight, because nobody had ever resisted Mort before.

Max descended in the lift to underground parking and got in his Porsche, roaring it up the ramps and out into the sun. It was the brief mid-morning lull on Macquarie Street and traffic was light – maybe he'd take a quick spin across the Harbour Bridge before turning around and coming back to town. The top was down and he loved the light and air as he drove across the bridge.

Bright bands of sunlight alternated with the shadows from the girders as he roared north over the bridge. He was free but he would have to decide how to use his freedom, not just don another yoke – or become a full-time surfer.

First, he'd have to negotiate a fair deal with Mort, of course. He'd love to get a piece of the McConnochie Consortium personally. Max looked up at the flags flapping furiously in the breeze. He didn't know McConnochie well, but the man had nothing against him, and Richard Wander, who advised McConnochie, would probably support Max. But the Tunnel Deal was only for the anointed. Even though Luke Terry was blocking Mort, not him, it would take more than just being neutral to win him a personal position in the Tunnel Consortium. A deal as hugely profitable, and as certain, was available to only a tiny circle of privileged insiders—and would come with a lifetime of strings attached.

Before anything else, he had to ring Ilona with the news. He dialled her mobile but it went to voicemail. That's right – she was at Nightingale meeting with Headmistress Whidbey. What was the meeting about, Max wondered, and why hadn't Ilona told him?

No, the Tunnel Consortium wasn't the right deal. But maybe he'd take a closer look at ZettaData. He might be able to help Susan Casner and her friends.

It was time to go see Luke Terry.

Chapter 14

'And accordingly, I thought it would be best if we met and discussed the issues arising from the behaviour of your daughters.' Miss Whidbey regarded Alexandra Norton and then Ilona Ring with a look as dour as the dark-wood atmosphere of the headmistress's office.

'Right-o, Miss Whidbey,' Alexandra smiled. 'Thank you for inviting us to meet with you today.'

'My first goal is to ensure the girls enjoy healthy peer relationships despite the distress experienced by Selena Woodbridge this past weekend,' said Miss Whidbey loftily.

'My second goal,' continued Miss Whidbey crisply, 'is to ensure the girls flourish as part of their on-going educational journey together at Nightingale School.'

Ilona allowed herself to feel a thrill of hope at the phrase "on-going educational journey together". It didn't sound like expulsions were on the table this morning.

'In short, Selena Woodbridge is still feeling hurt,' said Alexandra. 'Did she feel better today?'

'Yes, I believe she did,' said Miss Whidbey.

So far, Miss Whidbey seemed to be focusing on the Snapchat messages, and she had discussed Selena's panic attack without making any lurid accusations –yet.

'I'm so sorry –' Ilona began, hoping to make amends and also quickly establish how much Miss Whidbey knew about the weekend's events. The Snapchat messages had been regrettable, no doubt, but the real issue was whose Brazilian was posted on Instagram, how and by whom. Ilona was in agony waiting to hear how Miss Whidbey would address the horrible, embarrassing, scandal.

Alexandra cut her off with one look. 'Now, Miss Whidbey,' she began, crossing her legs.

'Yes, Mrs Norton.'

'Words were exchanged? Typed?'

'Certainly, Mrs Norton. According to the latest neurological research, our brains light up in the same places whether we experience insulting language or actual physical pain. Emotional damage, measured by detectable cognitive responses, is inflicted. That's the scientific foundation for Nightingale's policy that girls treat each other respectfully.'

'I'm just trying to understand the disciplinary context,' said Alexandra. 'The parameters of the offence, if you will.'

'Of course, Mrs Norton,' said Miss Whidbey, steepling her fingers. 'The incident involving your daughters and Selena was the equivalent of a fist fight, as far as Nightingale School is concerned. Selena was assaulted. I'm glad you're ready to address this matter with the appropriate seriousness.'

Ilona suddenly realised Miss Whidbey was treating what happened as exceptionally grave. A niggling doubt appeared in the back of her mind: was Alexandra truly planning to protect Ilona's Sammie—and Ilona herself—this morning, or was she planning to advocate with Miss Whidbye only for her own Trixie?

It was Ilona's worst nightmare. Fears coursed through her chest and stomach like fireworks dropping through a New Year's Eve into the harbour.

'So you're saying you believe the messages sent on social media by our daughters to their friend Selena to be the equivalent of punches or kicks,' said Alexandra.

'That's right, Mrs Norton.'

Ilona listened with bated breath. The one gap that had opened up between her and Alexandra during Covid was when it turned out Alexandra had been letting her cleaning team back into the Norton mansion for weeks, albeit with masks. And Mort had resumed playing with his tennis coach, outside and with both masked. The point was that Ilona and Alexandra had been resolute about not letting anybody but grocery deliveries enter their homes without a fourteen day quarantine. When Ilona found out through Sam, Alexandra just laughed it off and said she'd thought she had told Ilona.

'Reading words on a phone is the same thing, according to Nightingale policy, as being physically hit?'

'Yes – correct – Mrs Norton.' Miss Whidbey was being so stern it wasn't clear how much she knew but hadn't yet divulged.

Was Alexandra somehow setting up Sam? The suspense was becoming unbearable.

'Let's say for example ... that the girls had shaved one another's foo foos,' said Alexandra.

'I beg your pardon!'

Ilona was as shocked as Miss Whidbey. Was Alexandra planning to confess in order to beg Miss Whidbey to spare Trixie, and leave Sam to be thrown under the bus?

'What – you object to the term "foo foo"?' asked Alexandra coolly.

Miss Whidbey coloured. 'Do you mean that they shaved one another's ...'

'I'm not saying they did, Miss Whidbey, but I am using as an example of bad behaviour – physical behaviour, not words – the notion of girls shaving each other's foo foos.'

'You do mean ...' Miss Whidbey gasped.

'Yes, Miss Whidbey, foo foos. Vaginas – or rather their vulvas, to be technical about it.'

'Mrs Norton – that's appalling! The very idea!'

Ilona recognised that her mother, having worked her entire career at the Family Planning Association would have thoroughly approved of Alexandra's forthright language.

'Oh, come now, Miss Whidbey – is this, or is this not, a girls' school?'

'Yes, of course it is – the finest in Australia!'

'Do your blushes prevent you from speaking to the reality of your students' experiences as adolescents? Did you stint in any way from the hard truth about Covid and what had to be done to prevent it from devastating our Nightingale community?'

'No, certainly not, Mrs Norton! But this office isn't the forum –'

'Oh? Surely your office is the very centre of pastoral care as well as pandemic measures and disciplinary sessions,' Alexandra said. 'If you're as reluctant to speak candidly as you appear, how can the Nightingale community have confidence our daughters are being properly prepared with education about their bodies and how to make healthy choices?'

Alexandra looked at Ilona with a thoughtful expression, holding her gaze with a questioning arched eyebrow, and then she turned back slowly and deliberately to face Miss Whidbey. 'I hope there's no need for us to be concerned about your commitment to our daughters' wellbeing.'

Miss Whidbey sat back in her chair. 'Of course not, Mrs Norton! As you know, I was in the forefront of leadership when it was necessary to counter the pandemic—in advance of our Premier if you recall. And one of my special points of pride is Nightingale's PP & E course – it is best practice for introducing girls to healthy self-confidence and high self-esteem as a life-long approach to celebrating their womanhood and bodies.'

'Then you have no objection to my hypothetically floating the possibility of exploring their emerging femininity ... by shaving their foo foos? Consensually, of course.'

'Of course not – as long as they would be exploring from a place of mutual respect and self-esteem.'

Miss Whidbey was unknowingly echoing Alexandra's exact position on what had in fact actually happened. Ilona knew her own mother would heartily agree as well. So why did Ilona feel some mystery was being ignored? Their daughters' bodies had a personal meaning deeper than the discussion acknowledged – Ilona sensed obscure regions in their daughters' beings where damage may have been done, even though Ilona couldn't imagine what it might be. With Sam's well-being at stake, even as Alexandra seemed to be wonderfully ameliorating any threat posed by Miss Whidbey's previous self-righteousness, Ilona resisted the reassurance offered by Alexandra's confident but simplified world.

'Right – exactly. Well, as we're all in resounding agreement, can you please remind me why Selena and her mother have their knickers in a twist – so to speak? To be frank, I don't see what all the fuss is about.'

Alexandra glanced quickly, triumphantly, at Ilona before allowing her eyes to return and bore into Miss Whidbey.

Miss Whidbey, her face slightly flushed, remained resolute. 'Mrs Norton, you're ignoring the fact Selena was very upset – she suffered panic attacks after receiving those messages.'

'Right, so you said before – well, I think sticks and stones can break my bones, and razors can shave my mons veneris – but names can never hurt me.'

'Mrs Norton, we don't tolerate intolerance in the Nightingale community.'

Alexandra regarded Miss Whidbey blandly, perhaps assessing how far she could be pushed. Now it was clear Miss Whidbey knew nothing about the Brazilians, Alexandra seemed to be losing interest.

Suddenly Ilona remembered how she had felt, all those years ago, after her first weekend with Max. She was intensely aware, for the first time, of both her and Max's bodies together in a way that produced a personal meaning deeper than sexuality, as if they were one flesh. Then, when she realised she was only the latest of his lovers, these feelings vanished and her body lost its special personal meaning and seemed to be only territory for appropriation by Max. This was the mystery she felt was being ignored by Alexandra and Miss Whidbey, their daughters' bodies were more than just territories to be appropriated – even by themselves.

'I couldn't agree with you more, Miss Whidbey,' Alexandra said grandly. 'You may recall my husband and I made a major donation to funding Nightingales' Inclusiveness and Diversity seminar. Furthermore, as you know Mortimer and I are hosting the gala charity for the Nightingale Eighteen.'

The highlight of the new term would be a fundraiser just before school holidays to raise money in memory of the eighteen members of the extended Nightingale community who had died of Covid.

'So let's speak with complete frankness,' Alexandra continued, ' – we're all coming from the same values and vision. What was the nature of the hate speech? Was it racial? Sexual? Homophobic?'

Miss Whidbey coloured. 'No.'

'Well, what did they say?' asked Alexandra.

Miss Whidbey said primly, 'Unco.'

'Unco?'

'Yes, as in 'uncoordinated'. They also threatened not to invite Selena to their sixteenth birthday parties – which was exceptionally cruel and demeaning.'

Ilona tried to conceal her relief. It was clear Miss Whidbey, with all her research and hyper-vigilance, had no clue whatsoever about the Instagram post.

'Do you believe my daughter is disrespectful of the community of differently abled individuals?'

'No,' Miss Whidbey said reluctantly.

Miss Whidbey's cluelessness would have been laughable, except, Ilona thought furiously, for the real threats to their daughters, to which Miss Whidbey seemed oblivious. Did Miss Whidbey have any idea how many Nightingale students were likely to be struggling with eating disorders? Ilona's terrified sense was the truth was substantially higher than published statistics. How pervasive under-age drinking and drug use actually was? Risky sexual practices? Self-harming? So much for Miss Whidbey's research.

'Good, because I can assure you that's not how I brought up my daughters,' Alexandra said. 'I will add that I am truly sorry my daughter Trixie – very regrettably – said to Selena that she couldn't come to her sixteenth birthday party. That's in four years, Miss Whidbey, and I can assure you Selena will be invited.'

'And my Sam and Selena are already back on good terms,' said Ilona.

'Good-o,' said Alexandra briskly. 'I undertake to ensure Trixie acts fully in compliance with the Nightingale code from this moment forward.'

'I'm very glad to hear that, Mrs Norton.'

'Now, Miss Whidbey, if you'll excuse us, do we have anything further to discuss?'

'No.' The word was almost inaudible.

They stood up and said their goodbyes. It was clear Miss Whidbey knew only what happened on Snapchat, which meant Selena probably wasn't involved in the Instagram post. That narrowed down the possibilities of who had been displayed naked to the Ring and Norton girls themselves. While Ilona was relieved Alexandra had so definitively established Miss Whidbey's ignorance, as they walked across the grounds under the fig trees, she struggled to emulate Alexandra's blasé attitude towards what had, in fact, actually happened. Somebody had been objectified and the totality of their rich personhood exposed in a most callous and traumatising manner. Although the meeting had resolved any risk of action by the headmistress, it also seemed to confirm the Instagram image was now, almost certainly, of one of their daughters.

Chapter 15

'Just a second, honey – this is the crux,' Max said.

Ilona had taken the news much better than he'd expected. He splashed the two tablespoons of orange juice into the fluffy mixture, whisking busily with his right hand. After how disapproving she'd been with his stoush with Mort at the AGM, when he had to tell her about being kicked out of Norton & Ring this morning by Mort, he more than half-assumed she would demand a divorce.

'This is the last bit,' Max said, glancing at Ilona before he dropped in pinches of orange rind. Instead, she had been understanding and supportive.

'Another variation of the mother sauce?' asked Ilona. Her expression was patient, and he thought he detected a trace of compassion. That didn't happen often.

'That's right,' said Max. 'Notre Dame de Hollandaise.'

He dribbled in melted butter as he briskly whisked, watching alchemy produce Sauce Maltaise. Slow and steady would do it. 'Everything's possible if you have the right mother – that's why our girls are going to conquer the world.'

Ilona returned his smile.

Max removed the mixing bowl from the boiler, which they'd use for the asparagus. 'I think Sauce Maltaise goes particularly well with asparagus,' he said.

'Whatever you say, darling,' she said.

Amazing. He'd just delivered the worst news of their entire marriage, and there were few times he could remember when she had treated him this well.

Ilona was showing belief in him similar to the woman at the AGM, Susan Casner. In their very different ways they were making Max feel he could accomplish anything. He felt energised.

Ilona handed Max three handfuls of freshly rinsed asparagus.

'Now –' said Max, laying out the stalks in two rows on the cutting board. He picked up the knife.

'Are we going ahead with the reno?' Ilona blurted out. It sounded like she had been suppressing the question for so long it had forced itself out of her.

Max looked at her in surprise and stopped cutting. 'Sweetie, full speed ahead on the reno. We have three million dollars in the bank and another five million in short term securities I could sell at a moment's notice. The only thing that has changed is Mort thinks he's cut my balls off –but actually I'm going to cut his off.'

He could see hot blood rush to Ilona's temples.

Tink, tink, tink. Max resumed cutting the asparagus. 'The reason I work so hard and take risks is because I love you and the girls and I want you to be happy. I'll do everything I can to make that happen – no matter what Mort does.'

'You just said you're going to cut his balls off,' Ilona said, pronouncing each word slowly and distastefully.

'Bloody oath,' Max nodded.

'What does that mean exactly, Max?'

'Oh, Mortie's going to settle. He cooked this up himself, which means it's a lame idea. A big scandal is the last thing Alexandra will want Mort to get tangled up in. What he did at the AGM was bad enough—a lawsuit with me will be just another embarrassing example of how out of control Mort can be. He'll get frozen out of boards, he'll lose any chance of being admitted to the Royal Sydney Golf Club. Don't worry, Alexandra will sort him out. I wouldn't be surprised if we settle within a month and he pays me out my third of retained earnings.'

Ilona's face was warm with anger.

'What's the matter?'

'Alexandra will sort him out?'

'Yes, I'm sure she will.'

'Alexandra has such an easy time influencing Mort while I seem to have no influence at all on you.'

'That's not true, darling – I'm always trying to please you, I just don't seem to have much luck getting it right.' His big mistake had been telling Ilona about all his previous relationships. She had been so upset and despite the fact he humiliated himself and abjectly apologised, he had just ended up in purgatory permanently, unforgiven, forever tainted and morally inferior to Ilona herself.

Max concentrated on cutting the ends off the fresh asparagus.

He had tried to earn forgiveness, but even agreeing to return to Sydney didn't seem to make much difference.

Asperges me. Sprinkle me, and I shall be cleansed ...

He'd had enough guilt.

'I've already told him to stick the Deed up his arse.'

Ilona blushed more deeply, and was now looking quite cross. 'I don't even know what that means, Max. Talking so crudely is not a solution. Mort warned you it'll cost us a million dollars and ten years to sue!'

"We're going to get on with our lives just like normal while I deal with Mort,' said Max. 'He just got elected to the Board of Nightingale, and he and I are still on the Board of the Eden Street Theatre Company together – in fact I've thought about trying to get him kicked off – and having his daughter sacked from ASMing the new play ...' He rolled the stalks under his fingers, inspecting the ends to make sure they didn't look too fibrous.

'Could you do that?'

'Probably.' The stalks looked good.

Ilona frowned. 'It would be so petty.'

She was probably worried about her relationship with Alexandra and how it would all play out at Nightingale.

'I just said I've thought about it, I didn't say I was going to do it.'

Ilona looked at the row of fresh asparagus lying on the countertop. 'You've only cut one centimetre from the base of the stalks. I would've cut perhaps half a centimetre more. That'll eliminate any danger of the asparagus being too chewy.'

'Ok, will do.'

This was how she always started. Maybe it wasn't going to work out so well this evening, after all.

'One of the reasons Mort is acting the way he is, at the AGM and with me – apart from sheer greed – is because he thinks all his new board positions make him more powerful.' Max grinned. 'Actually, it's the opposite – his reputation is now much more important than it ever was, at least if Alexandra wants to continue enjoying her life. Soon enough Mort will figure out he can't litigate while he's trying to show everybody he's become "Good Mort".'

Max chuckled, looking at the bright green stalks with the ring of dusky purple between their heads and the sharply cut ends.

'Asparagus please,' Ilona said, holding out her hands to Max. 'I certainly hope you're right.'

Max deliberately gathered the asparagus stalks and held them over the steamer so they hovered above the boiling water. He didn't want Ilona to risk her hands being scalded. He carefully inserted the fasces of asparagus into the steel tube and released the stalks into the steam, his hands flying up.

Two minutes was all the asparagus would require.

'Ok, I need to concentrate,' said Ilona, rapidly grilling a dozen prawns she had previously wrapped in nearly-forbidden prosciutto. Six for Max, two for each of them.

Max watched Ilona's deft movements above the stove grill as the prawns sizzled and spat and the edges of the prosciutto curled.

Behind him Max could hear the water boiling furiously in the steamer, and he could smell the aroma of the asparagus. Did it matter, really, what he ate? In a way, Max had always considered what his body did to be irrelevant. It was his consciousness that mattered in a random, meaningless universe. His awareness floated above it all. In that sense, Max thought, he had always been quite a spiritual person.

'I'm going to keep seeing Alexandra, you know,' said Ilona as she set the wrapped prawns on a plate covered with a paper towel. 'I don't want what's going on between you and Mort to make it awkward with Alexandra, or between our girls.'

'Of course—good idea! She's the sane one.' Max leaned against the bench, set down his glass of chardonnay, and crossed his arms.

He thought tenderly about Ilona and her days with the girls. They had two wonderful daughters and Ilona was mostly responsible for that. Max smiled and took her in his arms. 'It's ok, darling. I'm going to start my own funds management company and in two years we'll be laughing about this. I promise.'

He held her tight and she went still for a long moment. Max let Ilona go and stepped back, still smiling, only to be startled by a look of alarm that appeared suddenly on her beautiful face. 'The asparagus!'

Time had run away from them – and the asparagus was close to being ruined. The stalks were limp and grey, drooping into each other in the rising steam bearing their over-cooked smell. Ilona extracted the drooping asparagus with tongs. They were edible, only just.

Ilona called the girls down and as they set the table she assigned stalks to each plate, and then deftly set the prawns into aesthetically pleasing juxtaposition next to the asparagus.

'How was your day?' Max asked their daughters after they had all sat at the table.

'Oh, fine,' said Sam as she cut a piece of asparagus.

Billie nodded. 'Good.'

'You're welcome to as much of this as you like,' Max said as he spooned Sauce Maltaise on his asparagus.

Ilona looked at him reproachfully.

Max knew what she was thinking, but he had begun to sense growing tension around meal times and was determined to do everything he could to ensure they were relaxed about food. Sam was a hearty eater, but Max had noticed Billie was starting to eat slowly, discriminatingly. He knew Ilona did her best by insisting on the purest, organic food and cooking that was as natural as possible. But perhaps Ilona might be inadvertently aggravating any food issues their daughters might be developing – although he knew the suggestion drove Ilona wild. But it was so important that despite the way the issue contributed to the growing rift between them, it was one of the few issues Max refused to give up on.

He had a sudden impulse. 'I have an announcement to make,' he said.

Sam and Billie looked at him expectantly, and Ilona's brow furrowed and she froze.

'Mort and I are going our separate ways. We just decided today.'

'Yay Dad!' Sam exclaimed immediately.

'Go Dad!' sang Billie.

Max was still ashamed of the way he and Ilona had fudged the truth in their last conversation with the girls about Mort. Of course, he had crossed the line of deception with Ilona and there was no going back, but he wanted to remain as honest as possible with Sam and Billie.

'I have to admit it was Mort's timing. Your mother and I have been talking about it for some time, but it was Mort who brought matters to a head this morning. I'm glad it happened, and I want you to know everything's going to be ok.'

'Who gets the tunnel?' asked Sam.

'I don't think either of us will get the small piece we were hoping for,' said Max. 'And remember, please, this is our private family conversation. Don't talk about this at school, even if you hear Trixie say things you don't like. If you have any questions, just ask me.'

'And girls,' Ilona said, 'remember Trixie and Anastasia are our good friends, and Alexandra is a dear, dear friend of mine, too. Just because your fathers are sorting out important business matters doesn't mean the rest of us can't be good friends. In fact, it's even more important now that we are. We certainly don't want to gossip.'

Sam rolled her eyes and her gaze clouded and went blank.

'The gossip all comes from Trixie,' said Billie.

'Billie!' Ilona said reproachfully.

'It doesn't matter,' said Sam. 'Nobody really cares what Trixie says.'

'That's changing,' said Billie. 'I heard Rory Bastille asked her out!'

'Really? How lovely!' said Ilona with a satisfied smile.

Sam looked at her mother with a congested look on her face. 'Yeah,' she said.

'Rory who?' asked Max.

'He's a very nice young boy – one of the most popular boys at Cranbrook, I believe,' said Ilona complacently.

Ilona certainly deserved some credit for the improvement in Trixie's social standing, Max thought. Trixie was a fairly unlikeable girl, but somehow that sleepover seemed to be making a difference.

Max could tell Sam was unhappy about something, and maybe Billie, too, but he didn't know about what.

He spooned more Sauce Maltaise onto his asparagus.

Ilona must have it under control, whatever it was – or so he had to hope.

Chapter 16

Ilona was so exhausted from Max's news she started to feel quite dreamy after dinner. It was such a relief that Sam and Billie seemed perfectly fine, except for their jealous snit about Trixie. But even that was indirect evidence there were no more serious issues. It looked like the Instagram crisis had blown over.

She and Max drank another bottle of wine after dinner and a show on Netflix eased the evening further. As they were getting ready for bed Ilona found herself feeling safe and hopeful. Her contented tummy, full of asparagus spears and the two yummy prawns wrapped in prosciutto, together with more than a slight feeling of exaltation from the excellent wine, awakened other appetites she normally prided herself on suppressing.

As she lay under the covers listening to Max clean his teeth, which normally annoyed her, she found to her surprise she was feeling grateful to him. He'd had a traumatic day and didn't bring home the stress. There was no talk of school fees, the reno, cancelling overseas holidays, or economising on the household budget. She felt so lonely in her marriage most of the time. He had been considerate this evening, taken her into his confidences, seemed to show his emotions for once, and really cared what she thought.

When the bathroom light blinked out and the mattress tipped and shifted under his weight, Ilona waited until Max leaned over in the darkness to kiss her on the cheek. She turned her head and with blind perfect timing met his lips.

'Good night,' he said, sounding a little startled.

'Mmmm,' she responded, his surprise giving her a sense of control. She nestled her bum against him and pressed her back against his hard chest. There was nothing comforting about Max except his strength.

He stayed motionless, and Ilona smiled to herself in the darkness and reached back, letting her fingertips lightly graze the side of her husband's thigh.

Max shifted his weight and moved close to her for the first time in a month or so. He remained obediently restrained as they kissed while she felt herself becoming warm and wet. After a few minutes affectionate phrases floated through her mind, and she stifled the urge to murmur them into Max's ear. It was too risky to express how she felt other than the mute truth of her body. Words might show too much. Her chest felt congested with the endearments ready on her lips.

She stopped kissing Max – otherwise he would have gone on forever – and withdrew in order to remove her nightie. She was mildly but pleasantly excited as she rustled in the darkness and the soft silk slipped off. Ilona reached around to grope for the pillows, and adjusted herself into her favourite position. She wasn't about to cede control over her boundaries, physical or emotional.

This was her favourite position. As far as she could tell, Max had never tried it with another woman, and it allowed him to pleasure her while she looked after him. In the first couple years of their marriage he had tried to impose himself on her in all kinds of unexpected ways she loathed: the positions distracting and the techniques disconcerting. They were, obviously, things he'd done with earlier girlfriends. Ilona had eventually succeeded in reining in Max until he stopped being distracting, and learned to be almost as predictable and satisfying as warm water flowing over her in the bathtub.

Max seemed happy enough now, and Ilona languidly allowed herself to drift in tranquil play towards that inner place of private pleasure, happily keeping him at a distance, a somehow abstract presence.

Ilona had another secret she'd never shared with Max: at about the same age as Samantha and Trixie, back in Erskineville, Ilona and Magda experimented and shaved themselves. But the real discovery they made was when they let warm water from the bathtub tap pour over them in order to wash off the shaving cream – and accidentally triggered that most delightful of all sensations which all through their teen years, they enjoyed alone and together. Had Sam and Trixie made the same discovery as she and Magda? Was that why Trixie kept denying any knowledge of what happened?

Max was being obedient, and knowing she had him under control Ilona relaxed completely. After only a few minutes the waves rolled over and through Ilona, catching her by surprise, and she continued to concentrate on Max, confident he would soon resolve himself. She hated it when she came first and he drew things out unnecessarily, just to prolong his own pleasure – it was so selfish. Before long, Max's breathing slowed, deepened, and Ilona could feel the growing tension in his cock until it was taut and throbbing – and then he caught his breath. She'd trained him well, and awaited the first traces of a taste that reminded her of some mellow oil she might use for baking, but without the sweetness.

'Come on, honey,' she managed to say. All she wanted now was a good sleep: it was time to get it over with.

'Yes, Headmistress,' breathed Max, and the primitive leaping began in her mouth. She actually didn't mind the taste at all. Max's pH was perfectly balanced. Still, she had to keep him in his place, so every time she made a point of spitting it out. As he collapsed in the darkness, she got up, languidly and triumphantly, disentangling herself from the bedclothes, and strolled to the sink. Ilona made sure Max could hear her spit and then turned on the tap. Her skin was still warm from Max's skin, and only minutes before he'd been inside her, but already she felt alone.

Tra-dee-la dee lee Parthenope we sing to thee. The stupid school song.

Of course she'd supported Max – what choice did she have?

Chapter 17

Richard Wander's smile was a hard one, but it softened the threat normally lurking in his features. In his own way, Richard was being genuinely friendly. They were mates.

'You're going to kill it. Let me know when you're ready to get organised. I can think of a lot of guys who will want to know.'

Wander's nod was worth a couple of hundred bars, maybe more. A couple of hundred million dollars. Max wanted to raise a billion dollars – a thousand bars – and Wander's support meant he was well on his way.

'Thanks, Richie, I appreciate it.'

Richard regarded him calmly. 'I'm here to help.'

Wander was only in his late thirties, but already exerted a powerful gravitational pull on the Australian financial markets. He was well into an extraordinary career as an investment banker reconfiguring the shape and relationships of many significant publicly listed corporations into a new galaxy – with himself at its centre.

Wander steepled his fingers. 'There are several big institutions considering raising their allocations to the private equity asset class. I assume your focus will be executing on classic Norton & Ring style deals?'

Max looked past the steeple of Richard's fingers to the magnificent view of the harbour – sunlight, blue sky and sparkling water glowing through the windows of the conference room of Wander, Fleagle & Co.

'I'm not going to get a piece of the McConnochie Consortium,' Max said. 'But there's plenty of other deals.'

Naturally, Wander was up to his neck in the Tunnel Deal. In fact, as Martin McConnochie's personal adviser, it was Wander doing most of the organising for the consortium led by Martin's family's construction firm, and liasing quietly with key advisers to the government. 'You'll find the deals,' Wander said with a smile.

CHRIS COFFMAN

'I'm not worried in the slightest,' said Max, who could tell he'd made the right call not to pitch for a position in the Tunnel Deal.

Wander wouldn't want to be seen to be choosing sides between him and Mort Norton, nobody did. He and Mort had signed the settlement just over a week after sacking Max. As Max predicted, Mort quickly realised that nobody wanted to get drawn into Mort's nasty public controversy with a respected former partner. Mort had plenty of money and the gutter instincts for a fight, but once Max refused to be intimidated, Mort quickly realised he was on the brink of alienating scores of allies and undoing years of PR work that had more-or-less repositioned his image. In the settlement Max was paid out all his retained earnings – just over thirty million – and was free to start his own financial firm without any restrictions or non-competes.

There was a reason his first meeting was here. 'In fact, I know my first deal.'

'Oh, really?' Wander said. 'What's that – if you don't mind my asking?'

'Not at all,' said Max. It was highly sensitive information, of course, but he and Wander routinely traded secrets of all kinds. Wander talked exclusively to people who either wanted to hire him, which only the largest corporations could afford to do, or could tell him something he didn't know, which was close to impossible. Max was one of very few who consistently did.

'I'm going to present you with a proposal in a couple weeks for a takeover of ZettaData, just like I promised at the AGM,' Max said.

Wander frowned. 'I thought you'd walk away.'

'Nuh,' said Max. 'I can do it.'

Wander shook his head. 'There's lots of deals, mate.'

'I thought I'd be doing you a favour by quickly snapping it up.' By all appearances, ZettaData was becoming an embarrassing disaster for Wander, Fleagle. Max could fix that.

Wander looked out the window without seeming to see the gorgeous view.

'I assumed you were just doing a favour for the Federal Government or the Americans,' said Max, referring to the two huge strategic investors who owned seventy percent of the equity in ZettaData. It was highly unusual for Wander's firm to be representing such a small company – and Wander was personally involved.

Wander looked at Max. 'Max, tell me something – is this about Mort?'

'ZettaData?'

Wander nodded.

Max rolled his eyes. 'No, Richie, it's not. I'm quite happy with the settlement.'

Mort's big win was getting the damn Mignano print. Of all things, something so trivial would have been the deal-breaker for Mort. In the end, Max let Mort keep it, knowing it was probably Alexandra who wanted it. If possible, he wanted to keep Alexandra happy, and therefore hopefully Ilona, despite the breach between Mort and him.

Most importantly, Mort cut him a cheque with the right number on it.

'The two of you made a great team,' said Wander. 'It's a shame it didn't work out.'

Max flinched. Being a great team implied he was more like Mort in Wander's eyes than he liked to think. A month ago he might have felt proud of the acknowledgment, Wander's recognition that he had arrived as a powerful player in Sydney, but now he couldn't ignore the feeling of disgust. 'Mort gets to do his deals now – and I get to do mine.'

'Right,' said Wander. 'Exactly.' He looked steadily at Max.

'I don't want ZettaData because of Mort, Richie – I wouldn't waste a second of my life, or put a dollar at risk, to get back at Mort Norton.'

'You know what I was thinking this morning, Max?'

'No, Richie – what?'

'I realised I could buy a new Bugatti every month if I wanted to.'

'Huh?'

'A Bugatti costs $2.5 million each. I could just keep buying them for years. Every month. I could probably buy them all. Kind of cool.'

'Ok,' said Max. 'What's the punch line?'

'I've arrived in a pretty special place,' said Wander. 'There's not many others up here with me. Once you're successful with your fund – and I know you will be – I can see you up here.'

'Yeah,' said Max. 'Thanks.'

'You can do anything you want to then.'

'That's probably right.'

'Oh, I'm right.'

Max nodded.

'Focus on that.' Wander turned around from the window. 'Forget ZettaData.'

'Are you saying you've got another investor lined up for it?'

There must be something Wander wanted to leverage for himself.

'What's this all about, Richard?'

Wander frowned. 'I can't get into it, Max. Neither of the strategic shareholders can focus on ZettaData. This is a delicate time for Luke Terry for reasons I'm not at liberty to discuss. And Todd Edgell is busy shorting the Euro – he's taking on opponents with trillions in fire power.'

Todd Edgell was sitting on hundreds of billions his hedge fund had made during Covid. He and Luke Terry were the two key decision-makers about ZettaData.

'Aren't you ignoring part of the share register?' asked Max.

Wander looked at Max blankly.

'The mums and dads, Richie – the ones who own the thirty percent that's traded on the ASX.'

'They're irrelevant, Max.'

'I know they're irrelevant,' said Max. 'But you're acting like they don't even exist – and they do.'

'Ok, Max, they exist,' said Wander. 'So what?'

'So you can't just fuck them.'

Wander regarded Max with very little interest. 'Well, in the first place, I can. Secondly, we're talking deals – what does the public float have to do with any imaginable deal for ZettaData?'

Of course, it was about Mort – in a way. Max was still angry about how casually Mort had been ready to destroy the little that was left of the investments of Susan Casner and the others.

'ZettaData isn't *Terra Nullius*, Richie. You can't just take the company away from these people.'

Terra Nullius, 'Nobody's Land' in Latin, was the basis on which Captain James Cook declared Australia the property of the British Crown in 1770, and remains the foundation of Australian law. Conveniently, it ignored the half a million to a million Aboriginal inhabitants who had arrived sixty to eighty thousand years before.

Cook knew they were there: cruising up the south eastern coast of the continent, he and his crew could glimpse Aboriginal peoples, their campfires and their smoke.

'What are you talking about, Max? I would never just take away something from someone.' Wander smiled. 'There's ways to do things.'

'That's my whole point,' said Max. 'Once Cook declared Australia *Terra Nullius*, everything became perfectly legal.'

'Hey, what is this?' Wander looked sharply at Max.

Cook's decision to deny the actual complexities he found in Australia was legally transformed into the appearance of truth through the complications of Common Law, subsequent government decrees and court cases.

'We can act like something is real but that doesn't make it real. You know what I thought about the lockdown policy.'

'Don't start Max.'

'You invested the way I did during Covid and you made a killing, too Richie. The markets would have collapsed if Corona was the Black Death.'

'You're going off in a very strange direction, Max. I thought we were discussing a capital raising for your fund.'

'The mums and dads in ZettaData are being treated as if they don't exist, by you and everybody else,' Max said patiently.

'ZettaData is a distraction.'

'ZettaData isn't *Terra Nullius*. Those people do exist.'

Wander shrugged. 'They were bloody lucky to have been along for the ride. If it had worked out, they would have done well. And I have no idea why we're talking about Captain Cook.'

'The small shareholders were fucked from the very start: that was how ZettaData was set up. Why were the Americans – and only the Americans, issued those weird securities – Compounding Convertible Preference Shares? What a fucking joke!'

'You *have* looked at ZettaData carefully, haven't you?' Wander's brows lifted to reveal large, dark-chocolate eyes that seemed to gleam with amusement.

'Those things limited the upside of the public float during the good times and now vaporise what's left of the value in the common shares,' said Max.

Wander yawned.

'Luke Terry and Todd Edgell aren't the only ones who matter at ZettaData.'

'So what's your plan, Max?'

'I'm going to Terry and Edgell and ask what they want for what's left of their investments.'

Wander rolled his eyes, then he smiled coldly and spread his hands, palms open. 'Ok, Max – knock yourself out.'

'I will.'

'You always saw yourself as an artist, Max – even though you pipped me at the post for the Eddington Prize,' said Wander.

They were both at Sydney Uni when Max achieved his MBA the year Wander received his undergraduate degree in Bachelor of Commerce / Law with First Class Honours.

'I've seen your artistic streak in Norton & Ring deals, Max.'

Max received the Eddington Prize that year for most outstanding graduate in the Business School, while Wander received the second prize Chandrasekhar Medal.

'As long as you focus on maximising returns to your investors you can count on my full support for your capital raising,' Wander said.

'Thanks, mate,' said Max. 'It's early days, when it matters most.'

Wander nodded and looked at his watch. 'Mate, I've got to go: I've been keeping seven hundred billion dollars waiting. One of the Chinese Army's main pension funds.'

They stood up and shook hands.

Suddenly Wander's hard smile appeared. 'I can't wait to see what you do next.'

Chapter 18

The laser machine sounded like a dishwasher churning, then it whirred and began a high frequency whine that rose to a crescendo. In the next instant there was the crack of an electric arc snapping across the centimetre between the tip of the instrument and the skin of Mortimer Norton's back.

'Ow – fuck me!' Mort said through gritted teeth.

The pain was intense but brief as the laser light streaked down several hair follicles to their roots where it exploded each one like a tiny star, incinerating it.

It had started with capping his teeth – The Duchess convinced him to do that within eighteen months of their wedding. Afterwards, he had to admit she was right, his new smile did make him look younger, more put together, ready for prime time. 'What was that?' demanded Richard Wander on the other end of the phone.

Mort lay on his stomach, swaddled in fluffy towelling. 'I'm having a procedure done.'

'Having your nostril hairs burned out with a match?'

'I should stick a blow torch up your arse and give you a sack and crack you'll never forget,' said Mort.

It was unlikely he'd be on the board of the Nightingale School with a mouth full of snaggled, yellow teeth from growing up vitamin-deficient and without dental care in postwar Communist Eastern Europe.

The clinic technician was a lean young woman named Felicia. 'The pain makes you feel alive, doesn't it?' she murmured in Mort's other ear. She had long dark hair, breasts that hung like fruit in the net shopping bags Europeans use, and plenty of ink all over what he could see of her body. He was glad she wasn't wearing a mask, he liked the look of her thin, elegant lips.

Crack! He exhaled a puff of breath. The pain did make him feel alive.

'Haha – a back, sack and crack, is that what you're getting? You're game, mate,' said Wander.

'So Max wants to take over ZettaData, hey?' grunted Mort, resting his head on his forearm. 'Do you think he's serious?'

The whirring began, crescendoed, and – crack! He'd had to suspend Alexandra's upgrade program for him during Corona, of course. But now everything was back to normal Alexandra's first priority was removing the pelt on his back.

Felicia was moving progressively down his back, just above his kidneys now. He knew he was alive, all right. Forget *j'pense donc j'suis*. It was pain, not thinking, that proved he existed. Thoughts aren't real: pain is real.

'Yep,' said Wander. 'He thinks ZettaData is a good investment – although I'm not sure I exactly understand his motives.'

'Really? What does he think it's worth?'

Crack!

His inevitable secret nickname for Felicia: Miss Fellatio. The name soothed the pain.

'We never had a chance to discuss what he thinks ZettaData is worth. He was being a sanctimonious prick.'

'Huh? 'Sanctimonious'?'

Crack! Mort puffed out another breath.

'He was bleating about *Terra Nullius* and comparing the public float to Aboriginals.'

It wasn't just pain – a weird thing happened as soon as he started these treatments: he would get hard as soon as Felicia zapped him. Hard like he hadn't been in years – even with The Duchess in her finest form.

'Aboriginals?'

'Max could be losing his mind,' Wander laughed shortly. 'Maybe you pushed him over the edge.'

'I should have pushed the cunt over an edge, all right—at The Gap.'

Crack! Crack! Crack!

Miss Fellatio didn't seem to like that word.

'Max is meeting with Luke Terry tomorrow,' said Wander.

'What – Luke Terry?' – Crack! – 'Fuck me!'

Felicia leaned over. 'Are you ok?'

Mort met her gaze – and saw the look in her eyes change instantly from concern to cool amusement. She'd probably be willing to get the sack if she had the chance to really stick it to him just once. He liked that about her. 'Yeah, yeah,' Mort said to her.

'Why the fuck is Max going to see Luke Fucking Terry?'

'ZettaData, so he says.'

Mort's mind raced even as his back was searing and he had a hard on so big he felt like it was curving his back from below. 'Bullshit!'

'What are you thinking?' murmured Wander.

'Pull your head out, mate! ZettaData is smoke and mirrors—he's going to see Luke about McConnochie!'

'That's what I was thinking,' said Wander.

It felt great lying naked in heaps of towels and being tortured by this sassy bird with her light gun – even better than how he imagined he would feel if she was blowing him.

'Well, what are you going to do about it?'

But pleasure wasn't intense enough to dispel *aboulie*, not for long – only pain could do that. He'd heard the word first from the old Romanian.

'Luke Terry isn't going to get Max into the deal. He's highly motivated to fuck you, he's not highly motivated to help Ring.'

Wander was right. Luke Terry liked to inflict pain. He wasn't in the business of helping anybody but himself.

'What if Max really wants ZettaData after all?'

'It doesn't matter what Max wants.'

Max's biggest problem was always trying to distract himself from the pain of being alive.

He thought of what the old Romanian told him on the flight all those years ago when he migrated as a teenager to Australia. Back then you could still light up on planes and the old guy chain-smoked hand-rolled cigarettes the whole flight. He was wrinkled and sallow, but glad to be alive – if in his sour, bleak way he could be said to be glad about anything. He'd explained he was possessed by *aboulie* – a gnawing emptiness combined with an utter vacuum of desire: the opposite of contentment. Worse than boredom. The eeriest form of depression, an agony so unbearable that anything, any distraction – pleasure, fear or pain – was preferable.

'After what Max said at the AGM the Board knows him: what if he buys ZettaData—right from underneath your fucking nose?'

'That's not going to happen.'

'What are you going to do about it?'

'I've already done what I'm going to do,' drawled Wander.

'With Whozit – the guy from Singapore?'

'Yeah. Ted Hector. CEO of Palisades, the big AsiaPac funds manager. One of his portfolio companies here in Australia is bleeding red ink. If he merges the company with ZettaData he buys more time to fix it.'

Wander had told him something about it. Because the company was privately held by Hector's hedge fund, the scale of the disaster was a closely guarded secret. That was why Wander's clients loved him. As successful and powerful as they were, they had problems of a commensurate magnitude – and they could depend on Wander to fix their big problems.

'Have you told the ZettaData Board about Ted Hector?'

'No.'

'Why?'

'I want them to get a little more desperate, so they'll accept the price Ted wants to offer.'

'Put me and this guy Hector together,' Mort said.

'Why would you want to get involved with ZettaData?' Wander sounded genuinely surprised.

'Max really thinks ZettaData is worth something?'

'Yeah. He seems to.'

'It's not just a smoke screen to go see Luke Terry about the Tunnel deal?'

She was zapping him in a steady tempo now and he could anticipate the pain – it was a change up from random agony and it was exciting – he felt another rush of blood to his old member, tightening it right up as if he were still twenty-five. He told her early on he could get her a job in a Darlinghurst dungeon, but she just smiled her superior smile. Definitely a dominatrix.

'Well – maybe it is. Who knows?'

'If Max does want ZettaData, that's all I need to know to take it myself – along with your mate Hector, of course.'

There was a pause on the line. 'How are you going to do that, Mortie?'

'I don't know – you're the fucking financial advisor.'

'Yeah, to the Board of ZettaData, not to you,' Wander said drily.

It was, of course, a massive conflict of interest to be discussing ZettaData like this. Just by having this conversation, he and Wander were breaking provisions of the Corps Act. He didn't know which ones, but Wander bloody well did.

'You must have a plan to get your mate Ted Hector into ZettaData. Besides, it might even stroke Luke Terry if I kick in some dosh to take that piece of shit off his hands.'

Wander snorted.

'What – you don't think it will help with Luke Terry?'

'You would know better than me, Mort.'

He was right. Probably not.

'Ok – fuck Luke Terry,' gasped Mort as lightning danced across his back. 'If Max does want ZettaData, that's enough for me. What's the deal?'

'Ted's doing this to solve a problem, Mort, not to make money. He wants to keep earning his bonuses for the next several years,' said Wander.

'How much could I lose if I help him?'

'How much would you put in?'

'I don't know, five bars.'

'Hard to say.'

'Do you think I could lose it all?'

'Possibly ... probably. Not sure.'

Dicking Max would be more expensive than the fight with Tori over Hugh's body, but he could afford it. Besides, he had to be careful with Tori, handle her with kid gloves so he didn't wreck his relationship with Peggy. He didn't have to do that with Max.

'I'm in,' Mort grunted.

The old guy from Bucharest told Mort his *aboulie* vanished during the war years when the Nazis were hunting him – and then popped right back up as soon as the war ended, feeling more real than war, mass murder, starvation, the long cold homeless winters, being hunted, the continual fear. The old man told him it vanished again when the Party purged him and threw him into prison. As long as he thought he might be shot he felt intensely alive. The moment he learned he was being sent into exile – and to Australia, which he was hoping would be a paradise – he felt the *aboulie* gnaw him hollow again, from the inside out. It was the real truth that appears when all distractions vanish. Pain was worth postponing its appearance.

He had learned his lesson from the old Romanian. That's why he was lying flat on the table letting Miss Fellatio give it to him, not flinching and instead accepting every agonising spark.

'I'll have a chat with Ted and get back to you, mate,' said Wander and the line went dead.

He put the phone on the towel next to him and turned his head to the side, laying it on the terrycloth and closed his eyes.

'Isn't it great to feel alive?' said Miss Fellatio.

Her lips were against his ear, and as his head rested sideways on his forearms he could see one of her breasts in the opening of her clinician's wrap. He almost expected to feel a warm, wet tongue pushed into his ear – but no – climbing up on the steel-frame bed, squatting, and pissing on him would be more her style.

Crack!

He hadn't known what the old man meant back then – he was young and feeling the enraptured bliss of being alive, after so many of his older relatives hadn't made it through the war and its aftermath – and then his cigarette smuggling got him in trouble after he slipped up and stopped paying bribes to a minor Party official. There were so many ways to die in those years. Unlike the old man, formally expelled from the Party and sent into exile at the expense of the people, young, friendless Mort had enjoyed no privileged protection from the doom closing in, but he'd been able to slip across the border at Trieste and make his way to Italy before earning enough money for a flight to Australia. He was full of hope about Australia, the land of sunshine, and every second he flew farther away from the killers in Europe, where in their myriads they still swarmed like lice.

Aboulie had finally appeared to him, many years later, in paradise, right here in Sydney. Just like what they say about LA – the perfect weather drives you crazy. Gauguin going to pieces in Tahiti.

At least he wasn't the imaginative type. Some guys who seemed to be the hardest of them all – real vicious rat-bastards – dreamed about the guys they burned. That had never happened to him. He could still remember little things, like the bird he strangled with his hands. She had taken a long time to die, which surprised him because her neck was long and thin. Elegant. Or one of the guys he'd pushed off the buildings being built in the CBD – that was because he sneezed just as he fell over the side – he only started screaming when he was already two stories below. Nobody else he'd burned ever appeared in his dreams.

Maybe by the time his back was smooth and hairless as a baby's arse he would get his sack and crack done after all – to please Alexandra. He would do anything for her, even though he didn't give a toss for the white teeth, the hairless back and scrotum, or the geegaws, board positions, fancy furnishings, and any of the other things that mattered so much to Alexandra.

Aboulie. Pleasure did work, back in the day, and so did fear. For years. But now it was only pain, or a combination of pleasure and pain. Hot and cold. Sweet and sour. The combinations were hard to process, so they kind of short-circuited awareness of that deepest of truths, the palpable nothingness of *aboulie*.

Once in a while Alexandra said something very bleak. If she felt *aboulie* too, she seemed to have a mild case – pleasure and their glamorous life still distracted her. He couldn't bring himself to talk to her about it because *aboulie* fed on thoughts – and even more on words. He went to a shrink once, and in the very first session as he talked about *aboulie* he'd suddenly felt transparent, hyper-aware of the sensation of being trapped inside his body – and the only way to escape was by dying. It felt intolerable being inside his own body with death as the only exit – like he was buried alive. He jumped up and ran out of the guy's office, and when he was outside in the hot sun pounded his fist against a wall until the *aboulie* disappeared.

Pain is good. Pain makes you feel alive – a lesson he was going to teach Max Ring.

Chapter 19

'I'm not saying Mummy lied,' Sam said anxiously. 'She really didn't know how it happened.'

Sam leaned against the bench by the big window in the kitchen as Max added less than a teaspoon of espresso machine cleaning powder to the blind basket he'd just inserted into the portafilter of the espresso machine, the black-handled device that normally contains freshly ground coffee beans.

Max performed the ritual weekly.

'Ok, sweetie. So what *did* happen?'

He was suddenly alert.

This was evidently one of those torrents of truth that well up from children on seemingly random occasions. Max had learned how precious they were.

'Well, we were drinking the vodka breezers Trixie brought over, and she was being mean to Selena.'

He pretended to be absorbed in the meditative process of removing the week's coffee bean oils to order to maintain the calm, familiar routine which had encouraged Sam to confide in him in the first place.

Max allowed himself to nod. The combination of alcohol, Trixie, and Selena could only refer to the infamous sleepover they'd hosted. Of course Trixie had brought over vodka breezers, Max thought. Mort's daughter. Max was suddenly aware of chaos that had been insinuating itself into their family like tendrils of cold fog - for weeks. He locked the portafilter into place feeling his fury rise. If he reacted Sam would clam up.

'After Selena's mum rang Mummy and we all got in trouble, Trixie laughed and said she was going to be even meaner to Selena,' Sam said earnestly. 'Trixie said she'd get even – she was going to post photos she had of Selena kissing Buster Impken last week when Buster had his hand under Selena's shirt.'

Be nonchalant, he told himself. Did Ilona know about all this? Max flipped up the lever and the rumble of the espresso machine pump filled the kitchen. The pressure gauges for the boiler and pump darted to the right as boiling water, diverted by the blind basket in the portafilter and unable to flow through the dispersion screen of the group head, instead soaked through the cleaning powder lying in the blind basket and backflushed up and inside throughout the group head. Five seconds – he counted.

Deep down he probably yearned for such a thorough cleaning himself.

Sam tossed her head. 'Trixie's jealous of Selena – she likes Buster too! So I said we should celebrate by taking some of Mummy's pills.'

'You said what?' Max looked sharply at Sam and flipped the pump lever up, closing it. 'Darling, that was so naughty – those pills are dangerous.'

Ilona regularly used Max's Ambiens – which he had been prescribed for his long international flights from Australia – to sleep in their own bed. The girls must have discovered the pills.

From the machine came a great aspirant woosh and a foamy crema, chocolate-coloured from being infused with residual essential oils and traces of ground espresso, spurted through a stainless steel tube and heaped up like tainted whipped cream on the grate of the drip screen. There were plenty of residual oils in the machine this week; he'd had more than the usual number of espressos, thanks to all the work he'd been doing on organising financing for the ZettaData deal. Max looked reproachfully at Sam and kept flipping the pump lever open and closed at five-second intervals.

The hidden stainless steel interior of the machine was being purged of any trace of last week's coffeemaking.

'I know, Daddy – I know – it was the wrong thing to do. But I'm telling you the truth.'

Sam's eyes were bright and as transparent as seawater.

The last time he'd seen Sam's eyes look so full of trust and love they'd also been standing in the kitchen – exactly where they were standing now.

Max put his arm around her shoulders, pressed her gently to his chest, and kissed the top of her head. 'I know, my darling, I love you.'

Sam was confessing a truth every bit as difficult for her to do in her world as confessing his affair with Claudia to Ilona would be for him. Max looked at Sam with even greater respect, aware of a sharp pang of guilt and shame inside himself. He flicked the lever and the pump rumbled, like Max himself clearing his throat. Five seconds.

'I don't understand why you suggested taking those pills,' Max said, trying to suppress the feelings rising within him. 'I don't know what there was to celebrate – it sounds like Trixie was being really nasty to poor Selena.'

Sam had a sly, amused look on her face. 'Well, that was the point – I couldn't stop Trixie from bullying Selena any other way, so I suggested the pills.'

'Oh, Sam ...'

'Of course, Trixie took two pills – she just snatched the second one from me, I couldn't help it – and then she drank another vodka breezer. She was out cold within ten minutes.'

Holy shit – two Ambiens – and two vodka breezers ... mixed up inside a sixty kilo twelve-year-old – Mort and Alexandra's daughter! That sleepover had been completely out of control. Max flipped the pump handle up, and the crema – white now – wooshed into the drip tray. 'Darling, that was so dangerous – your mother must be very upset about it,' Max exclaimed. Lately, Ilona had been depleting his Ambien stash more rapidly than normal – unless it was Sam. My God, what were they teaching the kids? Sam was lying like he was, and taking drugs like her mother. 'How long have you been taking my Ambiens? You know they're only for adults – you don't have the body mass to take them safely.'

And Sam was now proving herself more truthful than him. He certainly wasn't going to be confessing his affair to Ilona.

'Mummy doesn't know. I've only told you. I've never taken her pills before – honest – I was telling Trixie about them but she wanted to try them, and I didn't agree until Trixie said she would post the photo of Selena with Buster on Instagram – and I only gave them to her so I could stop her posting the photo on Instagram.'

Max sighed heavily. He and Sam were both lying to Ilona. 'Darling – thank you for telling me the truth, but that was a very dangerous situation. Why didn't you come wake us up?'

Sam looked at him. Stupid question.

The boiling water coming out of the group head was clear now, and Max removed the portafilter, rinsed out the blind basket with its dark brown oils and grounds, and locked it back into place inside the group head. He struggled to manage the swirling, toxic feelings inside him. Max flipped the switch and clean boiling water flushed through the group head again.

The dark chambers within the machine would be spotless at last. If only it were true of his heart as well.

Five seconds.

'That's when I sneaked into your bathroom and took your shaving things. It was my idea – Billie had nothing to do with it.'

Billie had been there the entire time. Great. She was ten and watching her sister and her sister's friend abusing alcohol and drugs. Max braced himself to hear about the new chaos involving his shaving gear. What were Ilona and Alexandra supposedly managing so well? The sleepover had been a fucking disaster, a free-for-all.

Max forced himself to remain mostly expressionless during the aspirant woosh as pure steam and boiling water spurted into the drip tray. He unlocked the portafilter from the group head.

'You mean my razor?' What on earth was she talking about?

Sam nodded. 'And your brush.'

He used a German-made aluminium razor with a unique dial in the handle set at the sharpest level.

'Darling, that razor is extremely dangerous.'

Max remembered his shaving brush that Sunday morning had been wet even before he shaved, which puzzled him at the time. 'And it was Trixie you shaved, or was it yourself?'

'Trixie, I shaved Trixie – because of what she did to Selena.'

'Did you use my razor as well?'

Sam nodded.

'You could have cut Trixie – very badly.'

'I've watched you change blades and shave yourself since I was a little girl. I know how to do it.'

'You know there are veins and arteries in the legs. What if she had woken up, or moved suddenly while she was asleep?'

'I know,' Sam said tearfully. 'I remember learning about the femoral artery. Trixie was completely asleep and didn't move, so I adjusted her legs very carefully. And I used nice warm water.'

What a strange idea to shave Trixie's legs.

'When Mummy found out from Alexandra, I told her I'd done it to myself, too. She wanted to see and at first I didn't let her.'

This wasn't the first time Max has witnessed an important disconnect between Sam and her mother. Six months ago, Ilona mentioned to Max that Sam had been irritable for several days and was complaining of stomach cramps. To Max, it was pretty obvious, but when he suggested Sam was about to have her first period Ilona ridiculed the idea.

'I understand,' said Max. At least Ilona had eventually figured out what was going on that night, except for the Ambien. That was somewhat reassuring.

'I realised I would have to show Mummy so I bought some shaving things at the mall in Bondi Junction and shaved myself in the lady's washroom.'

Naughty – but resourceful girl. Max shook his head, bewildered. 'Wow – are you and Trixie still friends?'

'Oh, she was very upset but didn't say anything until she went home – then she told Alexandra what happened but didn't say why – because, of course, she didn't know – and she didn't want to admit she'd been drinking and taking Ambien. Actually, everything turned out exactly opposite to what I expected: I thought Trixie should know what it felt like to have something like that on the internet, so I posted a photo of her on Instagram and it's made Trixie really popular even though nobody is really sure it's her.'

Max felt his head well and truly spinning. To steady himself, he filled the small sink with hot water, scooped a couple of teaspoons of sodium percarbonate into the rising water, and removed the blind basket from the portafilter putting it and the basket into the solution of hot, caustic solution to soak.

'Trixie is starting to get invited to parties and when she had a gathering last week everybody wanted an invitation. That never happened before. My Instagram made her famous. She's more popular now than me – she's the most popular girl at Nightingale. Even Buster started going out with Trixie – but she broke up with him for a boy who's on the Junior Eight at Shore. Trixie is getting everything she ever wanted.'

Her mum would be delighted too, no doubt. Ilona had been telling him for months how worried Alexandra was about how much Trixie's personality resembled Mort's. The way Trixie had delighted in tormenting Selena was an all-too-recent example. Alexandra constantly anguished over Trixie's lack of popularity, and hoped fervently Trixie might benefit from Sam's reflected glow.

'Am I worse than Trixie?' Sam asked tearfully, studying his face.

Six months ago, Max had been standing at the espresso machine, just like he was now, when Ilona and Sam appeared at the kitchen door and Sam walked to the big window and stopped. She had looked at Max with her eyes shining, full of love and trust, as transparent as seawater – just as they were a few minutes before.

Max stopped and looked from Sam to Ilona and back again – instantly he understood. 'Did it happen?' he asked Sam gently.

Sam nodded, her eyes shining. Max's heart filled with joy.

He walked to Sam and embraced her tenderly, kissing her on her forehead. 'Congratulations, my darling. I'm so happy for you.'

Sam had looked up at him and smiled. 'Thank you Daddy.'

'I'm so proud of you, my darling, so happy for you,' Max had said his own eyes filled with tears of happiness. 'This is a wonderful day. Today you join the long line of women, stretching back into time immemorial, who have brought the entire human race into this world.'

It was such a beautiful moment, and yet now, having a very different conversation with Sam, it felt as if everything was being subjected to futility. They were both lying to Ilona, whose performance as mother of their adolescent daughter he could never trust again. Of course, his daughter was more honest about her own transgressions than he was. His sense of moral inferiority paralysed him.

Max sighed heavily. 'Don't take revenge into your own hands, you can never tell how it's going to work out.' Max gave her shoulders an affectionate squeeze and kissed her cheek. 'As you now know. I wish I was wise enough to say more, but I'm not.'

Sam looked up at him. 'Daddy, please don't tell Mummy about this.'

'You know that's hard for me to do,' Max said.

'Please.'

He had lost all perspective on what to say or do. Who was he to confess Sam's sins when he couldn't confess his own? And what was their family turning into? Max felt numb. Perhaps it was enough he knew about the Ambien. He'd be more watchful from now on – and he'd put them away in the locked drawer of his nightstand. He'd find a way to hint to Ilona that they should be more careful with the pills now the girls were getting older – although he flinched at the thought of the scorn she would heap on him for intervening in the girls' upbringing – the authority she preserved with such fierce jealousy for herself alone.

'Ok, darling,' Max said.

He watched Sam disappear through the kitchen door. As disturbed as he felt in the wake of the conversation, her decision to confide in him gave Max hope – and the opportunity to hug her again was wonderful. It had been so long since his daughters hugged him and they held his hands less and less. Until just then, he'd gone all day without being touched, and earlier he had been having the eerie feeling he was becoming abstract, evaporating. Sometimes the only reminder that this was real life was the touch of something tangible, like the portafilter in his hand.

Max picked up a clean sponge, relishing its cool feel in his fingers, and peered at the bottom of the group head, which always reminded him of an arsehole, as if a stainless steel baby homonculous was crouched on the bench presenting its dirty bottom to him. He wiped the dispersion screen, first in circular motions then in straight strokes up and back, rinsing the sponge with warm water several times until the steel screen gleamed.

His mother had made her revulsion of his boyish body so clear Max had become empathetically calibrated with her disgust. When he transitioned from the baths of his boyhood, to taking showers as an adolescent, he found he was unable to touch the lower part of his body except indirectly, with a bar of soap. When he finally dared to actually touch himself, he began a long path towards connection with his own body that would eventually include sex – something else his mother had misled him about. She made it clear that sex was something brutish men selfishly imposed onto unwilling women. Realising it was a lie was the second great moment of liberation in his life. He'd never forget the girl who first took him inside herself one summer night in the cemetery near his home in Dover Heights, and how happy she had seemed to be having sex. It was not distasteful to her, and he was not a brute.

Max flipped the pump lever one more time, allowing boiling water to trickle free through the dispersion screen. He refilled the water tank and switched off the machine, now perfectly clean.

'Max, darling, have you seen Sam?'

'Yes, darling, she can't be far.' Max felt a rush of bitterness, confusingly mixed with guilt pangs. He had committed to conceal what Sam had said about the Ambiens – but everything else seemed to be fair game – except what he himself so needed to confess. 'By the way, she was saying a little bit about that sleepover. I didn't realise there was quite so much going on that night.'

'What did you say she sang?' Ilona asked sharply.

'Sorry?' asked Max, bewildered. He was a little off-balance, knowing he was concealing something from Ilona.

'Did you say sang?' Ilona asked Max.

Max heard Ilona pronounce 'saying', not 'sang.' 'Yes,' he said. 'Saying. And what she was saying was about the sleepover. The shaving. The Instagram.'

Ilona fixed Max with a curious gaze. 'What was it that she sang?'

'I said saying.' Why wasn't Ilona addressing the outrageous events of the sleepover?

'I know,' said Ilona. Her gaze was not yet quite a glare.

'Well – do you think it was ok for all that to happen? Don't you think you should have mentioned it to me the next morning? Who knows – maybe now I'm starting to understand why Mort was so pissed off – assuming Alexandra told him more of the truth than you've told me.'

'Sang,' she said deliberately.

Max's face flushed. 'No – saying. Sam was talking, she wasn't singing. She was saying.'

Ilona looked coldly at Max. He was familiar with the expression of loathing that crept over her face – and it infuriated him. She obviously wasn't sure what else he was going to bring up about that evening, and so she instantly decided the best defence is a good offence.

'No,' she said.

Max tossed his head. 'What do you mean, 'no'? I was here just now with Sam, and you weren't.'

Ilona calmly regarded Max. 'You told me you were listening to what she sang.'

Max's face was now tawny from the blood that had rushed into it. 'But that's not what I said! That's what *you've* been saying!'

'No ...' Ilona started to correct him. Once again she succeeded in making him angry, and his anger was now like a big wave risen from a calm sea – one she knew exactly how to surf. 'You said sang.'

'No I didn't! I said 'saying.' And I want to talk about how Trixie tormented poor little Selena Woodbridge!'

'Yes, you did,' Ilona said. Her expression hardened. 'I asked it twice and you said 'yes.' Sang.'

'I thought you said saying,' said Max, grinding his teeth. 'I wasn't saying 'sang'. Sam was *saying*. And you asked once, not twice – and then you misheard. Or misunderstood. Or whatever the fuck!'

'Don't swear,' said Ilona. 'I heard sang.'

'But that doesn't make any sense,' said Max. 'No sense whatsoever. Our daughter and I were talking about the sleepover, and it was pretty fucking atrocious, frankly. And we were talking, not singing. That doesn't make any fucking sense.'

'Max, don't swear at me—and of course it makes sense – the girls sing all the time,' said Ilona, raising her voice for the first time. 'Don't try condescending to me!'

Max recognised he was being manipulated, but the knowledge only increased his fury. He was almost overwhelmed by a powerful sense of injustice – and by the sense that he was in no position to appeal to justice when he himself was lying to Ilona and having an affair. She was the wronged party, not he. Brain lock. Max felt himself looking past Ilona, seeking a way to escape the kitchen. 'For Christ's sake!' he said, flinging down the damp dishtowel on the bench, and staring at Ilona, who returned his gaze unblinkingly. Max caught his own reflection, upset and bewildered, in the clean machine.

He glanced back to see Ilona inspecting him with a mixture of contempt and satisfaction. She was looking at him as if he were a child. 'You're just a bomb waiting to explode!' she exclaimed.

Ilona pivoted on her heel and disappeared.

Chapter 20

'I thought you would be the boring one – otherwise, Mortie would already be in jail where he belongs,' said Luke Terry.

Max looked at the cones of tarnished light that emerged from the ceiling and seemed to levitate the ceiling above the carpeted floor of Terry's vast office. They sat across from each other at a low table, on facing sofas, in the massive executive suite that was Terry's reward for party loyalty. Servant of the people.

'Why should I trust you?' Luke Terry asked.

'Because I left the partnership with Mortimer Norton. Old logic.'

The enemy of my enemy is my friend.

'Logic doesn't always lead to one conclusion. You might be trying to use standard logic as a trap. That's what a smart guy might do,' Terry said, looking at Max with dark, watchful eyes. 'Who knows? You could be smart.' His stern, sour expression suggested he was skeptical about that.

Max smiled. 'I was smart enough to leave Norton & Ring, and I didn't do it to set a trap for you.'

'You were his partner for over five years. That says things I don't like.'

'You wouldn't hate Norton if you hadn't been involved with him,' Max remarked. 'I don't know what your issue is, but you probably did business with him too. Judging by the way you feel, I'll bet there was a time when you were pretty close to Mort.'

Terry regarded him expressionlessly. 'What do you want?'

'ZettaData,' Max said. 'What do you want?'

'Whatever it may be,' Terry said, looking with distaste at Max, 'there's no chance of me getting it from you.'

'Do you want Mort stalking ZettaData? Do you want him creating any more dramas that might be embarrassing during your campaign?'

Terry frowned.

'Once I buy ZettaData there'll be nothing Norton can do.'

Terry's frown tightened until he was glaring at Max. 'As long as my arsehole points to the ground, Mortimer Norton will never touch ZettaData – or the McConnochie Consortium.'

He looked up at the ceiling, and then out the window.

Max smiled. 'You're a man who wants many things. I can help you with one of them. You're one of the two strategic shareholders, so out of respect I've come to see you. I'd like to buy the whole company, but I'd be very happy for you to continue to be a shareholder when I've become majority shareholder. I'm here to introduce myself. I think we can do business.'

'Yeah, you said something about putting an investment proposal to the board at the AGM. I wondered how your partner would feel about that,' Terry said, allowing an almost imperceptible smile at the corner of his mouth.

'Ex-partner. And my word is my bond.'

Terry laughed – a short, bitter laugh. 'I haven't heard that in years. Nobody says that anymore.'

'You don't have to believe what I say, but you'll believe what I do. I've talked to the bank group. As you know, they're ready to declare ZettaData in default on its loan covenants and hand the company to the first guy who promises to pay them back. That would be me.'

'So?'

'If they do that, it'll wipe out your equity – ANG's, along with Edgell's and the mums and dads. I don't think Edgell cares less that he got thirty-five percent of an Australian subsidiary when he took over the Texas parent company last month. The mums and dads can't do anything about it. That leaves the banks and you. I know what the banks want, and if I can give you what you want, I will.'

'What would you do that's any different?'

Terry's office was hung with Australian art, important and boring. Max's glance fell on an enormous painting of a gloomy paddock full of lean cattle under a blue sky, probably once cobalt blue but now darkened by old varnish. *Terra nullius*. 'First of all,' he said, 'I believe in ZettaData – and neither you nor the Americans ever did.'

'Why do you say that? I invested two hundred million dollars.'

It was Max's turn to laugh. 'ANG never risked a dollar. You got all that cash right back in the construction contracts ANG was awarded to build ZettaData's computer facilities and communications networks. Nice juicy margins on those, I'll bet.'

'It's called jobs, Max. In the union movement we look after our own.'

'Fair enough Luke, I guess. But because ANG got its thirty-five percent in ZettaData almost for free, in return you agreed to let the Texans invest in those wonky CCPS securities which quietly gave them majority ownership because there was no chance ZettaData could ever pay the coupon – and so every year they converted into more shares, setting up the Texans to take it over.'

'Water under the bridge – at five cents the Texans are fucked anyway. I doubt Edgell cares what happens to ZettaData.'

'Probably not,' Max agreed.

'So what's the problem?'

'Your deal-making was funded by the small investors,' said Max. 'They're the ones who didn't get their own special deal.'

'I said we look after our own,' Terry retorted.

'The only problem is that now ZettaData isn't worth anything. You're ok, because you got all your money back. The Texans got fucked, but for totally different reasons they went bankrupt anyway,' Max said. 'It's a pity about the small shareholders.'

Terry allowed himself a thin smile.

It was hard to believe they were almost sixty storeys in the air. It felt like they were underground.

'There was never any secret about those CCPSes, Max.'

'Oh no, of course not. The Prefs were fully disclosed in the complicated and ambiguous prospectus text the average person can't possibly understand. Everything was completely legal.' Like *Terra* fucking *Nullius*.

Terry was part of the rule-making elite, too, busily spinning his share of the many, many intricate complications enmeshing the economy and society. He looked away and seemed to study the dozens of framed photos of himself with two generations of union leaders and politicians displayed behind his desk. 'I hope you're not planning to stir up trouble, Max. Was Mort's little speech at the AGM your idea?'

'I didn't have a clue he was going to do that. He had the staff brief him up. You saw what I did the moment I heard what he said.'

Terry nodded. 'Those CCPSes weren't my idea, either.' He interlocked his fingers and flexed them by cantilevering his palms back and forth, his elbows resting on his massive desk. The people's business. 'That's capitalism – that's what you and your former mates at Norton & Ring believe, right?'

'I'd say it's a buggerised form of capitalism,' said Max.

Terry shrugged.

'Luke, have you ever read those software licensing agreements where we have to click 'I Agree' in order to get the latest update or app for our mobile phones?'

'No,' said Terry. 'What's the point?'

'Exactly,' Max said. 'We've probably signed away our children along with all our rights to privacy. How are ANG's agreements with consumers and small businesses to be supplied with natural gas any different?'

Terry regarded Max. 'The government and utilities regulator impose strict requirements on what we are allowed to put in those contracts,' he said sternly.

Max tried hard not to burst out laughing. Terry was the government. Besides, government is one of the main sources of complications –the proof was ANG's onerous gas supply contracts. Only ANG's biggest corporate customers had any hope of fairly negotiating the provisions of their gas supply contracts.

'Ok, Luke,' Max said. 'Let's agree you're the working class man's best friend. How did that affect in any way what happened with ZettaData?'

'It made all the difference in the world, mate,' Terry frowned. 'For my part, I made sure my boys had jobs that paid well – we just took the money, we didn't put our hands out for any upside from the capitalist casino. The Texans and investment bankers are the ones who fucked the little investors with those CCPSes, not me. I don't believe in capitalism.'

'ZettaData isn't capitalism. ZettaData is just another dirty deal like the McConnochie Tunnel,' said Max. 'It's cake frosting on a piece of shit.'

Terry shrugged. 'If I had my way, air, water – and electricity – would be free. The means of production would be owned by the people.'

'And administered by the unions,' said Max. 'In other words, by you.'

'I made sure the people who matter were looked after in ZettaData – workers who built the real assets of the company for the greedy shareholders.'

'You're one of the two biggest greedy shareholders,' said Max. 'But if you don't care about your shares, I'll buy them.'

'I'll put it on my list of things to think about.'

'Put this on your list of things to do immediately: introduce me to Edgell. It seems I'm the only one these days who's ready to save ZettaData from bankruptcy. A bankrupt ZettaData hurts you, too. I know I can do a deal with the banks, and I'd rather not wipe out shareholders – the little guys, you and Edgell. If you can't sell, I know Edgell can.'

'You want to meet Edgell?' Terry laughed.

'That's right,' said Max. 'All you have to do is hold on to ANG's shares and watch them go up as I run ZettaData. Trust me, you'll do well.'

'You think you can get ZettaData's shares away from Edgell?'

'It's worth a try.'

A sneer appeared slowly on Terry's tired, disenchanted face. 'Edgell is smarter than you, tougher than you, and he's got more money than most central banks,' he said.

Edgell would take his call because he was likely to be the next Prime Minister of Australia, not because of ZettaData. Edgell probably didn't know anything about ZettaData, and if he did, it would mean three fifths of fuck all to him.

'Will ANG be any worse if I try and fail?'

'Who knows?'

'Exactly,' said Max. 'And if I succeed, we'll all be laughing. What do you have to lose?'

'Ok,' Terry said. 'I can arrange the meeting. Just let me ask you one question.'

'Sure,' said Max.

'Do you know who Mort really is?'

'Of course,' said Max.

'Ok – if you say so,' Terry said, looking at Max. 'But if you don't, it looks like you're going to find out.'

Chapter 21

The tip of Claudia Bullivant's nose skimmed across the wool of Max's trousers as her head moved gently from side to side. She was still holding a cool glass of bright red, barely-tasted carrot, currant and ginger juice.

When Max arrived he was cheerful on the surface, but for the first time he was conflicted and had been behaving, he knew, differently than usual. Claudia was binge-watching cable shows, her mood lazy and languorous. With actor's intuition, Claudia immediately sensed something and responded by loosening her gown and, not even setting aside her glass, slipped off the sofa and sank to her knees. Max's scruples had faded immediately.

But as Max watched, in awe and wonder, an inconvenient thought appeared.

Was consent all that separated right from wrong? He no longer had his miserable partnership with Mortimer Norton to blame for acting out. Maybe he never really had.

Kairos.

'Hey, beautiful,' he said. It was time to own his own behaviour.

Claudia probably wanted a drink of that juice right now.

She murmured something, concentrating.

Was Ilona really to blame for this? His own daughter had turned out to be more honest than he was, and she had issues with her mother, too.

He looked at the glass of juice in Claudia's hand, which she hadn't tasted for almost ten minutes. She must be thirsty.

Claudia had landed a small role in the upcoming debut of *TransGod* at the Eden Street Theatre, but winning the role had nothing to do with Max. Their relationship wasn't some crude, direct trade.

'Hey,' he said gently, stroking her cheek with his fingertips. At the very least he didn't have to be so selfish.

She opened her eyes, looking into his. Max felt nearly hypnotised. While meditating he had seen eyes with that expression appear in his mind. A gaze beyond time and space. Some elemental knowing. Wisdom.

'Hey ... ' Max said again. He stepped away and sank to his own knees. She looked bewildered. 'Have a drink, darling,' he said, smiling, and kissed her with his eyes wide open.

Claudia folded sideways into a sitting position on the floor, drinking gratefully from the glass. She smiled. 'That was nice – now what?'

Max leaned towards her, gazed into her eyes, and they kissed. Claudia's eyes were open because she knew he liked it. They kissed slowly and deliberately, watching each other.

Max loved kissing. It was intimate and personal, a delight in itself – and a promise of good things to come when a woman kissed like Claudia, deeply and full of soul. Max savoured her tongue in his mouth, remembering Tiresias. For Max, kissing was the only sexual act totally equal and symmetrical between man and woman, a union of similar shapes dancing with each other, man and woman taking turns leading and following with lips and tongue, flaunting prowess by alternately initiating contact and being receptive.

Tiresias was the blind prophet of Apollo, who had been changed into a woman for seven years. Afterwards, he famously settled a debate among the gods by confirming, as the only human to have had sex as both a male and female, that women experience nine times as much pleasure as men.

Claudia ran her fingers along the back of Max's head, allowing them to intertangle in his hair. To his dismay, Max's bad conscience reappeared.

As always, he was fully present with Claudia. Their shared present was charged with affection and desire. But their future was missing, and the future is the dimension of love. He was putting up with a miserable present in his marriage, because of the future he still hoped for with Ilona and their daughters—that's how important the future was to him.

He wasn't offering Claudia a future. Max began kissing Claudia along her cheekbone and then her throat, to conceal the troubled look in his eyes. The authenticity of their shared present veiled their future's emptiness.

Max sighed.

Claudia purred in response. 'Come on, lover.'

He took her in his arms and looked pensively at her. Claudia returned his gaze languidly, receptively. He was fully aroused, but he felt conflicted. She kissed him gently, then looked at him, her head back, resting in his hand. Waiting.

Over her shoulder, just past Claudia's shining blonde hair, Max's eyes fell on the script lying open on the sofa. He hadn't paid attention to it when he first arrived.

'I'm going to be your acting coach,' he said.

Weeks ago Max surprised Claudia by his interest in the play, when he not only told her he had read the script, but was able to talk about it with some insight.

'My what?' Claudia looked bewildered.

He kissed her. 'Lesson One: Focus.'

He reached and picked up the script.

Claudia crossed her legs, looking confused and a little annoyed. She brushed strands of hair out of her eyes.

Max presented her with the script. 'Where's your part?'

'It's so small,' she said. 'I've got some good lines in Scene 3 – what is this? What are you doing?'

Max looked at the tabs Claudia had added to the pages and found her part, the role of the Secret Service Agent. 'Well, let me see, the beginning is a very good place to start. Right, here's your first entrance. Let's start with some of the lines before you make your entrance.'

Max handed her the script.

'What are you doing?'

As Max eased off her gown, leaving her completely naked, he said, 'Read all the parts – the Secret Service Agent, Pandemia and Dion's, too. But stay focused. No mistakes, and read with feeling.'

Claudia leaned back against the sofa and as she moved Max covered her with kisses, gently and fluidly, his kisses gradually descending to her belly.

'Oh, honey,' she said, stroking his cheeks with her free hand and then tousling his hair. 'Oh, honey ... darling ...' He could hear the smile in her voice.

'Read,' he said. 'No mistakes – focus.'

'President Donald, the two asylum seekers have arrived for their interview with you,' Claudia began in the voice of the Agent.

Max savoured her.

'What troublemakers! Throw them into a detention centre where they belong!' Claudia continued, sounding like the coarse President. 'Millions of my citizens are dying and these illegal immigrants think they can violate our borders!'

Claudia's gruff voice was sexy, and actually Max liked everything about Claudia, especially her cute little belly wick. Ilona's bald lips gave him the creepy feeling of being a paedophile, and he had to concentrate not to lose his arousal, but now he could enjoy the satisfaction of a woman.

'More trouble than you know: I am Dion, allow me to introduce my most committed activist, Pandemia—here to rock your world.'

Claudia's voice was low and husky. She no longer sounded like a haughty stranger who might or might not reveal mysterious powers.

'I love the world the way it is!' Claudia exclaimed in her gruff Presidential voice.

Max was, if possible, even more aroused than before. He could feel Claudia's warmth on his face.

'Then you won't be in it much longer!'

It wasn't clear the role of the mysteriously powerful stranger Dion required speaking so slowly.

'Stay in character,' Max said softly, and resumed what he was doing.

She tangled the fingers of one hand in his hair.

'A new race of women will claim your throne ...'

'I claim you,' murmured Max. He felt little ripples in her thighs against his cheeks.

'....stronger ... faster ... more brilliant ...bold and beautiful!'

Claudia was panting, barely able to pronounce the words.

'My advocates!'

She was speaking in little rushes now, trying to get the words out as she tried to adopt the imperious tone of Pandemia.

'I'll unleash the invisible on the visible! I'll hale unbelievers through the streets by their hair ...'

As a breeze stirs the surface of the waves, Max felt the ripples spread rapidly through Claudia's body.

'– until they eat strange flesh ...'

'...Like flesh-eating birds devouring baby turtles on hot sand!' Claudia sighed heavily.

Max suddenly realised the unique sensation of *omophagia*: warm flesh – slippery and wet like sushi.

Her breathing was audible as she fought for control, and then almost miraculously managed the next sentences: 'You deny science! You're a disease vector! You say a virus sanctified your nature? You will die by my new virus!'

Claudia dropped the script, clutched Max's head in both her hands, and began to lunge against his lips.

Max was silent, listening to sounds like waves lapping against the black sand of a beach on a Galapagos Island.

'You're dear to me only as turtle flesh....!'

Claudia groaned and cried out in her clear beautiful voice, her tones rising and becoming more urgent, the original source of all music. The primordial notes resonated in his DNA across millions of years in a melody that had never been surpassed.

'Oh my god, oh my god,' whispered Claudia, leaning her head back against the sofa. At last she wiped a sweaty strand from her face.

Max sat up and kissed her. He could feel his own sweat in his hair and he ached painfully. 'That's a 'Fail', darling.' He kissed her. 'You're not ready for opening night yet.'

Claudia opened her eyes and laughed to the ceiling.

'Ok, coach – let's see what kind of an actor you might make.'

Claudia helped him to undress, then they changed positions and Max picked up the script.

Max let out a short exhale, and then with determination focused on the script he was holding.

'... I'm responsible for maintaining order in this community ...' Max said, channelling President Donald.

Claudia was making it as difficult as she could possibly could, but Max continued to read, hearing his own voice slow and his words thicken.

'Oh,' said Max, breaking character. 'Here is where you make your entrance. You come on stage ...I'm about ...to ...come myself ...'

'Agent– that's you.'

'Unh-huh,' said Claudia indistinctly. Her poise seemed unaffected.

'Arrest these two and have them locked in Biohazard Quarantine!'

Claudia wasn't playing fair – she knew he especially loved what she was doing.

'... I want them sanitised and all their hair cut off!'

'My hair is sacred to science, and Pandemia's spikes can't be cut—only covered.'

Max stopped, and cycled through two complete breaths. Like a judo champion whose mastery of an esoteric hold permits her to throw her bigger and stronger opponent around the mat as she pleased, Claudia completely controlled him with her ability to expertly perform the daunting technique.

'My sweet Lord' – I'm... reading the script ...,' panted Max. 'It's Pandemia ... who says... 'My sweet Lord -'"

Almost inaudibly, Claudia indicated she understood.

'Let ... let him bluster,' Max panted out Dion's words to Pandemia.

Pranayama.

He tried to maintain his composure, fighting rising waves of pleasure, by fiercely concentrating on the script, barking out the threats of President Donald. 'I'll have you quarantined all right! ...' he managed to say. '... and that's the last you'll see ...' he gasped. '... of your curls and spikes!'

He couldn't bear it any longer. 'Get ready, baby, I'm coming ...' he murmured.

Max surrendered and sank below roaring waves of ecstasy.

When Max returned to consciousness it was with a vision of how President Donald meets his comeuppance for ignoring science and promoting self-centred freedom of choice over the common good: a heap of orange shreds and fluorescent hair mixed into what looks like a mound of turtle meat, with blood splattered all over the stage. The image was more vivid than any of the dialogue he and Claudia had just been practicing.

Max shuddered and looked to see Claudia's blond hair falling over her shoulders, a sweaty strand plastered across her forehead and cheek, her soft skin, her curves, the lovely plump chin: she was beautiful because she was kind and good.

Beautiful.

Max felt a nameless longing pierce him.

It was Aristophanes in Plato's dialogue the 'Symposium' who says lovers don't actually know what they want from each other. Aristophanes was the great comic playwright who used his comedies to mock his hated rival Euripides.

It's obvious, says Aristophanes in words Plato attributes to him in the philosophical dinner party where the dialogue unfolds, that the souls of both lovers are thirsting for something other than pleasure. But neither soul can express this other thing for which it yearns because their souls have only a vague premonition of what they actually want.

'Is there any juice left?' asked Max. The soul speaks to itself in riddles. His certainly did. 'If not, I'll get some water ... in a second.'

Max ran his fingers along Claudia's thigh. Plato was right – her beauty was giving him the healthy shock which destroyed his contentment, and by making him suffer, set him back on the path of his original quest.

'Sure, honey – a bit,' said Claudia, handing him the glass. It was just slightly less than half full.

'Thanks, babe,' said Max taking a small sip and giving her back the glass.

He watched her drink the rest, and then set the glass aside on the floor, her breasts swaying slightly as she turned back to him.

Claudia smiled, looking at Max steadily, and then she lay down next to him, flat on her back.

Max felt his thirst kindling into fire.

Chapter 22

'Have you had a look at the Campani Athena Lappato?' asked Alexandra, surveying the new entrance hall being constructed in the gaping hole torn into the façade of the Ring family home.

'I'm having my architect collect a dozen kinds of tiles to show me,' said Ilona, trying to prevent resentment from creeping into her tone. She was proud of herself for insisting to Max that she and Alexandra would remain friends no matter what happened between Mort and him. This morning, however—as so often—Ilona found Alexandra overwhelming.

'Mmm,' said Alexandra appraisingly. 'Make sure you bring home all the tiles you're considering, and look at them in the morning, during the day, and in the evening. You'd be amazed how different tiles appear when the light changes.'

'He's selecting different varieties, not just Georgian Lappato Clarus and the Campani Athena Lappato but other terracottas, marbles, and sandstones,' said Ilona, subtly trying to deny Alexandra the credit for convincing her to use tiles in the front entrance instead of timber.

'Tiles are best for high traffic areas, believe me,' Alexandra said. 'Incidentally darling, you and Max seemed tense the other night.'

'Oh really?' Alexandra had been sitting with some girlfriends at the bar of a Woollahra bistro where she and Max had been having an early dinner. Ilona scanned her memory for any incident, but they had maintained perfect civility as far as she could recall, not the slightest public sign of a crack, she thought.

'I just thought I saw pain in your face, and Max seemed detached,' Alexandra said. 'I just want to make sure you're ok. Now—'

'Mmmm,' said Ilona. Alexandra was right, as usual. She'd been feeling even more isolated since Max left Norton & Ring. Despite the initial warmth when she gave Max her full support, she had no idea what he was thinking or feeling now. Sometimes he didn't even seem to know she was there. The universe seemed to be collapsing into a tiny, airless, lonely prison. 'Max has never been a comforting man, and I've felt quite pushed aside lately. I suppose I've lashed out at him, more than a few times probably–but just because I'm trying to get him to engage with me.'

Alexandra inspected the raw brick wall revealed by the demolition. Its vertical edge was crenellated where the last bricks in every row had been knocked out. The remaining plaster was wrinkled by long rising cracks and soiled by grime and floating dust. Tradies' footprints intersected continuously like game trails on the dusting of plaster that coated the newly poured concrete floor.

'I'm sure if he paused and gave it some thought, he would realise he's at fault for how you're treating him, you poor darling,' said Alexandra.

'Oh, I don't know if Max even notices. I'm beginning to wonder if I should just give up.'

Her poor dismantled house. It distressed Ilona to walk through the disembowelled carcass of her home. It was once so comforting and safe, even if she was always dissatisfied with its lack of glamour.

Alexandra turned from the scene and looked at Ilona with a piercing glance that was also somehow sympathetic. 'Men always think of their egos first,' said Alexandra. 'We're so much better than the boys at working things out.'

'Of course!' said Ilona. Something bruised had unexpectedly appeared behind Alexandra's eyes, and Ilona was taken aback.

'I feel awful about the way Mortie and Max have fallen out,' said Alexandra, stepping nimbly over the crosshatch of steel reinforcements where the new front room floor and terrace was about to be poured. She was scanning to place her next step, so whatever Ilona had seen so suddenly in Alexandra's eyes was now hidden, perhaps accidentally, perhaps deliberately. 'I think it's so important for the girls and us to stay strong and keep the families together.'

'You're so right,' said Ilona, surprised to realise she meant it.

Trixie Norton was now the most popular girl in Year Seven at Nightingale: the invitations were flooding in to all the alpha girls' birthday parties, and Trixie was being invited to at least a dozen parties a month given by boys from the best schools: Cranbrook, Shore, Grammar and Scots. Trixie had even been invited to a sixteenth birthday party given by a boy from Kings on his family's vast station outside Moree – but Alexandra put her foot down on that one: no stay-over parties like that for Trixie, just yet.

'Presumably you're about to move out?' asked Alexandra as they passed great plastic sheets that sealed off the part of the house still occupied by the Rings.

'Yes, the removalists come tomorrow.'

'Hmmm,' said Alexandra, darting appraising glances in all directions. 'It's so stressful. Has Max been any help?'

Ilona shook her head, and Alexandra sympathetically mirrored the gesture.

Ilona sighed.

As she and Alexandra stepped into the not yet fully demolished kitchen, Ilona forgot her troubles with Max for a moment as a pall settled over her. Good old-fashioned social humiliation.

'Oh dear,' said Alexandra.

'You can see why we're so desperate to renovate,' Ilona said weakly, thinking of Alexandra's magnificent kitchen and informal eating area. Arguably, Alexandra had miscalculated slightly, as her decision to add a kitchen that resembled the sound stage of a TV show fomented a rebellion amongst their neighbours who baulked at the way the cathedral-like cornices jutted above the treetops, and the extension had cost almost $400,000 in extra legal and architectural bills, never mind the cost of actual construction.

'Right,' said Alexandra, stepping into the kitchen with an air of practicality she might assume for inspecting a dirty stable or the oily engine room of a yacht. 'I assume you're going to knock all this out and open it up? Is there a view on the other side of this wall?'

'Yes,' Ilona said gratefully, catching the note of absolution in Alexandra's voice. It was like being forced to confess Max had erectile dysfunction, only to have Alexandra offer the best practical remedies for the condition. 'All this will be demolished ... not that there are any water views, really, from here, just Bondi Junction and across the valley to Woollahra ...'

'Aga?' asked Alexandra, nodding to the spot where Ilona had just indicated the new stove would be.

'A Savoir-Faire Royal,' replied Ilona, looking anxiously at Alexandra, who just nodded.

'Side-by-side Liebherr.' Another nod, an approving one.

'Zip tap for boiling and cold filtered water.' A nod – of course.

Alexandra looked up through the shrouds of plastic sheeting at the kitchen ceiling, already eviscerated. 'Now, what kind of extractor fan are you putting in here?'

A blizzard of foreign names swirled in a panic through her mind: Italian, German, French, mostly unpronounceable and, at that moment, all disconnected from the products and services that made them famous.

'Is it a Schweigen?' Alexandra gently prompted, pronouncing the name with the assurance of an Oxford Don invoking a German philosopher.

'I ... don't think so.' All her awareness was concentrated on Alexandra's face. Alexandra was protecting her. She could be trusted.

'Darling, you must get a Schweigen,' said Alexandra firmly. 'You know all those awful noisy range hoods everyone has?'

Ilona nodded.

'They're noisy *because* they're not doing their job! First, they suck the smoky, greasy air off your stove and then blow it up the pipe and out the top above your house. Think what a silly business that is! First suck, then blow!'

Ilona knew Alexandra had clear concepts for what worked and no patience for things that didn't.

'Schweigens look quite glamorous – did you notice the one over my range? No? The point of it is that its powerful motor fan is placed on the roof—*not* next to your head above the stove—and it sucks all the smoke and greasy air right up the pipe and away!'

Alexandra was so capable, and always so positive; such a problem solver.

'Thank you, I'll get one,' said Ilona. How could she admit to Alexandra how all the pressures and responsibilities sometimes made her feel so small, and that she just wanted Max's arms around her, but could never imagine telling him that? She despised herself.

'Let me show you the bathroom. We've already torn one out, and we're waiting to move before gutting the rest of them.' What would confident Alexandra think of her, if she knew?

'Darling, Mortie has been very worried about you and the girls,' said Alexandra as they walked down the hall.

Ilona was surprised. She didn't know what to say.

'Max has been acting erratically for at least a year,' Alexandra murmured, as if to herself.

'Erratically? What do you mean?'

'I hate to say this, darling,' Alexandra looked at Ilona significantly. 'Mortie said there were more than a few complaints ... by female staff members. Especially the receptionist and one of the analysts, apparently. A young woman. German.'

Ilona suddenly imagined a young, blonde Valkyrie, like Alexandra but fresh and nubile, voluptuous and athletic. Flashing white teeth, fingers flying rapidly across the keyboard as she generated huge financial models with her expertise from some German university. She was probably also a fencer and an equestrian.

'Do you mean ... sexual harassment?'

Alexandra raised her chin in a way that was spirited, defiant but somehow non-committal. 'The real issue, darling—what has Mortie so concerned for you and your precious daughters—is Max acting very recklessly in the financial markets.'

Ilona was stunned.

'What is Max doing?'

'Max seems to be going around looking for support to buy a sick company called ZettaData ...'

'I remember ZettaData,' Ilona said.

'ZettaData was Mortie's idea, originally, but he was going to go about it very differently. He has no intention of taking risks. Now Max seems to want it only because Mortie wants it. It's got one hundred million dollars in bank debt!'

A chill cascaded down Ilona's ribs and tingled through her spine. A hundred million dollars of debt! 'Surely ... surely Max wouldn't be liable to repay that much debt?'

Alexandra shrugged. 'I wouldn't know,' she said loftily. 'But Mortie thinks your husband is mad.'

It was consistent with what Max told her weeks ago. He had nothing but contempt for Mort's plan. It hadn't occurred to her that Max might be placing them all at such huge risk.

'My father gambled and speculated away most of our family's fortune, darling. I've seen that kind of grandiosity before. ZettaData is worth fifty million on the ASX. Max only got thirty million when he left Norton & Ring.'

That was a sore point, but Ilona brushed it aside.

'Even if Max does find backers,' Alexandra continued confidently, 'he'd be crazy to put all thirty million into ZettaData. He could lose it all – not to mention the debt that might be left hanging around his neck.'

'Is ... is ... that what Mort thinks Max is going to do?'

Alexandra nodded. 'You have to protect yourself, darling. I won't tell you what happened to me with my first husband – it was a dreadful financial disaster. Mortie and I think you should contact a lawyer recommended by Allaway, Davis.'

'Why?'

'Mortie is very concerned, and as your friend I told Mort we couldn't just let you and your girls be victims of Max's midlife crisis.'

'Thank you darling,' Ilona said, suddenly feeling emotional about Alexandra's caring.

'Allaway, Davis don't do matrimonial law, of course, but after I insisted we support you and your darling girls, Mortie called the lead partner there, one of his oldest and closest friends, who recommended a solicitor specialising in Statutory Declarations of Divorce.'

Ilona was frozen in place. 'What?'

They had stopped a few steps away from the first bathroom that was to be renovated. Alexandra put her hand on Ilona's shoulder. 'I know this is hard, but for at least the last year Max has been in some kind of midlife crisis. If he operates in the markets without Mortie to steady him, Max might make a dreadful mistake. If you and Max stay married you and the girls could lose everything along with Max.'

It was her worst nightmare—poverty and a divorce with nothing left. 'What is a Statutory Declaration of ... '

'It allows you and Max to legally divide your financial assets as if you had already divorced. You don't have to actually divorce, but if Max goes bankrupt, yours and the girls' assets are no longer included. And he can't give personal guarantees that commit any of your assets for any of his deals.'

'I wouldn't dream of divorcing Max!' But to her surprise, the moment she said the 'D' word, Ilona realised the possibility had in fact been hovering just beyond her awareness, hidden behind the horizon of thought to which she limited herself.

Grief overcame her.

'This isn't divorce,' Alexandra said consolingly. 'It's just a legal document that outlines what would happen *if* you divorce. I know couples who filed one years ago and are still married. But it's all you need to protect your assets for the sake of yourself and the girls. Don't you think it's worth asking Max to sign one?'

Ilona felt warm, and then cold. 'It feels like ... death.'

'I understand, darling,' Alexandra said reassuringly. 'But it could also mean a wonderful new life for yourself and the girls.'

Ilona nodded, reluctantly. Wonderful new life? She didn't see it; she just imagined herself being thrown, at forty, into the Eastern Suburbs meat market.

'Think of it as a termination,' said Alexandra briskly.

'A termination ... ?' Ilona was bewildered. 'But you just said we weren't terminating, it was just a Statutory *Intention* to Divorce.'

Alexandra looked at her patiently.

Ilona blushed. Her mother would be throwing her hands up with exasperation if she could hear this conversation.

'Nobody's idea of fun, but necessary, sometimes,' Alexandra said firmly. 'A re-set button that makes it possible to have the bright future you deserve.'

Her mother's firm conviction, too. Your dignity and freedom comes first, not being humiliatingly trapped by your body and subjugated by men—the most important thing for a woman to understand was her biology was *not* her destiny—nothing could get in the way of Ilona achieving her full potential.

'You must feel like you're in a struggle for survival,' Alexandra said. 'And maybe you are: but it doesn't have to be that way always. Focus on abundance. Start thinking about the future.'

'Thank you so much,' Ilona said, feeling teary. 'I'm, I'm ... certainly not ready yet for a divorce.'

'Oh, never mind, darling,' said Alexandra, her arms wrapped around Ilona in a brisk, comforting squeeze. 'It's not like the police will come around knocking on your door a year from now and ask if you've actually divorced yet. The important thing is, once you sign the Stat Dec and agree on the financial settlement, you and the girls will be safe – no matter what Max does. It's like a termination—difficult in advance but then you never look back!'

Ilona nodded, tears of gratitude filling her eyes, even though she'd heard very different accounts from a couple friends who'd undergone the procedure in uni or early in their career. The point was Alexandra was trying to help her when there was nobody else who could, or would. Least of all Max—who was the problem. 'I'm sorry,' said Ilona, raising a finger to stem the tears hovering on her fluttering eyelid.

'Enjoy it – you deserve it.' Alexandra's voice was surprisingly husky. 'Sometimes I wish I could have a good cry too – but if I let myself cry, perhaps ... perhaps I'd never stop.'

Ilona saw with shock that Alexandra's eyes were brimming with tears, a delicate tracing of rose suddenly outlining her eyelids.

'What if I totally lost control and cried forever?' murmured Alexandra.

'What? Why?' Ilona barely managed to ask.

Alexandra turned away. 'Oh, it's nothing, darling. I'm just being soppy.'

'That reminds me,' said Alexandra briskly as they walked the last steps to see the first eviscerated bathroom. 'One of Mortimer's old mates can get the lowest prices on Wesaunard Eutopias in Australia. He has a big warehouse in Mascot.' She winked. 'He assures me it's all totally legal.'

Thank you,' Ilona said, and putting her hand on Alexandra's arm, she asked, 'Are you ok—really?'

'Yes, of course, darling,' said Alexandra with a short laugh.

'I'll ask my architect to contact him if you give me his details.' Ilona was still totally bewildered, but beneath her shock she felt a tiny pang of resentment. Always bloody showing off. It was a reminder that actually Mort had pulled the strings to arrange the secret shipment of Pfizer vaccines, even though Ilona liked to think that Mort and Max were responsible. They'd both paid for it, of course, but that wasn't the hard part: Mort made the phone calls. Still, they were buying nine of the expensive heated towel racks, not just for the bathrooms but also for the laundry room, the kitchen and pool house. She swallowed her pride: mate's rates would help a lot.

'Oh no, darling, when you're ready just give Bruno a ring yourself. I'll give you his number, too. He also does bathtubs. Are you getting a Kaldewei?'

Ilona smiled weakly. She suddenly felt faint.

She was meant to be building her own fairy castle, homey but glamorous and full of little luxuries. A setting so perfect she and Max would have to be happy, have to love each other. Everything else would flow from getting it right. Instead the universe seemed to be already wrecked, and she would have to salvage what she could.

'Now, enough of this darling. The other topic I really wanted to talk to you about today was to see if you might be available at the last minute to join me for lunch on Friday.'

'Well ... ' Ilona hesitated. The last thing she needed was one more obligation, one more complication. At the moment, she felt hardly able to see Alexandra to the door.

'Would you join me, darling?' said Alexandra. 'It's time to begin planning for the Nightingale School Charity Auction on behalf of the Nightingale Eighteen, and I thought I would invite you along so you and Sylvia Trebuchet can start really getting to know one another. We're discussing new candidates for the Charity Committee.'

Sylvia Trebuchet! The monarch of Sydney society. Sylvia Trebuchet was the wife of Lionel Trebuchet, an ex-Prime Minister. The youngest of their two daughters was in her last year at the Nightingale School. Sylvia was twenty years older than Ilona, but she had stunning looks and the star power to overshadow any other mother at Nightingale.

'Sylvia just loved you when you met,' said Alexandra. 'The two of you will get along famously. You have so much in common.'

Now Ilona knew that Alexandra must be having her on. What did she have in common with Sylvia Trebuchet? A nose and two eyes?

Ilona felt her heart flutter with both yearning and dread at the prospect of lunch with Sylvia Trebuchet. But it was a lovely cause, commemorating the grandparents and great grandparents of Nightingale students who had died of Covid; there was even one thirty-seven year old uncle of one of Billie's friends who had seemed perfectly healthy who was a Covid victim. It was a cause close to Ilona's heart. 'Thank you, darling,' she said, smiling faintly. 'Of course I'll join you.'

Chapter 23

B efore Max could fly to New York and negotiate with Todd Edgell for the stake in ZettaData, he had to make sure he had all the necessary capital for the deal.

Kent Logan was worth a hundred times Mortimer Norton. The Logan family investment company had invested several times in Norton & Ring deals.

'How the fuck are ya, Max?'

'Hi Kent,' said Max. 'Good.'

'You're not looking too good,' said Logan, studying him as pulled on his cheap cherry-flavoured cigarillo. All of Max's life, Logan had been the minotaur at the centre of the Sydney labyrinth.

His desk was laden with an array of metal and plastic miniature planes, mining equipment, cars, boats, and intricate models of other industrial machines: totems of the many businesses comprising the Logan billions. Large, silver-framed photographs of Logan with his wife and seven children glimmered in array on the credenza. For almost two decades they had been released into the top of Australian society and the Australian economy to feed like locusts.

'I feel like a million bucks.' Max did feel a bit tired and stressed, but he was surprised his appearance reflected it.

'Ah,' said Logan, nodding his head sagely. 'Just what I thought—not a hundred percent.'

Max smiled. 'I'm fine, Kent.'

Logan squinted at Max through pungent smoke. 'Mortie can be a bit rough – on the way in, and on the way out. Hope he used a little soap, at least.'

'Ah, he was all right – no worse than expected. We're sorted.'

Logan flicked ash into an enormous ashtray. It was like a sacrificial altar, carved out of a polished piece of fossilised coral from the Great Barrier Reef. 'Well,' said Logan philosophically, 'you went into partnership with that cunt.'

Logan took a long drag from his cigarillo. 'Mortie is one of me oldest mates,' said Logan. 'You're a young fella making his own way in the world now. So what d'yer got?'

'I want to take over ZettaData.'

'Going to buy it for a dollar from the bank group?'

'No, I'm going to put a deal to shareholders.'

The carapace of Logan's face hardened against his skull. 'Why?'

'Because it's worth it.'

'What's Luke Terry got to say?'

'Luke's fine.'

'Is he going to sell you his stake?'

'Maybe, maybe not. It doesn't matter. He's organised for me to see Todd Edgell in New York.'

Logan sat back and considered Max. It was like being assessed by a snake trying to decide what kind of meal Max might make. 'You didn't waste any time, did you?'

'Finding a deal?'

'Getting in Mort's grill.'

Logan clearly assumed Max was focusing only on the two strategic investors. But it wasn't true: he was focusing mostly on the thirty percent of the shares held by Susan Casner and the rest of the small shareholders.

'This isn't about Mort, Kent.'

'Sure, if you say so.'

Wander, Terry and now Logan all assumed he was after revenge. Exhale. 'It's about making money. A shitload of money.'

'Do you think Luke Terry needs your help against Mort?'

'I'm not helping Luke Terry.'

'He seems to be helping you.'

'Kent, I'm here to offer you a piece of the ZettaData deal, but if you're not interested, that's fine.'

Logan smiled faintly and sat back in his chair. 'There's this great whorehouse in Vegas behind Caesar's. They get the girls in by the busload at Caesar's of course, but it's more fun once in a while to toddle over to this joint.'

Logan paused and sized Max up, seemingly satisfied Max was a carnivore of similar predilections. 'They've got Francoise, who gives the greatest blow jobs in the world, and when I mean greatest blow jobs, think pole dancing on your pole. It's like an acrobatic performance and all you gotta worry about is getting your head clipped by her knees as she flies around and does somersaults with her lips glued to your knob. Know what I mean? Hey?'

'Sure, Kent,' said Max. It was exactly the kind of story Logan and Mort had liked to swap.

'Anyways they've got girls from Venezuela, Japan, Canada, fuckin' Kenya, you name it – they've got girls with slits running in every direction ... Ha ha.'

Max had always felt contemptuous as he listened to the two old, unattractive rich guys boasting about how they sexually exploited women willing to take their money. Logan obviously thought he was no different, which was embarrassing.

'But the one girl I've never forgotten we called Thumper, and she was a hooker in the Cross, right here in Sydney. This is going back years ago. And you know why we called her Thumper?'

Max felt shame welling up inside for himself and everybody who had convinced themselves that they took away more from these encounters than they left behind of themselves – and he suddenly felt deep compassion for these women, their kindness, and for the fierce resilience he hoped shielded them from the likes of Mortimer Norton and Kent Logan.

Suddenly he thought of Claudia.

'She had big boobs, real ones, and she wasn't bad lookin', but she'd lost one leg below the knee, and whenever she fucked you, her leg thumped against your thigh as you drove it home, know what I mean?'

Logan gazed steadily at Max. Max no longer believed the man was just being mindlessly crude; there was something old and full of guile in Logan's expression. He nodded, watchful. As imperceptibly as possible, he exhaled the smoky air and its pollution, then eased reluctantly into another defiling inhale of smoky air.

He wasn't the same as Logan and Mort; he and Claudia genuinely liked each other. Sure, he had total dominance based on his economic power and social position, but their relationship was truly affectionate.

'My old friend Mort is like the Thumper of deals. He ain't the best looking whore in Sydney, and he doesn't have the biggest tits, and I'll be goddamned if he's got any cute tricks like Francoise, but when I'm in the mood for making money the old-fashioned way, with just a little something extra, I look forward to seeing what Mort's got for me.'

Logan stabbed out his cigarillo. 'I know you've always brought your own special sauce to the deals I've seen from Norton & Ring. I get it. I can't quite tell where to draw the line between Mortie and you, but I'm interested. Cause you probably both have something to offer.'

Logan exuded a sense of necessity, of the indifferent forces of nature that are what they are. Max realised Logan saw Mort and himself down on their knees servicing Logan the way Claudia had serviced him.

'Thanks Kent. I'm eager to prove it to you.'

What else could he say?

'See that building?' Logan pointed with his thumb at an old black and white photo of a three-storey brick building standing in what looked like blinding sunshine somewhere on Victoria Street in King's Cross.

Logan turned back like a dinosaur, very slowly, and squinted at Max as he lit a new cigarillo.

'That's where Thumper worked. Some friends of ours owned it, but Mort was on the title. Understand?' He looked primeval.

Mort had been the official owner of a brothel in the Cross on behalf of silent owners.

'I guess,' said Max. 'Were the owners silent because they were part of the mob and didn't want the cops to know how much money they had, or the opposite—because they were too respectable to be publicly associated with a brothel?'

Logan grinned. 'You act like those are two different things.'

Mort would have been a young man back then, not long off the plane from whatever European hellhole he'd escaped. He'd told Max he owned hotels with some of his poker buddies. 'That was a while ago, judging from the photo,' Max said.

'Oh, hell yeah,' said Logan. 'That building was torn down twenty years ago. It's part of the land where a forty-storey apartment building now stands, right in the middle of the Cross. I thought it's time you know a bit more about your former partner,' he said.

He pulled on his cigarillo. 'Go ahead,' Logan said softly with smoke boiling up around his face in fantastic spiky shapes. 'Put me down for five bars.'

Five million. 'Sure thing,' said Max.

Getting the funding for ZettaData was now a done deal. Even though Logan's money was only five million of the required fifty he'd use to buy out Edgell and fund ZettaData for future growth, now Logan was in the deal Max could raise the rest of the cash in about half an hour. Richard Wander might even drop his objections, too. Max intended to put up five million himself, as much of the family wealth as he felt he should prudently put at risk.

Logan looked directly at Max. 'Don't misunderstand, son. This is just about money. If Luke Terry suddenly changes his mind about you investing in ZettaData and sends a couple of his bully boys to re-arrange your face, don't come crying to me.'

'Of course not, Kent.'

'I don't think Mortie will take his gloves off,' Logan said, as the smoke snaked between his teeth. 'His missus wouldn't let him. I can't imagine her risking their chance to get into the Royal Sydney Golf Club. She's part Scottish and a mad keen golfer—bloody good, too, from what I hear.'

'On the other hand,' Logan said, pointing a leathery finger at Max, 'if Mort *does* decide to get cranky, it's your problem, understand? I'm just a financial backer. I'm not stepping in as umpire if one of you decides not to play cricket.'

'Understood.'

'Now, about the money. I'm not expecting a ten to twenty bagger in your debut deal.' He meant a return of ten to twenty times his five million. 'But I do expect at least a five bagger—or it's the last deal we do together.'

'Got it,' said Max.

'So go ahead, pop your cherry.'

Logan didn't invest because he needed more money. His investment winnings were confirmation of being a special favourite of the universe in his brief moment of light between two eternities of darkness. Max had sensed that about Logan before—because for years it was how he himself had climbed out of bed in the morning. He loved his daughters, but his relationship with them didn't confer the strength he needed every morning to face life. The prospect of pleasure helped, too, no doubt – surfing, his Porsche, and now Claudia. The thrill of adrenaline had been another part of it, the sheer delight of competing to take something wanted by somebody else. But without a sense of being anointed, without proving yourself smarter than the next guy—the type of confirmation only closing a deal and releasing a new torrent of cash could prove—what was the point of being alive?

He could see how Logan had ended up the way he was now; not knowing anymore why he was still playing, but getting up every morning, still eager to be struck by what was next, still totally determined to keep winning.

Max shuddered. He hoped there was more to it and that he'd find out what it was some day.

He felt he'd woken up out of a trance when he left Norton & Ring but he still had to play by rules enforced by people like Logan, Wander, Terry, and Mortimer Norton.

'Ok,' said Logan, dismissing him.

'Thanks, Kent,' Max said, and stood up.

Deals were Logan's last real consolation. He'd better get ZettaData right.

Chapter 24

Max stretched out on his yoga mat as dim forms around him engaged in various stretching poses. He breathed in. He breathed out, and there it was again, the mild pleasure, and a subtle sense of calm. If he were truly indifferent to what happened to his body, why wasn't he taking a cold shower, or wearing a hair shirt? Why was he on a yoga mat? Why did he surf and drive a Porsche? It was embarrassing how self-serving the idea he was a spiritual being really was, that what he did with his body was irrelevant. It had allowed him to feel morally superior while doing exactly what he wanted to do—most recently, fucking Claudia any time he wanted to.

He was in his favourite place in the studio, near the corner next to the wall with empty sisal carpeting on each side. He'd asked Juanita about Peggy but she refused to tell him anything. Max wasn't sure if it was jealousy or something else. She'd even told him to stay away from Peggy, which of course made him more determined to meet her again.

You never know. He knelt in the middle of his mat, getting his buttocks down against his heels, feeling a hard stretch across the tops of his thighs, an almost painful tightness in his knees. He bowed deeply, his chest pressing against his thighs, his head hanging upside down in front of his knees, the top of his head pressed against the mat.

The floor flexed under a heavy step on the side open to the rest of the yoga room, and there was a rustling on his left. He didn't like the leaden footfall. Max could sense brittle, uneasy energy radiating across his back. Please don't let that be Peggy – so disillusioning. His forehead still on the mat, he peeked.

A woman in her late twenties or early thirties, frowning, unloaded a blanket, mat, straps, and a bolster with a thump on the sisal carpet next to Max. She unrolled her mat in a flurry of hurried, impatient gestures and sat on it with another definitive thump. A moment later she twirled around to grab her water bottle, gulped from it, then almost slapped the cap as she screwed it back on. Like a soldier preparing her weapons for combat.

Whew. Max rose into a downward dog pose.

A few moments later a shadow passed above his head and he felt something like a breath in the space between his mat and the wall.

'Hey,' a familiar voice said.

Max turned his head. Peggy was kneeling on her mat. Her grey-green eyes glowed in the shadows and she smiled as she stretched her arms straight before her, slid forward, and rose gracefully in the cobra asana.

'Good to see you,' he whispered.

Max folded his downward dog and knelt with his weight on his heels. Those piercing eyes were framed by a fringe of cedar-coloured hair and high cheekbones, and seemed to penetrate him. For weeks he had been aware of her in the background of his meetings and various conversations, but when he tried to remember what she looked like he recalled only a jumble of features, a graceful figure – and something in the air around her. He found himself hoping she wasn't really as beautiful as she seemed on that Bondi morning.

She nodded, her upper lip curved to a point in the middle, her lower lip like a sea swell parted by the prow of a sailboat.

Perhaps out of instinct, Max had tried to recall Peggy as—what was the French expression? – *jolie laide* – ugly cool. If she were unattractive it would keep things simple. Still, it was what she had said that mattered most to him.

He wanted to start another conversation, however brief, but Heather, the teacher, walked to the front of the room and positioned herself on the soft sisal. Max, Peggy and the others followed her as she led them in the opening chant and then through a series of vinyasa asanas.

Max now realised the flaw in his plan to maximise the chances of Peggy choosing to lay her mat next to his: she was effectively behind him, and as he watched Heather his eyes were turned away from Peggy. Still, it was a pleasure to be close to her, and several completely different imaginary conversations floated spontaneously through his mind as Heather led the class through the asanas. At the very end of class, as he lay in shivasana, corpse pose, side by side with Peggy, his eyes closed, Max thought about what he remembered of Peggy's wise heart. That it was a deep well, and he wanted to draw out its water. He wanted to understand the things she talked about. But as they lay next to each other the image of her body shimmered against the inside of his eyelids. Max could hear her breathing and smell the aroma of her hair and skin.

Heather led the class in the closing chant. Juanita must have told Peggy to stay away from him, too. Yet she'd come to class anyway. It was an exciting thought.

Heather pressed her hands together in front of her face, bowed her head, and farewelled the class with 'Namasthe'.

His life was already thoroughly tangled with compromised loyalties and betrayal: Mort, Ilona, Claudia, Sam and Billie. He was going to play it straight with Peggy. Learn from her. Be friends.

The answering syllables 'Namaste' had hardly passed Max's lips when he turned to Peggy. 'Would you like to go have a cup of tea?'

She paused to consider. 'No, thanks, I'm meeting a girlfriend now.'

'I'm leaving tomorrow evening for New York,' Max said. 'Why don't we have tea after class next week when I'm back?'

She looked at him with those grey-green eyes, considering, then she started to roll up her mat. 'Sure – why not?'

Max began to roll his mat, too. 'You know, I wish I could remember more about what you said to me on the beach –'

They were kneeling side by side and she looked at him and smiled. 'That's honest.'

' – but I feel like your words were seeds that germinated and have been growing ever since.'

She glanced at him, looking a little surprised. 'I'm glad.'

They collected their things, and Peggy slipped past several women waiting to speak with Heather, and she and Heather exchanged a quick hug and kissed one another's cheeks.

Max held back the curtain and Peggy stepped through the sliding glass door as she slung her mat's carrying strap over her shoulder.

It was cool and blustery outside. The air felt moist as if it could rain any moment.

Peggy's eyes were dark and challenging. 'You know, I can't tell whether you're a good guy who doesn't know his life is empty, or a dick who'll say anything to crack onto somebody.'

Max smiled. 'You say 'dick' like it's a bad thing.'

'You know what I mean.'

'You know what *I* mean,' replied Max.

Peggy arched a skeptical eyebrow, as if she'd met more than enough of his cocksure type. 'Yeah.'

'Why don't we table this conversation until that cup of tea.' Max glanced at the low clouds scudding in from the ocean. 'Can I give you a lift?'

Peggy shook her head. 'Thanks, it's a short walk.' She reached out and delicately touched the back of his hand, as if to soften what she had said a moment before.

He'd found a parking place right outside the yoga school. 'Sure? This is my car.'

'Nice wheels,' said Peggy when she saw his 911 Turbo SC. ' – for an eco-terrorist.' She started walking down Wallis Parade. 'See ya ... '

Chapter 25

'So, the public takes the idea of "cloud computing" literally,' said Ormsby. 'They think their photos and playlists float somewhere up in the blue sky, and the internet is just pulses of light flashing around the world without any environmental impact.'

Max smiled. It was exactly what the students in his Bondi yoga studio thought; he'd heard them talking about how global warming would be solved if everybody drove electric cars. They had no idea how electricity is generated.

'Google searches and cat videos and Netflix shows require data centres – that's what the cloud is,' said Ormsby, taking a long swig of his Diet Coca-Cola, which he pronounced "Co-Cola".

'I know,' Max said. 'Data centres have an extremely heavy industrial footprint – like steel mills, coal mines, aluminium smelters – they're worse than car factories. Hundreds of billions have been invested.'

'Walk lightly', Ormsby scoffed. 'If the Global IT industry were a country, it would be the third biggest contributor to greenhouse gas emissions behind the US and China.'

'Yeah,' said Max. 'Those data centres use as much electricity as a city with a million people and very few people understand that. The industry generates as much CO_2 as the airline industry—that's the cloud—it's a cloud of carbon dioxide around the planet. I get it.'

He thought briefly of Peggy. She was perceptive, sure, but with all that Bondi spirituality she couldn't have a clue how the world works, either.

'I'm glad to hear you say that,' said Ormsby, 'because ZettaData hasn't got the credit it deserves for defining a new model of environmentally responsible data centres. We're located in one of the coldest locations in Australia and we use almost entirely renewable energy for power. As big users figure that out, it's driving our growth.'

'Covid was a huge help, too,' said Max.

'Oh yes,' said Ormsby. 'Far more people started using Zoom and ramped up their shopping, gaming and porno versus the few who died.'

'Not to be cynical about it,' said Max.

'Not to be cynical about it,' nodded Ormsby.

Unfortunately, thought Max, it was almost too late for ZettaData. Or so he hoped.

The man's office was as bedraggled as his company's stock price, fake walnut veneers on the furniture and boxy black leather sofas and chairs with ugly steel frames. Not a bad sign in itself – Ormsby wasn't squandering shareholder's money on himself.

'Google and Amazon built data centres in Finland,' said Max.

'Yeah, but we started the trend,' said Ormsby. 'ZettaData only generates 3 grams of CO_2 per kilowatt hour.'

'That's impressive!' Max exclaimed. These things mattered when the average Google search uses as much energy as turning on a lightbulb for seventeen seconds. 'It's about 100 grams in France, and about 300 grams in California.'

'Yeah, and up to 1000 grams in parts of China,' said Ormsby.

'Ok,' said Max. 'You're on the leading edge environmentally – I like that. But before we go any further, I need to understand something.' He hadn't left his partnership with Mortimer Norton to do business with another bunch of crooks. 'Why haven't you announced the cryptocurrency project? It's an open secret – all the pros know about it.'

Ormsby grimaced and shrugged. 'We didn't want to create a false market. That was our advice, and we wanted to be fair.'

'Right,' said Max. ASX Listing Rule 3.1B – it was a tricky one. 'Because your total public float is small investors, who aren't necessarily qualified to evaluate the crypto opportunity, your board didn't want to risk creating unwarranted enthusiasm about its potential to save the company?'

'That's right,' said Ormsby.

Actually a pretty noble position, given how badly ZettaData needed good news.

'Well, the public doesn't know about it yet – but the pros know, and if they thought it was worth anything they would have bought the stock cheap from clueless small investors,' said Max. 'Which they haven't. So the experts think your Zetta idea is a fizzer.'

ZettaData directors were up to their necks in serious personal and professional risk, both reputational and financial.

'We did our best,' said Ormsby. 'We can't control the way you guys operate in the market.'

Max shrugged. 'The board was trying to do the right thing, that's the main thing as far as I'm concerned.' He looked at his notes. 'Tell me, how big is a zettabyte in practical terms?'

'The total amount of digital data in the entire world a couple years ago was about a zettabyte. ZettaData is an aspirational name, obviously.'

'What's the physical equivalent of a zetta?' asked Max. 'Is there a zetta of sand on all the beaches in the world?'

Ormsby thought for a moment. 'There's about five.'

'Aren't there more stars in the universe than grains of sand on all the beaches on Earth?'

'Oh yes,' said Ormsby.

'It's hard to believe,' said Max. 'You'd think that's too many stars: even the sand on Bondi Beach would be a mind-blowing number of stars.'

Ormsby looked at Max and smiled through his whiskers. 'At the low end, there's at least ten zettas of stars in the universe. At the high end, there might be 200 zettas of stars.'

He couldn't imagine that many stars. The few hundred grains of sand that stuck to Max's feet when he walked across Bondi after surfing was the equivalent of the night sky above Sydney. 'That's a hell of a lot of stars.'

'The universe is a big place.'

'It just seems like vast, random chaos,' said Max. 'Pointless.'

Ormsby offered him a can of Coca-Cola from the personal refrigerator behind his desk, but Max shook his head. 'You know, meaninglessness is just the absence of order. The *apparent* absence. Meaning depends on our ability to imagine order.'

'But that's just it—order is imaginary,' said Max. 'Order is an illusion.'

'No, sir,' said Ormsby. 'Order is very real.'

'But constellations for example are imaginary, just tricks of perspective.'

'Yes, that's an ancient, naïve attempt to discern order,' Ormsby said. 'But we've learned a few things since then, like the scientific revolution and the theory of relativity and quantum mechanics. Insisting on chaos is ignorant, too.'

Max flushed angrily.

Ormsby leaned forward in his chair, more professor than executive. 'Think about it, Max: have you ever asked yourself how atoms that behave so unpredictably—we can't even tell their location and what direction they're going at the same time, that's Heisenberg's Uncertainty Principle—can behave so predictably, for example, as the steel in our buildings? One steel molecule is completely unpredictable, but we rely on the steel beams holding up this building to keep us this high in the air safely.'

'Metal atoms behave differently than other atoms, don't they? The atoms bond somehow which allows metals to be bent and pulled and still maintain strength.'

'Right,' said Ormsby. 'Steel molecules freely exchange electrons with other steel molecules and this flow of electrons creates a three-dimensional lattice that provides paths for steel molecules to move when a piece of steel is subjected to stress. It's hidden order. But when steel molecules are moving, and each individual molecule moves through the lattice in an unpredictable way, how can we be confident the piece of steel as a whole won't behave unpredictably?'

'Let me think about it,' said Max. They were on the 22nd floor. 'In large enough numbers, atoms behave predictably.'

'Right.' Ormsby smiled and tossed a handful of roasted nuts into his mouth. 'Reality goes from unpredictable to predictable as you increase scale. Zettas of atoms, for example – or Zettabytes of data. What is individually random turn out to be highly predictable.'

'Got it,' said Max, feeling a bit sheepish. 'Large numbers are the bridge between random chaos and the order we see all around us.' In a nutshell Max's view of the world was an atom bouncing around like a mote of dust floating in the sunlight, randomly going up and down and spinning around in a totally chaotic, unpredictable fashion. It was the basis for his belief that life was random and chaotic, and that only his consciousness mattered. He was beginning to realise he had missed an extra step, and he knew why: his supposedly scientific conviction in the pointlessness of life gave him a philosophical excuse to do whatever he wanted to with his body.

'And I'll tell you something else – the mathematical laws that describe the natural order are short and simple. $E=MC^2$. Three terms – and it changes everything!'

'The alphabet of DNA has four letters,' said Max. 'And it specifies the unique individual architecture of every living being.'

'Yeah, so why do we need twenty-six letters in the English alphabet?' Ormsby asked. 'The Korean alphabet requires fewer characters. It's probably the most efficient alphabet in any language.'

Ah – thought Max – now Ormsby was moving back on ground he had thought about before. Ormsby's question reminded Max of the difference between complexity and complications. 'Well, the English language, and especially the way we write in English, is a completely human invention – using 'ph' or 'f' for the same sound is arbitrary, there's no deeper meaning to it. That's partly why ...'

Ormsby interrupted him. 'True—but why do humans multiply details beyond what's truly essential? The laws that describe nature's processes are simple and profound – they're the opposite of arbitrary. They're hints that indicate a deep order by showing the true relationship between a few, powerful, absolutely essential details. That's why natural laws produce a reality that is incredibly rich and complex,' said Ormsby. 'And endlessly surprising.'

'And beautiful,' said Max.

'And elegant,' said Ormsby, tossing another mouthful of nuts into his mouth. 'Shannon's equation for information has five terms: less than the letters on a parking sign! And yet it's the basis for the entire data industry.'

'Maxwell's equations have fewer letters and numbers than the ingredients on the back of a cereal box!' Max said, laughing at the thought of any random page of the Corps Act and how packed it was with intricately specified trivia.

'We humans create incredibly complicated laws to generate simple results,' said Ormsby. 'As an engineer used to building real things and the CEO of a publicly listed company, my brain goes numb at the thought of the Corps Act, ASX Listing Rules, and all that crap I have to stay on top of.'

'I must admit, I often ask myself what possible difference does it all make?' asked Max.

'Well, I'll tell you,' said Ormsby. 'Millions of pages of legal code generate the same result every time: the strong dominate the weak, and the rich dominate the poor. It's really monotonous—and of course totally unjust.'

Ormsby was beginning to sound like somebody Max could work with.

'You've put your finger on the problem,' said Max. 'Look at your own data centre. What has Cloud Computing, Big Data and AI produced – top down rule by the global one percent and increasingly joblessness for everybody else.'

'Hold on, pardner, that's not a law of nature,' said Ormsby. 'That's the way humans are applying the laws of nature – and the power nature is giving them.'

'What do you mean? It's just the order that's emerging from the law of large numbers you were just talking about,' said Max. 'The privatised surveillance state offers us everything for free in return for sucking up all our data, and then applies Big Data and AI algorithms to turn us from individuals to standard deviations on a Bell Curve.'

'The grander the order you can imagine, the bigger the meaning you create,' said Ormsby. 'You're describing the modern version of an old, limited, impoverished vision for how humanity might really live and thrive on this planet.'

'How can you tell that any particular meaning isn't just an illusion?' said Max, irritably. He'd begun hoping Ormsby was going to actually tell him something he didn't know – but now he sensed Ormsby was just trying to baffle him with bullshit.

'Meaning's not an illusion. It's a priority we assign to the orders around us.'

'What are you talking about?'

'For example, we can treat humans like atoms and use Big Data techniques to mine all the information we collect about them and generate large-scale averages of human behaviour. That way we can deliver millions of consumers to advertisers. You're right – that's dehumanising.'

'And it's your business.'

'Well, that's one meaning that could be assigned to it.'

'And? Any other suggestions?'

'We humans have evolved with everything else. We are part of nature – we're not more complicated than nature, we just pretend to be,' said Ormsby. 'If we can figure out how to measure galaxies and how many stars there are in the universe, why can't we understand society and the economy? Why can't we create a political system that doesn't institutionalise social injustice?'

'Why, indeed?' asked Max.

'It's partly, my friend, because we think meaning is an illusion. We're not observing reality carefully enough. We don't see its more subtle, profound orders,' Ormsby said. 'For example, because I operate a data centre I noticed that those supercomputers we carry around with us—because that's what a mobile phone really is—are hardly used at all. All the processing is being sucked into the big global data centres like mine that are heating up the planet, leaving the computers in phones hardly used except to process Instagram and TikTok and report your location to Facebook and Google Maps.'

'Ok,' said Max. 'True.'

'Processing power is what block chain protocols, such as cryptocurrencies, require,' said Ormsby. 'And we're carrying around billions of unused supercomputers! Look, for most of human history we needed microscopes and telescopes to access the true orders of reality, but not anymore. We can already detect and measure physical phenomena everywhere that remains completely mysterious to us, because the physicists haven't caught up yet with theories to explain what we're measuring. Our imaginations aren't big enough. But just as DNA is an indelible record of your ancestors and their origins going back millions of years, block chain technology also creates an indelible record of every transaction generated by a particular user. And so I realised that block chain technology is a way of reversing the top-down authoritarian compression of humanity into broad averages, because it creates a user as unique as every human being – and for the same reason, because it produces an indelible, confidential record as detailed as DNA.'

As Ormsby began to explain the commercial model behind the cryptocurrency project, Max thought about the time when he'd been awed by the surprisingly wonderful order of the universe: witnessing the Transit of Venus. The Transit of Venus is is visible when the orbits of Venus and the Earth line up so that Venus can be observed from Earth passing across the face of the sun. It is the rarest of recurring astronomical phenomena, happening once every 120 years or so, and then occurring twice, eight years apart, as if every five human generations the sun, Venus, and planet Earth spend eight years in a period pregnant with the possibility of *kairos*.

Max saw the Transit of Venus because his friend Rob owned a vineyard in the mountains three hours south of Sydney. They just happened to agree to visit the vineyard on the day of the Transit of Venus. The coincidence didn't seem to matter because Sydney was cloudy that morning, but as they climbed into the mountains the skies began to clear, and Rob got excited. As soon as they arrived, Rob ran around the winery and vineyard collecting sunglasses from his employees. Then he put all the sunglasses together, creating a combined goggle of eight separate lenses, and positioned his car—an elegant old Mercedes—directly facing the sun so they could gaze through the additional protective glass of its sunroof.

Rob gave Max the first turn. Venus was the size of a pinhead against the great flaming disc. Tears welled in Max's eyes as he watched gallant Venus floating so close to the source of light in the solar system, intrepidly making her way through the fierce storm of electromagnetic radiation on her journey past the sun. He and all humanity were simultaneously participating in the sublime cosmic dance of Earth and Venus, while almost no one else had any way of sensing the celestial synchronicity of their orbits around the sun.

He climbed out of the back of Rob's car and handed back the makeshift goggles. One by one, Rob's team sat in the back seat, wore the goggles, and observed the cosmic drama performing in the sky. They emerged matter-of-factly, as Max stood a few metres away under a tree, blinking back tears, deeply moved. He never understood why he was so affected, but listening to Ormsby describe the cryptocurrency project, Max realised something else Ormsby had said might explain it. He had been a man sitting in a vineyard observing a secret mystery of the universe. He didn't know how to interpret its meaning, but Max had felt it in the beats of his heart.

The Transit of Venus had been occurring for 4.5 billion years every 130 years without being observed by a single conscious being from Earth. It was a *kairos* that could only have been identified by applying the human mind and imagination, because the sun is far too bright to observe directly. First Newton and Kepler had to imagine an order more expansive than what appeared to be the sun shining blankly in the sky, and then calculations had to be made, ships had to be outfitted, instruments had to be invented, and men intrepid enough to sail around the planet had to be dispatched. But the moment of wonder existed and kept recurring in a secret mystery through what appeared to be millions of years of the tedious flow of *chronos*. It was humanity who had to evolve enough to recognise the *kairos* and reveal its mystery.

The spooky wonder of Kepler's Second Law was also the perfect example of what Ormsby had just said about simple laws producing beautiful, incredibly rich – and utterly astonishing reality.

Ormsby was right.

Max tried to focus as Ormsby was summing up his discussion about the cryptocurrency project by talking about gigas, and petas and zettas, but what really mattered was a much smaller number: the value of ZettaData.

'Well, thanks Donald,' said Max. 'This has been a very illuminating meeting. I'd like to provide the funding ZettaData needs as it goes cash flow positive, but I have to confirm a few things first.'

All Max needed to imagine—as accurately as possible—was the sum of all the cash ZettaData earned now and could be projected to earn in the future. Much simpler than imagining a universe that expressed Kepler's Second Law. Find the *kairos* inside the chaos.

'I'm all ears, pardner,' said Ormsby.

Max couldn't reveal the order he was beginning to imagine yet. He couldn't tell Ormsby he was leaving that evening on a flight to meet Todd Edgell. Max wouldn't know if he could save ZettaData until he'd met Edgell. He had to keep it vague and contingent for now.

'I'm planning to table my proposal at the next board meeting.'

'But that's two weeks away.'

'I know.'

'That's it?'

'Yep, for now.'

'Right,' said Ormsby, struggling to hide his disappointment. 'Well, I prepare the board pack and I normally need all the information two weeks before the meeting. That was yesterday.'

'I'm not going to have something for you for another three or four days,' said Max.

'That's pretty tight timing,' said Ormsby.

'I'm going to do my best.'

'Ok, pardner.'

Max smiled and stood up. Ormsby didn't just want him to save ZettaData, he wanted him to do it on time: typical engineer. It was understandable. He'd been living for months not knowing, day to day, whether ZettaData would survive.

'Ah'll walk you to the elevator,' said Ormsby. 'The lift, I mean.'

'Thanks, mate,' said Max.

Chapter 26

'My god, Max. Have you lost your mind?'

Ilona's eyes blazed across the small table as they sat above Redleaf Pool, their regular Saturday morning brunch spot.

'No, I haven't, actually.'

He'd arrived that morning from New York and was hoping the bright sunlight would help his jet lag. The girls were down on the sand, Billie playing in the tiny waves while Sam lay on a towel and sunned herself, surrounded by dozens of teenagers and young women.

'Is that all you have to say?'

Nobody in Sydney would have believed he could buy the ZettaData stake from Todd Edgell, but it was his now. Admittedly, he'd had to immediately transfer a deposit of five million dollars, but getting the entire stake held by Edgell's hedge fund for less than twenty million—a stake once valued at close to two billion dollars—was a coup.

But not to Ilona.

'What else do you want to know?'

'What about the five million?' Ilona tossed her head. Her heavy dark hair, shining almost red, fanned out like a battle flag in the dazzling sun.

A familiar intensity had appeared in her voice and it filled Max with dread. He stifled an impulse to jump up from the table.

'It's a deposit. If the board doesn't approve my proposal, or it gets voted down by shareholders in the EGM, I get it back.'

'But that's *our* money, Max!'

Max recalled how Knights of the Round Table received encouragement and inspiration from their ladies as the knights embarked on their search for the Holy Grail. Their ladies gave them personal tokens as keepsakes and tended the wounds the Knights received in battle.

'Darling, nobody thought I could pull this off. I took on the biggest hedge fund in the world and talked its CEO into selling me his stake in ZettaData.'

Max sighed, he hoped imperceptibly, and felt himself physically hunch.

'Maybe that guy sold it to you for a reason. You told me yourself the company is almost bankrupt.' Ilona looked at him coldly. 'But that's not my point; I never questioned that you're a terrific *investment banker*. This is a question of trust.'

Ilona was actually right about trust, she just didn't know why. She knew nothing about Claudia, but he did, and so he didn't have the heart to defend himself. 'I have been withholding things from you,' Max said.

Recently the bougainvillea next to their table had been harshly pruned to open up unobstructed views down the slope to the beach. Max looked away from Ilona and searched for the girls.

Ilona took a deep breath. 'Ok Max, I'm glad you admit it. So why don't we start by talking about that five million? We didn't discuss it – you just transferred the money after you met the American guy. Can you get it back?'

Max shook his head and reached out, putting his hand gently over one of Ilona's hands. 'Not unless the board rejects my proposal or shareholders vote it down at the EGM.'

He spotted Sam and Billie, each doing her own thing.

Ilona contemplated their hands. 'I don't know what to say, Max, or how to say it. I try and break through to you, and I know that comes across as an attack, and you end up playing defence until you just shut down. But if I do the opposite, stay calm and try to have a reasonable conversation, I feel you don't engage with me.'

'I know you're not happy with me.' Was it possible Ilona's continuous attacks and complaints were actually her way of trying to tell him how much she wanted them to be close? 'I want to do better.'

' ... we just lead these separate lives, Max,' Ilona said, still not looking at him.

She was his wife and he felt oppressed by a sense of guilt that was almost suffocating. 'I do withdraw, honey, because I can't bear when you're so angry with me. I love you and really, really care what you think of me.' Max took a deep breath, palpably aware of Ilona's distress.

Ilona looked startled. 'I had no idea you felt that way when I get cross with you.' He felt the warmth of her hand under his.

'I didn't think I was having any effect on you whatsoever,' she said. 'I just thought you're this big strong man who likes everything your way, and goes totally cold when you don't get it.'

Perhaps, all along, Max thought to himself, *Ilona has been fighting for our marriage and girls. She's not trying to subjugate and humiliate me, after all.*

'I've been a coward,' Max said. 'I've just avoided these issues and distracted myself. I'd like to tell you everything ... everything you don't know.' Whether because of jetlag or the prospect of confessing he suddenly felt giddy. 'But I'm afraid that if I do, it'll only mean you'll reject me, once and for all.'

Ilona looked at him with her full attention.

She hasn't chosen a way out by finding a safety valve like I have with Claudia. Instead she tried to survive the tension by telling me honestly how she was feeling.

And he'd just tuned her out. No wonder Ilona was so angry.

'Ok, Max,' Ilona said, pulling her hands out from underneath's Max's hand and then holding his hand in both of hers. 'Get the five million back.' She gave his hand a little tug with her hands.

'I might not know for ninety days whether I can get the money back.'

'Didn't you say you get it back if the board rejects your proposal?'

'Sure.'

'When is that?'

'Late next week.'

'So don't put in a proposal – or put in a crap proposal.'

'But darling, ZettaData is going to make us a lot of money, and in the mean time we have plenty of cash left for your reno.'

Ilona sat back in her chair, her eyes focused sharply on Max. 'Don't patronise me Max! And it's not my reno, it's our reno, Max. I thought you said you wanted me to trust you. Is this any way to start?'

'I do want you to trust me.'

'Max, you're stalling. You transferred that money without asking me, and we need a fresh start. Get it back and find a new deal. There must be plenty out there – for Christ's sake!'

'Ilona, you've never had anything to do with my deals.'

'This isn't financial, Max—or it's not just financial. It's about trust. It's also about you acting normal. First, you break up with your partner, then you fly to New York to meet some billionaire so you can buy his stake in a bankrupt company. Then you transfer our money without discussing it with me. And, by the way, are you trying to wreck Sam and Billie's lives, too?'

Max tried to remain calm. He didn't want to lose his temper again the way he had done at the espresso machine. As subtly as possible he exhaled, looking out at the view. Behind the boardwalk of Red Leaf Pool, millions of lights gleamed on the water and delicate waves slid slowly between Darling Point and Point Piper.

'How could I possibly be wrecking Sam and Billie's lives?' he asked evenly.

'Well, that's just it, Max—you don't even have *any* idea what goes on in our lives. You only want that damn company because Mortimer Norton wanted it first. Do you think it's ok to be feuding with your former partner? It's so childish! And he just happens to be the father of the most popular girl at Nightingale! What do you think it's like for our daughters every day when they go to school?'

Oh my god, Max thought, *I am so fucking miserable.* At least his heart rate hadn't accelerated and he didn't feel his temper rising. Yoga was having an effect.

'Maybe you have Asperger's, Max.' Her fingers moved the spoon deftly around the saucer. 'You don't seem to have normal human feelings. I thought for a second you did, but now I've realised you're just manipulating me by telling me what you think I want to hear. Everything is a deal to you.'

Taken aback, Max took a sip of his macchiato. He'd been feeling so guilty for his inability to make her happy he hadn't realised she didn't even like him. But was it possible that Ilona still loved him, the way a mother might love a son, no matter what he did?

'You can take a banker out of the markets, but you can't take the markets out of the banker,' Ilona said, as if to herself.

He looked into her eyes, but immediately Ilona avoided—rejected—his gaze and made darting glances up and down the beach, looking for the girls.

'Is Mort trying to get to me through you and Alexandra so I pull the plug on ZettaData?'

Ilona's eyes burned into his. 'How are we meant to start trusting each other when you make such a horrible accusation? As if nothing I had to say has any validity. I knew it all along, Max! I can't stand this. I think you may be literally going crazy, Max.' She grabbed her purse. 'I'm taking the girls home.'

In the old days, the girls would finish their pastry and babycinos or Chinottos and call, 'Daddy, Daddy, Daddy!' running along the beach, jumping up and down and twirling in the sand to coax Max to walk out on the boardwalk with them. But today they would go with Ilona. 'I'll stay a while and walk home,' he said.

'Fine,' Ilona said bitterly.

Max followed her down the stone steps.

'I can't tell you how disappointed I am, Max,' she said quietly, not looking at him. 'People are talking.'

'About what?'

'About your midlife crisis.'

'People—you mean Alexandra?'

Ilona turned and faced him. 'It's not just Alexandra, Max – it's not even mainly Alexandra. Everybody is talking. Lots of people can't believe you and Mort broke up. Why do you always point fingers at everybody but yourself?' She whirled around and descended the remaining steps.

The girls saw them arrive on the footpath and began walking towards them, at first skipping and then as they read their parents' body language the girls slowed to a cautious walk. Sam was already tall and thin, suddenly a head taller than Billie.

As the girls come towards them, Billie suddenly tripped, cried out and fell outstretched on the sand. Sam turned, frozen.

Instantly Max instantly ran towards Billie, and heard Ilona say, 'No, Max, she'll be all right.'

Max wasn't having any of it.

As Max reached her, Billie lifted her head and tried to brush the sand off her face.

'You'll be ok, sweetie.'

He kneeled down and gently stroked Billie's forehead and eyelids so the grains of sand fell away from her eyes, then he combed his fingers through her hair, gently shaking the tresses to shed more sand. Max helped Billie to her feet and held her hand as the three of them walked towards Ilona. She watched them approach with her appraising gaze.

Max could feel the girls wilt and almost undetectably withdraw from him. Ilona hurried the last several steps towards them and knelt and gave Billie a big hug, kissing her and lavishing attention on her.

What if he had followed Ilona's instructions, done nothing, and let her be the only one to comfort Billie?

'Sam, Billie, let's go home, darlings. Your father wants to walk home by himself.'

'That's not true,' said Max.

Without looking back, Ilona began marching up the stone steps, holding Billie's hand as Sam slouched behind.

Max turned and crossed the beach, and with a heavy heart walked onto the boardwalk.

Chapter 27

The planks were springy above the closely arrayed steel rods that emerged from the water to support the boardwalk. It was a public amenity that also discreetly formed a steel cage to keep sharks out of Redleaf Pool. It was windier than on land and the sun's glare from the waves was intense. The dry planks clanked noisily under his slow steps. The girls had loved to run ahead of him out over the water; he could still hear echoing across the years the sound of their lithe little heels thunder on the wood. A small flock of drifting clouds seemed to graze across the blue sky.

Max had never trusted Sydney's beauty, even though he knew there was a possibility Venus was floating in the sky above him along with the hosts of stars shining invisibly above the veil of the atmosphere. Beauty and order couldn't soothe his foreboding. Concealed above the sky, behind the slopes across the Harbour, or just beyond the horizon of time, it always seemed to Max that something monstrous was preparing to emerge. He had never been able to shake the feeling everybody was marking time until the apocalypse. The mansions and luxury apartment buildings of Darling Point and Point Piper faced each other across the water of Double Bay, resembling the tombs and sepulchres of South Head Cemetery. Max sighed and looked across the tranquil water at Redleaf Beach.

Several women sunbathed on the sand near the esplanade, their naked torsos shining. A baby pram was parked in their midst, with a shade cloth of white muslin draped across the top as protection from the sun, and one woman in a malachite-coloured bikini bottom lay on her back, a straw hat over her face. He remembered the unusual colour from somewhere.

Max came to the end of the boardwalk and started across the sand.

The woman in the green malachite bikini bottom was now kneeling in front of the baby and changing its nappy as Max walked towards them, tiny waves lapping at his feet. He observed absentmindedly as she expertly wiped the baby's bottom and, opening a fresh nappy, slipped it underneath the baby boy. Then she paused for a moment before fastening it. She was almost nude, and her figure was beautiful – elegant and healthy. The baby boy gazed at her happily, eyes full of love, his expression a kind of rapture of adoration and gratitude. Below the rim of her straw hat Max could see her aristocratic chin, neck and her indulgent smile; he walked along happily imagining the woman's loving gaze as she looked into the baby boy's eyes.

The light straw brim tipped and fluttered in the breeze, revealing her face. 'Peggy,' said Max.

Peggy turned with surprise. 'Oh, hi Max,' she said, fastening the nappy. She leaned over, held the baby's cheeks in her hands and gave him a kiss. Then she scooped him into her arms and stood up, as one of the baby's completely relaxed arms dangled in the air.

'I didn't know you had a baby,' Max said, stopping in front of them and admiring Peggy and the baby. 'He's beautiful.'

'Oh, Lockie's not mine,' Peggy laughed. 'His mum Rebecca just went up to the loo, and—what do you know!—mummy and baby were in perfect synch.'

She turned and bounced him on her hip, not making any effort to hide her breasts. 'You love your mummy, don't you, darling boy?' The baby laughed happily and she kissed him.

'I'm impressed,' said Max. He'd changed his daughters' nappies hundreds of times. 'You're a good friend.'

'Oh, he's such a smunchie. I adore Lachlan,' she said. 'Besides little boys are held so much less than little girls, and for much shorter periods. If I had a little boy, I'd give him extra cuddles.' She brought Lachlan's face up to hers and, cheek to cheek, she rocked him back and forth. 'You love extra cuddles, don't you?' she said. She and the baby laughed.

A tall, athletic woman with a cascade of blonde ringlets around her shoulders purposefully descended the stairs, and Max sensed she must be Rebecca.

'So, how are you?' Peggy asked.

'Couldn't be better,' he said, wishing it were true.

She smiled. Her friends, their oiled bodies shining in the light, ignored them, even when Rebecca arrived and took Lachlan into her arms. After Peggy introduced Rebecca and Max, he knew he should either sit down or say goodbye. 'I don't mean to intrude.'

'It's fine,' Peggy smiled and shook her head. 'You're not intruding.'

He certainly had no intention of making the same mistake he had made with Claudia. But he couldn't bring himself to say goodbye, either. 'Have time for a walk?'

Peggy looked at her friends. 'Sure,' she said. She grabbed a top out of her bag, a Moroccan style breezy thing in light fabric, shrugged into it, and put on her straw hat. 'Back soon,' she said quietly. One of her friends languidly lifted her forefinger.

The clouds had fattened slightly and were slowly spiralling in a vast pinwheel across the sky. They walked through the gate in the fence onto Seven Shillings Beach. Tenders were stacked against the fence and along the wall of the estate that fronts the beach. The Rose Bay seaplane droned in the sky. It all seemed so serene.

'Look,' said Peggy, pointing towards the water.

A mother duck was paddling a couple of hundred metres ahead of them, followed by her little brood of half-a-dozen ducklings. The ducklings were round and fluffy, and in the tiny waves of the harbour they bobbed up and momentarily disappeared from sight. A hundred metres ahead, dozens of seagulls gathered on the sand intently watching the little flotilla of mother and ducklings. The gulls were tipping their necks towards the family of ducks, wings back and folded high, as they screeched challenges.

'Fucking gulls,' said Max.

It didn't surprise him. It was just like what happened in the play *TransGod* being produced at the Eden Street Theatre. *Sparagmos* on a beautiful, idyllic, seemingly perfect and tranquil morning. The beauty and glory of a perfect winter day in Sydney as the setting for the last stand of the mother duck and the massacre of ducklings.

The duck paddled towards the beach, but lost her nerve as the gulls gathered in force. She turned back, heading out into the open water.

'It'll be ok,' said Peggy.

'No, it won't,' said Max. He knew exactly what this was—it was the truth of evolution. Tennessee Williams had written about the massacre of baby turtles by raptors in the Galapagos, and his play was one of Reed Michaelis' sources when he wrote *TransGod*.

'My mum has a duck farm,' Peggy said. 'Watch.'

'A what?'

'She breeds Muscovy and Pekin ducks on her farm outside Byron Bay.'

They kept walking up the beach, watching the mother duck repeatedly steer in an arc and paddle towards the beach with her little line of yellow puffballs appearing and disappearing behind her, only to turn back as the volume of the seagulls' shrieking increased. The gulls jostled one another into tightly closed ranks along the waterline across a front of ten metres, massing at exactly the point where the mother duck was landing.

At any moment that flock might fly off the sand and swoop to attack the mother and her ducklings. 'I'm not going to let those ducks get torn apart,' Max said as the ducks neared the beach. The water the ducks were paddling in was shallow, probably less than a metre. He started to run. If he had to, he'd wade out to the ducks and bat away diving seagulls with his arms.

'No, Max!'

To his amazement, Max was whipped around just as he planted his foot – Peggy had grabbed one of his arms with both hands and was holding him back, her heels scoring the sand.

'What are you doing?'

He tried to shake her loose so he could get to the ducks in time. Peggy managed to maintain her strong grip even though her hands slipped down his arm to his wrist. She intertwined the fingers of one of her hands with his and held on.

'You don't understand – they're going to be torn apart!' Max said urgently, not wanting to hurt her and trying to shake loose her grip as gently as possible. 'I can't bear it: *Sparagmos.*' She wouldn't know what the word meant but he didn't care.

'Look, Max!' Peggy panted. 'Just stop and look!'

The mother duck was paddling determinedly in the direction of the beach and now was only a few feet from the sand.

The gulls began to shift their positions on the beach like iron filings arranging themselves around an approaching magnet. Agonisingly slowly, as the seconds passed an open arc formed amongst the seagulls at exactly the point towards where the mother duck, now less than two metres away, paddled to her landing.

Was it a pincer movement? Were the gulls withdrawing only to attack from both sides on steeper angles? But no, like iron filings nudged by a magnet, the seagulls steadily fell back, and now several in back were actually turning away.

'I can't believe it,' Max said, looking in wonder at Peggy. 'Look at that.'

The mother duck, carried onto the sand by a last wavelet, splashed onto the beach. Successive rippling waves carried the ducklings to the beach, some toppling head over tail out of the water and others scrambling up with a bit of poise behind their mother.

The seagulls spread out, opening a wide avenue of sand in front of the mother duck as she led the ducklings to a spot in the sun by the seawall, shielded from the wind.

Max shook his head. 'That was amazing.'

Peggy was right. It was what Ormsby had said about observation. Peggy's vision of the true order was right.

Peggy smiled at him. 'Given what that duck probably went through to have those ducklings, a flock of hungry seagulls is nothing.'

'What do you mean?'

'Evolution is not just the strong eating the weak, and the fast eating the slow,' said Peggy. 'It's also about love and protecting those we love. Look how that mother duck faced down an entire flock of seagulls.'

'Very impressive,' Max said, waving his arm towards the glistening towers of the CBD and North Sydney. 'But she's just a duck.'

Max understood that paying attention was more important than he'd realised. Sometimes it meant listening to Susan Casner. Other times a creative imagination could tell you where to look, how to look, and when to look to witness the Transit of Venus.

But watching a duck swim towards a flock of seagulls? A fluke.

'I know the truth about evolution,' said Max. 'I work in the Darwinian world of the financial markets every day. The race may not be to the swift or the battle to the strong, but that's the way to bet. The markets are about pitiless natural selection. Trust me, that's evolution.'

'It is, huh?' said Peggy, trying to suppress a smile.

'Yeah, it is,' Max said, a little irritated.

'You're not the only investment banker I know,' Peggy said, looking at him with amusement. 'The business world is a man-made environment. You think you get it—but what do you really know about the natural world?'

'Quite a lot, actually,' said Max.

'Can you tell me about duck sex?'

'Duck sex?' Max asked, puzzled.

'Yep.'

'Why duck sex?'

'Because we just watched a duck face down a whole flock of hungry seagulls, and they backed off and left her and her ducklings unharmed. That's evolution, too. You guys in business and the financial markets make the rules the way it suits you and pretend it's evolution. There's nothing natural about the ASX. You're operating in a completely man-made environment. You're pretending your rules are laws of nature.'

Max was hearing too much, too fast. Peggy kept surprising him with ideas he either didn't know—or did know but didn't want to admit. 'Listen, there's a play being produced in Sydney right now which opens next month. It's about Covid and how badly it was handled by governments who weren't willing to acknowledge how rapidly viruses evolve, but it also has lots of literary references to Greek tragedians and to Tennessee Williams. It's all about how nature operates through mass killings and deaths. That's evolution. I'll take you to see it.'

'I know the play you're talking about, and I know the Tennessee Williams play, too. There's no annual slaughter of turtles in the Galapagos,' said Peggy.

'Why? Have they all been exterminated?' asked Max.

'No, because it's a myth,' Peggy said. 'It probably started with that play.'

'The birds don't swoop down and eat baby turtles?'

'Nope. Turtles hatch all year on the Galapagos. There's no annual dash to the sea by baby turtles. Google it.'

She was certainly full of surprises, and Max liked it. 'Ok, I take your point. Actually, I've come to some of the same conclusions. The Corps Act isn't the law of gravity. I agree with you on that. So what is evolution?'

'From what I've seen affection and cooperation is even more important than killing. We just saw what one mother duck can do against a flock of seagulls. What are you going to believe—a play, or something you saw with your own eyes?'

'What I've seen, of course,' said Max. 'But the mother duck wasn't being affectionate to the seagulls—that was a conflict. She just has brass balls and called their bluff. I've never seen affection work in the capital markets, either.'

He suddenly remembered the intense emotion he'd felt while watching the Transit of Venus, when he had sensed some kind of enigmatic meaning, but couldn't quite grasp what it might be.

'There's nothing more evolutionarily successful than love,' Peggy said. 'It's the core survival code.'

'Love?' Max repeated sceptically. He he'd been hoping for another Transit of Venus moment and was disappointed. He felt mildly annoyed. 'Sex, I can see, it's kind of obvious.'

'Sex, sure, but also love.'

Max shook his head. He had just begun expecting Peggy to keep saying cool things, but it was over.

'Sorry, that's just not true. It can't be.' He felt a little bored.

'Your problem, Max, is you don't know anything about duck sex.'

'That's true!' he laughed. 'And you know what? I'm fine with that. I'd better start for home - I've got a half an hour walk, straight up Bellevue Hill. See you soon at yoga?'

'Sure,' Peggy smiled.

Chapter 28

L ogan nodded. 'I like it. Tell me more.'

That was a relief – not what Max had expected when he told Logan he was planning to offer a participating role in his takeover to shareholders like Susan Casner. It was a big call to include parties in the deal who could just as easily be ignored—or exploited.

Nobody understood capital and the capital markets better than Logan. He, like Max, knew that the nature of money changes qualitatively as its scale increases quantitatively. After it accumulates above the amounts required to sustain daily life, money evolves and acquires special powers. Money becomes capital.

Logan nodded. 'Uh huh. So why not just squash the little guys?'

'Just because we can do something doesn't mean we should do it.'

The lockdowns, once they were finally implemented, had ruthlessly shut down daily life for Australians. Maybe it saved millions of lives, but there was nothing like that at stake in ZettaData. Sure, the system gave him the power to wipe out the small shareholders. It's what he and Mort would have done a year ago, and Max himself would have engineered the pitiless terms of the proposal. 'I like the idea of giving small shareholders the chance to invest with me.'

Logan's position at the top of the system gave him a stake in its stability. As a public company, the ZettaData takeover would be widely reported, and either further diminish public confidence in financial markets, or affirm the public's wavering confidence. Logan was a stock market operator himself, and he was wise enough to leave crumbs for the punters, too. He knew an occasional jackpot in a pokie keeps the casino crowded.

'So I'll offer every existing shareholder a right to buy another share of ZettaData for each share they already own,' said Max. He studied Logan's face closely.

'Yeah, ok,' said Logan. 'A rights issue.'

'Kent, I'm going to price the rights at one cent a share,' said Max.

Logan squinted uncomprehendingly at Max. 'I thought you said you were going to give the punters a break – you must be fucking nuts,' he grumbled. 'What's the stock trading at? Five, six cents?'

'It's up to about eight cents since I spoke at the AGM,' said Max.

'Fuck! Why are you proposing to let existing ZettaData shareholders buy more shares at one cent a share? You're giving away seven cents for every share they buy. Craziest fucking thing I've ever heard!' He plucked a cigarillo out of his ornate gold box like a hawk snatching a field mouse.

'It's a signal of confidence,' said Max. 'One that can't be faked. If I price the rights issue at one cent, ZettaData shareholders who believe their shares are worth more than seven cents will gladly pay one cent per share to buy more shares. And new investors who don't already own shares will buy ZettaData shares on the ASX at eight cents in order to participate in the rights issue and buy the same number of shares again at one cent – so the share price will continue to rise, well above eight cents.'

Logan looked at Max through narrowed eyelids that almost completely concealed his eyes. 'This isn't a Norton & Ring–type deal, that rights issue isn't fairy dust sprinkled over the structure. It's the real thing.'

'That's right, Kent.'

If he was going to give small shareholders a fair go, he was going to have to encourage them to ascend to the realm of capital. He had to educate them, reveal the truth.

Capital naturally stratifies into layers, and each layer has subtly different characteristics, the way the atmosphere cools and thins as the altitude increases. When in balance, the stratas of global capital create an enormous and complex phenomenon like the planet's atmosphere between sea level and its upper reaches on the dark, inhospitable frontiers of space, shielding the planet and generating the abundant moisture required for all life on Earth to thrive.

'Those bastards could make a serious profit.'

'Yeah, that's right. I hope they do.'

'What if the punters can't figure it out?'

'Easy. I'll buy all the shares myself, and for twenty-five million dollars and the other twenty-odd million that I'm going to pay Edgell, I'll control ZettaData. But I'll know I tried to help the little guys.'

Logan's nostrils flared. 'Five bars of those forty to fifty bars are mine, son.'

'I know, Kent,' said Max. 'Trust me. The company's worth a lot more than eight cents a share. If it's managed properly it should be worth at least a dollar a share.'

Max had decided Peggy was right – it wasn't a law of nature that required him to crush helpless parties in a mergers and acquisitions deal – he was just used to doing it because he could. But the Corps Act wasn't Maxwell's equations, and he wasn't a lion who had to kill in order to eat. In his new approach to M & A Max was determined to include the Susan Casners in the fertility made possible by the ecology of capital, and introduce them all to the wonderful order operating far above their stressful day-to-day lives getting and spending money.

'You know the board isn't going to understand what you're doing, either,' said Logan. 'Grimson is a boring old fart and O'Toole is a high class paper-pusher – neither of them are real investors.'

They both knew Wander wouldn't like it. He had mastered the existing Darwinian rules of capital and would see Max's ideas for the threat they were to him.

'As long as I succeed in explaining that my offer will both create value and result in a group of shareholders who really support me and believe in the company, the board will back it,' Max knew it wasn't going to be an easy outcome to achieve. 'It's a bloody good idea for shareholders.'

'It is a good idea, son,' said Logan. 'But why are you doing it?'

Max knew Logan has already calculated the surplus value he was planning to distribute, unnecessarily in Logan's view, to irrelevant and completely powerless parties in the deal.

'In the longer term it makes sense to look after the little guy.'

He was going to offer them the deal they originally thought they were getting when ZettaData was founded by its two strategic shareholders, the Australian Government and the now-bankrupt Texas electricity conglomerate. The opportunity to co-invest as equals with the big boys. This time, in Max's deal, there would be no special contract and no artfully crafted special class of securities solely designed to benefit Max and his investor group.

'Makes sense to whom?'

'To the system, to the community, to society, to everybody,' said Max.

'What? Are you becoming the Robin Hood of the Australian Stock Exchange?' Logan drawled the words sarcastically.

Capital in the enormous amounts that energise the global economy is like air at the highest altitudes, thin, light, arid, offering little nourishment. The upper strata of capital swirls restlessly, in continual stiff breezes that desiccate and freeze, and this strata of capital is almost disembodied, valueless, empty in itself. What Max had realised was that, just as human activity can influence Earth's atmosphere and put at risk the future of all life on Earth, the mechanisms for generating and allocating capital can also release malignant forces with the potential to extinguish human society. And unlike greenhouse gases, which have taken centuries to accumulate, capital moves as fast as thought. Max sensed that economic climate change was toxifying the global economy faster than greenhouse gases were suffocating the environment and stifling people's wellbeing as completely as the lockdowns—but for the benefit of only those at the top.

'Kent, Zettadata's common shareholders got fucked. You might argue they're too stupid to make money, that they deserve to lose their money—that's certainly the position of people like Mort and Richard Wander. But destroying trust doesn't help anybody. The ASX will dry up and blow away if punters lose trust. I'm going to let them buy, when I buy, at the same price I do. No tricks, no more of the usual scam where I advise them to do something while I personally do nothing, or the opposite.'

Logan inhaled and then exhaled cherry-flavoured smoke.

'I'm still going to make money for us, Kent, I just won't make it quite as fast.'

'Are the rights renounceable?' Logan asked.

The question surprised Max. A renounceable rights issue gives shareholders the right to 'renounce' their entitlement to buy additional shares, and to sell that right for cash.

'No,' said Max.

What Logan was suggesting was even more generous than Max's proposal. Making the rights issue renounceable meant allowing all the small ZettaData shareholders to make money—even the ones who chose not trust and join him investing in the future of ZettaData—by selling their rights.

'You'll have to make them renounceable.'

'Why?'

'If you want to herd sheep, Max, you have to learn how to be a shepherd. You gotta give them the freedom to reject you, or they won't follow you.'

'I don't know, Kent,' Max said resentfully. 'Why should I hand out money for free to shareholders who don't trust me?'

'Look at that sour expression on your face!' Logan hooted.

'I just don't get it, Kent. Why should I allow people who don't support me to make money, too?'

'Max, you can't force people to trust you! What's the matter—now you don't like letting people make decisions for themselves?'

Max struggled to pull himself together.

Logan grinned. 'Why should the punters trust you? Look at your history. You're just a crazy wolf to them. You might change your mind any day and then decide to pounce and devour them. Sheep have a deep, primitive wisdom, Max – that's why there's so many of them still around, even though they're slow, fat, defenceless, and stupid.'

'How about if I get back to you on that, Kent,' Max said.

Logan had put his finger on the last vestige of Max's ego left in his ZettaData proposal: Max's desire to benefit only the small shareholders who supported him.

'You can't do things halfway, Max. You can ram it down the throats of the common shareholders in a deal with the board – which I'm sure the board fucking wants you to do – then pay out Edgell and take the keys from the banks. Or you can run your charming exercise in shareholder democracy. But if you do that, you have to give up control, otherwise they can't really trust you.' Logan pulled on his cigarillo. 'If that's what you fuckin' want, that's how you gotta do it. Real choice. I can't imagine why you want to give them that, personally.'

A properly functioning financial system circulates capital and money back into society and the economy where most people live, just as warm air rises to high altitudes, cools and settles, then returns to lower altitudes as breezes and rain to cool and water the Earth, producing abundance in which everybody and everything thrives.

Logan was adamant that Max benefit all small shareholders. Perhaps Logan had seen even more keenly than he the emptiness hidden inside the pocket of the ZettaData wave. Max had been so focused on crafting the fine details of his takeover proposal he had forgotten the fecund zero that makes all form possible, the fertile nothingness that generates all that is.

A dry smile appeared on Logan's lipless mouth. 'Do what you want, Max,' he said. 'But do it right, whatever it is. In the end, you'll have to make those rights renounceable.'

Max suddenly understood Logan as a man with a comprehension of the world capable of discerning illusion layered on illusion layered on illusion. Logan understood the difference between complexity and complications, always had – and he had just taken his sword and cut away the last web of complications shielding Max's ego.

Max looked at Logan thoughtfully. Logan sat on the pinnacle of Australian society all his life and had watched others far below feverishly struggling for the things of this world without ever knowing why they wanted those things, only that others wanted them, too.

He had always thought of Logan as a great nihilist. Logan was not amongst the small number of the world's billionaires who had pledged to give away most of their capital, partly because, Max suspected, Logan was so acutely aware of capital's extraordinary power, for good or ill. He didn't want it controlled by the wrong people.

But even the generous wealthy minority who announced their intention to divest most of their wealth first dedicated their lives to accumulating as much capital as they possibly could without sharing with others on the way up. Like Max, they hadn't been able to bring themselves to trust the fertile emptiness, the nothingness that produces everything that is. He hadn't sensed until this moment the paradox of representing bigger and bigger numbers with more and more zeroes – until even the myriads of stars in the universe could be described by a numeral followed by twenty-one zeroes: a Zetta. It pointed to a mysterious truth.

Perhaps, Max realised, it was Logan, not he, who had first fully understood how zero, the nothing that is, unites emptiness and abundance through the ultimate, most esoteric law of physics: we generate more energy by giving away what we own than we do by keeping it.

Kairos.

Chapter 29

'Its emissions are better than you would think – EC regulators are all over Porsche's arse,' Max said.

'Oh, come on,' said Peggy. 'These things throw off so much heat, I can feel it on my skin when they drive by. And if one's in front of me in traffic the exhaust is incredibly toxic.'

The Porsche leapt from the curb, paused for a moment at Campbell Parade, and then surged into the turn and roared up Military Road like a breaking wave.

'You're right,' said Max. 'As a matter of fact, before I got married I had one of the first Vespas imported into Sydney. That's how I used to get to work from Woollahra.' He smiled. 'By the way, it has a dirty, two-stroke engine like a lawn mower, but I used to fly past the Porsches and the Range Rovers and the BMWs stuck in traffic on the way to work, and I'd think to myself, "I'm having the fun they think they're having".'

Peggy patted the dashboard. 'So what happened?'

'Life,' Max said. 'Now, I'm one of those middle-aged guys in a Porsche myself.'

'No, you're not.' Peggy looked at him.

'Well ... I am.'

Peggy shrugged. 'It's a choice.'

'You're about to have a lot more fun than you would have had on that bus,' Max smiled, changing the subject. 'In fact, you're about to have more fun than you've ever had on the way to Vaucluse.'

Suddenly Max saw an opening and plenty of visibility. 'Now, don't worry,' he said.

Max crossed the centre line and accelerated down Old South Head Road. The world outside the cockpit disintegrated into a misty blur and streaks of gooey-looking lights from headlights and taillights as Max deftly threaded the Porsche perfectly back into an eye of the needle of the traffic.

Kairos.

'Wasn't that great?'

Max had no vision of a downed driver lying on the road now. The waking nightmare only afflicted him when he was driving alone.

'Surfing's more fun.'

'True. You surf?'

Peggy nodded. 'Not in a few years, but there are plenty of other things as much fun as this car – and they're free, too.'

'Very true.'

It was a rebuke – but it felt like something else, too.

Max nodded to the left, determined to resist whatever temptation there might be. 'You know, I grew up over there, just down and out of sight, in Dover Heights. It was the darkest, wettest house on the darkest street up here. Our house was the last one to get the sunlight when the sun rose above the cliffs in the morning.'

'It was still Dover Heights,' Peggy said. 'Right between Vaucluse and Bondi.'

'It wasn't expensive back then. My dad was a third-tier accountant who did ok until he tried to set up an investment management business with his accounting clients. It didn't work out.' Heavy clouds hung low above them as they climbed the escarpment, and the first sprays of rain struck the windscreen and misted into the air passing above their heads. 'Just so you don't think I grew up with lots of money.'

'It doesn't matter to me.'

'Yeah, I know you don't like Porsches.'

She laughed. 'Right!'

What was he doing?

On their right the ocean was out of sight as they drove along the top of the great cliffs, but its dark water absorbed all light, and the blackness seemed impenetrable. On the left, street lights and houses dwindled as they approached the dark expanse of South Head Cemetery. Max made a decision.

'You know, the rain's not too bad, and we're almost at Princes Avenue. Let's stop for ten minutes. I want to show you something.'

'Ok,' Peggy said.

Max slowed down, pulled over, and eased to a stop. 'Here we are.'

Peggy looked to the left, puzzled, at the line of modest houses.

Max raised the roof of the Porsche and switched off the engine. They stepped out in the road, as half-a-dozen cars passed by, dangerously close. 'Not this side,' said Max. '*This* side.' In the sudden silence wind rushed over the car and a spatter of rain smacked plump drops onto the car and beaded their faces and hair.

Another bunch of cars was speeding towards them. 'Come on,' Max said, and offered his hand. They crossed Old South Head Road, their hands lightly together until they crossed to the side where the cemetery is located.

'This way,' said Max.

A line of taxis waiting for fares were parked under large cypress trees next to the low cemetery wall, and behind the dark stones rose a dense cluster of funerary monuments and large, old-fashioned tombstones.

Peggy glanced about as she walked with Max. She stopped abruptly in the darkness and mist at the massive, crumbling stone pillars of the yawning entrance of South Head Cemetery.

'Hey,' Peggy sounded suddenly alarmed. 'Where are we going?'

'Into the cemetery. I want to show you something cool.'

Peggy looked around, crossed her arms, and shook her head. 'Nuh – this is too strange.'

Max wasn't surprised. 'Well, it *is* strange, but is it *too* strange? Look –' he pointed through the darkness at the long dim lines of tombs and headstones illuminated with the pale, furtive light cast by a bus stop next to the taxi rank. 'See that line of tombs over there on the right? It's just past there.'

'I can't believe you brought me to this fucking cemetery.'

Real anger made her words vibrate in the air. 'What's the matter?' asked Max. 'This is just a short stop – I know it's a bit weird, but fun.'

'Why here? Why this awful cemetery – of all places?' she cried, her voice escalating. She leaned her face towards Max and almost shouted. 'Why did you bring me here?'

What had happened to the calm, poised yogini who talked about water and evolution and love? Her sudden, intense anger reminded Max of someone he knew all too well. Repelled as he felt, Max also knew he must have done something to upset Peggy, but he had no idea what it could be.

'Look, I'm really sorry. I didn't mean to distress you. You just seem – I thought, until now – like the kind of person who could take a quick visit to a cemetery in their stride.' Max raised his hands and let them drop. 'When I was a teenager my friends and I used to come here all the time. After we went sea-cliffing at The Gap we'd lie in the grass among the tombs and smoke pot and drink beer and look at the stars.'

Max turned away and watched cars drive into the roundabout where New South Head Road and Old South Head Road merge. 'Back in the day, I found something kind of cool in here, and after all our conversations, I thought it was the kind of thing you might like, too.'

There was only silence behind him. He turned around. 'Forget about it.'

'I ... can ... walk ... to ... my friend's,' she said deliberately.

Max considered, still silently amazed at her outburst. 'You won't get as wet if I drive you. It's up to you.'

Peggy's face was going in and out of the shadows.

She sighed and rested her hand on Max's arm. 'Let's see the cool thing you wanted to show me.'

'Are you sure?' Max took a long inhale of cool, damp night air.

'Yeah—might as well, we're here.'

Max raised his eyebrows and waved towards the gate and the avenues of tombs and graves stretching into the darkness, letting Peggy know it was her decision.

'Just down there, right?' Peggy indicated with her chin where Max had pointed a few minutes before.

'Yeah, a couple hundred metres.'

Peggy nodded. 'Ok,' she said, pushing back some strands of damp hair. 'Let's go.'

They strode through the gates and Max started towards the wide central avenue of the cemetery but Peggy stopped in her tracks and pointed to the right. 'We're going this way, right?'

'Yes.'

'Ok, let's go down here, it's more direct,' said Peggy, nodding to the dark, narrow path near the wall.

They walked down the path, through the tombs and graves arranged on either side, with the central avenue of the cemetery on their left. Although the right side of the cemetery along Old South Head Road was the brightest area, the cemetery wall blocked all light below their knees, and the contrast with the dim light on the tombs and the darkness of their way made it impossible for Max and Peggy to see where they were stepping. Their shoes seemed to vanish into the dark grass as they walked.

'Are you ok?' asked Max, reaching out so that his fingers touched her arm lightly and protectively.

'Oh sure,' Peggy said.

The tombs and graves hemmed them in on both sides, and soft rain settled silently into the blackness at their feet, as they stepped carefully, feeling graves outlined on the ground by stones or covered with a slab of granite or marble. After Peggy stumbled twice Max took her hand. The sound of traffic seemed remote.

'Once we get to the end, it'll be all right,' Max said. 'The tombs are organised differently over there and the path is wider. It'll be easier for us to walk.'

But their destination was still lost in the darkness ahead, and Peggy's sandals made her going slippery and her feet vulnerable. Max could feel her weight on his hand as she steadied herself. 'We could always cross to the central avenue,' offered Max as they arrived at a path connecting to it. He didn't understand why Peggy seemed to want to avoid the central avenue. 'It would be much easier.'

Peggy stopped, letting his hand drop.

'Come on then, I'm not afraid of you!' she cried, and started walking resolutely down the side path to the main avenue.

'I should certainly hope not!' said Max, walking by her side.

'You're just more devious than I expected,' Peggy said hotly, tossing her hair, her eyes catching the dim light as she glared at him. 'I guess I should have known.'

'I don't know what you're talking about,' Max said.

'Sure!'

They arrived at the end of the central avenue of the cemetery, where a great Gaelic cross rises towards the sky, and near it squats a hulking mausoleum like a German pillbox, opposite a great sepulchre that looked like a piece had fallen off some gloomy English Victorian cathedral, its faux-Gothic stone ornaments convoluted, forbidding and outlined by grime from bus engines.

'Wow, look at this,' said Max in surprise. 'I can't remember who they built the cross for, but that's the tomb of the Boylston family,' he said, pointing to the mausoleum pillbox. He indicated the great faux Gothic sepulchre. 'That's where the Logan family are all buried,' he said.

Next to the Logan family tomb was a construction zone.

'I didn't expect to see this,' Max said, looking at the great heaps of freshly piled-up earth rising out of the shadows. Silhouetted in the flickering light was earth-moving equipment, reflective safety barriers, and steel bars planted in a concrete foundation. It looked like somebody was building a house. 'This must be the tomb my ex-partner is building for himself and his family,' Max said, shaking his head. 'I had no idea it was so huge.'

'That cross was built for a Premier of New South Wales, I think,' Peggy said quietly.

'Really?' said Max absently, still gazing at the mud and equipment.

Max heard her take a deep breath. She turned to him. Her face was gently illuminated by weak light from the bus stop. 'I haven't been here since Longbranch Logan died.'

'Kent's father?'

Peggy nodded.

'You were at his funeral?'

'Yes, my father is a good friend of Kent's,' Peggy said.

'Really!' said Max.

'They go back a long way,' said Peggy.

'Really,' Max said, wondering if he'd heard of her father. He'd thought she was a country girl raised on a duck farm in Byron who came to Bondi. Max scanned his memory for tall, elegant, patrician country landowners who were known to be close to Logan—someone whom she resembled.

'You just don't get it, do you?' Peggy asked.

'Get what?'

'My father's building this tomb for our family.'

Our family. Max looked at the mud and chaos. He looked into the darkness of Peggy's face. All at once—as if he could suddenly understand the contents of an entire page without registering any individual words – he got it.

'You're Margaret Norton.'

Six months ago, when the board was told that the Eden Street Theatre had just hired Mortimer Norton's daughter Margaret as ASM, Max vaguely imagined a tough, crop-haired, wide-hipped, bulldozer of a woman, with a low centre of gravity and an understandably disillusioned view of men—who would probably be an excellent ASM. Somebody who could kick arse and take names, keep rehearsals on track and performances moving smoothly.

Peggy nodded.

'That's how you know about the baby turtles and the raptors. You're working on *TransGod*.'

Peggy had been toying with him.

'I am, but I learned that when I went to the Galapagos on a Nightingale School excursion.'

'Nightingale!' Max exclaimed, secretly surprised Mort had a daughter enrolled in Nightingale School so long ago. Before he married Alexandra he was certainly not the Nightingale type.

'I went there my last two years as a boarder after my parents broke up. It was Uncle Kent's idea.'

'Kent Logan?'

Peggy nodded.

'I didn't see baby turtles getting slaughtered when I went to the Galapagos, either,' Max admitted. 'I just assumed I was there at the wrong time of year.' Max shook his head. 'Margaret Norton. It's hard to believe – for all kinds of reasons.'

'My friends call me Peggy,' she said. 'Dad's about the only one who still calls me Margaret.'

'How long were you going to wait before you told me?'

Peggy took a breath. 'Max, I wouldn't have let it go on much longer like this.'

'I guess you knew who I was when we met on the beach?' Max asked.

'Yes, Juanita told me as you were walking up.'

'So the whole time we were talking on the beach, you knew?' Max tried to hide the disappointment in his voice. 'All that stuff about water and thirst? You knew I was your father's ex-partner?'

'Yes,' Peggy said evenly, and reaching for Max's shoulder she held it, firmly but gently. 'But I never thought I'd see you again.'

'It probably would have been better,' said Max.

'Oh, come on, Max. I liked the way you surf. I didn't know who you were. I was watching you before Juanita recognised you.'

Max wanted to believe her. He wasn't sure. 'Peggy, how can I trust you?'

'For all I knew, you had found out who I was, yourself. That's why I was so angry with you by the gates. I thought this was your way of letting me know – by bringing me to the awful tomb my father is building.'

'I'm not as much like your father as you think,' Max said.

They had two choices: they could enter a labyrinth of mutual paranoia until they'd lost one another forever – or they could be even more honest with each other.

'I have to admit I wasn't telling you everything about myself, either,' Max said reluctantly. 'I should have told you myself I'm married. I have two beautiful daughters.' That much she knew already, of course. He still wasn't being truly honest with her. 'And – in fact – I'm seeing Claudia Bullivant, whom you work with.'

'I know,' Peggy said. 'She talks about you, and she likes you a lot.'

'That's not what this is – I'm not cracking on to you,' Max said. 'I admire the way you see things.'

His feelings for Peggy were stronger than he'd just admitted, but he'd described his intentions sincerely and accurately enough. It was hard to believe this sylph could be flesh of the flesh, bone of the bone, of Mortimer Norton.

Peggy was gazing at the dark, chaotic mud. 'There is something else I've been meaning to tell you.'

'About what?'

'About some deal you and my father are both working on.'

'The McConnochie Consortium – the Tunnel deal – WholeSydney?'

Peggy shook her head. 'That's not it – it's a funny name.'

'ZettaData?'

'That's it.'

Max laughed. 'Oh, that's old news. It's ok, don't worry about it—but thank you.'

Peggy put her hand on Max's arm. 'Max, that's not right: I'm talking about conversations my dad has been having this week with Alexandra.'

'Mort doesn't have any pieces to play with, Peggy I control them all. But I really appreciate you telling me. It's all ok.'

Peggy's eyes were troubled. 'Don't be so sure, Max. He's mates with almost everybody, including Uncle Kent. They go way back.'

Max smiled. 'Kent is actually investing with me in my takeover of ZettaData.'

'I don't know the details, because he doesn't really explain them, but he's coming after you. That's what he said.'

The fifty million he needed for ZettaData was already over-subscribed—he could have raised a couple hundred million easily. He had Kent, Luke Terry, and Donald Ormsby on his side, he had an agreement with Todd Edgell, and soon he'd have the approval of the Board of ZettaData. 'Your dad is wasting his time.'

'Don't be over-confident, Max. Daddy gets what he wants in all kinds of different ways. What if he sues you? He's ruining my mother with legal bills.'

'He didn't sue me when he had the chance,' said Max. 'He won't sue me now. Why is he suing your mum?'

'I didn't come down to Sydney to work on a play,' she said at last.

'I came back because of this,' she said, pointing at the muddy construction site.

'I don't understand,' said Max.

'I don't want Hugh in here!' Peggy continued, her voice unnaturally bright. 'After he died, my father took out an injunction preventing my mother from removing Hugh's body from the morgue.'

Max spoke softly. 'Your mum doesn't want his body here, either?'

'Oh absolutely not.'

'What do you and your mother want?' Max asked gently.

'We ... we ... we want Hugh's body cremated, and now that Covid is behind us we want a big funeral with his ashes scattered on the waves at Byron in a Vedic ceremony, with all our family, including dad, and all Hugh's friends.'

The words all came out rapidly, in a quick, sure rhythm, and her tone remained even, although to Max she seemed to be hurrying to finish the sentence before breaking down.

'That's a long way from here,' Max said, looking through the gloom at the muddy construction site. 'And a very different farewell.'

'I came back to try to talk my father into keeping my brother's body out of this awful thing,' she said. 'Instead, his lawyers have stepped up the pace.'

'Same old Mort,' Max said carefully. Was this the real reason she was seeing him?

Max fought an urge to plunge himself head-long into another confrontation with Mort and realised he was struggling with a terrible suspicion Peggy was setting him up.

Peggy nodded, and Max could see her eyes shining with tears.

'Hey,' he said gently, 'it'll be ok.'

She shook her head vigorously.

He was reluctant to admit it, but she was right: it wasn't going to be ok.

'Oh, it's just a matter of time ...'

Tears trickled down her cheeks.

Mort was playing to win as always, and once the Mortimer family tomb was built, Peggy's brother's body would be enclosed inside it, only a few metres from where they stood now.

It was so confusing. Max reached into his pocket, pulled out a handkerchief of Irish linen, and with the soft, rich cloth he wiped away her tears.

She was sobbing quietly now. 'I'm sorry,' she managed to say, at last.

He didn't want to be manipulated by another member of the Norton family, yet he couldn't bear to stand by while she was so alone and abandoned.

'Hey,' Max said. 'Don't be.'

He stepped beside Peggy and enclosing her in one of his arms, gave her a firm, brotherly hug, a friendly kiss on her hair, and he released her.

'Come on, let's get away from all this,' he said softly. 'I'll show you what we came to see.'

Max turned his back on the mud and guided her away from the great blocks of stone, old and freshly cut, that dominated the cemetery centre.

They walked slowly through a dark wilderness of obelisks, pillars, arcs of pediments and curves of urns, outlines of angel wings, saints' robes, and crosses. Crowds of carved figures, slick with rain and faintly gleaming, seemed to pause as they passed. The sound of traffic grew remote as Max guided Peggy along a narrow path between graves.

A ghostly head stared fixedly at them. Peggy gasped.

'It's the grave of Phil Garlick,' Max said. He was aware that Peggy was far more emotional than he had anticipated she would be when he first thought of bringing her here, as he showed her the life-sized marble sculpture of a driver in an old-fashioned race car, his arms gripping the steering wheel. The driver was wearing a marble replica of a leather helmet and high collar, and a faint smile was visible beneath his tidy marble moustache.

'He was killed in a car crash on the Maroubra race track back in the twenties,' Max said. 'He was one of the biggest celebrities in Australia when he died.'

'What happened?'

'The race track at Maroubra back in those days was built right by the sea. It was called "Australia's killer track" because it was shaped like a concrete saucer with very steep sides. If a driver went too slow his car could drop into the middle and crash, and if he was going too fast, he could drive right over the lip of the track and die.'

'"She'll be right",' said Peggy ironically, invoking the most ominous of all Australian reassurances.

'Exactly,' Max smiled, glad Peggy's spirits seemed to be recovering.

'It's kind of sweet,' Peggy said.

'Phil looks so happy and full of life, doesn't he? He was one of the best drivers of his day, until one race when he was in the lead and about to win, when he drove around the curve at almost one hundred miles an hour and went up and over the lip, and hit a light pole.'

It was too dark to read the elaborate inscription carved into the marble, and Peggy found her phone in her purse, knelt in the wet grass, and moving her hand back and forth across the marble illuminated several lines at a time:

PHIL GARLICK

A tribute to the memory of

REGINALD GORDON GARLICK

Beloved husband of Nellie

Accidentally killed at Maroubra Speedway

8th January 1928 – Aged 38 Years

A most popular highly skilled sporting devotee

of automobile speedway racing, whose career was tragically

ended, whilst about to achieve another of his triumphs.

ERECTED BY HIS MANY SORROWING AND RESPECTING

PALS

Max knelt next to Peggy. 'I first heard about Phil Garlick when I was a boy, from the news agent where I'd stop to buy newspapers for my dad.'

Max stood and helped Peggy up. The rain had stopped.

'The way the news agent, old Andy Fullerton, told me the story, another driver was thrown from his car just ahead of him, leaving Phil only two choices. He could hit the driver and kill him, which was the only way Phil himself could stay inside the race track, or he could swerve wide, but at the speed he was going it was certain he'd lose control and drive over the top the track. But the only way to save the other driver's life meant certain death for Phil, and Phil knew it.

'Andy Fullerton told me Phil made his decision in an instant: he swerved and went over the cliff to save the other guy.'

Peggy put out her hand and touched the cold stone head, letting her fingers run along the faint smile on the cold features. 'I thought you told me he hit a light pole.'

Max smiled sadly. 'That's right, I did. The story Andy told me wasn't true.' He looked at Peggy. 'It's true Phil Garlick was trying to pass another driver. He did go wide and up over the top of the lip. But he just made a mistake.

'He didn't have to pass the other driver. He had already lapped him and no other driver was close. He was about to win. There was no downed driver in his path. He didn't make a split second decision to save a stranger's life and sacrifice his own.

'I've found out that Phil was famous for being a mild-mannered, friendly bloke, until he got behind the wheel of his racing car. Then he became aggressive and hot-tempered. That day his temper probably got the better of him, and in a moment of reckless fury at being blocked by another car, he tried to pass him.' Max shook his head. 'It was just a mistake, and it was caused by one of his faults, not his virtues. I believed Andy's version of that story from the time I was about eight until a few years ago, when I thought to Google Phil's death.'

Max laughed shortly and fell silent.

'I don't understand,' said Peggy, at last. 'Why are you telling me this story?'

'When you told me the birds slaughtering the baby turtles wasn't true, I thought of my Phil Garlick story.' Max shrugged. 'We believe all kinds of stories, without even realising they're stories. We've been taught that Bible stories are just myths and fairy tales, but the way most people think they understand evolution, that it's kill or be killed, isn't necessarily science—maybe it's just a story, too. What does it even mean to say "Believe the science"? That tells you that what most people think of as science is just a story to them, whether they realise it or not. If they were thinking scientifically they'd say "Understand the science" not "*Believe* the science."'

Max laughed humourlessly.

'I don't blame Andy. Maybe that's the way he heard the story himself. That's not the point. The story didn't make me a good person,' Max said. 'It made me give up on being a good person.' He laughed shortly. 'Maybe that's why I was so happy to learn a few years later about evolution. It let me be the person I decided I wanted to be.'

'Why did Andy's story about Phil Garlick make you give up on being a good person?' asked Peggy.

'Because it was too high a standard,' Max said. 'I knew I couldn't do something like that.'

It was the ultimate *kairos*, a sudden moment of opportunity when the stakes couldn't be higher: but a negative *kairos*, when making the right decision would cost his life, and saving his life required making the wrong decision.

'I see, in a way,' said Peggy gently. 'But you're not a bad person.'

'Really?' said Max. 'I feel like an imposter, at best.'

'But why?'

'The part that haunted me about Andy's story was that Phil Garlick made the decision in a split second. Even when I was eight I'd read this inscription and I knew he had a wife named Nellie and lots of pals. How could he do it, I wondered? Such courage, such goodness. His life for another man's life: and he made the choice in an instant!

'Or so I was told—what a relief it was when I found out the truth a few years ago. Because I try to do the right thing, or at least I used to try, and often my first impulse is a good one. But with the stakes that high? Would I be able to give up my life—and willing to do so in a second?'

Max looked at Peggy, wanting to explain the idea of *kairos* and what it meant to him, but he decided it would be too much, at least for now.

'So the story seemed to prove I wasn't good enough—could never, realistically, be good enough. Finding out that Andy's story wasn't true is still one of the two greatest things I've ever learned in my life.'

'So you should be ok now that you know the truth about Phil Garlick.'

Max shook his head. 'In some ways, it's too late. I've accepted the idea we reveal ourselves in a split-second. I agree with it. But by the time I learned that Andy's story wasn't true, I'd spent a couple decades as an investment banker making instant decisions all the time, knowing those decisions were valid indications of who I really am. So the belief didn't go away when I discovered the real Phil Garlick story. It still bothers me. When I'm driving I sometimes see what looks like a body on the road – it's like a test of courage and goodness I know won't pass.'

The truth about Phil Garlick had also taught him the terrible consequences of mistaking a false *kairos* for a real *kairos*: it had cost Phil Garlick his life. Could Peggy represent a false *kairos*?

'You'd pass the test.'

'No,' Max shook his head. 'Not likely.'

'Yes, you would.'

'No, I've given up, actually.'

'No, you haven't,' whispered Peggy. 'Didn't you stand up to my father at that company's shareholder meeting? That's why dad's coming for you. Were you planning to do that?'

She was right. 'No, I had no idea what he was going to do and no way of planning it. But that was something different. I can't really explain it. Rather than feeling like I was looking down a tunnel that might close in the next instant and suddenly being aware that I had to make a split-second decision, I just suddenly realised that I had showed up, I knew I was there for a purpose, and I had to do something about it. I knew what to do without even thinking about it.

'By the way, I'm not even necessarily sure I was being a good guy – maybe I suddenly realised I hated your dad—and myself.'

'Maybe it was grace,' she said.

'Whatever that means,' said Max.

'Whatever that means,' agreed Peggy, taking his arm in hers. She walked in a short circle, turning Max around with her. 'Ok–come on, mister, let's get away from all this.'

They began the long walk back through the cemetery. As they passed the construction site, Max sensed a moment approaching to make another decision.

'Who did Mort hire to litigate against your mum?'

'Allaway, Davis.'

Max smiled grimly. 'That would be right,' he said. 'Your dad probably doesn't even have a case, or he only has a weak one. So he'll have Allaway, Davis generating utterly meaningless motions and filings that will force your mum to pay her lawyers to respond to them – until she bleeds out. As long your dad funds them, Allaway, Davis could keep that going for centuries, but from the look of the construction site he'll want control of your brother's body fairly soon, so he'll have them step up the tempo.'

'That's what's happening. They're escalating the number of motions they're filing.'

'Of course.'

He had worked with both Philip Allaway and Anthony Davis. They owned the most prestigious law firm in Sydney and charged their clients enormous fees to operate the legal system in a way that ensured the strong dominate the weak, and the rich dominate the poor. They were so expensive even Norton & Ring had hired the firm only for special situations. Mort was pulling out all stops in the battle to control his son's body.

'I'll pay your mum's legal fees,' said Max.

'What?'

'I'll pay them.'

Peggy shook her head. 'I can't let you do that.'

'Sure you can!'

'No, you only want revenge.'

She was right, of course. So what? 'I'm not going to let Mort get away with it – Not if I can help it. And I can help.'

'No, Max.' Peggy patted his arm.

'Why the hell not?'

'Because you're angry.'

'I sure as hell am,' Max agreed. And he was – he was starting to sweat.

'Your father's only doing it because he thinks he can get away with it,' Max said. 'It will be my pleasure to stop him.' His whole body was glowing now with anger. It felt almost as good as coming.

'What will my father say when he finds out?'

Max shrugged.

'Max, dad is angry, too. You know that. But do you know this? I know it's going to sound weird, but dad is the most justice-obsessed person I know.'

Max laughed bitterly. 'Justice-obsessed? Do you have any idea how many times I've pulled Mort back from the brink of breaking the law? He'd rather breach the Corps Act or ignore ASX Listing Rules than grab the last *biscotti*!'

Peggy smiled. 'He likes his biscottis, doesn't he?'

'He likes breaking the law even better—as long as he's sure he can get away with it.'

'Still, he's obsessed with justice. Believe me, Max, my father is the biggest accuser of them all. He doesn't see himself as breaking laws and committing crimes. As far as he's concerned, he's acting according to his own code, which is the truest of them all. In his mind, he's the highest and purest person in his world – everybody else is a hypocrite. He judges everybody. And anybody who crosses him is dirty, corrupt. He's indignant about it.'

'You're right,' Max admitted.

What Peggy said was true. It was exactly the way Mort talked. Max had listened to countless diatribes by Mort heaping contempt on other people.

'Max, I know him. Listen to me. He's capable of having you torn limb from limb—while convinced you are the one who is wrong. He's always totally right in his own mind.'

Sparagmos.

'Funny you mention that,' said Max.

'There's nothing funny about it, Max, when he gets angry, my father demands a sacrifice, it's the only thing that propitiates him.'

Unless she was playing a very deep game, she seemed to be totally sincere.

Max suddenly felt grimly determined. Peggy was describing exactly the man revealed by their five years as partners.

'Mort needs to be stopped and I'm the one to do it.'

'Be realistic, Max. My father is capable of anything.'

'He'd better bring help.'

'Max, don't you realise we turn into our enemies?'

'You're fighting your father,' Max pointed out. 'And you're not turning into him, are you?'

'I can explain that, another time.'

They reached the gates and stopped. Peggy was silent.

At last she stepped to him and gave him a quick hug, holding his shoulders firmly in her hands and keeping her body slightly away from his. 'Thank you, but I can't accept,' she said.

'Peggy, I'm not going to accept 'no' for an answer.'

'It has to be my mother's decision.'

'So ask her.'

'Why don't you come to Byron? You and mum should discuss your generous offer in person. You can stay with us at the farm.'

He smiled. 'Done. Now, are you really going to a friend's house, or did you just tell me that?'

'I really am,' Peggy said.

'I'll get you there in less than a minute.'

'I'll bet,' Peggy said.

Chapter 30

From her position just behind the curtain on the OP, or Opposite Prompt, side of the stage Peggy listened to stage manager Hamish Lawson call the show for the tech run. She breathed the comfortable close air of the theatre, with its smell of a closet in summer, trying to stay calm and professional despite the fact Claudia Bullivant stood next to her, waiting her cue to step on stage in the minor part of the Secret Service Agent protecting President Orange.

'I'll unleash the invisible on the visible! I'll hale those who don't believe in science through the streets by their hair ...' exclaimed Joan Perrone, the actor playing Pandemia, to the actor Trevor Walker, who played President Orange. Walker had never acted before, but his casting was considered a coup by the producers because in real life he was host of the widely watched TV program *Mighty Money*. In rehearsals he had proved the perfect choice to bring President Orange to life on the Australian stage.

It was difficult to concentrate while they stood together. Peggy was struggling to ignore her guilty feelings as she stood beside Claudia now that she had invited Max to Byron Bay.

'Standby LX 29, Sound 13, Flys 28.'

Golden interior light bathed the stage. The smell of sweat and human essence floated on the shimmering air.

Max wasn't the only guy Claudia was seeing, of course. The thought momentarily made Peggy feel better.

Joan Perrone stood at centre stage right on the setting line, intoning her speech exactly as she intended to give it to a live house. Perrone was born John and inspired as a boy by the character Divine in John Waters' film *Pink Flamingos*. Like her idol Divine, Perrone looked voluptuous – *zaftig* – with sweeping hips that curved like a cornucopia and seemed able to cradle enough fertility to breed an entire civilisation. Her breasts undulated like the billows of the sea, and her brown eyes and wide full lips conveyed a wild and untamable vitality that registered as an insatiable and destructive, not a life-giving, force. Even though

Joan Perrone was not in costume because this was the tech run, her Pandemia looked like what she was: a global storm.

'– until they eat strange flesh like flesh-eating birds devouring baby turtles on hot sand!'

Peggy glanced at Claudia. Claudia wasn't wearing stage make-up so Peggy could see her face was suddenly a little flushed. That was odd. Peggy checked the pre-set for her: the props person had laid out the handcuffs and the pistol on the prop table positioned deep in the shadow of the wings. Regardless of how attentive she was to Claudia's welfare, Peggy knew she was betraying her trust.

The main goal of the tech run was to confirm that the centrepiece of the production operated properly: the main prop was a huge flock of raptors lowered at several key moments in the play. The crew called it 'the skull flock' because it comprised thirty or forty birds, fashioned from twisted and partially melted pieces of metal, arranged to form great gaping eye sockets and a nose hole in the three dimensional shape of a human skull. The flock looked naturalistic when viewed front-on from the audience, but when the spot shone on it from above, the cunningly shaped flock transmogrified into a huge human skull and projected a great death's head shadow onto the back drop.

Lawson's voice in Peggy's ear calmly ordered: 'LX 29, Sound 13, and Flys 28 ... go.'

The sound cue came up perfectly. Harsh bird cries filled the theatre making the seagulls on Seven Shillings Beach sound like cooing doves. Peggy had already heard it at full volume three or four times by now and it still made her nervous.

Now Claudia's neck was rosy, too, Peggy noticed. Claudia's eyes were bright and skittered away and back, held Peggy's gaze, and then skittered away again to look at the stage. Claudia seemed slightly agitated, which was unusual. By now she had normally already disappeared into her character.

'Max and I read this part together,' Claudia whispered.

Peggy momentarily blanked on the lines Trevor Walker and Joan Perrone were saying to each other as a searing pang of jealousy flashed through her. *There was that much depth to Max and Claudia's relationship?* Peggy glanced at Claudia, shocked by her own jealousy–and realised she had assumed—and hoped—that Max and Claudia's relationship was just physical.

Peggy made a small tick on her script as Claudia shifted her weight restlessly between the balls and toes of her feet and her heels.

'You've denied science! You're a disease vector! You say a virus sanctified your nature? You will die by a new virus!'

'LX 30, Sound 14 go,' intoned Lawson.

Rays of light shot across the stage and turned a cool blue. A shadow appeared on the back of the set depicting a jungle-like Sydney pullulating with invisible swarms of a killer virus, and a sinister Dionysian flute began playing.

Joan Perrone projected a hoarse stage whisper that would be heard in the seats all the way in the last row of the theatre. 'You're dear to me only as turtle flesh—and I eat turtle flesh raw!'

'Standby LX31, Flys 14.'

Trevor Walker in his role as President Orange barked authoritatively, '... I'm responsible for maintaining order in this community ...'

'LX 31, Flys 14, go.' The most crucial part of the tech run was the rate of speed at which the skull flock was lowered over the stage. The complex lighting changes that preceded and followed the moment the skull flock became visible to the audience had to work perfectly to ensure the shadow of the skull evolved at just the right moment into a high-contrast outline of a death's head, just before the horrible metal skull flock itself appeared to the audience.

It was also her cue to remind Claudia to prepare her props. Peggy looked significantly at Claudia, who wheeled and reached the prop table in two silent steps.

Claudia grabbed the handcuffs in one hand and the pistol in the other.

Perrone looked wildly out towards the theatre seats as a shadow appeared behind the characters playing Pandemia, President Orange and Dion.

There was a three second pause and then 'LX 32, Sound 15, go.'

The great shadow resolved steadily and horribly into a huge human skull that hovered like a collective hallucination behind the actors as the flock of birds slowly appeared from above.

Claudia walked briskly out on stage along the setting line. Her costume would include heels that clicked decisively as she progressed to centre stage, but in her trainers she was almost noiseless. Nevertheless, Joan Perrone, Trevor Walker and Bill Atkinson all cocked their heads and paused on cue as if Claudia's steps were clearly audible. As Claudia arrived she seemed to radiate an indefinable energy into the little ensemble Peggy had never noticed before.

'LX 33, go. Standby LX 34.'

The bright lights of the stage dimmed and spots suddenly shone on the skull flock that had emerged above the three actors, its twisted metal birds now collectively and unmistakably transformed into a huge human skull as the huge, stark shadow of a skull was projected onto the backdrop.

Even Joan Perrone seemed cowed.

'LX 34, go.'

A spot shone on Claudia as her arm reached out, incandescent under the lights.

'You're coming with me, sir,' said Claudia, as she pointed a pistol which looked huge in her small hand at Dion.

What else had that hand held, wondered Peggy, surprised at her own thought.

'Oh, indeed I am!' exclaimed Bill Atkinson gleefully as Dion, the god Dionysus in disguise. 'Here's my wand, officer, it's for you.'

He presented her with the traditional symbol of Dionysus, and turned around, allowing her to handcuff him.

Peggy could see the producer and director watching from the third row, smiling with satisfaction at the way the scene had come together under the huge skull.

'Use it wisely, often and well!' said Bill Atkinson as Claudia marched him off stage.

The producer and director chuckled at the line.

The great skull hovered in the air. Death revealed as the Lord of Life.

The effect was perfect.

Chapter 31

'**G**ood morning, Mr Ring,' smiled Susan, an elegant honey-coloured wave rising from her coiffure and revealing her high forehead.

'Please, call me Max.'

The Casners lived on a shady street of substantial houses rising out of lush gardens. He had come along a walk lined on either side by an English box hedge as he approached the front door, and the rest of the front garden was a mixture of European trees and native flowering shrubs, the non-natives a violation of the latest standards of cool, according to Ilona.

'Come in, Max, you're very welcome.'

The front rooms were full of English furniture, Persian rugs and various paintings and framed photos. Max started to relax, after the stressful drive up the contorted, under-sized Pacific Highway to Pymble. He didn't know the Pacific Highway very well and hated driving it. Both he and his Porsche had baulked at the ugly, twisting stretch of road as it unfurled through the Northern Suburbs. Every several seconds it seemed he was cut off and boxed in by experienced locals at the maddeningly frequent right turn lanes, or hemmed in behind trucks and meandering weekday cruisers. What a relief it was to turn off Pacific Highway at last and motor quietly down the tranquil streets of Pymble.

'It's lovely,' said Max, not entirely sincerely. The Casner home was traditional and there was nothing dramatic or attention-getting about it. No wonder Juanita was indifferent to real estate listings from Pymble in her cutting-edge Eastern Suburbs publication.

'How long have you lived here?'

Max followed Susan into a sunny side room with walls of glass on two sides providing a view onto a quietly tasteful back garden. The branches of an oak and two Japanese maples, abundant with fresh, newly sprouted leaves, bright green and the colour of wine, framed the view, which included another box hedge, this one chest high. A sofa and two armchairs covered in pale gabardine faced each other, and Susan waved Max to the sofa.

'We moved here thirty years ago. Would you like a cup of tea?'

'Yes, thank you,' said Max.

The sofa was extremely comfortable. There wasn't a single piece of furniture in the Ring home as comfortable as this sofa, and the chairs looked inviting, too. Everything about the Casner's home was elegant and tasteful, but Ilona's renovations were probably going to cost as much as the Casner's entire house.

Still, he had to admit he was becoming deeply relaxed. Max looked around. On a credenza were framed photos of two handsome young men, both clear eyed, square-jawed, purposeful, smiling into their futures. At the edge of the credenza was a stack of five small, leather-bound books that looked like they might be rare.

How nice to have successfully launched two children. Sure, the Casner's lives seemed fairly conventional and routine, but they must enjoy security and a sense of satisfaction in their simple world. That was attractive: if only he could feel that way.

Susan returned to the living room, poured tea, and sat with Max on the large sofa, rather than across the tea table in one of the comfortable upholstered chairs. There was something confident in the gesture and Max admired it.

He sipped his tea. 'Wow, this is great. What is it?'

'I make my own blend—half Earl Grey, half Darjeeling. Earl Grey provides perfume and Darjeeling gives it rich body and flavour.'

Maybe this was the life. Not too exciting, but nothing to worry about apart from the occasional dud investment. And he could fix that.

The tea tasted delicious. As Max set down his teacup a tall, rangy man in his late sixties, vigorous but slightly stooped, appeared in the doorway. Max stood up.

'Harold Casner,' he said, extending his hand. 'Call me Hal.'

'Max Ring.'

Hal shook hands and waved Max to his seat on the sofa and sat in the armchair across from his wife.

He and Max exchanged brief introductions. Hal was a semi-retired government research scientist at the CSIRO, the Commonwealth Science and Industrial Research Organisation.

'I understand you're here to talk about ZettaData,' Hal said. 'The worst investment of my life.'

'Yes, I am,' said Max. 'I'd like to describe my proposal to you, Susan and Hal. You just have to tell me what you think, that's all.'

'That's very considerate of you, Max—I doubt it could possibly be worth coming all this way.'

Hal and Susan exchanged glances. Hal had both hands on his knees.

'When did you make your investment?' Max asked gently, conscious Hal felt humiliated by what happened.

'Oh, we bought shares in the IPO. We held them all the way up, to five dollars and never sold—and then followed them all the way down.' He and Susan exchanged glances, but her thoughtful, sympathetic expression didn't change. 'Susie suggested we sell near the top, at four dollars, seventy-one I think it was.' He smiled sadly and Susan slightly nodded. 'But I thought of ZettaData as a long-term investment, and saw no reason to sell. It was worth half a million at the peak—and I thought I was a genius.'

Hal laughed ruefully.

'So, you invested fifty thousand or so in the IPO?'

'Yes,' Hal sighed. 'A huge amount of money, I know.'

'My word,' Susan said softly, and reached out and patted her husband's knee comfortingly.

Max smiled encouragingly. 'It happened to lots of people.'

Max's eye caught movement in the garden. A plump young woman had just appeared pushing a wheelchair, in which sat a young man with a blanket over his knees. They had been seated out of sight just on the other side of a box hedge in the sunlight, and now she was gently pushing him up a walkway of finely crushed rock to the house.

A door creaked open and closed, and there was a faint rumbling noise from the corridor.

'This is our son Lachlan,' said Susan when the young man and his nurse appeared in the door to the sunroom. Max glanced at the photos of the two young men on the credenza. He couldn't tell which of them was now in the wheelchair. Lachlan's seated body was contorted, his head tilted at a steep angle above his right shoulder, his chest straining out from the back of the wheelchair supported by his elbows, which were each firmly planted on the armrests, his legs pressed against one another and sticking out at an angle from the direction in which his chest was turned.

'G'day, Lachlan,' said Max, hoping his voice was level and empty of the sudden horror he felt washing over him.

Lachlan made inarticulate noises and his body quivered. His right hand was oscillating above the armrest.

'Lachlan would like to shake your hand,' his mother said softly.

Max steeled himself, stood up, and walked over as the young woman pushed Lachlan into the room. He smiled at Lachlan and reached out his right hand, fitting his fingers into the curled fingers and folded palm of Lachlan's hand. 'It's good to meet you, Lachlan,' Max said. He pressed Lachlan's hand and Lachlan responded with a strong three fingered grip that caught Max's hand like a softly tenacious grappling hook.

Lachlan looked up into Max's eyes. His gaze was alive with vitality even though the rest of his body was broken and atrophied. Lachlan's face was twisted into a meaningless expression, but Max could see everything about him in those warm, trusting, intelligent eyes. If, in good health, the kid had interviewed at Norton & Ring, he and Mort would probably not have hired him because of that warmth and trust, and if they did, *in spite* of the goodness shining in his eyes, they would have done everything possible to turn Lachlan into another predator on their team like themselves.

'Lachlan, your father and I are chatting with Mr Ring about something he visited us today to discuss,' said Susan. 'Bea will take you to the kitchen and fix your lunch now.'

Lachlan held Max's gaze as he was wheeled out.

'We have two sons,' Susan said as Max regained his seat. 'Tim is a barrister at Mallesons. Lachlan was doing even better than his older brother and had just completed his HSC the night he was hit by a car as he was walking home. He topped his year in the HSC.'

Max glanced back at the photos on the mantelpiece. One of them was now recognisable as Lachlan, before his face became slackened from paralysis. 'How long ago was that?' Max said.

'Ten years ago. Lachlan's twenty-eight.'

Hal cleared his throat. 'The driver was drunk, just a kid himself who'd had a tough week the night he had too much alcohol and then tried to drive home. I wasn't going to sue the kid, and only did so when we realised it's the insurance company who pays, not the driver—we didn't want to bankrupt the young man, and wreck his life, too.'

'I wouldn't have given it a thought, if it was me,' said Max. 'I'd say bankrupting the bastard would have been just a start.'

Susan shook her head gently. 'There was no point blighting two young lives. Punishing Johnno wouldn't have helped Lachlan.'

'The insurance proceeds weren't much, but they gave us a start,' said Hal. 'Once we knew we were going to receive some funds I was determined that we would look after Lachlan at home ourselves.'

'I so wanted to prevent Lachlan from being institutionalised, but I wasn't sure we could manage his care, and at first I thought it might be our only choice.' Susan leaned forward and took Hal's hand. 'Hal convinced me we could do it, which I so wanted to do, if there was any way it was possible.'

'Thank God it's worked out so far, by hook and by crook. I focused on organising the insurance and various government assistance programs to maximise our resources,' said Hal. 'I effectively put together a family business case for how we could do it, and it's worked out pretty closely to how I projected. When ZettaData took off, I thought we were assured of being able to look after Lachlan ourselves.'

Susan nodded and smiled sadly at her husband.

A chill tingled in Max's spine. When Mort stood up at the AGM to attack Luke Terry, he almost wiped out the last of the Casner's investment. If Max hadn't spoken up in the nick of time they'd have nothing left of it.

'Through all the ups and down—'

'For ten years,' Max said softly.

An even more troubling thought occurred to Max: how much pain and suffering had he caused during his career, without giving any thought to who was suffering? The frightening part was he hadn't even noticed for all those years.

' – it was Susie who stepped in and took over managing people, and the logistics, and all the comings and goings, and making sure Lachlan gets the care he needs, even if she's the only one here to provide it. Susie's brilliant daily management is what, in practice, has made it work. It's Susie who makes it possible to provide Lachlan with the care he needs.'

'Hal started worked part-time even though he was leading a major research initiative, to help me with Lachlan,' said Susan.

'In retrospect, if I'd only waited another year Covid would have forced us all to work from home and I could have remained full-time and received the credit for our discoveries. But of course nobody knows what the future holds, and Susie was struggling at the time with Lachlan's needs. So I was quite clinical about constantly evaluating the contribution my money-making provided to our situation versus my ability to help Susan and Bea, and when I felt I could be of more assistance at home I stepped down to part-time.'

'At just the moment when his entire career of research was beginning to bear enormous fruit,' said Susan. 'And Hal allowed others—his own protégés and the others he had trained—to get the glory for it.'

'Knowing what I knew at the time, it was the right decision,' said Hal. 'I wish I could say the same for my decision to hold on to ZettaData.'

The Casners demonstrated how a couple could work together: Hal was abstract and not very practical, and Susan's insightful and energetic approach to solving problems transformed Hal's principles into the reality of high quality medical care. Neither one could have looked after Lachlan individually, but together they had triumphed over inadequate resources.

'It must be expensive to look after Lachlan,' Max said.

'Yes, we do as much as we can ourselves, and Bea is an angel, but it certainly is expensive. It's what will happen as we grow older that concerns me.' Susan glanced down, and seemed to catch her breath.

'I'd like to help you,' said Max. 'Let me explain the proposal I'm considering putting to the ZettaData Board. The most essential part is that I've decided to offer you and other small shareholders the opportunity to invest on the exact same terms as I will invest. But only if you want to.'

'We don't have any money to invest, Max,' said Susan.

'I know that. But you do have your existing shares, and my plan is designed to make them worth a lot more.'

They looked expectantly at Max.

'If and when my proposal is approved, and announced on the ASX, the lawyers will have turned it into almost incomprehensible mumbo jumbo. So let me tell you what it really means.'

'Something like that,' nodded Hal.

'Ok, beneath all the complications, the essence of my proposal would be the same deal as if I offered you, and everyone who owns a house in Pymble, the right to buy another house in Pymble just like the one you already own—for just one cent. If you have a small house, you could buy another small house. If you have a big house, you could buy another big house. My Pymble proposal would be a public vote of confidence in Pymble. So even though I was doubling the number of houses, if *more* than double the number of people who now live in Pymble decide they want to live in Pymble too, the demand for Pymble real estate will drive up the value of your house, and all the other houses in Pymble. That's because even though I am doubling the supply of houses, I've more than doubled demand for houses in Pymble. Do you see that?'

'I think so,' said Hal. They looked doubtful.

'So by drawing attention to the value of Pymble real estate, you expect to generate more demand than new supply, lifting the value of all houses here,' said Hal.

'That's right,' said Max. 'It's a signal of confidence designed to benefit firstly the people who already live in Pymble. But a company is different than houses, because it generates cash. So by offering my one cent rights issue, I'm telling the market I think ZettaData is going to start generating lots more cash than it does today. Current shareholders like you will be the first to benefit because you already have shares—just like you already have a house in Pymble. It's a loyalty bonus.'

'Yes, I think I can see how a rights issue priced at one cent wouldn't make the share price fall,' said Hal.

'Perhaps there is something poetic in it,' said Susan.

Max knew that in ancient Greek, the word *poesis* means "making things". Perhaps by developing his proposal he was becoming a true poet, a "maker", not an exploiter like Mort, and like he himself used to be.

'So … does your deal mean we won't lose any more money?' Susan asked hesitantly. 'I trust you, Max, and I want to believe in you.'

'I'm taking over ZettaData to make money, Susan, not to lose money,' Max said. 'But if something goes wrong, at least you'll know I'll lose millions—that's as sincere as I can possibly be.'

Max turned and his eyes caught the rare books on the mantelpiece. As a distraction, he walked over and picked one up. It was an old pocket Bible; it looked like a relic of the nineteenth century. He looked questioningly at Susan.

'I'm descended from five generations of Methodist ministers,' she said. 'Those have been in the family for years.'

Ilona's remote ancestor Erskine was also a Methodist minister. She had applied the simplicity and directness of her Methodist heritage to shaping a worldview in which the existence of God was completely unnecessary. 'Does this help?' Max asked.

'Words matter only when they're living and active,' Susan said.

Max replaced the Bible on the stack and nodded.

He could accept the idea that human consciousness had repeatedly generated, across history and cultures, complex expressions of inner human potential referred to as the divine: Lord Krishna, the Lord of Hosts, Athena Pallida, Lord Buddha, and the Lord Jesus Christ, amongst others, but Max had never been motivated to investigate the impenetrable theology surrounding those mysterious events. Theology reminded him of the tax code, the only difference was that he knew there was value in mastering the complications of the tax code.

'Well, you've been very generous with your time, but I think I should probably go,' said Max. 'Do you mind if I say goodbye to Lachlan?'

'What a lovely idea,' said Susan, standing up.

Max followed her into her kitchen, which was orderly and homey, a fraction of the size of the kitchen in the Ring home.

'Goodbye, mate,' said Max, intertwining his fingers in Lachlan's fingers and gently shaking his hand.

Lachlan's warm brown eyes were full of love and something else Max didn't immediately interpret. As he turned away, he realised what he'd seen in Lachlan's eyes: peace.

Hal and Susan showed Max to the door, and as he stepped out onto the front step he turned around to say goodbye.

He shook hands with Hal, gave Susan a kiss on her cheek, and walked to his car, got in, switched on the engine, and sat as the roof opened. They were still standing at the open door. Max waved, and they waved as he pulled away from the kerb.

For the first time he felt an obligation to help the Casners and countless people like them. He had the skills, experience, contacts and capital to do it: he just had to stop thinking only about himself and his family and raise his eyes to the needs of all the others he was well-qualified to provide for.

The languid throbbing of the Flax Six sent soothing vibrations up and down his spine as he drove slowly under the leafy branches of quiet Pymble streets. Hal and Susan were like the tea they served, an appealing blend of distinct elements that produced a unique, wonderful result.

He knew corporate finance.

They knew something he didn't.

Chapter 32

Hugh Grimson was the ZettaData Director who first broke the silence after Max finished his presentation. 'What if the rights issue triggers a backlash?' he asked.

He was a merchant banker and the fear in Grimson's voice was palpable. Logan was right about him.

'A backlash?' repeated Max politely. 'You mean, in the market? A collapse in the stock price?'

'Well, that would be bad enough. A fall in the stock price would be a very serious reverse for ZettaData,' said Grimson. The anxiety in his eyes discredited the air of confidence he had donned that morning along with his crisp shirt and elegant necktie, the dignity of the grey hair combed straight back from his forehead, and the stern lines on his face. 'What I mean is, what if a group of shareholders decides to take action after the proposal is approved?'

Max understood. Grimson meant *what if there's a shareholder lawsuit against us directors?*

'My proposal treats all shareholders equally,' said Max. 'Small shareholders are going to love it.'

Bernice O'Toole, the former Head of Strategy at one of the biggest corporations in Australia and a director of five other public companies besides ZettaData, glared at Max. He didn't take it personally – O'Toole was no doubt furious with herself for not resigning a couple years ago, before it was too late.

Company Secretary Leonard Whyte sat at the table, busily taking minutes, so directors had to be careful what they said on the record.

None of the directors had yet grasped the benefits to shareholders offered by Max's proposal.

'How do we know the punters are going to get behind this thing?' asked O'Toole.

'That's the essential point, isn't it?' asked Telford.

Max sized him up, aware his feelings for Telford were shifting and becoming more positive. Telford seemed genuinely to be trying to do the right thing.

Telford's main responsibility was to do Edgell's will, but he displayed stubborn loyalty to Grimson and O'Toole. If ordinary shareholders objected to the proposal, it was Grimson and O'Toole who would be targeted by shareholder lawsuits for breach of their duties as directors representing ordinary shareholders. They were facing grave risks of being forced to fight financially ruinous lawsuits, and perhaps lose even their homes if, by approving the proposal, they were convicted of breaching their duties as directors. The reason their dilemma was so excruciating was because they might also be successfully sued if they rejected the proposal and ZettaData went into liquidation.

'Gentlemen, I am sure common shareholders and the wider market will welcome being given a fair go after all this time,' said Max. 'That's what this rights issue is – the chance common shareholders have deserved all along.'

'There's no need to rub anyone's face in it, Max,' said Wander.

Although very aware of their personal conflicts, Max was here to obtain the support of the directors, not reprimand them for transferring value out of ZettaData, or the cosy relationships that made those arrangements possible.

He was offering ordinary shareholders a fair deal, and at the same time offering directors a real solution to their personal predicaments.

'Chairman,' Max said, surveying Telford politely but still with very little respect. 'I'm inviting existing shareholders to share the future of the company with me.'

The Telfords were Dallas aristocracy. At the turn of the last century, Luther's great-grandfather founded the Dallas electricity company which eventually grew into the gigantic holding company SpecTel. Telford was certainly a gentleman, but the intellect and entrepreneurial vinegar had leached out of the Telford bloodline at least one generation before Luther IV was born.

Telford sat back in his chair, clearly unconvinced.

'Perhaps I can solicit the view of our financial advisor, Mr Wander?'

They all looked at Richard Wander.

'A rights issue is like a tax on shareholders,' Wander said flatly. 'The higher the tax, the more the stock price falls,' Wander continued. 'A rights issue at one cent might be perceived the way Mr Ring is describing it, as a "freebie" to shareholders, and if it is, the stock price will rise to match the perceived value. Of course, this gentleman,' waving an insouciant arm to indicate Max, 'is also converting at one cent the capital he's agreed to buy from Edgell for control of ZettaData.'

Telford looked at Max, silently inviting a response. Wander's reference to his new boss had suddenly sobered Telford. He seemed to have remembered that the first step in Max's proposal to the board had been to agree to a deal with Todd Edgell, who held Telford's fate in his hands.

'That's true,' said Max. So far, Wander had been neutral and objective. 'And that's exactly my point: I'm offering the small shareholders the same price I'm proposing the board approve for myself.'

'Any shareholder who doesn't take up their rights will be diluted to buggery,' Wander replied.

'Unless the share price rises,' said Max.

'Unless the share price rises,' agreed Wander.

Max suddenly realised that Wander was probably the one who dreamed up those special securities the Texans had used to try and steal control of ZettaData. It would have worked brilliantly except for ZettaData's cash flow crisis. His rights issue was the vaccine for the virus with which Wander had infected ZettaData.

Wander fell silent with a sardonic smile, having accurately stated for the official record the financial benefits to shareholders of Max's proposal. It was clear to Max that he actually opposed it, but Wander still hadn't said a thing that hinted why.

Telford's face was expressionless, but his eyes were bewildered. He leaned back in his chair and grandly turned his head from side to side, surveying the board, as if offering the directors an opportunity to express their opinions. Luke Terry cleared his throat and leaned forward towards Max. 'I'm not sure how all these extra complications work better for ordinary shareholders?'

It was an ironic question coming from Luke Terry, who had told Max he didn't believe in capitalism or the financial markets. Terry was clearly speaking for the record.

'I can assure you we share the same objectives, Luke,' Max said solemnly. He couldn't resist – but he didn't want to be too cheeky and put at risk Luke Terry's support. Acknowledging, or pretending to acknowledge, while the company secretary was busily taking the official minutes of the meeting his concern for ordinary shareholders was helpful to Terry, given his ambitions to become prime minister of Australia. 'I've tried to offer ordinary shareholders something good and simple: the same deal I have. This is about equality, real equality, for all shareholders.'

Terry, in fact, probably cared very little for the fate of the Casners and the tens of thousands of ordinary ZettaData shareholders, because most of them probably voted for the opposition party, not the party currently in power who had appointed Terry.

Terry nodded. 'Thanks.'

He seemed satisfied, and why wouldn't he be? If Max took over ZettaData, it would cease to be a weekly, if not daily, public spectacle. Max was likely to be safe hands for at least a couple years, by which time Terry was probably already going to be prime minister. Besides, as the ZettaData Director appointed by the Australian Government, Terry was in the unique position of having a full indemnity against anything he might say or do on the board. He could do anything he wanted as long as his minister supported him—and the minister knew Terry was likely to be his next boss.

Grimson squinted through his spectacles, studying Max's proposed transaction timetable. 'Now, you're saying that if we execute the agreement with you tomorrow, we can appoint the Independent Expert to begin work on the rights issue and announce it in two weeks?'

'That's right,' said Max.

'Let's see, then ... from the announcement to the EGM,' the Extraordinary General Meeting of ZettaData shareholders, 'would be just over four weeks ... and then once the rights issue is approved, there's another month before the issue closes.' Grimson frowned.

Grimson didn't like the extra month before he was off the hook, that was clear. He'd lost his taste for creating and shaping events, for seeing the consequences of his influence in the world. He just wanted to find an orderly retreat into retired life that preserved as much of his wealth and reputation as possible.

'Once shareholders vote, nothing else can really happen,' said Max. 'The deal will be done by the end of October. The remaining four weeks in November are just procedural.'

The directors were silent, but from their expressions Max could see they yearned to ask: But why do you insist on the extra step of the rights issue? Why not just crush the common shareholders and get it over with? They all wanted to ask the question, but none of them could figure out quite how as the secretary looked around the table, waiting to record the words of the next director to speak.

Max sensed their desperation – but they didn't have another offer. His offer was it – and he was going to bring Hal and Susan along with him.

The Chairman, Luther Telford, looked at Max, his expression muted by his air of resignation. 'What I hear you saying is you're confident the market will support your proposal?'

'Yes, Chairman, I am extremely confident ordinary shareholders will support the rights issue,' said Max.

'And could your idea work in a general way across the capital markets?' Terry asked suddenly.

'Well, yes, in principle Luke. The idea that any institutional investor or investment bank would allow small investors to invest on exactly the same terms as they did in a deal, that could be a general rule. And it should be.'

'To make the markets work for everybody,' said Terry, clearly aware he and Max were continuing the conversation they had begun in his office.

'That's right,' said Max. 'They'd finally evolve to a form that truly benefited everyone, which should have happened a long time ago.'

'Got it,' said Terry.

Max now knew Terry could see what Logan had seen: the emptiness inside ZettaData was brewing up something powerful: a new storm of capital – a fierce brew of energy capable of cleansing the Australian financial markets.

If Max succeeded in turning around ZettaData, the capital he restored to the Casners and tens of thousands of shareholders would benefit their lives and quicken the energy in the Australian economy. Their money would accumulate into capital, and Max would return additional capital to investors, including ANG and all the small shareholders who decided to support him. Life would flourish. Maybe even Luke Terry himself would come around.

'Richard, in your considered view, is the proposal before the board today likely to result in a rise of the share price?'

Wander's brows were drawn together, seemingly in concentration, but he seemed displeased. He was silent, and his face gradually reddened. 'Chairman, it's impossible to know. Mr Ring is asking the board to accept the extraordinary risk that the average ZettaData shareholder will understand this proposal and recognise that it is in their interests.'

'Is it in their interests, Richard?' asked O'Toole sharply. Wander was not only being condescending about the acumen of ordinary shareholders, he was subtlely reminding the board they had hoodwinked shareholders before on several major occasions. That is what apparently enflamed O'Toole.

Wander paused and regarded O'Toole for several beats with his intimidating gaze. 'It may be for some. I can't speak to the interests of all shareholders,' he said coldly.

'But if they do understand their own interests, Richard, for the most part they're likely to support the rights issue?'

'If it's not too complicated for them to understand, yes.'

O'Toole had had enough. 'This proposal seems simple to me, compared to some of the schemes you've presented us for approval over the years, Richard.'

Wander didn't like that. He stared at the wall across from where he sat.

'Well, it's not like we haven't heard plenty of criticism already from the press and social media,' said O'Toole. 'And I suppose the process of a rights issue is better than just agreeing a deal with the banks as a *fait accompli*.'

There, it was – out on the table. There was no way to suppress the public shareholder debate that was coming – no matter what they decided to do – and doing Max's fair deal that could stand on its own merits in public discussion, was better than forcing through an expropriation of the poor and the weak just because the system permitted it.

The one woman director and the men gazed at each other as their minds calibrated, and then the Chairman, confident that he had assessed the will of the board, nodded. 'Yes, giving shareholders one last choice is much better, Bernice,' said Chairman Telford. 'I've got to think so.'

For Max, suddenly everything seemed especially satisfying. He was no different from Grimson, O'Toole or the rest of them – there had been many times he had failed the test presented by events. So many times as Mort's partner his fault had been that of Sir Perceval in the legend of the Holy Grail: he had failed to speak out.

Like him, Grimson and O'Toole's tests probably appeared suddenly, and out of surprise and fear they'd done the easy, wrong thing. He understood.

Max realised that he was smiling towards everyone—the directors, Company Secretary Leonard Whyte, who was scribbling away with a harried expression—and even Richard Wander, whose face had settled into an indifferent scowl.

This time *kairos* had appeared and drawn him into the future without him becoming aware of the choice. It wasn't the same as the way he felt when he stood up at the AGM and intervened in Mort's plan to destroy the company, but it felt more like it than his obsessive Phil Garlick-haunted sensation of facing *kairos*.

Max suddenly felt a premonition that this quiet, diplomatic discussion amongst the directors of a small, financially weak company was possibly invoking a form of fertile emptiness that was both creative and destructive: this calm discussion might prove to be the eye of a great national storm.

'Hmmm,' O'Toole grumbled enigmatically.

Telford glanced around the table. 'Well, have we heard enough? Is there anything else we should ask Mr Ring?'

There were nods around the table, and the tension seemed to go out of the room.

'On behalf of this board,' said Chairman Telford in his deep drawl, 'I thank you for your time, Mr Ring.'

Chapter 33

'You also like the window?' Max asked Peggy, realising she was stepping into it even though he had the window seat. 'Please, take it.'

'Thank you, I will.'

They were headed up to Byron Bay for two days, and Max quickly stowed their small bags in the compartment and settled himself into the aisle seat. He had told Ilona he was going to Melbourne on business. He had always been able to compartmentalise his affair with Claudia, recognising in a detached way his own capacity for dualism, but the lies he told Ilona about this trip troubled him. He was becoming aware of a yearning for a way out of the tangle of lies his life had become.

The morning sun shimmered on Botany Bay as the aircraft taxied. Peggy untangled her earbuds from her phone and flicked through the playlist.

Peggy turned to Max. 'Have you ever heard Sigur Rós?'

Max turned his head to look at Peggy's beautiful face, lit by the warm glow from the window. Max smiled and shook his head.

Their lips were centimetres apart.

Peggy put one ear bud in Max's left ear and the other bud in her own. Max closed his eyes, shocked and deeply satisfied by her intimacy. A Bach-like organ started to play, morphed into a piano playing something that sounded like Chopin, and was then joined by a high, ethereal voice.

'Love it,' he murmured. 'What is it?'

Peggy turned to him with a happy smile. 'It's 'Vaka', one of my favourites.'

'This would make a great soundtrack to lots of things.'

'I just like listening to it myself,' Peggy said sleepily.

'Nice,' Max murmured.

He wondered if Peggy played Sigur Rós when she was having sex. He hoped so.

As the aircraft began to rumble down the runway Peggy said 'Try this.'

They listened to another piece of aethereal music as their stomachs dropped lightly, and then there was air under the wheels as they soared into the sky.

Max was entranced. 'What is this?'

Peggy looked at him dreamily. 'It's 'Njósnavelín.'

For that matter, what kind of trip was this? What did he want it to be?

Max had paid for the tickets and the rental car, fully intending to cover all expenses in Byron Bay, and they were staying at Peggy's mother's house—in separate rooms.

The plane levelled off and they tracked the coast of New South Wales on the way north. 'So how do I know you're not setting me up?" Max asked.

'You mean, using my seductive arts to lure you into bailing out mum?'

'Exactly.'

'How do I know you're not trying to get into my pants?'

'You don't,' said Max. 'Neither do I, for that matter.'

Peggy laughed. 'I had no idea what you were doing when we stopped at the cemetery. Are you saying I set that up?'

'No, of course not, it was all my idea.'

'And I only told about the lawsuit over Hugh's body when we were standing right in front of the tomb daddy's building. Which I tried to avoid but you kept drawing me towards.'

'All true.'

'And you spontaneously offered to fund the lawsuit.'

'Yes, I suppose that's all true.' Max smiled. 'But you're Mort's daughter, not just an improbably pretty face, and I give you all kinds of credit for possibly being a step ahead of me.'

Peggy laughed. 'Mum is much brighter than dad. Dad has low cunning in abundance, and a naturally aggressive approach to life that's worked out very well—for him. But mum is head and shoulders above dad."

'So, why did she start a duck farm? That's an interesting choice of business.'

'I don't know where she came up with the idea,' Peggy said. 'But it has worked out. Now she supplies the best restaurants in Australia.'

'Ok, I'm convinced,' said Max. 'I'll relax now and trustingly put myself in your hands.'

'Right decision.'

'Is this where I say something utterly convincing that proves to you I don't want to get in your pants?' asked Max.

Peggy settled into her seat. 'Sure, I can't wait.'

'I can't think of anything,' said Max. He wasn't absolutely sure he meant what he was saying but he was having fun.

'So, how are things with you and Claudia?'

Max smiled. He wasn't going to let Peggy make him uncomfortable about the fact Claudia was discussing their affair, at least with Peggy and perhaps with the rest of the cast and crew. 'They're great.'

'Yeah? I saw her a lot this week.'

Was that a vague threat? While Claudia would probably feel awkward approaching Ilona or Mort, nothing could be more natural for Peggy.

'Are you two serious?'

'What do you think?'

'I don't know.'

A game of cat and mouse—or was Peggy revealing genuine interest in him. Did he want that? At some level, of course he did. 'Do you think a twenty-five-year-old actor is going to be serious about somebody like me?'

'I don't know. It depends.'

'I doubt it,' Max said. 'And she's very talented—I can't imagine her putting her career on hold for me. Being in a committed relationship with me, or anybody else, would reduce her options at this point.'

'That seems a bit cynical.'

'Why don't you ask her?'

'It's not my place. Why don't you ask her, Max?'

'I'd be stunned if Claudia really sees me as her life partner.'

'Do you know that?'

'Do you know something I don't?'

Peggy shook her head. 'And you're ok with that?'

'Sure – why not?'

'You don't feel any … confusion, or tension, about being married, and in a relationship with Claudia?'

Max sighed and leaned back in his seat. 'This is going to sound self-serving, I know, but when my children were born I learned something about love I hadn't realised before. When Sam was born, she was this brand-new person who had never lived before, and the moment I saw her arrive in this world I loved her with all my heart. I didn't think I could ever love anybody else as much, and it worried me when we talked about having a second child. But when Billie was born I loved her too, with all my heart, and there was no lessening in my love for Sam, no need to ration my love in any way. My time—yes; my energy—yes. But not my ability to love both Sam and Billie. My capacity for love expanded each time, and I'm sure if we'd continue to have children, my capacity would continue to grow.'

Max looked at Peggy. 'Since returning to Sydney after those years in London, I've run into women I used to go out with before I left for New York and London. Some of those relationships weren't that great, often it was my fault and most of them ended fairly badly. But what I found out when I ran into these women again was that the love was still there, living and fresh. The old issues and hurts had faded away, but still there was something alive.'

'Love,' said Peggy softly.

'Yes, that's what I realised,' said Max.

'So did you re-start those relationships?'

'Not romantically,' Max said. 'And some felt awkward because they were married and didn't want their husbands to be jealous.'

'Sure.'

'So they didn't want us to continue to see one another, but for the most part, it was just an opportunity to meet again as loving friends, who really care for one another, and don't have any agenda. I am glad they have husbands and children and great lives.'

'And you have a wife.'

'Well, as you can imagine I've compared my love for my daughters, and for women with whom I was once in a relationship, with how I feel about Ilona. Is our marriage still alive? I think the living energy of love must be there, because that's what I've found to be true about every other relationship I've been in. Even tough ones. I think Ilona and I still love each other, but to be honest with you, I really struggle to see it these days. I wonder how Ilona really feels about me and our marriage.'

'Have you ever asked her?'

'Have you ever been married?'

'No.'

'That's why you think I'd get a straight answer,' smiled Max.

Peggy smiled, put her earbud back in, and gently put the other into Max's ear. Together they listened to more Sigur Rós as Max inhaled the fragrance of her hair and skin, considering what had been said to him.

Preparations for landing at Ballina began soon afterwards, and Peggy chose another Sigur Rós song for their landing. Max watched the flat, lush fields of the shire wheeling under the window as the music soared. Listening to the song with Peggy as they flew through the air, Max felt at peace for the first time he could remember. Temporarily.

After picking up the rental car at the tiny airport, they were on their way through the flat open country towards the coast and Byron Bay. The climate was perceptibly more tropical than Sydney, and if anything, the sunlight was even brighter. Peggy seemed subdued as Max drove, and said very little. Max wasn't in the best mood either. He had been aware, while he was doing every little thing necessary to get them from the plane into the car – taking out his credit card, signing the rental papers, picking up their bags, opening the boot – that hidden motives could be undermining everything he was doing. That was apart from the fact he'd lied to Ilona about where he was. A depressing feeling settled on him and he began to think the whole expedition was fundamentally compromised, and probably a big mistake.

When they got to Byron Bay, Peggy asked Max to stop and park on Bay Street. 'Mum's a tea drinker,' she explained, and she led him to a little organic shop where they stocked up on ground coffee, and basic coffee-making equipment. Then they wandered down the street and stopped in at an organic food store where Peggy knew the proprietor, and bought some soaps, shampoo and conditioner. 'I never know what weird stuff mum's using.' Peggy laughed. 'I just like to get something basic for myself, to be safe. Sometimes mum has found something amazing, but often she's using products that don't suit me at all.'

The extra shopping was harmless, but it reminded Max that Peggy, despite her Byron Bay hippy, love-the-world side, had also grown up as an attractive Sydney private school girl from a privileged family. She was well-travelled, sophisticated and smart. How pure were her motives? Why was she seeing him, and why did she invite him to Byron? What secrets was she hiding?

They got back in the car and worked their way through the usual Byron traffic. Following Peggy's directions, Max took them along and past streets named after literary men and poets: Carlyle, Ruskin, Cowper, Tennyson, and Burns, and finally Gordon, named after George Gordon, Lord Byron. Byron Bay itself wasn't named after a poet, nor was

Skinner's Shoot Road, which they turned onto next. After ten minutes they pulled off the road, drove through a gate under a stand of trees, and then followed a dirt road for half a kilometre through paddocks and outcroppings of tall grass, until they approached a tranquil copse of trees surrounded by a garden, with farm equipment parked neatly on the left and, in the middle, a modest house with a broad wrap-around verandah that cast a deep shade in the blinding sunlight.

The barking began as the car passed through a fence line that defined the garden from the surrounding bush. Two big Kelpies burst around the side of the house and began running around the car in rapid circles, prancing and bucking at the windows.

'Ooh, it's Angel and Bernie, my babies!' said Peggy, holding out her hand through the open window.

As soon as the dogs recognised Peggy, their canine Wagnerian chorus became eager and delighted, and by the time the wheels slowed under the crunching gravel and Max brought the car to a stop, the dogs sounded pleading and frantic. Peggy flung her door open and kneeled down, and the dogs ran into her arms as she kissed them and held them, letting them cover her hair and clothes with dust and mud.

Max unloaded the car in the heat, ignored by Peggy and the dogs. As he carried their bags up the steps of the verandah the screen door opened. An attractive woman in her fifties, a few centimetres shorter than her daughter, with a Scots-Irish complexion, high cheekbones and auburn hair stepped into the hot shade of the verandah.

'Hello,' she said, shaking Max's hand with a firm, dry grip. 'Welcome. I'm Tori.'

'Max. Thanks for having me.'

'Of course,' Tori nodded and descended the steps.

Max dropped the bags next to some wicker furniture and followed Tori down the steps again to where Peggy was still kneeling in the gravel and dirt, having caught one of the dogs by its great furry face and neck. She was pressing her smooth cheek into the dog's jowls, her eyes closed and a blissful expression on her face.

'Hello, darling,' Tori said, a mixture of affection and disapproval on her face.

Peggy got up and flung her muddy arms around her mother, who recoiled slightly with a tight smile. 'Hello, mum! Thanks for having us!'

'Of course, darling.'

Tori showed them inside, taking them down a central hallway with a high ceiling, onto which large, gracious rooms, dim and breezy with big French doors, opened onto the hallway. If being her former husband's partner had made Tori suspicious or curious, or felt either grateful or awkward about this offer of financial support, her dignified, circumspect Australian reserve prevented any sign of it.

Above the doors were panes of coloured glass, and their blues, green, purples and reds seemed dark and mysterious in the dim light after the glaring sunlight outside. Tori led them to their rooms and Max unpacked and made several phone calls, the final and most important to Richard Wander, who told him the board was still considering his proposal and it was too early to even come back to Max with any questions they might have.

He walked down the hall into the beautiful, large living room with a gorgeous old Persian carpet and elegant British furniture that was neither dark nor heavy, somehow perfectly adapted to the tropical climate of Byron Bay. Peggy was sitting on a sofa talking to her mother; she had brushed the dust and dog hair out of her own hair, tied it back in a sloppy bun, and changed from her muddied top into a long-sleeved, pastel green linen shirt and faded jeans.

Tori stood up. 'Max, I'd like to thank you for your incredible generosity,' she said, quietly but firmly, taking his hand in her hands. 'But we can't accept.'

Max coloured. 'What do you mean? Of course you can.'

Tori continued to hold his hand in hers. 'If my former husband were to find out you were funding our legal expenses, there's no telling what he might do.'

Max gently extracted his hand and placed it protectively on her shoulder. He liked the way these Norton women touched other people. 'You mean, do to you?'

'Oh, possibly,' said Tori. 'But we're most concerned about what he might do to you.'

Max laughed. 'Don't worry about it.'

'Max, you have no idea,' Tori said. 'There are people no longer on this Earth because of him.'

'Are you saying Mort killed people?' He could see the fear, and also the kindness and concern, in Tori's hazel-coloured eyes, a distinctly different shade than Peggy's which were more blue than green.

Tori nodded.

'How long ago?'

'I don't want to talk about it. Early in our marriage.'

Max smiled. 'He'd better bring help if he tries it these days.'

Tori reminded Max of Susan Casner with her presence, the keen, intelligent way she focused on him, and, as aware as she was of her own predicament, her concern for others.

'He can do that, Max. Easily.'

Mort was in his sixties. He was on the board of the Nightingale School and half-a-dozen others, and he and his wife wanted to become members of the Royal Sydney Golf Club. There was no way he'd put all that at risk. Besides, Max had no intention of letting Tori, still being victimised by Mort, remain vulnerable.

'Listen, Tori, these days Mort has too much to lose to act the way you remember. He fights in the financial markets and the courts now, and I'm going to take the fight to Mort. I'll get my mate Robert Henninger on the case. He's as smart as anyone at Allaway, Davis and if there's any way to win this, Bob will know what it is.'

He wasn't about to be intimidated by the fears of these gentle women – much less their submissive strategies for coping with Mortimer Norton. Max was getting angry.

'Bob's going to take your case, and I'll pay him, and that will be that. How can Mort find out who's paying Bob? And besides, I don't care if he does. I really don't.'

Tori's eyes teared up. Max glanced over her shoulder at Peggy and back again at Tori.

'I couldn't bear for something awful to happen to you,' Tori said.

'Nothing's going to happen to me,' Max said. 'Mort can't operate the way he did back in the day.'

'How can you be so sure?'

'I'm sure.'

'Really?'

'Really.'

Tori was fighting hard now to retain her reserve. Her eyes were watery and her fair complexion was flushed.

'Thank you so much,' she said softly.

'No worries,' Max said. 'I'm so glad to be able to do something.'

'But what a terrible hostess I am! Would you like some lunch?' Tori asked, turning and looking at Peggy as well as Max.

'I think we're fine, Mum – I thought we'd go look at the ducks,' Peggy said, standing up. 'Perhaps we'll have a bite to eat later.'

Max grinned. 'Are we going to want to have duck afterwards?'

'Sure,' said Peggy. 'Why not?'

'Bismarck said, "One should not inquire too closely into the making of laws or sausages." I just wondered whether ducks might be the same.'

'You decide.'

Peggy showed Max out the side door and to the small barn and equipment shed, where a powerful-looking ATV with two seats and a roll bar was parked. 'Would you like to drive?' Peggy asked.

'Absolutely!'

'I thought so.'

Max took off down the dusty track, its course gnarled into what had been muddy ground and enjoyed gunning the loose, stretchy suspension and grippy, nobbled tyres as they flew down the hardened gyrus, Peggy gripping one upright with a strong, relaxed hand. The dogs managed to keep up while barking enthusiastically.

They blasted through the shimmering heat until they approached a dip that had turned into a deep, muddy wallow of brown-green water of uncertain depth. Max looked at Peggy and raised an eyebrow. Peggy nodded.

Max gunned the engine and smashed into the water's surface, the chassis twisting in the liquid and then snapping back on the vector Max was steering as a great sheet of scummy water exploded on both sides and boiled up through the chassis. The dogs were totally drenched and Max and Peggy were soaked half way up their shirts. Laughing, they continued through the trees until they came to a fence line.

'This is it,' Peggy said.

They got out and the dogs arrived, silent, with their tongues hanging out. Max was looking out at hectares of chest-high fences that penned in hundreds of ducks. The ammonia smell of duck excrement hit him on the wave of heat just as both dogs braced where they were standing and violently shook themselves, sending a geyser of pond water, warmed by dog fur, showering onto Max and Peggy.

They wiped their faces with their shirtsleeves and then Peggy showed Max through the gate, carefully keeping the dogs on the other side, where they ran along the fence barking. Max had noticed Peggy was wearing Blundstones and he was glad he'd brought his pair, too. They were equal to anything as long as it wasn't more than ankle deep.

'What kind of ducks did you say these are?'

'All ducks descend from the common wild duck. Mum breeds Pekins and Muscovys.'

Hundreds of white ducks with patches of red skin around their eyes and across their prawn-coloured bills walked around in the slimy mud, mostly in groups as small as two and as large as eight or ten. Their pale webbed feet were somehow pristine despite the mud.

The ducks seemed highly social; it looked like a Nightingale parents' cocktail party.

'What are the males and females called?'

'The male wild duck is called a mallard. But males in the domesticated species are called drakes. Females are called ducks – as if they're the essential duck.'

The smell was overpowering in the heat, a shocking contrast to the elegant, civilised home where Tori lived. 'Does your mum come here often?' Max asked.

'Oh yes, every day,' said Peggy. 'She has help, but she supervises and does a lot of work herself.'

Max stepped around the little green coils of duck faeces. Apart from its rural location and Tori's strong grip when they shook hands, there was nothing in her elegant home that had prepared Max for Tori's earthy qualities. He looked around, wondering whether there was some sort of clue here to Tori's attraction to Mort – and to the still-hidden part of Peggy she had in common with her father.

A sudden burst of wings erupted to one side, accompanied by hissing and guttural squawking, as two ducks launched into a full-on fight. Max and Peggy stopped and watched them bite and beat their wings against each other, until one duck, who looked no different except that he was almost fifty percent bigger than the other, lunged forward, bumping into the other duck and, slipping through its opponent's vicious wings, knocked the smaller duck into the filthy mud. Instantly the big duck was on top of the downed duck and covered it with its own body, hemming it in with its wings.

The top duck began moving rhythmically while the bottom duck lay grimly, eyes open, bill in the mud.

'Is that a male and a female?' Max asked, appalled.

'Yep, that's duck sex,' said Peggy. The male duck periodically nipped at the neck of the female duck in what looked like retribution. 'The erotic male is not politically correct,' said Peggy.

'This guy could give us all a bad name,' said Max.

'Now do you understand why I wasn't worried about that mother duck getting her ducklings safely through that flock of seagulls?' Peggy asked as they watched the mating.

'Sure—now that I can see what she'd gone through to conceive those ducklings in the first place.' Max watched the female duck being subjected to the steadily increasing tempo of pounding, her bill sliding back and forth in the mud, slowly blinking her eyes.

'Makes you wonder how there are any ducks,' Max said.

Peggy must have seen it countless times. 'Ducks can't stop drakes who behave like that,' she agreed. 'But having said that, they've evolved an ingenious way to thwart those drakes who do it.'

The duck lay under the drake, resigned, without seeming to interfere with him in any way.

'What could she possibly do?' asked Max.

Peggy pointed around the vast pen. 'Look around,' she said. 'See how the ducks and drakes are getting along?'

Max looked up, confirming his earlier impression of a Nightingale School cocktail party.

'It seems relaxed, doesn't it?' asked Peggy. She pointed. 'And when the males and females have disputes, it seems kind of balanced, doesn't it?'

A few metres away two smaller ducks had arched their necks, and were flapping their wings and hissing at a big duck, who turned and waddled away. 'There's two female ducks intimidating a drake.'

Peggy swept her arm across the vast pen. 'For the most part, ducks and drakes live in harmony.'

Max could see pairs everywhere, grooming one another or quacking quietly, and groups of ducks waddled quietly through the pen, seemingly unconcerned and showing no signs of being stalked by drakes.

'Even though it's not what most drakes do, this happens all the time,' said Peggy, indicating the brutal male in front of them. 'But ducks have evolved a special way of responding to violent drakes.'

'I'll bet I know – they forgive them,' said Max.

'No, not exactly.' Peggy reddened to her hair line, but her expression remained calm. 'But consider this – only about five percent of coerced matings produce offspring, in comparison to matings in which the females cooperate – those impregnate the duck about half the time.'

'Is that right!' said Max. He looked around again at the hundreds of ducks, male and female, interacting peacefully in the pen. 'How do they accomplish that?'

Peggy held up one hand with her fingers and thumb together. 'Female ducks have evolved a multi-chambered vagina, and only one chamber leads to their uterus. Without the cooperation of the female duck, the male duck is likely to be rooting her in the wrong chamber.'

Max stared at Peggy's hand and then looked back down at the mating ducks, still grimly going at it. 'You're kidding me.'

'No, I'm not,' Peggy said.

'That's genetic war!'

'It's evolution. Female ducks guide the evolution of their species through their mating preferences. Their preferences for their mates shape the evolutionary path as females breed with males whom they find attractive. Everything from the appearance of males, with their colourful plumage, even to their own anatomy, seems to result from female preferences.'

'So female ducks are gradually breeding the offspring of rapists out of the species,' said Max.

'Right,' said Peggy. 'But it's not a simple process.'

'It never is, when sex is involved,' said Max. 'Even duck sex.'

'Something must have gone wrong in the evolution of Pekin and Muscovy ducks. Their evolutionary path has degenerated into violent confrontation between males and females, and other ducks aren't like that. But these female Pekins and Muscovys demonstrate to all of us we don't have to give up when we find ourselves in a seemingly impossible situation – as painful, humiliating, and violent as it may be – even if we seem to be temporarily defeated.'

Peggy gave him a dubious smile as the mating session at their feet continued. 'She couldn't stop him – but she's probably going to succeed in preventing him from reproducing any offspring with her. His line will finish. She'll win in the long run.'

'Makes me want to give him a kick,' said Max.

Peggy shook her head. 'You might hurt her.'

Max nodded.

'By the way, the drakes are evolving too, you know,' said Peggy. 'The sexual conflict between the males and the females shapes both. In response to the evolution of the females, the male ducks have evolved a penis shaped like a fly fishing rod, the better to probe the female's vagina.'

'Really?'

'Really,' said Peggy.

'It's hard to believe bodies morph that way,' said Max.

The pair in front of them were beginning to decouple, and the male backed up and started to wobble away on uncertain webbed feet. The female waited until he had left her proximity, then rose to her full height and began shuddering and beating her wings violently, stretching out her neck and opening and closing her bill silently, as if cursing her tormentor.

'That one's spent,' said Peggy. 'Do you see why I don't like hearing about evolution as an excuse for bad behaviour by humans?'

'Oh sure,' said Max, shuddering.

'Well, you told me at Redleaf Pool the financial markets are Darwinian,' Peggy said. 'That's what my father says, too.'

'We just call it like it is,' Max said. 'I haven't seen anything just now that disproves it – on the contrary.'

Peggy looked at him. 'Let's find another male.'

'A kinder, gentler male?'

'We'll see,' said Peggy. 'I'll fluff him for you.'

'You don't mean ...'

'Come on.' Peggy strode towards a group of ducks and waved over her shoulder for Max to follow. She pointed silently to a large male duck surrounded by seemingly tranquil female ducks. Then she quickly stepped up and threw her arms around his wings.

Immediately the male duck started hissing and flapping his wings as the females scattered. Peggy's grip slipped as one of the duck's wings swung free and she fell to her knees in the mud in order to smother him with her weight. The male duck fought hard, his powerful wing battering Peggy's face and neck.

Max ran up, gripped the free wing and enveloped the male from behind with his other arm. He and Peggy were folded together, her shoulder in his stomach, and for a few seconds the male duck in his fury beat them emphatically with his wings. It felt like being hit on the arms and face by a tennis racket, and the duck had sharp little claws concealed in the feathers that cut Max's hands and arms.

Already, after only seconds of struggle, Peggy had several scratches and a splotch of duck shit on her forehead. After the paroxysm of anger, the duck's strength subsided and the two of them were able to bring their weight and strength to bear down, furling the metre-and-a-half wing span tightly again the duck's body. Why was Peggy doing this? Max caught his breath and crouched in the mud, trying not to lose his balance and fall back into the goo.

'Got him,' Peggy said. 'I'm ok now, thanks.'

Panting, she rose one leg at a time, holding the duck in a tight embrace with both arms. Max had let his arms slip away from the duck and Peggy now turned towards him, holding the duck. 'You and my father operate in the financial markets, which are almost entirely determined by human factors, and yet you justify your selfish behaviour by claiming it's somehow inevitable because of evolution. There's nothing inevitable about it: markets express collective human choices, not fundamental physical laws.'

'Fear and greed move markets,' said Max. 'Those are fundamental forces.'

Peggy shook her head impatiently. 'They're choices. Evolution produces beauty and increasingly complex beings, and its main mechanism is love and affection – including most kinds of sex. We can choose to change from being motivated by fear and greed to being inspired by love for others.'

'Are you saying you have no more agency than a duck?' she asked, as one arm gently slid down the duck's body and her hand disappeared between his legs. 'Ducks have more limited choices than humans, not the other way around. That should be obvious to a smart guy like you.'

Max watched for about a minute until suddenly the long wand of the duck's penis snapped into the air directly in front of him, pale and urgent as Peggy watched Max with the same feline look in her eyes he'd seen in Mort's. A spurting spray of semen flew at him and splattered against his shirt, neck and chin.

Peggy opened her arms and let the duck drop back into the mud and waddle away, bewildered, disgruntled, but sated. 'Don't think I'm not grateful you're being so generous to mum. But make sure you act like a man, not a mallard.'

Peggy looked at him expressionlessly.

'That's incredible!' Max exclaimed, wiping semen off his face with the side of his hand.

Max reached into the back pocket of his jeans and pulled out a handkerchief. It was a huge call for Peggy to treat him like this when he had made his offer to save her mother's farm—which he could withdraw any time he chose to do so. He was also her only chance of obtaining her brother's body. She had put everything she cared about on the line.

'Irish linen,' Max said, flourishing open its generous folds. A huge respect for Peggy's bold integrity was welling inside him. He realised he could completely trust her. He wiped his chin again, and along his neck and jaw, then his fingers, and did his best about his splattered shirt. He started laughing. 'If I'd known we were going to have this much fun, I'd have brought two of these.'

Max watched Peggy's eyes become human again. She smiled, took the handkerchief from Max's fingers, and finished cleaning him. Peggy put one hand on his chest, right on his heart, while with the other hand she scrubbed him with the handkerchief, studying him intently. Peggy frowned, put her finger in her mouth to wet it, and scrubbed at a couple of patches on his face. Then she nodded and smiled.

'All done.'

Peggy gave Max his handkerchief.

'Thanks.' Max flicked the soiled linen in the air and folded it up, returning it to his back pocket. 'Do you mind if I do laundry tonight?'

'Of course,' Peggy laughed. 'That was cheeky of me.'

Peggy leaned towards him as she said it, and spontaneously he kissed her gently but lingeringly.

Her eyes closed and then tenderly, furtively, he felt the faintest beginning of a response. Peggy abruptly pulled away. They looked at each other, their eyes centimetres apart.

'What you did with that drake was unbelievable,' said Max.

Peggy smiled. 'It's certainly got wow factor.'

Chapter 34

Tori had prepared steamed and raw squash, pickled eggplant, and couscous along with homemade tofu, radishes, oyster mushroom, mushroom broth, and a big garden salad. No duck.

Max and Peggy set the table, and when they all sat down and the savoury-smelling food was served on their plates, Max waited expectantly for Tori to offer a toast or say *Bon appetit*.

Instead, Tori and Peggy held hands, Peggy took one of Max's hands, and to his astonishment they bowed their heads while Tori said a simple thanks for the food, the day, and for Max's visit.

Peggy released Max's hand while he tried to conceal his confusion. Mort's family saying a prayer!

Peggy smiled at Max's expression.

'We started this when Peggy had bulimia,' said Tori. 'To help her recover.'

'I couldn't actually metabolise food very well because I'd been bulimic for so long,' Peggy explained. 'I had to take my body out of survival mode to get the adrenaline and cortisol out of my system. In the lead-up to every meal, I'd flood my body with these hormones, and they blocked my digestion. When mum began praying before every meal, it helped put my body into gratitude, which re-set my neural and immune systems. They switched out of survival mode and allowed my body to metabolise food.'

'I'll bet Mort loved that,' said Max.

'That was the least of the issues, at that point,' Tori shrugged. 'Besides, what's a mum meant to do? She always has to try to help the weakest. Back then, Peggy seemed weakest.' She and Peggy looked sadly at each other. 'At the time, Hugh seemed fine.'

Apparently to change the subject, Tori asked Max what he thought of the ducks.

'I still can't believe it,' Max said. 'How did you get involved?'

Tori smiled. 'I've been interested since I was a little girl, and an aunt had a farm with chickens and ducks and geese.'

'But how can you preside over what the drakes do to the females? I think I'd cook all the drakes who acted like that.'

'It's a good question,' said Tori. 'We don't have to accept life the way we find it,' Tori said. 'Watching Peggy's heroic and successful recovery from her eating disorder, and extricating myself from my marriage, taught me we can try things that seem impossible and actually figure out how to do them.'

'What's going on in your duck flock is full-on,' said Max.

'I'm making a difference with my flock – a small difference – but a positive one,' said Tori. 'I've found that introducing more female ducks cuts the violence a lot, because it reduces competition amongst the males. I'm actively cooperating with the female ducks to more rapidly breed the genes of the violent males out of the flock. Violent couplings only produce offspring five percent of the time, while cooperative couplings produce offspring ten times more frequently. It's my mission to breed as many gentle Muscovy and Pekins as I can.'

'Are you trying to affect the course of evolution?' Max asked.

'It's a long shot, I know,' said Tori.

Max thought about the female duck flattened in the mud, her bill moving back and forth in the slime, her eyes blinking stoically. 'It's certainly pretty slow. How can you tolerate the suffering of the females instead of intervening more actively?'

'I'm not sure a quick fix would work, and I find it inspiring that although female ducks do try to defend themselves, often successfully, violence isn't the fundamental response of the females.'

'The way they've evolved to handle rogue drakes is so crazy it's hard to believe –and totally ingenious,' said Max.

'Isn't it amazing? The thing is, Pekins and Muscovys didn't evolve into chickens. They're not dimwitted little domestic birds. The reason I don't want to interfere too strongly in evolution is because we can't possibly understand the deep logic unfolding through the preferences of female ducks.'

'You—a human—are respectful of duck logic?' asked Max.

'Yes, and with good reason: duck evolution has produced a kind of super-bird. Ducks aren't nearly as big as geese but they have comparable range. They're incredibly hardy. They're also very fast: they can fly a hundred kilometres an hour.'

Peggy smiled at Max.

'I like that,' said Max.

'Let your inner duck come out,' smiled Peggy.

'I never thought I'd aspire to be a good drake,' said Max. 'Perhaps it would be an improvement.'

'And not all duck sex is bad,' said Tori. 'In fact, bird sex as a whole is very peaceful. I'm trying to nudge the Muscovys and Pekins back towards the main line of duck and bird evolution. Non-violently. Using love to empower love.'

'You mean sex,' said Max.

'Not only sex, I also mean love. Observation doesn't tell us that evolution is about the stronger killing the weaker, and the faster killing the slower. Reptiles are great killing machines. If survival of the fittest really meant being the most efficient killers, evolution could have stopped with reptiles.

'We humans have become the world's greatest killers only because we think of ourselves that way. I don't think that's why we evolved our big brains.'

'Maybe not, but that's what plenty of people use them for,' said Max. 'The Americans, Russians and Chinese have enough nukes to take out our corner of the solar system. And look at all the countries building their own nukes.'

'If we have any hope of saving the planet, we have to commit to cooperation and kindness.'

'Good luck with that,' said Max.

'It already works – billions of times. I think of a mother breastfeeding her baby,' Tori said. 'We evolved our big brains in order to see one another's faces so we can interpret expressions and body language, and to develop speech. Why? So we cooperate socially. Killing doesn't need the kind of processing powers our brains have. Our challenge is to use our minds and hearts to influence evolution, not just accepting what we see in nature and using it to excuse ourselves. That's what I'm trying to do with my ducks, as small a difference as it may be.'

They all cleared the table and Max helped Tori wash up while Peggy dried the dishes. Tori invited them into the living room where they sat on the sofa and chairs arranged on the luminous Persian carpet, one of the vestiges of her old life with Mortimer in Sydney. Tori drank only half a glass of wine at dinner, the one discernibly un-Australian thing about her, but Peggy and Max not only finished off the bottle between them, but after what had happened that afternoon, Max had no intention of slowing down, and Peggy opened a second bottle before dinner was half over. Max brought their glasses and Peggy carried the remainder of the second bottle into the dining room.

The dogs stirred and started growling. Max heard the rumble of a diesel engine in low gear. Angel huffed her sides in and out like a bellow and let out a sharp bark as Bernie leaped to his feet and headed towards the hallway and front door, his head low.

'Who could that be?' Tori asked. She and Peggy both looked out the windows into the darkness and then at each other. Shortly they heard the crunch of gravel under slow-moving wheels.

The blue-white light of headlamps glared onto the wall behind them, and by now the dogs were baying in full chorus at the front door. Tori stood up and with Peggy and Max headed to the front door.

They stepped out onto the porch and as the dogs ploughed past them into the yard, they were illuminated by the glare of headlamps pointing straight at them from a ute that had pulled up halfway around the circular drive. A row of hunting lights on the ute flicked on, blinding them.

The dogs swirled around the cab, barking and snarling. The driver's door opened, and then the passenger door. A low command was given to the dogs who, to Max's shock, instantly went silent and came to heel. Three large, shadowy figures ambled out of the ute and stood in front of the headlamps, silhouetted from behind.

Max sized them up. The smallest was about the same build as he was, but a little thicker in the legs, and wore a battered Akubra. The shadows of the other two were even bigger and more powerful. The man on the right wore a cap, and the big man in the middle was hatless. He turned to look at Peggy, and from the light across the side of his face Max could see he was a handsome Aboriginal man. Because the dogs recognised the men Max assumed they were friends, neighbours, or farm workers.

'Charlie?' breathed Tori to Peggy.

Peggy nodded. Her face was stark white in the glare and she looked completely stunned. She hurriedly descended the stairs and stopped at the bottom.

'Hi, Charlie,' she said.

'Hi, Peggo,' said the largest of the three men. The ute's engine, running in neutral, seemed to pant quickly like a winded dog, the biggest one in the pack.

Tori crossed her arms nervously and pressed one closed hand against her chin.

'Is it all right?' Max murmured to Tori. Were they bringing a report of some accident – a broken fence or water line?

Tori looked at him with concern and shrugged almost imperceptibly.

'Why are you here, Charlie?' Peggy asked. Max could hear the strain in her voice over the ute's engine.

'I heard you was in town, darlin',' Charlie said.

'Yeah?' Peggy responded.

Whatever was going on, it didn't feel right. A neighbour or employee wouldn't have spoken to Peggy that way. Max couldn't tell how Peggy felt, but he sensed standing next to him that Tori was on the verge of panic. Max could dimly make out the dogs, lying watchfully beside the truck. For whatever reason, it didn't look like they would protect Peggy and Tori.

The men didn't seem particularly menacing, but they were totally in control.

The hands of the man who had spoken were empty – he could make out his individual fingers in the brilliant light – but perhaps the other two were armed. Whatever was going on, the Norton women were taken by surprise and overmatched.

Max walked down the stairs. The dogs pricked up their ears and cocked their heads at the sound of the wood creaking under his tread. He could see all three men now, but their expressions were unreadable. Max stood beside Peggy.

'How long you here for?' Charlie asked Peggy.

'Not long,' she said.

'Why didn't you tell me you was coming?'

'Why should I?'

Charlie shrugged. 'My bros and me broke into the morgue and got your brother. He's in back.'

Peggy's face went rigid and she took half a step back. Max turned and put his hand lightly on her shoulder.

From up on the porch, Tori said, her voice shocked, 'Hugh's body is in your ute?'

'Yeah.'

'What?' gasped Peggy.

'He belongs with you and your mum.'

'What do you want us to do with him?' cried Tori.

'Charlie, you can't do this!' Peggy rushed forward and began beating on Charlie's chest. 'You can't do this! You can't do this!' she cried wildly, throwing punches that really seemed intended to hurt him as her hair tossed in the light.

'Hey, Peggo, hey ...' Charlie said. He put an arm lightly around her shoulder and brought his other hand up to stifle the strikes from Peggy's free arm, but she twisted away and stepped back, weeping.

Here I am.

Max stepped forward. It looked like Charlie and Peggy had been – at the very least – childhood friends. Perhaps lovers. He put his arm around Peggy for a moment and then turned and put out his hand to Charlie.

'Hi,' he said. 'Max Ring.'

Charlie took Max's hand in his own and they shook.

'So, you and your mates broke into the morgue and took Hugh Norton's body?'

Charlie nodded. 'That's right.'

'How'd you do that?' Max asked.

'It was snack,' Charlie said. 'There was an old log splitter that was left out for a couple years on the Lyne property, so I just hooked it up to the ute, towed it to the morgue, put the ute into reverse, and used the log splitter to ram the door.'

'Nobody was there?'

'Nuh, only on Tuesdays and Thursdays, unless there's a new body.'

'Nobody saw you?'

'Nuh.'

Charlie, whoever he was, had committed a crime. Clearly Peggy and Tori knew him well. Unless they reported him immediately, they were all accomplices.

Max put out his hand to the big man in the cap. 'Max,' he said. 'How're you goin'?'

'Good,' said the man. 'Bobby.'

Max put out his hand to the man in the Akubra. 'How you going? Max.'

'George,' said the man, shaking his hand.

Max turned to Peggy, and looked up at Tori, who was still standing on the verandah. Wordlessly he spread his hands, and cocked his head thoughtfully before turning on his heel and facing the three men.

'Let's have a look,' Max said. He walked around the ute with the three men, their boots crunching on the gravel in the heavy silence, avoiding the dogs, who lay obediently but twitching uneasily. As soon as Max passed the cab he knew why: the sweet, putrid, black odour of death hung heavily over the ute. The four men walked to the back and Charlie dropped the back panel of the tray.

In the darkness, Max could make out a long, oddly flat-seeming body bag strapped to the tray, next to a rectangular object under a tarp.

Charlie and his three mates had thwarted Mort with a ute and an abandoned log splitter.

'Well done, mate,' said Max, putting his hand on Charlie's shoulder.

'He was my bro,' Charlie said simply.

There would be hell to pay if they didn't return the body. In a way, Charlie had done exactly what Mort had done with his teams of lawyers and hundreds of thousands of dollars: taken control of Hugh's body. But Mort had done it legally, and that made all the difference. If he got tangled up in this Max could be prosecuted, and if convicted he would lose his Financial Services Licence. He wouldn't be able to operate as an investment banker or funds manager. He wouldn't be able to take over ZettaData. Ilona was already upset with him – if he got involved in this she would definitely divorce him, and considering how he would be entangled with Tori and Peggy, Mort's ex-wife and daughter, the divorce would be vindictive, ugly and extremely expensive. He would lose most of his wealth – and his means of making a living. He could even be sentenced to prison.

Hugh's body, or ZettaData? A grisly crime – or his freedom, reputation, and marriage. After a long look at the body bag, Max walked back. He knew what he had to do.

Tori had come down the verandah steps and she and Peggy were standing together in one another's arms. Max walked up to them. 'What do you want to do?' he asked.

Peggy looked at Tori and then back at Max. He suddenly had the sensation that he and Peggy both had one ear bud each in their ears and were listening to the same music. She looked at her mother again and then at Max.

'I can't give him back,' she said. Yes, they were hearing the same song.

'Ok,' said Max. 'I'll help.'

He turned around and waved for Charlie, Bobby and George to join them.

'What do we do?' asked Tori.

'We have to bury him,' Max said gently to Tori and Peggy. There was no way to cremate the body.

'I want to see him,' Tori said. 'I never got to see him after Mort put the injunction in place.'

'He don't smell good,' Charlie said.

'He's my son.'

'All right,' said Charlie.

Max and Charlie walked to the back of the ute, let down the panel, and Max jumped up into the tray. Charlie helped Tori and Peggy position a foot on the tow bar and Max pulled them up by the hand one after the other. Charlie quickly climbed up into the tray. The half moon was high and shining down with a cold, blue light. The throbbing of the diesel engine sounded reassuring for some reason.

They stood in the tray of the ute looking down on the bag. Peggy and Tori were suddenly frozen.

'I'll do it,' Max said.

'Oh, Max,' Peggy said. She raised her hands to her face.

Max leaned forward and tugged the zipper, opening it as far as the chest of Hugh's body. A wave of sweet stench hit Max and he stood up quickly, exhaling in a burst and, turning his head over his shoulder, inhaling clean night air. Looking down, he could see pale features in the shadows of the open body, eyes closed, hair plastered across a white forehead, skin that looked like bone.

'Oh God,' Max said, shaking his head and stepping carefully back. Tori's and Peggy's faces were anguished in the moonlight, their bodies bent forward as if weighted by heavy burdens. Tori clasped her hands, and Peggy held Tori from behind, one hand on her mother's shoulder.

Max stood at the back of the tray with Charlie, whose face showed his compassion for the women.

'You're sure nobody saw you?' Max asked softly.

'Nuh,' said Charlie.

The odour of flesh and formaldehyde flowing back was overpowering, and Max had to keep his face lifted towards the sky.

The women stayed with Hugh's body far longer than Max expected. They made only the smallest animal sounds. At last, Tori straightened, and with her arm around Peggy she returned to the back of the ute. Max could see tears on her cheekbones in the moonlight. 'I don't want Hugh buried in that body bag,' said Tori softly. 'I'm going to get a sheet to wrap him.'

Max turned. 'I think this is a—' he tapped with his boot against the tarp, and there was a hollow sound. 'It's a coffin.'

'Still,' Tori said. 'Peg and I are going to wrap him in a sheet before we put him in it.'

Charlie jumped to the ground and he and Max helped the women down.

Max stood with Charlie, Bobby, and George until Tori and Peggy returned with white sheets and a wicker basket full of bottles of essential oils. 'I don't want to bury him on the property,' Tori said. 'I couldn't bear it.'

Charlie looked at George and Bobby. 'We can bury him with our people.'

'What do you mean?' asked Max.

'We got a cemetery. Hugh can go there. He's family.'

'Oh, Charlie!' said Peggy. 'Isn't it sacred to your nation? Do you need to ask the elders?'

Charlie looked at George and Bobby again and they nodded. 'It'll be ok.'

Peggy hugged Charlie, and he gently patted her back. 'He's my bro.'

Tears running down Peggy's cheeks.

So that was it – Charlie had been her brother's friend.

Charlie said the Aboriginal burial ground was about half an hour away.

Tori rode in the cab with Charlie and his friends and Max and Peggy sat on the tray in back next to Hugh's body, the bag zipped closed again.

Once the ute got to the main road and picked up speed, the perfumed tropical air snatched away the odour of putrefaction. Max sat with his arm around Peggy, and she curled into his side, although Peggy seemed to be trying to avoid Charlie seeing them seated so closely together in his mirror. They rode silently under the half moon, sitting in the rushing night breeze, until Charlie again pulled off the highway and went down a dirt road for ten kilometres under gum trees stretching across the sky above them and threw spangled patches of moonlight over Max, Peggy and Hugh's body.

When the ute came to a halt, Peggy quickly stood up. It took three hours to dig the grave, and Max did his share of the digging with pick axe and shovel. Charlie positioned the ute with the roo lights angled down to give the men light as they worked. As the hole got deeper and deeper, the smell of fresh earth and the darkness at his feet became increasingly oppressive to Max. Max had never felt so unready to die. It was a huge relief when Charlie or George reached down and pulled him back up in the cool night air, where the fragrance of the gum trees mingled with the smell of the earth.

Finally, the men carefully opened the bag and took out Hugh's body, cold, slippery and rigid. Tori and Peggy applied the oils over Hugh's face and torso and helped the men wrap him in the sheets.

George and Bobby retrieved the coffin from underneath the tarp and laid it on the ground. It was made of particle board with a simple lid that fit over it like a shoe box.

'It's all we could get without making a big deal,' said Charlie.

The four men carefully lifted Hugh's shrouded body and lowered it into the box and set the lid onto it.

Using straps from Charlie's ute, they lowered it into the grave. Max handed the straps back to Charlie and, stepping around the grave, walked to where Peggy and her mother stood by the large mound of dirt. He put his arm around Peggy.

She turned her face and rested her cheek against his neck.

In the deep shadows thrown by the glare of the ute's roo lights Max could only discern Charlie's outline, but Charlie had stopped, was standing still, and seemed to be contemplating Max and Peggy.

At last Charlie spoke. 'Ready?' he said softly.

Tori nodded. She sank her hands into the mound and scooped up a heaping double handful of dirt. 'God bless you, dear,' she said, and let soil drop through her fingers into the blackness of Hugo's grave.

Max flinched at the terrible hollow sound as the clods struck Hugo's coffin. The thuds and the immediate silence seemed so final, so beyond appeal. It was the same sound, the same chilling awareness of irrational, irreparable death he remembered from the hot, bright afternoon when his mother threw the first clods of earth onto his father's grave.

Max took a deep breath and plunged his hands into the mound of dirt that he and his new friends had piled up beside the profound darkness in the grave. Immersing his hands to above the wrists in the cold, gritty, resistant soil, gravel and stones, he almost willed the Earth to rend his fingernails and scour his skin, then, drawing out a huge double handful of soil with a hissing trail of falling dirt, Max turned, breathed out slowly, and let the earth fall into the darkness at his feet.

Max stepped aside, and wrestling with a swirl of emotions, he hardly noticed as the rest of the little group continued throwing in handfuls of dirt. Charlie handed Max a shovel and for half an hour as he, Charlie, Bobby and George steadily filled the hole his world shrank to the bite of its edge in the mound of earth and the sudden lift as he tilted it into the grave. They erected a small cairn of stones in the middle of the fresh earth, the sides of the stones glowing dully in patches of light as the setting moon hovered just above the western horizon.

As they drove back up the dirt road towards the highway, the moon disappeared below the horizon and in the darkness the bright cone of the ute's headlamps resolutely preceded them all the way home.

Chapter 35

M ort picked up his phone and punched in a number. 'Denis rang this afternoon,' he said as soon as the line clicked to life.

'That's never good news.'

Denis was Mort's old mate Dinny, the Deputy Police Chief these days, and the voice on the other end of the line belonged to Bobby Allenhurst. Bobby was one of the meanest cops who ever lived. He had been kicked off the force years ago, something that wasn't easy to achieve in New South Wales. Great bloke to his friends, savage to his enemies. A legend.

'Hugh's body is gone,' Mort told Bobby. 'Somebody broke into the morgue last night.'

'They took Hugh's body?'

'Yep.'

'Holy fuck.'

'Yep.'

'Did they take anything else? Vandalise the place?'

'Nope. Denis says the official line those boufheads in Byron are investigating is that it was some larrikins, a home invasion, a case of mistaken identity. A couple of ice addicts, or stoners. You never know, that's what the local bronze said.'

'Bullshit.'

'Stupid cunts. Anyways, Denis is dispatching a forensics team from Sydney to find whatever they can. But my guess is it'll be buckley's. They smashed the door with an old log splitter. The video camera didn't work. They were probably wearing gloves, whoever they were.'

'Weird deal.'

'Yeah, weird. But who wants the body?'

'You do.'

'Yeah, me and the ex. It's gotta be her. She's about to run out of money and so she came up with the damn-fool idea.'

'You really think she'd do something like this?'

'I dunno. Go find out.'

'Sure thing, Mort. But it seems like a bit of an intense card for her to play. She didn't strike me as that type, at all.'

'Well, who knows?'

'It's not the kind of thing a bird would dream up. Especially Tori.'

'I don't pay you for your opinions.'

'Right-eo. Got it.'

'By the way, I saw the rent hit the account over the weekend,' said Mort, referring to the lease of one his buildings on Broadway near the train station. It was only a small fraction of the total yield of that particular building, a small amount, but he still monitored all the debits and credits in his accounts daily. A Leb who ran the barbershop there was ninety days behind on his rent. He said his kid had started on ice and was stealing from the shop. Bobby and a couple of mates beat the shit out of the kid. 'Well done, Bobby.'

'No worries.'

Mort hung up. He scratched his forearm vigorously through the superfine wool of his coat and the crinkly starched sleeve of his Egyptian cotton shirt. It would have been good fun to slap the Leb punk around himself – how long had it been since he'd slammed some arsehole's head into a wall? He had to keep his distance from the action these days. He'd kicked himself upstairs.

He sat in the half-light, the heavy shades pulled down on both sides of his corner office to block out the blinding sunlight bathing the 57th floor. Now that he was a solid citizen he had to leave the action to others. It went against his grain, even now in his mid-sixties, but there was no help for it. All he could do was wait.

Chapter 36

P eggy knocked tentatively on Max's door.

'Yep?' Max said, rolling on his back in bed.

She stuck her head round the door. 'Mum's gone to yoga,' she said. 'Want to go surfing?'

'Sure,' said Max.

'I'll make you a coffee.'

He had seen a proper old-fashioned espresso machine last night on the bench in Tori's kitchen, and wondered if Mort had once used it. 'Can you make a macchiato?'

'No worries!'

'Awesome,' said Max. 'Thank you.'

Max lay thinking for a few moments about the previous night. There was more to the relationship between Charlie and Peggy than a bond through her brother. Tori's comments over dinner about evolution came back, was she mad?

Max got out of bed and dressed haphazardly.

Max found Peggy in the kitchen. His timing was perfect, she had just finished frothing the milk.

'Have you heard from Charlie?' Max asked.

'No, and I don't think I will,' she said.

'He and his mates really stuck their necks out for you guys.'

'You never know what Charlie is going to do.'

'That's not very generous,' said Max, taking a sip of the macchiato.

'Charlie and I went out, for a couple years.'

'Going to see him again before we go back to Sydney?' Max asked.

Peggy shook her head. 'Not unless the cops come and grab us all.'

'Let's hope not,' said Max. In the light of day, the risks they'd taken last night seemed hard to imagine.

Peggy led Max across the garden to the barn by the house. It was cool and dark and he smelled the odour of wood and leather and oiled steel mixed with the musky, almost animal smell of jacaranda blossoms through the open windows. He noticed Peggy's confidence as she moved through the midst of equipment and farm machinery and led him to a rack on the side wall which held less than a dozen surfboards.

'I think it's two or three metres at Main Beach,' said Peggy, reaching out to a pink five footer crusted in ancient wax. 'I've had this board since I was thirteen,' she said. She wrinkled her nose, then smiled. 'I love this board.'

'He had quite a diverse quiver,' Max said, inspecting everything from a long board almost nine feet long to a short board, hardly longer than a boogie board and without fins.

'He was always playing around,' Peggy said. 'Trying new things.'

Max picked out a 5' 10" Gunther Rohn, lifted it off its rack and balancing it on its tail, twirled it around by the tip with the fingers of one hand, gently brushing and tapping it in various places with his other hand in an exploratory way. It was strange to look at the green tether, which had been tied so many times around Hugh's leg, the cold, white, stiff limb he'd handled last night. These objects Hugh had loved and used so well in life spoke eloquently. The myriads of bumps of old wax had been individually applied by his fingers. Max contemplated the logic of the way Hugh had applied the wax to the stick and agreed with the way he did it.

'I'll take this one,' Max said, glancing at Peggy's board. 'They both need fresh wax.'

Peggy found a couple sets of sawhorses folded against the barn wall, and they set them up, lay the boards down, scraped off the old wax, and then re-applied fresh wax. Max worked respectfully, conscious he was removing a bit of evidence of Hugh's life as he scraped the wax off his board. When he re-applied fresh wax he emulated Hugh's logic.

They decided to forgo wet suits and loaded the boards in the back seat of the rental car. Max drove into Byron and parked in front of Main Beach.

He was glad to see Peggy's first genuinely happy smile as they walked across the sand, a breeze gently stirring the ends of her hair. The lighthouse was shining white against the blue sky to the south. Although it was close to full tide, the beach was still very wide. A rounded wave with a full base bulged out of the water and then began to break right, its edge clean and hardly affected by the breeze.

Peggy pointed to the left. 'I thought we'd surf The Wreck.'

'Let's do it.'

Max knew about The Wreck: the *Wollongbar* was a 2000 tonne ship that was caught in the sandbars during a big storm in 1921 and destroyed. Its hull rests a couple hundred metres from the shoreline, depending on the tides, and a sandbar has formed around it, creating one of the best surf breaks in Byron.

Peggy began to run into the surging white water, her slim ankles flashing as she kicked forward flat seashells of spray, knees high. As Peggy's strides reached deeper water that enveloped her thighs, she brought her board up and vaulted forward—landing on the board with perfect timing as it splashed into the swell.

The waves were breaking perfectly across The Wreck, peaking on the south, curling right and furling steadily along their length, generating a perfect pocket for a long, gentle surf. Peggy expertly piloted herself into the rip-tide, paddling quickly out the thirty metres or so that separated her from the next wave rising out of the chaos. As Max paddled easily behind her, he realised how he'd unconsciously allowed the shadow of Mort to shape how he thought of her. Out here on the water and in the bright air, he saw that Peggy was strong, eager for life, and full of joy.

A wave was rippling rapidly towards them, its steep flank gleaming in the sunlight as it reared up directly in front of them. Peggy quickly raised herself into a kneeling position and rammed her straight arms against the surfboard, driving its nose underwater and disappearing below the surface just as the wave crashed right in front of them.

Max waited the extra split second to see Peggy's duck dive and it was almost too late as a metre high of whitewater exploded towards him just as he pushed his board below the surface: the current caught his shoulders and neck and began to suck him back up into its raging turmoil but he fought deeper. He opened his eyes in the clear water below the cloudy wave swirling directly above him and saw Peggy swimming five metres ahead through the clear water with the relaxed power of a mermaid. As she reached the other side Peggy suddenly disappeared upwards except for her legs and the tail of the board.

After several strokes Max surfaced in the light and air. Peggy flashed him a gay smile and exuberantly tossed her head sending glistening drops of water flying off the tendrils of her hair in every direction. Another wave was building and they stroked up the face of the wave and smiled at each other as they breached its crest and dropped down the back.

'This is great, isn't it?' Max said.

'Yeah,' said Peggy, lifting her chin as she inhaled the clean, salty air.

The Wreck wasn't far.

A subtle swell in the water forty or fifty metres long began to emerge out of the chop in the ocean. As it approached its swollen line blotted out the horizon. It was going to be a decent slab. Max glanced at Peggy, uncertain whether or not she'd be ok. She was staring resolutely at the wave, totally focused. They swung their boards around in the direction of the beach at exactly the same instant. The biggest wave of the set, Max saw, was bearing down on them, rising higher and higher until it enclosed their world inside a long, heavy wall of shining water.

Peggy was on Max's right several metres away. They paddled furiously in a suddenly smooth sea, the water level dropping as it flowed into the wave rising above them. The wave was upon them and its roar was almost deafening. Their boards lifted up and rose skyward on the steepening slope of the wave.

Max was exactly in the pocket and Peggy was still on his right. A glassy slope appeared beneath the noses of their boards and descended about six metres as they were catapulted forward. Max sprang to his feet and cut right. Peggy was up an instant later, at first in a shock-absorbing crouch and then she rose and began rhythmically bending and straightening her knees as she carved a foaming line on the face of the wave above Max, her trailing arm floating gracefully behind her.

Peggy hadn't yielded the wave to him. Max had right of way and surfing in such close proximity was dangerous—he had no choice but to drop sharply down the face of the wave and concede the lip to Peggy.

He glanced up and saw Peggy charging along the wave, her hand lifted to shoulder height and gyrated in small rhythmic circles to transmit direction down her shoulders, through her waist, and into her swaying knees.

Max swung his shoulders and hips to carve deep curves through the wave and slow himself down as the foam cascaded right behind. Max had little margin for error between the curling wave just behind him and its avalanche of foam – which could easily suck him in too – and the twitching, leaping tail of Peggy's surfboard just above and ahead of him as she knifed through the clean wave face.

Dropping in on him was a boss move, but it also expressed Peggy's trust in him as she hurtled across the face in flatter curves that maximised her speed, knowing a single mistake could severely injure or kill them both. Peggy's relaxed, expert moves showed she was totally at home, still and tranquil in the eye of a storm, and fully capable of managing her side of the risks she had created for them.

Suddenly, Peggy threw her left shoulder back, her arm sweeping in a circle through the air as she carved a huge rooster tail of spray and dropped down the wave where Max was surfing just behind her. Turning, Peggy came right at Max, who was in the bottom of the curve at the base of the wave. It was playful in a hyper-aggressive way – a provocation, an insane banzai charge – and Max suddenly felt Peggy's spirit merge with his like a ballerina making a *grand jeté* before her partner. Instead of catching her Max threw his shoulder right, and instantly his board tracked up the wave as Peggy hurtled past him and down the wave, like matador and bull. What could have been a violent collision unfolded in a split second into a beautiful *pas-de-deux* across tonnes of water moving at fifty kilometres per hour.

Max exploded through the curling lip and into the air above the wave, high enough into the air for him to dive, laughing with joy and relief, into the sea where the wave had just been.

Max pulled his board to him by the tether as he floated in the foam, watching Peggy's head appear and disappear above the crest of the wave, her wet hair flying, as she rode the wave all the way to shore.

A few minutes later Peggy paddled back out to where Max sat in the line up.

They looked at each other with huge smiles, both aware they might have killed each other and still exhilarated by the beauty and danger of what had just happened.

'You're a real terror on a wave,' Max said.

'Thank you.'

They sat quietly for a few minutes, looking around from the lighthouse to the mountains in the distance. Max took in the beauty of Byron Bay, thinking Hugh knew these same sights and had spent many days just like this. Was he as crazy as his sister?

'Did Hugh surf The Wreck?'

Peggy shook her head. 'Nah, he preferred The Pass and Cosy Corner.'

'Speaking of crazy, what Charlie and his mates did last night was an incredible thing,' Max said.

'Yeah, I'm grateful, even though there's going to be hell to pay with dad. He'll blame mum.'

'He can do what he likes, he has no proof.'

'Yet.'

Max looked at Peggy. She was beautiful sitting on her surf board, alert to the waves, her eyes fierce, her wet hair tangled and briny.

These Nortons were intense, all of them.

. 'Charlie still loves you.'

'Yeah, but it's over, and he knows it.'

Chapter 37

T he wind was picking up.

Peggy watched Max look around, and she could see him surveying the stiffening breeze and the way it was pushing up little wrinkles on the clear skin of the water.

'That was probably the last clean wave we'll catch this morning,' said Max.

Peggy liked the fact he had said so little about her dropping into his wave, and especially her sudden cut-back. He faced dangerous surprises calmly, before and after. Last night there turned out to be so much more to Max than she had imagined.

'The water's pretty clear. We can probably see the hull of the *Wollongbar*,' Peggy said. 'It's only about ten or twelve metres down. Have you ever done any free diving?'

'Not really,' said Max. 'My ears start to hurt when I go down much more than ten metres or so. I can probably just make it down to the *Wollongbar*.'

'You can probably fix that by pinching your nostrils with your fingers and blowing your nose,' said Peggy. 'I can try and work with you. Do you want to have a go?'

Max smiled and shrugged. 'Of course!'

He certainly didn't need the five thousand dollar suit he was probably wearing in the photo on the website. Stripped down and wet, sitting on Hugh's surfboard next to her in the waves, he was more of a man than he seemed to be in the Eastern Suburbs. It was hard to imagine his wife Ilona appreciated that. His marriage seemed incomprehensible. She knew Ilona before she and Max met on Bondi, and she'd taken it for granted that beautiful, fastidious Ilona was just along for the ride and the sumptuous lifestyle. Nothing she'd seen in her brief encounters with Ilona, or what Alexandra had said, alerted her to the kind of man Max was turning out to be. Ilona had probably never seen the Max who was bobbing on the waves next to her, totally at home in the ocean. Peggy liked that.

Peggy dropped to her belly and started to paddle to the left. 'The Wreck should be right around here somewhere.'

Peggy rolled off her board and submerged, feeling the weight of her hair as it floated underwater while she scanned the sea floor. Visibility was good and in the clear water she made out the outlines of the sunken ship below. Peggy popped up, water streaming from her hair and face, and pointed to the north. 'The shore side of the hull is about twenty metres over there. We can see it pretty clearly today.'

'Right,' said Max. 'I'm in.'

They paddled over, sat up, untied the tethers from their legs, and rolled into the water. Who was Max really?

'Ok,' said Peggy. 'If your ears start to hurt, stop wherever you are, pinch your nose like this, and then blow – that should clear your ears.'

She liked what she saw the night before and on the wave just now, and she wanted to see more examples of how Max acted when he was out of his comfort zone. She tried and failed to do that on a wave, but maybe she'd succeed underwater.

'Ok.'

'Ready?'

Peggy jackknifed and dove. The radiant water was like glass, and the sandy floor reflected plenty of sunlight back up through the water, which darkened from sky blue to teal as she swam. Below was the outline of both port and starboard sides of the *Wollongbar*, with the seaward side more covered in sand. Peggy descended all the way and skimmed through the water just above the sand, tracking the hull.

The weight of the water was comforting, so different from its intimidating landslide-like power when massed into a wave on the surface. Down here the water expressed completely different qualities, and she felt embraced, her body rocked gently by the subtle underwater currents. She felt like a baby again in her mother's womb, and wished she could stay underneath the surface all day, far from the reach of lawyers and her mother's legal bills, far from her father, far from Hugh's cold, hard, motionless body decomposing in secret in the dirt and rock.

She hadn't always felt that way underwater.

She looked back and couldn't see Max. It didn't worry her. He must have returned to the surface, but she couldn't make out his legs in the dazzling water above her.

Chapter 38

'What happened to you?' Peggy called from almost fifty metres away. Max had collected their drifting surfboards and was bobbing in the water between them. Peggy swam over and he gently pushed her surfboard to her.

'I had pain in my ears,' said Max.

'Did you get to the wreck?'

'Just above it, but the pain didn't go away, so after a while I came straight back up.'

Peggy smiled. 'I'm sorry, I should have stayed close to you. Do you want to keep trying? You don't have to, you know.'

'It's something you do, so I'd like to know what it's like, too.'

Peggy laughed. 'Ok then, you're in.' She held out a closed fist for him to tap with his closed fist. 'I'm going to teach you my deepest, darkest secrets of power, pain and breathing.'

'Bring it on.'

'Ok, why don't we try the *Tassie*?' Peggy said. 'It's deeper, but it's a better place because you'll have to really relax to learn.'

'You mean to learn your deepest secrets of power and pain,' said Max.

'Right – if you dare! But they're not something you're going to master on one dive.'

'We'll see!'

He knew relaxing was essential. He'd learned that paradox as he acquired mastery in surfing and fast driving: survival depends on not being concerned about surviving.

The *Tassie* was the other major wreck still visible on the sandy floor of Byron Bay, an old American ammunition ship that sank in World War II. They paddled straight out to sea to get beyond the zone where the waves were breaking, then turned and paddled north a few hundred metres until Peggy said, 'I think this is it.' They sat up on their surfboards and Peggy looked to shore. 'Yeah, it's right at the end of where the Old Jetty used to be.

We're going to have to let our surfboards float again. This is a lot deeper. The *Tassie*'s probably about ten metres down.'

'Ten metres? My ears were hurting pretty bad at less than three.'

'Keep trying to clear your ears when it starts to hurt. There's different ways to clear your ears: swallow, try to yawn with your mouth closed, or tilt your head from side to side. You're just trying to open your Eustachian tubes so that air from your nose and mouth flows into your middle ears.'

'Ok,' said Max.

'Watch me – and then do this, too.' Peggy began breathing slowly and rhythmically, inhaling through her nose and exhaling through pursed lips, finishing with a series of sharp, brief inhalations, puffing out her cheeks as she exhaled while Max did his best to imitate her. Inhaling one last time, Peggy jackknifed and suddenly her legs lofted in the air and she disappeared. Max breathed one last mouthful of air, hoped his ears had cleared, and dove, not as cleanly as Peggy, and saw her swimming below like a frog, her hair streaming behind.

Max followed her down but as he reached three metres he felt sharp needles of pain in his ears – the squeeze – as his inner ears failed to equalise pressure. He stopped diving, turned right-side up, and tried to follow Peggy's instructions. Schools of fish swam around him as he tried clearing his ears by pinching his nostrils and blowing his nose. The fish circling him in all their colours, clearly relaxed and happy, some catching the light, were a calming sight. Max shook his head from side to side. He nodded his head. He blew again, but it didn't seem to help. Peggy was now so far below she was almost disappearing into the dark water.

Max looked up. The water was beautiful – clear and radiant with long shafts of sunlight penetrating through swirls of gleaming particles. When he looked down now he could see only the dark water into which Peggy had disappeared. He felt uneasy, and although he would be able to stay underwater for at least another two minutes, his chest felt tight, as if he didn't have any oxygen left.

Max recognised the tricks his mind was playing: ten seconds turning over and over in a big wave feels like a minute, thirty seconds feels like an eternity. Stress had made him alert and he was automatically scanning the situation for threats. Great whites had been sighted at Byron – and the thought of sharks confirmed his mind was playing its tricks. He was passively floating underwater, discouraged about the possibility of ever clearing his ears and performing a decent free dive. He was paralysed with indecision. He glanced up again at the bright water above. It looked so welcoming. He glanced down again into the forbidding darkness below and with an icy jolt of fear saw a dim form moving beneath him.

It was Peggy, stroking straight up, moving rapidly and fluidly.

Seconds later she was floating in front of him. She cocked her head and pointed with her thumb questioningly towards the surface, and Max shook his head and spread his hands from the middle of his chest to indicate 'no'. Without masks, not every detail was clear, so they both gestured broadly.

Max tapped on his ears.

Peggy nodded and showed him the open palm of her hand, and then pointed two fingers toward her eyes in the sign indicating 'look at me.' Nothing in Peggy's movements was pre-emptory, every aspect of her body language was gentle. She pinched her nose with her thumb and forefinger and inclined her head slightly, pantomiming blowing through her nose. Max gave Peggy the 'ok' sign and imitated her, but his ears remained tight, locked in the squeeze.

Peggy gave a hopeful 'ok' sign but Max shook his head and made the 'not ok' sign by extending his hand flat between them and tipping it from side to side. Peggy smiled and nodded understandingly.

Again she made the 'look at me' sign. Tilting her head back, her face upwards and shining in the light, and baring her throat to Max, Peggy stroked her throat with graceful fingertips to suggest Max try swallowing. Max lifted his chin and swallowed and he felt a slight pop in his left ear. Immediate relief. He pointed to his left ear and gave Peggy the 'ok' sign, then pointed to his right ear and made the 'not ok' sign.

Peggy gave no sign of impatience or irritation. She made the 'look at me' sign and then cocked her jaw, hollowing her cheeks in a yawn and then for good measure tilted her head from side to side. Nothing in her gestures suggested Max should feel unworthy or humiliated. Her graceful swan-like neck was so flexible Peggy's ears almost touched her shoulders.

Max was becoming aware of dwindling oxygen in his lungs, but in Peggy's calm presence he felt himself arrive at a state of relaxed, focused, heightened awareness: it was almost that he felt loved. Max imitated Peggy, and somewhere between the yawn and tilting his head towards his shoulder he felt his right ear pop, and the squeeze vanished completely.

Max knew from surfing that he could have either locked up and given in to fear – or he could break through into this awareness.

Joyfully, Max pointed to his right ear and gave Peggy the 'ok' sign. His entire being seemed in relaxed harmony with the fish swirling around them, with Peggy, with all other sentient beings, and in effortless synchrony with the energies of the universe.

Peggy mirrored his gesture to confirm she understood, and then reached for his hand and pressed it gently and encouragingly. She pointed towards the surface with her thumb, asking if Max wanted to terminate the dive and return to the surface. There was no judgement coming from her. Max made the thumbs down sign, indicating he was ready and eager to descend.

Peggy nodded, turned upside down, and dove. Max followed. He had about a minute of air left and wanted to shake off the flashes of ego that appeared before Peggy returned to help him, and in other ways while he was following her demonstration of how to clear his ears. Max was determined to maintain his current full, clear awareness for the rest of this dive.

He descended another three metres – almost two thirds of the way to the bottom – before needles started jabbing his ears again. There were still lots of fish in the water around him, but as Max paused to clear his ears again, he realised he didn't like being where he was: the sea into which Peggy had now disappeared curved away below him, dark and ominous, with only the faintest glimmer of the sandy bottom visible through the murk. Suspended in the cool, dark water far below the surface, Max felt intensely uncomfortable. He hesitated, feeling vulnerable in the gloom, and looked up at the safety of the dim sunlight on the ocean surface.

He cleared both ears and, stifling his growing anxiety, breaststroked down to just above the floor of the bay. Through the schools of fish he saw dark structures resting in the sand not far ahead. The area looked inhospitable, even threatening, the lack of light made him very aware of the limited amount of air in his lungs. Panic started in his stomach and despite his best efforts continued moving along his spine until the base of his neck tingled. Objectively, Max knew he could stay underwater for at least another minute. He glanced upwards at the light, which seemed so far away he was reminded of a cathedral ceiling. Feeling ashamed, he swam back up towards the light.

Max surfaced and gratefully breathed the salt air. He spotted the surfboards and swam slowly to them as he breathed luxurious lungfuls of ocean air. A few seconds later Peggy exploded to the surface with a huge exhale and then gulped in air, and when she recovered enough to speak, she said, 'You did great! I saw you coming pretty far down.'

'Not far enough,' Max said. 'I didn't get to the *Tassie.*'

'That's ok.' Peggy reached for the board which Max had just collected. She wiped the water out of her eyes. 'Wow, it's really beautiful down there.'

Max shook his head, feeling embarrassed. 'I got close, but I wasn't having any fun. It's too dark for me. I basically fucked up.'

'You were great, Max. Most people have to clear their ears a couple times when they descend. It's normal,' Peggy said, busily splashing water up her nose and on her face.

Max had a dim memory of his mother frowning at him. The sting of a slap on his face. Then he remembered Peggy kneeling in the grass at Redleaf Pool and changing the nappy for her friend's baby.

'Maybe,' he said, cautiously, a sudden sense of being unlovable slowly dissipating.

Peggy treated him so differently from the way, deep down inside, Max expected to be treated.

He also knew he'd felt fear at the bottom, and a secret humiliation and shame.

'You did such a great job clearing the squeeze with me,' Peggy was scrutinising him. 'Were you afraid?'

Surprised, Max instantly said, 'Yes.'

Peggy nodded. 'We're all afraid of what we don't know – and besides, it's deeper than that. We really don't know anything about how life works. So fear is always in the background, ready to appear in an instant. Sometimes when I take my last breath before I dive, a voice pops into my head and says, "This is the last breath of your life. You're going to die this time".'

'Really?' Max said. 'What do you do?'

'It happened to me just now, right before our dive. I call the voice my Opponent. I just dive. Actually, I heard it again when we resumed our descent after you cleared the squeeze. I should have stayed with you – I knew you'd probably need to clear your ears again – but I wanted to swim straight at my Opponent and take it on.'

'How do you know it's not some sort of real warning – your intuition that something is wrong?'

'I can't know. There's no theoretical way to tell – I just have to keep practicing to challenge it in a way that's very uncomfortable.'

'I thought I'd do better,' said Max. He felt he'd had enough. Peggy's secrets of pain and power, whatever they might be, were now forgotten or discounted as irrelevant. But Peggy's sympathy renewed his desire to try again. 'I want to give it at least one more go.'

'Great!' said Peggy with a smile. 'Now, you first have to believe it's possible – that's when your mind starts to find the way. Push yourself, but take small steps. And relax. Believe there is a way, and that you'll find it. It might take lots of free dives. Who knows? So set little goals. When you've reached one little goal and feel ready to move on, set another little goal. Relax – but push yourself.'

'I get it – at least the idea,' said Max. 'When I'm surfing waves bigger than I can easily handle, I breathe in a special way to relax, and it works out fine. But you can't fake being relaxed – as you know.'

Slick, gleaming slabs of huge waves out in the bright air with their roar in his ears were one thing, while the dim, gloomy, silent depths from which he'd just returned, where what seemed like the weight of the entire ocean was pressing on his body, was quite another. 'I guess what's bothering me are two things: I don't like the darkness, and I can't breathe – a quick exhale is how I normally handle fear.'

'That was true for me, too,' said Peggy. 'Not breathing is a stress trigger, obviously. That's why it's such a powerful path to understanding yourself. You've had plenty of long hold-unders when you've been surfing, right? It's basically the same thing. You can relax.'

Max nodded. He'd learned long ago that adrenaline is very dangerous underwater because it raises the heart rate and makes the body consume oxygen faster. Without surrendering and relaxing, adrenaline can cause drowning during a long hold-under beneath a big wave, and unless he could relax, his adrenaline response could completely cancel his ability to free dive. 'I want to try again – no matter how much I kind of hate it.'

Peggy smiled. 'Just like you did with surfing, you'll gradually expand your comfort zone as you practice. Then you'll naturally relax, even at greater and greater levels of effort. You'll find you're calm and feeling good even on dives that were totally impossible for you a short time before. Just push yourself and accept the pain. Don't pretend to be making an effort when you're really not. It's truly a matter of time and honest effort before fear and discomfort disappear, and you're achieving a state where you're all the way down, swimming along, and just loving it.'

'I guess there's only one way to find out,' said Max.

'Ok, but you have to believe it in advance in order to set your mind into problem-solving mode,' said Peggy.

'Got it,' said Max.

Peggy began breathing again until she was inhaling and puffing her cheeks in fast, sharp exhales, gradually accelerating their tempo and strength, until she threw her head back and inhaled one last time through her nose, and then in a flash her head disappeared and her legs reared in the air, and then they disappeared too. Max dove too.

This time as he followed the triangle of malachite around Peggy's hips deeper into the water, Max didn't need to stop and clear his ears. He knew the growing darkness and drop in temperature of the water were sending alarms through his nervous system. He would have to break through these false alarms to reach calm, clear awareness – the same state he'd sensed in Peggy.

He was experiencing the fear of the unknown, as Peggy had said. The heightened state his fear had activated could switch into a state of panic or a state of expanded awareness. As he saw the dark outlines of the *Tassie* rising out of the sand ahead and just below him, he could make out the pale flickers of Peggy's feet as she swam above the wreck ten metres ahead. As he started to cruise over the sponges, and the hard and soft corals completely encrusting what was left of the structure, swimming through curtains of butterfly fish, sergeant fish and snapper, barred soapfish, angelfish and surgeon fish, bullseyes, fusiliers, and pipe fish, Max's whole body tingled and he felt the base of his scalp crawl as the cool, heavy water pressed into him from all sides.

Max had at least another minute of oxygen, but his lungs felt like they were on fire. He told himself to relax, to absorb the pain in his chest, not block out his fear and absorb that, too. He had to accept not being in control.

Max knew what was happening: his fear was producing an urgent desire for immediate relief – and was about to result in panic and defeat. His fear was confining him to his previous experience and current knowledge.

Kairos.

A pair of sea turtles swam lazily past an erect tower encrusted with coral thrusting up into the seawater, a beautiful sight, but his heart was racing and his ego was screaming at him to swim back up to the surface – the simple, wrong, solution. Max knew from surfing that the ego is almost always addressing a fear which it has generated: running out of oxygen, great white sharks, dark water, unknown damage to his ears that the pain might be signalling.

He focused on his swimming technique as he followed Peggy, ignoring the pain in his chest, determined to see off the baseless fears and enjoy the mad shapes of the coral and the clouds of fish flitting in every direction. His ego consciousness always operated within his existing limits and constraints and, inspired by Peggy, Max was determined to free dive to personal transformation.

Just when he felt a wild despair start to envelop him—*am I Phil Garlick?*—Max broke through to the calm awareness for which he had been yearning and found Peggy was right: he was swimming along behind Peggy and loving it. He matched Peggy stroke for stroke without struggling or stress.

But through the beauty of the fish, and the white sand and coral, the anemones and the anemone fish, the turtles, the long shafts of light fading into a kind of gauzy haze above them as they swam in the twilight through the various coral-covered structures and erect sentinel pillars formed by the *Tassie*, Max was aware of the subtle indications of his ego in flickers of pride and competitiveness with Peggy. His senses were full of the beauty all around, including swimming centimetres from a beautiful almost naked woman.

Peggy twice gave the thumbs up sign, querying whether Max needed to return to the surface, and twice Max shook his head. Finally she gave the thumbs up sign and it was clear she needed to finish her dive. Max gave Peggy the ok sign but stayed near the bottom and didn't begin his ascent until he saw her legs far above him, and then he began a slow ascent.

Let her get the boards this time, he thought to himself.

When Max was still ten metres from the surface he urgently needed to breathe. His chest was on fire. He swam up through the shining water, light all around him, looking at the golden ball of the sun flaring and swaying as its light refracted in the waves above him, so close to where there was infinite air to breathe.

The fulcrum of the universe seemed to be crushing his chest. Heaven and Earth slowly pivoted on his sternum and he suddenly remembered the agony in which Ilona gave birth to both their daughters. A holy moment. Where a human being overcomes their fear and pain to perform at their best is sacred space. Max twisted in his agony, arms outstretched, looking at the sun heaving and dancing in all its glory just above him. Suddenly he was full of clear awareness, a quiet joy, and he knew it was going to be ok. His last three strokes were joyful and his head burst into the bright air. Max felt like suddenly new, restored, and welcome in the world: it felt like redemption.

Chapter 39

They said very little and looked out at the magnificent cumulus clouds shining in the morning sun as he drove.

The car started up the steep, winding road, and Max looked back over the bay as they wound their way up. The entire bay was shining like beaten gold, and almost right in the middle near the curving shoreline was the location of the *Tassie* wreck.

They were almost up the mountain when Peggy pointed to a small parking area in a rare flat part of the hill.

They got out of the car and walked about fifty metres, around one bend and then into the middle of a second which formed a perfect semicircle above the eastern slope of the mountain. Peggy crossed the road and walked up to the fence. It was a beautiful spot, the easternmost point in Australia, looking directly onto the South Pacific. To the right, a saddleback mountain protected Tallow Beach, the scene of yet another shipwreck, which had resulted in a cargo of rendered animal fat – extremely valuable at the time – washing up on the beach and leaving it greasy for years. To the left, just past the lighthouse, they could again see the great curve of Byron Bay, framed by primordial-looking mountains outlined in the glare.

Peggy stood in front of a wooden fence post. 'This is where Hugh went over,' she said, putting her hand on the top beam. It was noticeably newer than the posts and the beams on either side. Thick tropical cane plants grew beneath a freshly chipped and scoured lower beam, and there was a gap in the vegetation.

'The police said it was an accident. But there were no skid marks, and Hugh T-boned right into the fence. I think he was riding on his back wheel, doing a wheelie when he hit the fence. He must have been going close to a hundred. His bike broke through the top beam and skidded down the mountain almost fifty metres before it got stuck in the brush.'

Max looked down. The slope dropped away for hundreds of metres until it met the ocean waves. Just around the base Tallow Beach stretched to the right. The slope was strewn with boulders and low foliage, and pocked with sudden vertical faces where erosion had carved away the mountain.

'He would have flown out a fair way,' Max said. 'How far down the slope did he land?'

It was breezy and bright where they stood, surrounded by the radiance of sky and sea.

'About halfway,' said Peggy.

'Where did they find his body?'

'In the ocean.'

'It's almost like it wasn't suicide,' said Max. 'Hugh would have been in the air for a long time. It was like flying, not falling.'

'You saw his body. He was a little bruised, but he didn't break anything. He was just knocked unconscious when he landed, kept sliding until he hit the water and drowned in the surf.'

Hugh's impact probably would have easily started a landslide in the volcanic soil, gravel, and small rocks that swept him into the sea to his death.

'He must have been totally relaxed,' Max said. 'You can't fake that.'

'No,' Peggy said. 'You can't fake that.'

'Did he leave a note?'

'No, but I know why he did it,' Peggy said.

'Are you willing to talk about it?'

'Dad demanded he become his own man – but the moment Hugh showed signs of independence, Dad crushed him.' She sighed. 'He came to Byron to set himself free from fear – but he realised Father had gotten inside his head. That's how small his world became. When he realised he couldn't escape him, he came here.'

'I think what triggered it was when my dad organised that shipment of Pfizer vaccines.' Max nodded.

'He told us he had one for Hugh and me. But not my mother.'

'I didn't know that,' Max said. 'All I know is we received ten vaccines, and we split them 50:50.'

Max looked out at the sea and sky, imagining Hugh flying through the shining air like Icarus, falling in a lovely arc until he intersected on the slope with his death.

'We refused to accept the vaccines because my mum wasn't included. It was typical of Dad, really. He's so vindictive and controlling. But it seemed to prey on Hugh's mind. He couldn't bear being controlled and manipulated, even up here, by Dad.'

'It must be really hard to be around your dad when you consider him responsible for your brother's death.'

'If you really want to love, you have to learn to forgive.'

Max looked at the gentle, understanding look in Peggy's eyes.

Peggy smiled. 'Ideally, we'd never have to forgive, because we'd never be aware of being insulted or injured in the first place, no matter what others said or did to us. That isn't really an option for me—dad is too intense and the pain of losing Hugh was too awful.

'I had to learn to forgive my father before then, about all the awful things that happened when I was growing up.'

'I'll bet,' said Max. But even as he said it, he was uncomfortably aware he was in no position to judge Mort.

'I realised I can't fix the way the hat is sitting on the head of the person in the mirror—I have to fix it on my own head. That made me realise I had to focus on changing myself, not my father ... '

'It's hard to believe you had as much to fix as your dad does. Unless you're a serial killer.'

'The point is I couldn't change my dad, but I can change myself,' said Peggy.

'How does that make much difference? Has it changed Mort in any way?'

'Because we're all connected. My dad and me. You and me. You and my dad. I don't know if it's changed him. I think he is changing, partly perhaps because of Alexandra, partly because of his new daughters ... I just don't know.'

'Maybe because he's so fucking rich now. Maybe he's starting to relax.'

'I doubt that's it.'

'Probably not,' agreed Max. 'But are you saying we're all mirror images of each other?' It seemed monstrous.

'Yes. Everybody in our life reflects a potential or actual version of ourselves.'

'What do you mirror back to me about myself?' asked Max.

'I'm not sure,' said Peggy. 'Maybe we're going to find out.'

Max made a thumb's up.

'So, tell me what you had to forgive Mort for—the biggest thing.' His question might sound prying, Max realised. 'As a father of two daughters, I'd like to know.'

'Sure,' nodded Peggy. 'To start with, I had to be really specific about how he'd injured me. He beat my mother.'

Max concealed his shock. *My partner of five years?* The thought made him feel dirty.

'It was terrible, and something my mum had to, and has to, deal with. But what about me? Could it be right to say Dad injured me by beating Mum?'

'Of course,' said Max. 'In so many ways.'

Peggy nodded. 'Yes, he did, but I wasn't personally beaten, so I couldn't forgive him for beating my mum. You have to be precise, Max, about what you can forgive, or it's pointless.'

Max realised listening to Peggy talk about forgiveness was ironically making him angry and judgmental. *It feels so good to be angry at someone else.*

'I developed an eating disorder. Was that related to how I felt watching my mother beaten? Yes, sure, but he didn't force me to put my fingers down my throat and throw up after every meal, either. He didn't force me to obsess constantly about food. In fact, the truth was bulimia allowed me to control my father.'

'How?'

'I'll tell you some other time. For now, remember forgiveness is a powerful energy, and we can't predict how it will affect us. It's one of those elemental life energies.'

'Like love,' said Max, remembering their conversation on the plane.

'Yes, like love. Like love, forgiveness is alive itself, it's a kind of conscious energy. Forgiveness is much older than human life, probably fourteen billion years old – as old as the universe.' She put her hand on his arm. 'I know you'll get that.'

Max did get it. As he had listened to Peggy he suddenly had an expansive vision of the universe permeated not just with energy and matter but with intelligence, forgiveness and love.

'Max, love is the true secret of evolution, it's the highest survival strategy of all. My father is suffering a kind of living death. Anybody close to him who can't see that risks dying too.'

'That's why I'm going to look after your mother – and you,' said Max. He was even more determined after what he had just heard. Nothing, and nobody, was going to stop him.

'Honestly, I'm worried about Trixie, Anastasia and Alexandra.'

'Really? He wouldn't do anything to them,' said Max. 'The last person I'd worry about is Alexandra. She can look after herself.

'I'm here to look after you.'

Chapter 40

'ASX/MEDIA RELEASE 28 SEPTEMBER

NEW INVESTOR OFFERS
ZETTADATA SHAREHOLDERS
A FAIR DEAL

A group of experienced and credentialed Australian investors intends to acquire the entire stake currently owned by SpecTel Holdings Inc. (USA), the largest shareholder of ZettaData Limited, and in addition will fund on a fully underwritten basis $50MM of new equity while offering existing shareholders the right to invest alongside them ...'

ZettaData's share price skyrocketed moments after the announcement was released on the ASX at 10:00 am. The stock price had been ticking up on light but steady volume for weeks, ever since Max's comments at the AGM, and reached just over eleven cents while he and Peggy were in Byron Bay – double the price before he'd confronted Mort at the AGM. This afternoon the stock price was trading between thirty-five and thirty-six cents, a level it hadn't seen for almost two years.

After landing in Sydney yesterday afternoon, one of his voicemails had been the news the board had agreed to his proposal. He'd gone right over to ZettaData offices to complete the documentation in time to release the announcement to the ASX next morning. The price cleared fourteen cents less than five minutes later, just enough time for a few pros to do the numbers and realise Max was offering to spread around a lot of wealth with his rights issue priced at one cent. As word flashed around the market, the order volume started to stack up from the initial purchases of a few thousand dollars to orders worth tens of thousands of dollars. Rapidly cleaning up the previous out of the money sell orders in the mid-teens generated buying momentum that powered ZettaData's stock to almost twenty cents before noon. The response on the sell side was sluggish, as the small investors who controlled the majority of ZettaData's publicly listed shares had largely given up hope and didn't appear to have seen – or understood – Max's ASX announcement, or weren't monitoring the sudden, dramatic jump in the share price. So brokers began scanning lists of top shareholders and ringing them with offers to buy their shares at slightly more than the rapidly rising stock price – which more than tripled ZettaData's opening share price.

By then, every board member except Luke Terry had rung Max to congratulate him and celebrate the success of his rights issue. By one o'clock Max was absorbed in a seemingly endless series of satisfying conversations with journalists, analysts, and the ZettaData management team as the scale of the market's reaction to the announcement became clear. Millions of dollars had poured into the stock, and Max hadn't even committed a dollar yet. He was already attracting the multiplier effect of new investment he had prophesied his rights issue would stimulate. Max also found it interesting the market seemed to be forecasting that the five bagger he had promised Kent Logan, as a minimum return, was almost certain. For most people involved with ZettaData, a morning that had begun in tremendous tension evolved first into relief, and then into almost incredulous joy and congratulations all around.

But not for Max. At his temporary offices made available by Bob Henninger, in between a meeting with Chairman Telford of ZettaData and an interview with the chief financial editor of the *Australian Business Digest*, Max stayed hard at work, doing everything he could to ensure he saved ZettaData.

Chapter 41

'One cent a share? Why are you promising average investors something for nothing, Max?' demanded Perry Hocking, a wide grin concealing his aggressive tone. 'It can't really be true—so isn't that unethical, not to mention illegal?'

Hocking gestured under the hot lights towards Trevor Walker, host of the widely watched TV program *Mighty Money*, who nodded wisely.

'Guys—ZettaData's stock price is up eight times,' said Max. 'I'm not promising something for nothing, and the market obviously knows it!'

Max knew the chances Hocking had actually read the ZettaData proposal filed with the ASX were close to zero. Hocking was a senior financial journalist working for the *Australian Business Digest* and Max had known him for years—Hocking never did his own research; he probably hadn't read a stock exchange filing in decades.

'One cent,' Walker intoned gravely. 'If it looks too good to be true . . . you know the old saying.'

Conventionally attractive and intelligent, as a TV host Walker was a good proxy for his viewers. His purple eyelids, which gave him an unexpectedly soulful look, had disappeared under the make-up. Max suddenly remembered Walker was about to make his theatre debut acting in the highly anticipated play *TransGod*.

'One cent isn't nothing Max, but it's bloody close!' exclaimed Walker, rescuing Hocking. It was clear Walker had been given an attack brief by his editors, who would be following instructions from the owners of the network.

'I'm sharing the wealth I create *while I'm creating it*. Existing shareholders of ZettaData have benefited from the increase in the value of ZettaData—not me.'

Max had known he was in an unfamiliar environment the moment hours before when he sat down and the make-up people began tapping skin-coloured lotions onto his face with wet sponges and then brushed powder onto his skin. He knew *Mighty Money*, the most established financial news show in Australia, was going to be a tough gig – its advertisers were the big establishment financial institutions most threatened by Max's new model of sharing value with small shareholders.

'You're telling punters that for one cent per share you'll make all their hopes and dreams come true!' said Hocking.

'Really, Perry—is that what I'm doing?' Max smiled at Hocking and held his eye.

Like most journalists, Hocking never read anything himself. Early every morning Hocking called daily his favourite contacts and gleaned their opinions. Max was on his list, and Hocking would follow up his call with an email to Max, the issue that interested him in the subject heading and just write 'What does it mean?'

The next morning Max would read his own summary in Perry's column in the *Digest*. As long as Hocking's articles satisfied the *Digest's* advertisers his career was safe: ordinary *Digest* readers had no idea how worthless Hocking's columns were.

Obviously somebody, or perhaps numerous market players, were feeding Hocking negative information about Max's ZettaData takeover.

'One cent!' barked Rupert Campbell, the Head of Investment Banking at Coldstream Holdings, the dominant investment bank in Australia. The skin on his wide, balding forehead was wrinkling like a pastry. 'You've bent the Corps Act as far as it can go, Max, I'm not sure how you can live with yourself.'

Max suddenly understood the *Mighty Money* segment was an ambush. Hocking and Walker were puppets who may not even have known they were lying, but Campbell knew exactly what was in Max's takeover proposal, and he was deliberately pretending it was a bad joke.

'You know as well as I do Rupert that I'm not claiming advantages I'm legally entitled to under the Corps Act. My proposal is dialed way over in favour of the small ZettaData shareholders.'

'I've never seen anyone apply the Corps Act the way you have, Max,' Hocking shook his head disapprovingly.

'With respect, Max,' said Campbell, laughing ghoulishly. 'You're a blithering idiot.'

Hocking chortled appreciatively. He needed to pretend to be one of Campbell's believers: Campbell was one of his most valuable sources, Coldstream Holdings was a major advertiser in the *Australian Business Digest*, and the *Digest* was barely surviving. Hocking had to deliver happy endings to his employer's customers—or he'd be out of a job. Max felt sorry for him.

'This isn't Twitter, Rupert, you need to rise above making insults,' said Max. 'How do you explain the stock price increasing eight times?'

'Oh, that's easy to explain. It's called the "greater fool theory",' said Campbell. 'Every fool who buys ZettaData stock is waiting for a greater fool to buy it from him. And besides, with penny stocks, ignorant punters can buy lots of shares for very little money.

'You offer an absurd rights issue for a worthless company, and the least informed investors have taken the bait. We've seen all this before,' said Campbell loftily, sitting back in his chair and crossing his legs. 'It's not some new model. It's an old, sad story.'

Campbell, Hocking and Walker laughed derisively.

There was scattered chuckling from the studio audience, herd behaviour as the audience tried to discern which of the panel members was the lead bull.

'I could have proposed a very different deal, Rupert – a deal fully within ASX rules and the Corps Act – and the two hundred million dollar increase in the value of ZettaData would belong to me. That's how the system is designed to work – and you know it, Rupert.'

Campbell and Hocking, both of whom he knew well, looked like animated corpses in the heavy pancake make-up required under the hot lights. He'd never met Trevor Walker in person until just before the show, but despite his conventional good looks, from a couple metres away and in his TV make-up, Walker looked like Frankenstein.

'It's called the laws of economics. You can't just pretend those laws don't exist,' snarled Campbell.

'Corporate law is not physics or economics, Rupert,' said Max. 'It's a tool to rig the system in favour of insiders like us.'

'I can't let you use this program unchallenged to spread conspiracy theories, Max,' Walker said, looking down and consulting his notes. 'Let's change the subject: a few weeks ago, most of our viewers had never heard of you. Now you've got over two hundred thousand Twitter followers, and you're adding thousands every day. I'm wondering whether some of the things you say are just meant to pander to the prejudices of the ignorant. Are you spreading misinformation?'

Sparagmos. He was being torn limb from limb without any factual discussion about his ZettaData takeover.

'It's not misinformation to acknowledge laws aren't neutral,' said Max. 'Laws are written by a certain class of people for their own benefit. That's the way people like Rupert Campbell get richer every year, and why we have so many billionaires in Australia.'

'Are you blaming the Australian legal system?' asked Hocking, who was little better than a marginalised sex worker servicing his paper's owners' advertisers—including the major legal firms.

'Yes, I am, Perry – remember this is the same legal system that declared Australia *Terra Nullius*. It can be used to eliminate an entire group of people at the stroke of a pen – and for any other purpose. It was done to the original inhabitants of this land and increasingly it's being done to average shareholders and voters.' He was thinking of the Casners, struggling to pay the costs of caring for their permanently disabled son. 'Everyone can be bought, any rule can be bent, new legislation can be shaped just to accommodate the selfish interests of a billionaire. The system is as rigged as Captain Cook's frigate!'

'And your one cent offer is the solution?' demanded Rupert Campbell, glaring at Max. There was total silence from the studio audience.

Charlie and his mates Bobby and George – ten generations of their ancestors didn't legally exist until the Mabo Decision. Hal and Sue Casner are being treated as if they don't exist now.

'A penny for your thoughts Max—or rather for your ZettaData shares!' said Hocking, who seemed to be melting under the heat.

The TV host and his other two guests rocked back in their chairs with more ghoulish laughter. The studio audience remained silent. Walker seemed to wipe a tear of laughter out of the corner of his eye as he consulted his notes. He turned to Max. 'You're telling your Twitter followers what they want to hear: misinformation. That's what you're peddling. You sound like an anti-vaxxer!'

'I can agree with that!' said Rupert Campbell. 'We have to be very careful about thinking this complicated world is as simple as my good friend Max Ring says it is. One cent a share!'

'Maybe I'm telling them truths nobody else is,' said Max.

'What is truth? You mean *your* truth, Max. By the way would you mind confirming to our studio audience and viewers around Australia whether or not you've been vaccinated?' said Trevor Walker, beads of sweat on his forehead.

'Yes, I am vaccinated – but frankly it was probably totally pointless,' said Max.

'What—did you say you're not vaccinated?'

'I am vaccinated, but I think for myself.'

'You think it's ok to selfishly endanger the community, Max?'

'I'm vaccinated!'

'What you are is a disgrace, Max,' said Hocking. 'Mr One Cent. Our viewers should never forget—you get what you pay for!'

'Now, Max,' Walker said, chuckling. 'Let's see what real Australians are saying about these wild things Max Ring has been using this program to say.' Walker looked up at a screen to the side. 'We've been getting tweets for a while now, and they've turned into a flood in the last few minutes. Let's bring up a sample.'

'"Onya, Max!" Well, that's a show of support from a real, um, Australian, of a certain sort,' Walker smiled sardonically into the TV camera.

'A real Aucker,' murmured Campbell.

'"Liar, liar, pants on fire, Ring". Hmmm, someone doesn't seem convinced. "You don't speak for me, Ring!" "Don't you dare tear down what we built, Max Ring!" "Ring off – Max!" "Shove it up your ring, Max!" Well, Max, looks like a lot of people aren't buying what you're selling this evening.' Walker watched Max without blinking.

It was public *sparagmos* – the show's producers were unleashing a mob to do what the other panellists hadn't accomplished – tear him apart on the show. But were the tweets legit? Troll farms. Young staff members operating fake accounts, their fingers busily typing up fake outrage. Max pulled out his phone as he watched the hostile tweets flood the *Mighty Money* screen, and looked at his Twitter feed. A blur of tweets in support of him were flooding his feed. Something wasn't right.

The show was almost over. He had one last chance to make his case. He wasn't going to use precious seconds to try to expose the fraud scrolling across the screen.

'Coldstream Holdings and other huge institutions dominate the system, consuming resources on a massive scale, pushing smaller and weaker entities to the margins. We've seen this all before.'

'And you know what happens?' Max looked into the TV camera and swivelled his chair to address the studio audience. 'There's a major shock – and these huge dominators can't adapt – and they become extinct.'

The panelists and the audience were silent. Max continued. 'A million years ago they were called dinosaurs – and the comet that struck the Yucatan peninsula started changes dinosaurs couldn't adapt to, so they went from being super-predators to extinct. We've created a global economic system in which dinosaurs dominate the planet: billionaire dinosaurs and their flunkies. It's an old order protected by a web of rules – I can't dignify those rules by calling them laws. The shocks that will push these fat dinosaurs to extinction are coming.'

'Do you remember who succeeded the dinosaurs? Weak, furry little mammals. The mammals hid in the jungle during the heyday of the dinosaurs—but they adapted after the comet hit. You know why? Because they weren't killing machines—they were social animals and cooperated with each other.'

'With full respect, mate – you sound like a crackpot,' said Campbell. 'Give me big teeth and claws any day.'

Walker, Campbell and Hocking grinned into the hot lights under what was left of their pancake make-up.

'That's what you've got, Perry, trust me.'

'What about survival of the fittest? Come on, Max!'

'Don't tell us, Max, you don't believe in evolution!'

The panellists laughed. Sweating profusely now, the powder of the TV make-up had become waxy – they looked like leering old clowns – ready to be torn apart.

The laughter of the studio audience was almost deafening, washing over Max and the other panellists in waves of sound that made it impossible to speak. The panellists laughed along with the audience.

Max looked out to the audience and through the hot lights could make out the darkened faces – nobody in the audience was laughing. It was a laugh track.

Max knew he didn't look much better. 'Survival of the fittest?' Max cried out. He thought of Tori. 'You know who that is? A mother breastfeeding her baby.'

Max looked from Walker to Campbell to Hocking and back as the laugh track was suddenly dialed down and faded to silence.

'That's your so-called truth,' Hocking said distinctly into microphone.

Walker's big teeth glinted towards the camera. 'Well, thank *you* Max One Cent Ring, and thank you, gentlemen – for an unforgettable, and memorably hilarious, show. That's *Mighty Money* – good night!'

Chapter 42

Ilona silently held up the *Australian Financial Digest*, folded back to Perry Hocking's column with the headline: 'The Greatest Fool?'

'Yeah, I know, I saw it,' said Max.

'Max, it wasn't some journo who called you the greatest fool – it wasn't even Mortimer Norton – it was Rupert Campbell, the head of the biggest bank in Australia! That's who the article is quoting – and we all heard him for ourselves on the tellie.'

Max looked at the strained expression on Ilona's face. She had just put down the fork she was using to nibble at a morsel of chickpea flour omelette still speared on the tip.

'Yeah, well what does Rupert Campbell know?' said Max testily.

Ilona had hit on a sore point: the eerie silence all morning from the vast majority of his colleagues. Even Steven Crossman, the head of the banking group lending to ZettaData, always so eager to please, always so ready with easy compliments – and so relieved and grateful for Max's proposal to inject new capital into ZettaData – hadn't texted or emailed, much less rung. No doubt Crossman was uneasy and waiting to see which way the wind would blow.

'What? Are you listening to yourself, Max? Who do you think you're kidding? You were called a fool by one of the most respected financiers in Australia. And I don't know why you consider yourself so superior to Mortimer Norton – he looks after his wife and children. They live in a comfortable home –'

Comfortable. A fifty million dollar mansion, not including its renovations.

They were sitting on the upper verandah of their ugly, fifteen thousand dollar a month Vaucluse rental perched on a sandstone crag on the east side of Hopetoun Avenue, well up the slope from the Nortons' waterside mansion, and boasting panoramic views of the harbour and CBD to the jaded gazes of its series of occupiers.

' – and they don't have to worry when they come home in the afternoon that their father may have lost everything in the market that day!'

'Oh, now darling, that's just ridiculous –'

Max recognised the silence that had settled over the financial markets in the immediate aftermath of the show as a sign everyone in the market was poised for a sign to appear; waiting like a heap of motionless iron filings to respond to a magnetic current from either of two dormant electromagnets that had just appeared in the midst of the markets, either Rupert Campbell or Max Ring, to arrange themselves into a pattern around the electromagnet generating the most powerful energy field.

He hadn't heard a word from anybody connected with ZettaData – not a single board member, or Don Ormsby. The paralysis in the markets might still end with a sudden flood of support – or it might end in *sparagmos*.

' – that's exactly what people are saying,' Ilona said indignantly.

This morning the entire traditional media ignored the show, but social media and blogosphere were full of comments about last night's airing of *Mighty Money*. The few minor references in conventional media outlets to Max's appearance on Mighty Money were generating hundreds of reader comments.

The majority of the more peripheral opinions posted supported Max, but the closer they originated to the establishment, especially the most prominent articles in the financial press and brokerage reports to institutional investors, the more they suggested Max was acting like a loud-mouthed American tycoon, cynically advancing his own interests in a most un-Australian way. Several analyst notes, not surprisingly from Coldstream Holdings and its allies, questioned whether he might be secretly acting for the ruthless American hedge fund predator Todd Edgell.

'Max, I don't think you have any idea how you come across when you say things on TV like, "I let other shareholders take two hundred million dollars instead of keeping it for myself"!'

That morning he had already been invited on several other talk shows, his email inbox was flooded with requests for interviews, and his Twitter followers more than doubled overnight, and were now well over a half a million.

'Well, maybe I do,' said Max, sensing the conversation slipping away, his hopes for their marriage sinking like a great stone into the sea.

'The girls and I were so embarrassed when you said that.'

'Really – the girls, too?'

'You sounded stupid, Max – and pompous. Who would walk away from two hundred million dollars? I'm not sure anybody believes you. Two hundred million dollars is serious – what do you call it? – 'fuck you' money. If it was real, you would have grabbed it.'

'No, Ilona, darling – that was exactly my point on the show. I don't want us to get obscenely rich by exploiting the way the system currently works. Why – so that, at the end of our lives, we can establish a trust to start giving away all the money? What's the point of that – why don't we share in the first place? I want to bring along others on the way – not give them small handouts of some of the money I shouldn't have taken in the first place!'

Max felt his pulse pounding in his temples and under his fresh shirt he was warm. If he didn't calm down, Ilona would accuse him of losing his temper – and he'd start sweating into his shirt and have to change.

Max's mobile rang. 'It's Kent Logan.'

Ilona's mouth snapped shut and she nodded angrily, curt permission to answer his mobile.

'Yes, Kent.' Max held his breath.

'Yer made some good points on the tellie, son.'

'Kent, about that line about a billionaire being a policy failure –'

'You overstated the case for effect, son, I get that. It's ok.'

A warm wave of relief washed over Max. They both knew hundreds of people, including scores they called friends, who must be feeling offended, at the very least, perhaps even threatened, after watching *Mighty Money*.

'I'm interested in the stability of Australia, son, it's my home and I want the system to work for everybody. I believe in it.'

'That's great to hear, Kent, I appreciate you ringing to tell me.'

Max glanced at Ilona and saw her chair was empty.

'You know how we started out, Max? My family employed millions of Australians over the last century, and we worked together with the unions and paid a living wage. Families and communities all over Australian have thrived because of Logan Industries.'

'Right,' said Max.

'What I realised while I was watching the tellie last night is that your ZettaData deal is like an election. The shareholders are voters. If they support you, you'll win. Now, I'm keeping my money with you – but you have to expect that some of the boys won't. You bent some noses out of joint last night.'

'I can imagine,' said Max, thinking again of the vast morning silence, until this phone call.

'These are forces of history, Max, and I never interfere with them. I just adapt to whatever they are. If you win this, you might find yourself standing for a real election one day, son – that's how big I think this might be.'

Max was stunned and flattered. 'Well, thank you, Kent, I appreciate everything you're saying.'

Max could hear Logan inhaling on his cigarillo across the line. 'I just want to remind you of the rules of the game. You've got my five bars, but the other mob are not going to be playing patty cake. You have to win on your own. Other than the five bars I've got with you, I'm not putting my thumb on either side of the scale. Not yours, and not the other fellers. Good luck to you.'

The line went dead.

Max looked up to see Ilona had returned with a freshly made soy latte. She was sitting erectly in her chair, her posture perfect, holding the saucer and cup with both hands, watching him through pupils that could be pinpoints.

Chapter 43

Ilona watched Max nodding his head as she sipped her soy latte. From his alert posture and attentive, respectful tone it was clear Max was super-gratified by what he was hearing.

She was ready – the decision had suddenly crystalised as she frothed the soy milk. Today was the day. She'd tell Max as soon as his phone call was over.

Kent Logan. The old lecher. On the few occasions when they had met at Nightingale School events he'd given her the creeps.

'Well, thank you, Kent, I appreciate everything you're saying,' Max said. He was no doubt proud to be treated like a confidante by Logan. She wasn't having a bar of it – Mort was closer to Kent Logan than Max was, and always would be. He and Kent Logan had known each other for forever and a day.

Ilona watched Max nod his head as he listened to Logan – my god, how many times could her husband bob on the billionaire's nob? She wasn't nervous about what she was about to tell her husband. Energised—that's how she felt: full of a warm feeling. Her breathing was relaxed and even. As she watched Max kissing Kent Logan's arse, Ilona wondered idly how Alexandra did it. Fucking Mort. Sucking his dick.

Max put the phone down.

Ilona took a tentative sip of her soy latte, feeling its warmth across her lips. Maybe she could stomach it too – but she wouldn't want to kiss Mort. Ugh.

'Well, he's on side,' Max said, with one of the self-satisfied smirks she loathed so much.

The evening before and this morning, she'd already had dozens of texts, messages and calls from friends, acquaintances and random Nightingale mothers, mostly gushing over how dashing Max looked and how passionately he spoke about the takeover. She must be so proud. If they only knew. Even Magda Wexroth had been caught up with enthusiasm, and swept away by her approval of Max's appearance and how sincere he looked and sounded on TV. Ilona had to have a few sharp words with her old friend.

'So, you're going forward with the takeover, Max? I want to be sure I understand.'

Max looked at her in surprise. 'Of course, darling. There's no going back.'

She knew what Mort thought. And not just Alexandra, but a few of the cannier callers who went beyond social niceties. Perhaps reflecting their husbands' reservations about Max's true motives, guardedly asking how sincere Max was being, or if he was perhaps on a bit of an ego trip – or had just found a controversial new ploy to add to his takeover tactics.

In fact, Alexandra didn't need to say a word. As soon as she saw the caller was Alexandra, Ilona announced, 'You were right, darling. Max is acting exactly the way you predicted.'

'Well, there's no going back for me, either, Max,' said Ilona firmly, even feeling a little triumphant. 'I've tried to explain how I felt about the position you've put me and the girls in, and you haven't done anything about it. Despite what you said a little while ago, I don't see any evidence you really care what I think. So I'd like us to sign a Statutory Declaration of Intention to Divorce. I want a financial settlement that protects the three of us, no matter what happens to your deal.'

Max turned pale. 'You want a divorce?'

'No, I want a financial settlement.'

'Do you want me to move out?'

Ilona felt she was in uncertain waters. She shrugged, trying to sense her truest self. 'That's up to you, Max. I'm not suggesting we separate. But I need us to sign that Stat Dec, because what I do need is a financial settlement.'

She felt a thrill – this was how she had been encouraged to be by Alexandra – acting according to her purest, highest self.

'Really? You mean it?'

'I need our finances to be completely separate, Max. Separate accounts, everything.'

'I'm sorry to hear it, but I think I can understand your point of view.' Max crossed his arms and leaned back in his chair, watching her. 'It's disappointing, but ok.'

'Look at the bright side, Max – if you make a billion dollars on ZettaData, it's all yours.'

She watched him redden. She didn't necessarily want Max to leave the family, she didn't want the disruption for herself and the girls, but she needed to live without fear, without anxiety—and most importantly, without compromise. She yearned for purity: her ideal when she was hungry.

'What are we going to tell the girls?' Max said.

'I'm not sure we need to tell them anything,' said Ilona, feeling a twinge of annoyance. As if Max actually gave a thought for the wellbeing of Samantha or Elizabeth. He didn't have to front up for the meeting with the Headmistress! Their Sam and Trixie Norton were the two most popular girls in their year, and Sam's popularity was despite her father, not because of anything he had done. Mort was a much less controversial father than Max—she would never have imagined it, but it was true.

'Well, let me think about it,' Max said, standing up. 'Is there anything else?'

'I'll send you a draft of the Stat Dec,' said Ilona. 'And I've retained Gottlieb, Teufelfreude to negotiate our financial settlement.'

Max shrugged. 'Ok, then let's get on with it.'

Max Ring – big, bad merchant banker and corporate raider, Ilona thought, sipping on her latte. Unmasked as a push-over.

She already felt slight contempt now. At a certain level, she realised she had probably wanted Max to be strong and scary, even if she liked him less for it. Years ago, when she still respected Max, and occasionally was even a little intimidated by him, the feeling made her feel safe and protected, as if her husband was someone who could truly look after her and her babies, come what may. It also conferred a satisfying sense of her moral superiority to her restlessly competitive and hot-tempered husband.

This morning he'd just caved with hardly a whimper. Who said nice girls didn't finish first?

Chapter 44

'I liked what he had to say,' said Luke Terry, looking across the table at Mort with unfriendly eyes as a waiter in a white coat laden with a large platter approached them. 'I reckon he was bloody sensible.'

'Oh sure, you would have liked that bit about billionaires,' said Mort, shifting slightly in his seat, suddenly not in the mood for reconciliation. 'Of course you did, Luke.'

'What – is that where you're up to these days, you old cocksucker? A billion? Taking what Ring said a bit personally, are we?' Terry grinned his menacing wharfie grin – often his opponent's last sight, back in the day, before his face got smashed in.

'If I'm not yet, I certainly plan to be,' said Mort. 'Meanwhile, have you twigged to how much Ring is going to shit all over you and *your* plans – or are you still too busy fantasising where you'll set up the guillotine in Martin Place?'

Terry wasn't listening, or pretended not to be. His craggy face was blank as he looked around the restaurant, taking in the fully prepared tables, the posh furnishings, the gleaming finishes, and the stunning view of the Sydney Opera House. It was a few minutes past six in the evening. The restaurant was completely empty like it was Covid all over again. 'This is a Thursday night – how did you pull this off?'

Mort smiled. 'If the Premier can do it, I can do it.'

After a certain point, money itself is irrelevant if you can't fuck with people, when and how it suited you, at your absolute discretion. Otherwise, where was the fun? 'We've got another hour, at least,' Mort said. 'No worries.'

Terry looked around suspiciously, like a cat in a new house. 'What did they do with all the people with reservations? It takes months to get a table here. This place has been jammed since the restrictions ended.'

'They're probably at the bar – or wanking in the toilet. Who cares?'

After a brief inspection, Terry waved away with a contemptuous grimace the platter of Szechuan yellowtail sashimi anointed with Szechuan ponzu and chili oil, Toro tartare rubbed with Japanese mustard and Sansho pepper, Black Sea Bass carpaccio infused with chili lime Tosazu and fennel, and Red Snapper rolls marinated in Yuzu avocado, lemon oil espuma, and mentaiko.

'I don't want that poofter fodder,' Terry said. 'Who do I have to blow around here to get a VB?'

Victoria Bitter, the working man's beer. Early in his union movement career, Luke Terry was deemed a genuine idealist, something that could never have been said – at any time – about himself, Mort knew.

Mort snapped his finger at the waiter and said, 'Get my friend here a VB, and get me a glass of the 2007 Clos Saint-Jacques.'

'Sir? The Gevrey-Chambertin? Apologies, we don't offer that by the glass,' said the waiter.

The idealist sitting across the table now lived in a five million dollar mansion on the Lower North Shore with meticulous mock-Tudor cabinetry throughout the entire ground floor, walnut wood-panelled walls choked with his first-class collection of contemporary art, and, under the staircase, a safe stuffed with three million in cash. Mort had heard about all of it.

But Luke Terry drank VB, and he still drove a Holden to work.

'Then open a fuckin' bottle, maybe I can convince my friend here to try a glass,' Mort said, watching Terry redden and curtly shake his head. He enjoyed the fact he'd succeeded in making both Terry and the waiter uncomfortable – a trifecta for the evening including the major domo, who was standing respectfully out of earshot, visibly mortified to have been ordered by the restaurant owner, Mort's mate, not to seat anyone else until 7:30 pm.

'Ring can't shit on my plans,' said Terry suddenly. 'Nobody can – including you.' He'd obviously been thinking over what he'd said while going through the whole charade about sushi and beer. 'I'm standing in Grayndler, and once we form government and I'm appointed minister, I can cut Ring's balls off any time I please – but yours will be first.'

Terry smiled his hard smile, one of the few times he revealed an expression that looked completely sincere.

'Yeah, knock yourself out, Luke,' Mort said thickly, using the tip of his tongue to push the mess of fish and rice out of the way so he could speak more clearly. 'Since when does a shadow minister get to cut anybody's balls off? You're going to spend most of the time on your own knees, with your mouth full, while you're in opposition for the next two to three years.'

'Fuck you, dickhead.' Terry watched with distaste as Mort picked up sushi with his hands and shoved the pieces in his mouth, one after the other. 'We can't lose this election.'

Grayndler, the seat where Terry would be standing in his maiden election, not only contained once-gritty East Balmain, where he was born, but was, quite apart from that fact, the safest Labor district in New South Wales.

The drinks came.

'Cheers,' said Mort, tipping his glass in Terry's direction, who sat motionless, just touching his glass of beer with his thumb and the tip of his forefinger. It was an old trick he learned working on the union crews: the best way to keep beer from going warm in the Australian sun, and he affected it in the posh, air-conditioned restaurant – while refusing to join the toast.

'Pull your finger out, mate,' Mort said, trying to dim the malicious joy sparkling in his eyes. 'If Max Ring wins his takeover of ZettaData, it's going to change the dynamics of your precious election.'

'Ballocks,' said Terry, sipping his VB.

'Yeah – what makes you so sure? What if Ring forms a new party? That might cause a three to four percent swing nationally. What if he joins the Greens and stands in the next election himself? That might cause an even bigger swing.'

Allowing himself to growl a little, like in the good old days, Mort said, 'Do you really want to suck Green dicks in order to form a coalition, when you're on course to govern outright?'

Mort inhaled the complex, savoury tang wafting from the platter of sushi, thinking suddenly of the smell of Max Ring's urine-soaked suit and the reek of his shit further fouling himself, rising from the open boot of the car as he gazed down on the fucker, bound and gagged. It was still only a daydream.

'Oh, is that right? You're saying Max Ring is the latest political phenomenon?'

'Do you know how many Twitter followers Ring has these days? He already thinks he's the messiah of small shareholders.'

'I know what's in his proposal,' said Terry.

'You'd better pull your fucking head out of your arse – it's not about Grayndler, matie – it's about all the other seats,' said Mort. 'Are you ready to deal with the fallout when Labor loses the unlosable election because of Ring?'

'You won't be the only one not happy about being in opposition. Forget Grayndler – that's given you a totally false sense of comfort. How's it going to look when the boys in

Chinatown start doing the CSI on who the fuck Max Ring is, how he rose to power, and who the fuck supported him at the beginning? You personally are in the crosshairs, mate, and make no mistake about it.'

'You're not making any sense,' Terry said uneasily.

'Once your crew have done the forensic, I sure wouldn't want to be the *single biggest shareholder* in ZettaData after Mr Ring himself, Luke – I'll tell you that right now. What a sad end to your brilliant career – and you'll be lucky if that's all you lose. When Max Ring put his proposal to the board, he shoved a live grenade up your bum and lit the fuse.'

'Let me think about it.'

Mort looked ostentatiously at his complicated wristwatch, a seventy thousand dollar gift from The Duchess for Valentine's Day, two years before. 'We've got forty-five minutes, mate.'

Terry's eyes narrowed, and he sat back in his chair, crossed his arms, and gazed sightlessly at the Opera House.

Should he have the boys keep Max's necktie on? What would be funnier? Leave it on, or tie it around his mouth? He'd probably cry into it if it's in his mouth, it's amazing how often men cry – tears and snot – before he was too dehydrated to piss, sweat or cry, anymore.

Maybe tie it around Max's balls and dick and leave it hanging out of his trouser fly. Haha. When he pisses and shits himself he'll make a real mess of that tie. Yeah, he liked that – more symbolic – Ok, Max – Mister Hot Shot Corporate Raider – show me your Hermès tie, why don't you? You know the one I mean! Haha.

Terry cleared his throat. 'I don't see why we can't be inclusive – you catch more flies with honey than vinegar. Say we give Ring a piece of the Tunnel deal in return for dropping the billionaire lines, the messiah bullshit, and keeping his mouth shut. He can just win ZettaData quietly – he's got Todd Edgell's piece, and I'm the only other significant voter on the share register.'

'No, you don't understand, my barrow boy cobber. You and the fucking Board of ZettaData created a monster when you approved Ring's deal. He's gone from being a sketchy loser I sacked, to being on the cusp of taking over a public company, making heaps of dosh, and becoming a talk-show star. We gotta shut him up.'

Terry looked stubbornly across the table. 'You say he's sketchy, so what's the big risk? I don't see it.'

'He'll be a lot less sketchy when he takes over ZettaData and makes money for tens of thousands of punters – and voters. This is fucking serious, Luke – you can't tell me he won't look for another public company like ZettaData. And why stop there? Why not call everyone's attention to the way things actually work in this town?'

He had to hit Terry where he knew it would hurt. 'What's stopping Max from making an announcement that the whole process for choosing the McConnochie Consortium for the Tunnel is rigged?'

Terry flinched. He'd extracted plenty of favours from McConnochie in return for supporting his selection. Terry's war chest was bursting now. Blocking Norton & Ring had been only part of a very lucrative package. 'He wouldn't do that. And besides, nobody would print it or broadcast it.'

'What makes you so sure?'

Mort said nothing further, just letting him process the idea. Luke Terry was a dealmaker to his fingertips, and nobody was going to take away his hard-earned right to make deals. He had worked too hard, suffered too much, made too many humiliating compromises and done too many dirty deals in order to reach his almost all-powerful status.

Terry took a sip of his beer and looked as if he'd just put something distasteful into his mouth.

'How do you propose to stop him?'

'It's too late to just get him kicked off Twitter.'

Terry nodded.

'What do you think? It's pretty fuckin' simple, innit?' Mort leaned forward. 'We gotta pull the plug on Ring's deal. Without ZettaData he's just another loud mouth. Unless he makes tens of thousands of punters rich, he's nobody.

'If he loses ZettaData, everything changes – tens of thousands of shareholders will lose money because they've believed him and invested in ZettaData. They won't love him – they'll hate him. Max Ring will be finished. He'll dry up and blow away. The job has to get done properly, mate.'

Mort chose another sushi piece, thinking of Max in the boot of the car, and as he placed it on his tongue he could almost taste the stale sweat of fear that would have soaked all the way through Ring's shirt, and the armpits and crotch of his suit.

It was something he and Alexandra shared in common; The Duchess could smell horse shit, or the shit in the intestines of a deer she was gutting, and love it. Like him, she didn't only find appeal in the aroma of Chanel Number Fucking Five.

And just as Alexandra didn't flinch at shooting and gutting deer, she was willingly helping him wreck the Rings' marriage. She had her standards, and he understood them: when she killed a deer, she insisted on a clean shot – no chance of maiming or wounding the animal by pulling the trigger while it was moving. Similarly, she wasn't on the nose at all about wrecking Max's marriage – or even bankrupting him – the first was certainly on the cards anyway and the second probably was, too – as long as Ilona and the girls were immunised by the Stat Dec and the financial settlement. No harm to women and children – just a clean kill. Of course, Alexandra didn't know, any more than Terry did, the full extent of his plans for Max.

'Ok, let's hear it – what's your idea?' Terry said heavily.

'Max Ring is the problem. Give me Ring!'

'What are you asking? I don't follow.'

'I said – give me Max Ring!'

'What do you mean?'

'Stop protecting Ring – cut him loose.' He leaned over the table, knowing Terry liked to negotiate like this: just one step away, one extra insult, one false move – from a fist fight, or worse. 'There's nothing Ring owns – or wants to own – that I can't take away. I'm going to buy ZettaData myself, which is going to be a fucking losing proposition, by the look of it – but I'm doing it for all of us. So, you can thank me by giving me a piece of McConnochie's Tunnel. The piece I deserved in the first place, you fucker.'

'Nuh,' Terry shook his head. 'No to ZettaData and no to the Tunnel. Ironically, ZettaData is the harder ask. I can't publicly let you invest. There's no way ANG, or I, or the minister, can voluntarily do business with you. Sorry, mate. The boys wouldn't like it. There's still some hurt feelings.'

Mort suppressed a smirk. Luke was talking about some of the toughest, most vicious blokes who'd ever shovelled Australian dirt. But they had gotten pretty passionate about the stupid fucking Green Ban, he knew that. And there was blood involved, and Mort was tangled up in the beatings, the kidnappings, the attempted contract hits, and the killing that did go down. Even though the suppression of the Green Bans happened decades ago, Luke Terry was probably right.

'You can't publicly do a deal with me?' Mort said, a little operatically, as if it were a big, hurtful surprise. 'Well, as a matter of fact I've got a perfect solution. We can work together and the optics will be fine – leave it with me, I'll explain later. Those are details – we're talking principles now. Do I get Ring?'

Terry glowered across the table. The outside corner of his left eye started twitching.

Terry had hired Mort not long after Kent Logan gave Mort his start in Sydney. Mort was recruited by Terry as muscle to handle violent strikers from a Maoist splinter faction in Terry's union. Mort had just arrived in Australia. Terry, the son of a wharfie on the Sydney docks, was a young union organiser already making his name. The Maoist fuckers were calling wildcat strikes on the construction sites of major office buildings in Sydney's CBD, reviving a trick invented during the construction boom after the War.

The wildcat strikes were killing the goose that laid the golden egg by sending property developers to the wall, and that was making the banks shaky. So something had to be done.

The Maoist fuckers would strike immediately after starting to pour the concrete for a floor. Once the pour starts it has to continue until the whole floor is poured, or it all has to be jackhammered up and and started again, because the concrete will crack like a biscuit right along the line where the two pours were made. Mort threw two of them off the top floors of the construction sites. That ended it.

It wasn't just his quick reflexes and strength that allowed him to overpower his victims. His low centre of gravity was essential when he planted a boot on the I beam, grabbed the stroppy Maoist fucker by his scruff and his belt and flung him into the void.

From the top of the building, the emptiness was so palpable it felt alive – and yet it couldn't bear weight. He'd had that experience first in the Carpathian Mountains as a teenager: in his struggles on the crags across those treacherous gorges the emptiness was more real, somehow, than the rocks and trees of the mountains themselves. Emptiness, *aboulie*.

Except that it was the antidote to *aboulie* – the only real one – as he stood, thrilled and a little shocked, full of life energy with every cell vibrating with its vital power, his pulse audible in his ears and pounding on either side of his throat, chest heaving with great draughts of air, the scream fading outrageously abruptly as he listened, the wind ruffling his hair, his boot planted like steel itself on the I beam, the pivot from which he had just flung the fucker into death's oblivion. He was completely alive – but when you look into the abyss long enough, it looks back at you.

'This isn't the Green Bans, Luke. We're on the same side now.'

Terry's face darkened with blood.

The Green Bans were arguably the most idealistic moment in the history of the Australian union movement – and back in the day, Luke Terry was all in. Mortimer Norton was, too – until he wasn't.

Terry shook his head.

'Mate,' Mort said, nodding encouragingly. 'It was years ago – decades ago. A lifetime ago.'

When Terry and his idealistic union mates tried to use the Green Bans to save King's Cross, Mort had to choose sides. He decided to stick with his real friends, the ones who gave him his first stake by making him the official owner of some of their buildings. He was only in his early twenties at the time.

'Yeah, you know whose lifetime,' said Terry bitterly. 'And she wasn't the only one.'

Mort sighed, he was going to have to let him have his little whinge. Terry was talking about the most famous victim of the fight for Victoria Street.

He'd killed her. They'd wanted him to cap her with a small calibre pistol – a pill in the brain. No sense of ceremony – but she was a queen in a way, and she was entitled to suffer in a royal way. The monarchs of Europe had always had inconvenient family members, rival claimants to the throne or whatever. If the inconvenience was official, they had them beheaded. If it was unofficial like what went down in Kings Cross, they had them strangled in their dungeon cells – or in their beds in the royal apartments. No desecration of the royal body, no punctures or cuts, no *lèse majesté*. You have to kill royals without encouraging the mobs to run amok. Bog-standard Aussie hoodlums back in the day didn't understand, didn't even begin to, it was something he had brought to his adopted country. But he did her right. He could still remember her face changing colour until it looked swollen and polluted, how she voided from every orifice as he maintained his death grip on her throat. Rapturous with his own strength, gazing at the dumb suffering in her bulging eyes, he wrested her mind from her body as if shucking an oyster from a great shell, becoming increasingly exhilarated as he could feel her body, transfixed with pain, begin dying around the consciousness that had led it into the fatal trap. Death at its most grim and stately. It was his contribution to an otherwise merely sordid crime: a proper sense of ceremony.

'I'm not saying I would have done things the same way if I'd been making the decisions, but I wasn't. I got the order, and I did it.'

'Sure,' said Terry.

'The point is, it happened decades ago. This is about now.' They were both speaking in even tones. He wanted Terry feeling confident, thinking clearly.

The truth was, Terry's grudge was the last vestige of his idealism. Terry knew it, too. Forget the VB and his other affectations, Terry was no longer the man he once was. If he and Mort did business again, Terry was going to have to relinquish the last traces of the man he had started out as. It wasn't a bad thing. In return, he'd remove the last obstacle to Terry becoming prime minister. It was an obvious decision.

When they went their separate ways back in the day, the only real difference was Mort acted first. Terry postured just long enough afterwards to be able ride his reputation as a reformer for the next three decades all the way up until he was in sight of the top.

Terry looked at him, reluctantly, no longer angry but not wanting to concede the point. Mort smiled.

Terry eyed him. 'Ring doesn't mean anything to me.'

'Good to hear, mate,' Mort said. 'By the way –' he snapped his fingers again at the waiter – 'I've brought something along for you on the chance I'd be able to present you with a token of my good will.'

Mort smiled, but didn't overdo it. Terry didn't need to know he was about to help him destroy, not only Max's takeover deal and his reputation, but his wealth and his marriage – as a warm up. He only needed his support for step one, and Terry didn't need to know anything else about his plans. He had planned for Max Ring a special therapy for cunts with bad attitudes.

Two busboys carried over a rectangular package, puffy with protective wrapping. The front of the package was clear plastic. As Mort expected, Luke Terry instantly recognised the print as a rare Mignano. 'I thought you'd find it amusing since Mignano accidentally hanged himself in the Tarleton Hotel. It's only a modest addition to your collection, I know. But I thought you might also like the fact it was on the wall behind Ring's desk for the last five years. He dearly loved it, mate, I kept trying to buy it from him but he refused. When I sacked the fucker, I kept his fucking Mignano print. Now it belongs to you, mate.'

Max had chosen exactly the wrong time to make friends with his oldest daughter. They'd obviously met through that bird in the theatre, the actress, who Max was bonking. But his timing couldn't have been worse – the very moment Hugh's body disappeared. At any other time, Max would still have had to pay the consequences for stickybeaking into Norton family business. It was just going to be worse now.

He watched Terry's eyes dilate. He and his senior union mates never set foot in the Tarleton Hotel because it was a non-union operation. Several years ago, Mignano had accidentally asphyxiated himself in a suite while standing on a chair with a rope around his neck getting a blow job from a hooker. Terry would appreciate that. The Tarleton was just across the water from where they were sitting. And besides, a copy of the print last changed hands for over a hundred thousand dollars.

Terry set the print carefully against the table and stood up. His face was expressionless, and for a second Mort wasn't sure what would happen next.

Terry stepped around the table and offered his hand.

'You better leave through the kitchen,' Mort said. 'We shouldn't let the crowd in the bar see us walking out together. No doubt there's more than a few blokes out there who would be very interested. The boys can take it down to your car and put it in the boot.'

The print was worth several times more than Luke Terry's car – which was just the way he liked it.

Max was going to finish his career in the boot, too. It was one of his favourite operations, back in the day. Grab the recalcitrant cunt, gag him and tie him hand and foot, throw him in the boot of a big-arse Holden and have the lads drive him around for a day or two. Just drive around. Give him plenty of time to think about where he might be going, what might happen to him. No food. No water. Of course they pissed and shit themselves – immediately or eventually – and got to lay in it. And then – after twenty-four or thirty-six hours – the lads pull up by the side of the road, pull the cunt out of the boot, cut him loose, tell him to keep his fucking gob shut, and drive away.

As he watched the major domo escort Terry and his package out through the kitchen, he had another idea: maybe throw a chainsaw or two in the boot, too. Give Max something to worry about – what's coming – and while he's rolling around in the boot and bouncing around as the boys drive over bumps, the chainsaws would be touching up his suit a bit, cutting it here and there, smearing him with cutter oil and petrol. Haha. He'd be a complete wreck, when the ride finally ended and they hauled him out. He'd expect to be castrated, or cut limb from limb, and then beheaded, probably, with a chainsaw. Haha. Have to keep it fun – thinking of new angles. Otherwise, what's the point?

Neither Luke Terry or The Duchess would ever know: like everyone else, Max would be too frightened to say anything about the ordeal, too aware of the hopelessness of his position.

It would just be a special memory for the two of them to share. Their little secret.

Chapter 45

'A dog collar,' said Alexandra languidly but distinctly in her upper class English drawl.

Ilona shuddered. 'Here you are darling,' she said, handing over a granola bar to a little Nightingale schoolgirl with thick glasses and glossy hair brushed under her regulation straw school hat. As Ilona accepted the girl's change, she realised she'd just understood something about Alexandra's voice for the first time.

It was their day to volunteer at the Nightingale Tuckshop and it had been a busy lunch period, with hundreds of girls choosing to buy their lunch today rather than bring a packed lunch from home. The food line was just trailing off, but in a few minutes the ice cream line would form. Ilona had so missed the chance to see their daughters and their friends together at school, and it was soothing to return to normal after what was increasingly seeming like the nightmare of the lockdown.

'That skinny, little pot-bellied man with his hunched shoulders ... ha, ha, ha! Can you imagine!'

Until that morning Ilona was always charmed by Alexandra's accent with its elegant tonic scale of amused indifference, but today for the first time she realised its secret power.

Alexandra used her voice the way a jazz singer does; she slowed it down so her inflection and pronunciation hovered in her listener's consciousness. It was as if she thought of conversations as unfolding within the thirty-two bars of a jazz song, but suddenly Ilona noticed her friend's delivery made it possible to hear the dark universe from which the beautiful, seemingly carefree music originated.

'That's awful!' said Ilona, conscious of her flat Australian twang, and more so of the clipped, business-like, unmusical sound of her voice. 'Martin is such an ... *unprepossessing* man – and what a revolting fantasy.'

The last girls in line buying their lunches had no idea what the two volunteering mothers were discussing, of course. For the past twenty minutes, as the two women handed out a seemingly endless flow of grilled free-range chicken, gluten-free brown rice pilaf, steamed organic broccoli, and lemon-oregano net-caught fish and non-GMO chips, Alexandra had managed to reveal the latest gossip about Martin McConnochie, in enigmatically cryptic, but graphically thorough, detail.

The story had been coming out in similarly innocent phrases: 'She finally smelled a rat … The guy followed him around for a few weeks … Took lots of photos and videos … She's in one of those new apartment buildings in the CBD.'

Everyone in the east knew how Martin had transformed McConnochie Construction, the company founded by his grandfather to erect houses after the war, into one of the biggest builders in Australia. McConnochie was also now a big contractor on pipelines, highways, oil and gas projects, and the company was one of the bidders on the short list to build the amazing new tunnel that was going to completely encircle Sydney and connect all existing tunnels and roads into a vast, high tech and efficient road network that would be one of the best transportation systems in the world. Apparently, Martin's wife had become suspicious of her husband's after-work activities and hired a private investigator to follow him around Sydney.

After some stomach-churning descriptions of Martin's wedding tackle, Alexandra had just revealed what Martin's mistress wore when he visited her. She'd said it right in front of the girls standing in line on the other side of the counter because it sounded innocent enough.

'Really … a dog collar!' echoed Ilona, the surprise in her voice bearing audible disgust in its wake.

The queue had briefly vanished, and not a girl was in earshot.

Alexandra leaned against the bench. 'The PI made a compilation video out of what he saw on Martin's visits and Bianca watched it – it took her several attempts to get through the whole thing. Martin puts a collar and leash around the hooker's neck, makes her get down on all fours, and she barks like a dog while he takes her from behind!'

Alexandra was laughing unnervingly. 'Martin!' There was that bitterly amused quality again in the way she pronounced his name. "Summer time …. and the living is easy". She sounded bereft somehow, as if she were all too aware of the tragic exigency the song proclaimed, the cold transactional heart of marriage: "Your daddy's rich, and your ma is good-lookin".

'It's so degrading,' Ilona said, listening to herself speak. She sounded like an old-fashioned typewriter.

'It must make him feel important,' shrugged Alexandra.

Ilona suddenly felt fiery hot, and knew her face had flushed so dramatically that any schoolgirl who appeared at the counter would notice immediately. Alexandra had just reminded her – oh, so painfully – of the way Max tried to excuse his years of bad conduct by blaming her – by accusing her of not making him feel important!

'Are you feeling all right, darling?' Alexandra was looking at her with surprise and concern, inconspicuously assessing her mottled complexion. 'Having a hot flush?'

'What is wrong with men?' Ilona seethed. 'I mean – really – what the *hell* is wrong with them?'

'Oh, darling ... ' Alexandra said lightly, evidently trying to soothe Ilona's anger by brushing it aside.

'Fucking a dog is important?' demanded Ilona. 'That's what important men do? I hope she divorces him and takes him for everything he's worth!'

Her heart was pounding and she was surprised her rage was still unslaked and, if anything, continuing to build. Was that Max's next move – putting dog collars on hookers? Why not – surely that would be her fault, too! Maybe Max just couldn't feel important unless he too had a naked woman on her hands and knees barking at him. She felt sickened.

'Well, in the first place, that's not going to happen,' said Alexandra. 'At best Bianca will get sixty percent of whatever he's officially worth, which is a fraction of what he's really worth.'

From fiery rage, Ilona could now feel herself going ice cold with contempt as she imagined the repellent scene. 'But what about her self-respect? How could Bianca live with a man who did such a thing? Husband or not! That actually makes it so much worse!'

'That's why Bianca wanted to talk to me,' said Alexandra. 'She asked whether I thought she should divorce Martin.'

'Of course she should!' said Ilona. She was offended by Martin's fetishistic need to humiliate all the women in his life, but it also made Bianca seem tainted by her willingness to possibly compromise. Ilona felt sick inside.

Ilona had been a little anxious about their relationship ever since Alexandra's daughter Trixie had eclipsed Sam as the most popular girl in Nightingale. Ilona had been feeling a little insecure, not just because of the catastrophic breach between their husbands, but because Alexandra no longer needed her, now that Trixie didn't need Sam's halo effect. The way Alexandra was confiding in Ilona had been so reassuring – until the conversation steered in this direction and evoked her own nightmares.

'What I asked her was, "Does he do it to you?"' said Alexandra.

Ilona looked at Alexandra. 'You mean ... ?'

Alexandra nodded. 'I asked her, "Does he put a collar around *your* neck and make *you* bark like a dog?"'

'She said, "No, he doesn't", and I said, "So – why do you care?"'

Ilona studied Alexandra. Alexandra obviously assumed she would agree that if Martin wasn't putting a dog collar around Bianca's neck, then Bianca should be ok with that. Alexandra seemed to be inviting her into her very innermost circle, which was very flattering in a way – in fact, more than Ilona had dared to hope – but part of being inside that elite group meant swallowing a set of pragmatic values, Ilona hardly dared even use the word *values*. Her problem was she found them unpalatable.

What did that say about Ilona herself – did she act, somehow, like a woman who would be ok with a rich guy degrading another woman? The very idea was repellent to every cell in her body. She understood Mort and Alexandra had a bleak, realist, even harsh view of life – they prided themselves on being the best of friends and the worst of enemies. They had certainly shown Ilona by their many acts of kindness to her and her daughters that they were the best of her friends.

'So you think Bianca should stay after seeing all those photos and videos?' Ilona asked, studying the bleak look in Alexandra's eyes from behind her sensuous lashes. It was unsettling to be confronted by this side of their pragmatism. 'Because there's so much money involved.'

'Not just money, darling,' Alexandra said, sounding like the opening bars of *Kind of Blue*. 'Family, lifestyle, their wide circle of common friends, companionship, their children. Everything.'

Of course she understood that Mort, at the very least, must derive some pleasure, and perhaps even some benefit, from the assistance he and Alexandra had been providing her and the girls. But it wasn't serious – it wasn't like they were asking her to vote her block of ZettaData stock against Max. She didn't have any actual power. Their kindness was private and purely personal.

Ilona wanted Alexandra to feel they were seamlessly aligned, but she had to be true to herself and she found herself shaking her head decisively. 'I couldn't do it. It would make me sick. I would burn the whole world down if I found out something like that.'

What could be the key to the mystery of Alexandra's relationship with Mortimer Norton? Alexandra certainly wasn't oblivious, after all, to a man's looks – not the way she described Martin McConnochie hunched over his hooker as he yanked on her dog collar. And her first two husbands, the Argentinian polo player and the Italian F1 driver had both been extremely handsome. Of course she wasn't. She was a woman and shared the same feelings as Ilona.

Alexandra smiled kindly. 'Well, that's why I waited until you'd already decided to sign the Stat Dec before telling you poor Bianca's story. I wanted to make sure you weren't being emotional in any way when you made your decision.'

'Mrs Ring?'

'Oh, hello Lucinda, darling!' exclaimed Ilona, smiling at one of Sam's best friends.

Half-a-dozen girls had started to line up for ice cream, and Ilona could see scores more converging from every direction in order to buy a treat before the bell rang.

A terrible thought appeared in Ilona's mind. There were still twenty girls waiting to buy ice cream, but she couldn't wait. 'What did you mean about not wanting me to make an emotional decision?'

Alexandra glanced at Ilona, but she was making change, and then asked the next girl in line what she would like to eat.

It couldn't be.

'Darling,' she felt embarrassed about being so crude, but she had to know. 'That dog doesn't have two masters, does she?'

'Thanks, darling!' Alexandra said brightly to her little customer. 'Who's next – quick sticks!' She looked quickly at Ilona, not meeting her eye. 'Oh, no – of course not!'

'But then why would the story make me act emotionally?'

Their eyes met. The hair rose on Ilona's neck as she sensed the dark calculations of her friend's world looming before her.

Ilona took a deep breath and served the ice cream. As always, she loathed taking the girls' money in exchange for giving them this fatty, sugary poison – they should be eating rice crackers and freshly sliced mango. It was enough to make her despise herself every month for being complicit when she and Alexandra had their rota at the tuckshop. Especially after everybody had already gained so much weight during the lockdown.

A feeling was welling up inside her, something big, it felt like a shift in tectonic plates. Something terrible and irrevocable had just changed deep inside herself.

'Alexandra,' Ilona said quietly but urgently. She felt fearless, riding a surge of personal power. Several dozen girls were now in the ice cream line, but if Max was doing something she had to know immediately. 'What do you know?'

'Well now, darling, it's not my place –' Alexandra continuing to efficiently accept change and hand out Golden Gaytimes, Key Lime Splices, Magnums, Paddle Pops, Drumsticks, and Frosty Fruits.

'This may not be the right time to talk about this,' said Alexandra, her eyebrows raised. 'Why, you mean here?'

Alexandra shook her head slightly. 'I mean, we're all going to the premiere next week.'

The Eden Street Theatre. Ilona's heart felt like it was in her throat. How stupid she was! How trite of Max! It wasn't just ZettaData – he was having a full-blown midlife crisis – just as she had thought! She knew it!

How boring, it *was* just like what Alexandra had said about Martin, except for the dog collar thing – Max wanted to feel important, so he was revelling in adulation from the nobodies who watched him pontificate on the tellie and followed him on social media – and now he'd acquired his own little mawwie – model, actress, whatever. He was pathetic.

Ilona watched one girl as she wandered away, a green Splice in her hand, beaded with moisture, glowing in the sunshine.

'An actress?'

'I really can't say, darling. I don't want to pass on gossip. It might not be right, anyway. And you know what I think – even if it is true, I think you should just forget about it.'

Suddenly, Alexandra's sultry voice sounded insinuating, like a diabolic temptation, a shining lure to live a lie, an utterly humiliating, soul-crushing but luxurious lie, for the rest of her life. But what was the fucking Stat Dec for, after all? Ilona savoured in her mind not just every word, but every syllable: Statutory Declaration of Divorce. Bring it, baby.

The bell rang.

The counter was empty in front of them.

'As long as Max doesn't put a leash on my neck, you mean,' Ilona said, aware that she was again incandescent with rage.

Alexandra nodded sympathetically.

So this is how it feels. Ilona didn't want to insult Alexandra, or confront her in any way, but she didn't care whether she got ejected from Alexandra's inner circle as quickly as she had been brought in – she wasn't going to let her husband put a dog collar on her neck – or the neck of any other woman – while they were married! She wasn't going to tolerate his sick, narcissistic, puerile need to feel important.

She laughed suddenly. 'I'm not about to forget about it.'

Alexandra looked Ilona directly in the eye.

This wouldn't be the first time she stood up to Alexandra and let her know that as much as she loved her and appreciated being part of her world, she adhered to a different, higher, set of values. Ilona had already gently reproved Alexandra for the way she and Mort were pouring resources into Trixie's rising social star: they were throwing a birthday cruise for Trixie on the Norton's thirty metre yacht and inviting fifty girls – a breathtakingly lavish celebration. But, even with Sam's invitation potentially at risk, and the possibility the war between their husbands might spread into their own relationship, Ilona felt she simply had to remind Alexandra of her promise to the headmistress and insisted Alexandra invite Selena Woodbridge as well.

'It's a much more valuable invitation now that Trixie is the most popular girl in Year 7,' said Alexandra. 'I didn't promise Miss Whidbey to invite Selena to the best party of the year.'

Ilona had looked sternly at Alexandra.

'Oh, all right!' said Alexandra with exasperation.

Ilona had felt quite proud of herself when an extremely reluctant Alexandra issued a fifty-first invitation only a few days after the rest.

This was no time to march to the beat of Alexandra's drummer.

'I'm sorry darling – I can't do what Bianca can do.'

Alexandra regarded Ilona thoughtfully.

Ilona hoped against hope Alexandra would understand.

Suddenly Alexandra leaned over to Ilona and hugged her. 'Good for you, darling. I respect your choice.'

Ilona was silent, returning Alexandra's hug, blinking back tears.

'You should go see Richard. He'll have good advice for you, darling,' Alexandra said.

'Richard? Richard who?'

'Richard Wander.'

On numerous occasions over the last several years, she and Richard had exchanged glances at various functions, events and gatherings. Ilona often noticed Richard gazing at her from across the room, and when she did, he wouldn't look away.

'Why do you suggest Richard?'

She would hold her own gaze for just an instant longer as he looked at her with steady eyes and the faintest smile possible – allowing their eyes to connect just long enough to be significant, but still ambiguous, and then she would look haughtily away.

Alexandra smiled. 'Darling, now that you've signed the Statutory Declaration and agreed to the financial settlement with Max, you'll need to get independent financial advice about what to do next. How should you invest your capital, what kind of budget should you put in place to protect your and the girls' futures? Nobody's better at that than Richard – with all respect to Max, of course.' This was the voice of the Alexandra who had ridden across the Kalahari on a BMW GS1200; it pulsed with the civilised power of a highly evolved Boxer engine: it was a warm steel sword. That's what was needed, a sword to cut through her illusions and Max's self-delusions. Ilona could feel the cleansing, purifying power of her anger.

An affair with a mawwie. Her husband.

'Thanks, darling,' Ilona said faintly, already feeling the descent of an eerie calm within her. 'That's an *excellent* idea.'

'I've been there, too, darling. It doesn't feel like it now, but I promise you're going to be better and stronger by the end of this,' said Alexandra soothingly. 'Look at me!'

Chapter 46

M ax walked under the massive Colonial-era fig tree on the grounds of the Nightingale School, enjoying its dense shade on the hot spring afternoon.

'Hullo, Max.'

Max smiled at Navneel Narayan, a successful orthopaedic surgeon whose brilliant
daughter Prema played first cello in Nightingale's Senior Orchestra, even though she was
still only in Year 7.

'Hello Nav – how's tricks?'

They fell into step on the way to the Father's concert and Navneel, who hadn't travelled
overseas in two years, told Max with relish about a medical conference in Las Vegas from
which he had just returned. Max smiled and listened, as girls of all ages in various editions
of Nightingale school and athletic uniforms streamed past them.

'And how is Samantha?' Navneel inquired.

'Oh, well, Sam's playing clarinet in the Junior Orchestra, of course –' said Max.

His phone pinged with an ASX alert: 'An investor consortium headed by Palisades
Futures Holdings (PFH) announces its intentions to acquire the shares in ZettaData, to
be followed by a recapitalisation of ZettaData through the investment of additional funds
through a pro rata rights offering ...'

A rival takeover bid. Max stopped short. Nav, ahead two steps, turned back and faced
Max. 'Are you ok?'

Max looked up. Nav's handsome face suddenly seemed to be looking at him through
the wrong end of a telescope. 'Sure, mate – sure ... See you inside.'

Nav looked at him curiously, then headed into the hall. The concert was about to begin.
Max had less than five minutes to figure out what was going on, and to start his response
– before he was locked away incommunicado for an hour or more. The worst imaginable
timing for the announcement.

There were only two days remaining to file a Bidders' Statement, and less than three weeks before the EGM. It was a last minute ambush. The structure of the new bid was similar to his offer, it included a pro rata rights offering, too. Whoever Palisades was, they had obviously pored over the details of his bid and adopted some of the same features.

Max felt ice cold in the bright, hot sunshine. At least he was starting to make a real difference in the financial markets – no matter what Rupert Campbell and Perry Hocking had said on TV. The new bidder felt compelled to make a fair offer to ordinary shareholders, too. The rules of the game were starting to change. Despite the shock, Max felt good – the markets were listening to what he was saying.

He read on – there was a key difference: Palisades was offering as a first step to acquire the shares of ZettaData, and then as a second step to offer rights in a different security class that would be more senior to remaining ZettaData shares.

Curious. He flicked down to the price.

A punch seemed to land in the middle of Max's stomach. He felt the breath knocked out of him as he read the price Palisades was offering for a ZettaData share: $0.03.

Three cents.

Three cents!

The shares were trading that minute at forty-two cents! What possible reason would there be for investors who bought shares at prices up to forty-two cents to sell their shares for just three cents? Who ever heard of a takeover offer pitched below the current price of a target's shares?

The Palisades offer seemed to boldly proclaim that the current ZettaData share price was a sham. Max suddenly saw Rupert Campbell sitting next to him under the hot TV lights, looking ghastly and uncanny in his heavy pancake make-up, saying, 'Oh, that's easy to explain. It's called the "greater fool theory".'

The sound of the orchestra tuning up through the open doors of the concert hall floated out to him on the breeze. Max looked around. There were no other fathers or girls in sight. The plaza was deserted. Miss Whidbey, the headmistress, was personally starting to close the front doors of the hall – Nightingale events were run with military precision – and Max realised he was in danger of being locked out.

Max raised a finger in the air from twenty metres away, imploring Miss Whidbey to hold the door open long enough to admit him. As he hurried towards her, streams of numbers coursed through his mind in every direction: at three cents a share, shareholders were basically wiped out. They would be worse off than before the AGM, when their shares were trading at five cents, at the time an all-time low.

The new bid was a disaster for ANG. The common shareholders? The Casners would be wiped out, but it had taken almost a decade for them to lose their investment, while all the new shareholders who bought ZettaData shares after Max announced his deal would lose almost their entire investment in only six weeks. The tens of thousands of people who had trusted him and his promise they could invest on equal terms with him would instead be shocked to find their investments annihilated. Max's reputation would be destroyed forever.

Miss Whidbey's face was deeply disapproving as he stepped past her through the door: fortunately, she liked Ilona, Sam and Billie. He quietly entered the top and back of the darkened theatre.

The new takeover offer was absurd. There had never been another takeover offer like it in the history of the ASX: how could Palisades, whoever they were, force ZettaData shareholders to sell their shares at three cents? What could possibly be the Palisades strategy? Max calculated Edgell's stake ... and suddenly it became clear.

The Choir Mistress was droning away from the middle of the still-empty stage and Max could see about a third of the fathers ignoring her, their faces glowing in the pale light of their phones. Max spotted a seat halfway down on the edge of a row and quickly slipped down the aisle and into the empty seat. From the stage the Choir Mistress was saying something about the fact the students would play Vivaldi and Pachelbel.

The Palisades bid was targeted at Edgell: he was the only ZettaData shareholder who would make a profit. At three cents a share, the Palisades offer was worth twenty-six and a half million dollars – exactly one and a half million dollars more than Max had agreed to pay.

The Palisades bid wasn't really a takeover offer – it was directed at Edgell alone. The Palisades bid wasn't patterned on his new model of takeovers at all, but it cunningly imitated, on the surface, Max's attempt to treat ordinary investors fairly. So much for changing the rules of the game.

Palisades' three cent per share offer, combined with a rights issue, appeared similar to his own one cent per share rights issue only as protective colouring to disguise how outrageous and unfair their proposal actually was. It was similar to the way certain insects pretend to be leaves in order to lure their unsuspecting prey. But there was a puzzle: he and Todd Edgell already had an exclusive and legally binding sales agreement: Edgell couldn't sell his stake to Palisades for the additional million and a half dollars. So what was the point of the Palisades offer?

Long lines of girls began filing on stage. The puzzle teased Max's mind as he scanned the stage looking for Sam. After much shuffling back and forth on the now crowded stage, the Choir Mistress raised her arms to conduct and the opening of a Vivaldi piece swelled. Max saw the top of Sam's head, just visible in the crowd of clarinets and wood instruments. Prema Narayan was playing at the very front as first cello, as relaxed and graceful as a bird in flight.

Max's muted phone came alive in his hand, vibrating and its screen flaring. Most fathers had put away their phones, but defying disapproving gazes Max watched as text messages popped up like popcorn on his phone, faster than he could read them. Everybody he knew in Australia, beginning with the investors in his group: Haddad, Maloney, Sterling, and a dozen others – along with everybody else, financial analysts, journalists – Perry Hocking the very first – and lawyers, accountants, everybody with access to Bloomberg and ASX feeds wanted to know what he thought about the Palisades bid. Most messages were very short: 'WTF?'

The sounds of Pachelbel soothed him as he typed 'I'm on it' dozens and dozens of times and released his own texts and emails like arrows flying back out into battle. It was too early to Tweet. He had to read the entire bid before he could respond.

Who the fuck was Palisades Futures Holdings, anyway – surely not the big Singapore funds manager? Max read more: yes, Palisades was the big Singapore funds manager. Its investors were some of the most prestigious financial institutions in the world—what was Palisades doing in Australia trying to acquire ZettaData? Why was a billion dollar international investor suddenly competing with him for obscure, unloved ZettaData, a company that only a few months ago had crawled off to die quietly in a corner of the Australian Stock Exchange?

The bid certainly proved him right, and Rupert Campbell wrong, about one thing – the unfairness of competition in the markets. Except this time the professionals weren't preying on small, defenceless shareholders: they were taking on Max. He'd aspired to defend the interests of small investors in ZettaData: now he was getting his chance.

Max glanced up several times and was able to glimpse Sam, depending on how she and the other girls swayed in their seats as they played their instruments.

After reading the string of prestigious financial institutions and funds management firms who were Palisades investors, his eyes froze on a sentence at the bottom of the announcement, in the section 'Information about the Palisades Futures Holding ('PFH') Investor Group.' The investment vehicle being used to launch the takeover was an unincorporated joint venture between Palisades and PowerPartners.

PowerPartners was an off the shelf company, a shell, owned by Norton & Ring. He'd actually bought it in the middle of Covid, along with several other shell companies, in order to have ready-made vehicles to launch quick bids just like this one; they'd been left in Norton & Ring when he and Mort settled. Stress jolts flickered up and down Max's arms. *Mort had partnered with Palisades.*

It had been a week and a half since returning from Byron, and there had been no sign of Mort. Now it all made sense – he had teamed up with Palisades and was going after Luke Terry, and Max was more-or-less accidentally tangled up in the duel between Mort and Luke, just as Wander had warned he would be.

Max sat back in his seat and slipped his phone into his suit pocket, ignoring the resentful sidelong glance of the guy next to him. So he was caught in the fight between Mort and Luke Terry over the McConnochie Consortium. By publicly offering three cents a share for Edgell's stake, the Palisades bid also suggested that ANG's investment was worth only three cents a share, which would represent a huge loss. Awkward for Luke Terry. But Max could save Terry along with the small shareholders. Terry would just have to ride out the public embarrassment for two-and-a-half more weeks until Max won the shareholder vote at the EGM, and then the value of ANG's investment would bounce right back. Luke could hang tight. The election probably wouldn't be called for another six months, plenty of time for the recovery of ANG's investment under Max's leadership. As long as Max won the shareholder vote at the EGM, all would be well—and how could he lose?

Mort was undoubtedly in the audience this morning. He'd noticed several texts he received from Nightingale fathers, who must be sitting in the same auditorium. Max looked around but couldn't spot anybody. He glanced down again at his phone, and tabbed down through the rest of the announcement.

The bottom of it read, 'Coldstream Holdings is acting as Financial Advisor to Palisades Future Holdings on this takeover offer.'

Rupert Campbell was the Head of Investment Banking at Coldstream. When Campbell said those things on *Mighty Money* he knew the Palisades bid was about to be unveiled. Hypocrite!

Max could sense an extraordinary mind at work on the other side, and he didn't under-stand what was motivating its actions. The sophisticated way the structure mirrored his own, the pitilessness of the plan to annihilate the investments of the ordinary shareholders Max was so determined to save, the surgical targeting of the interests of Todd Edgell – Max grudgingly acknowledged the signs of a twisted genius.

There was also a cynical aroma of black humour rising from the Palisades proposal that reminded him of Mort – but Mort was all thumbs when it came to finance, he totally lacked the expertise to structure something so elegant and diabolical. Campbell, although one of the most senior investment bankers in Australia, was a bureaucrat, not a great financial mind. Max would have suspected Richard Wander, he certainly had the flair. But Wander was financial advisor to ZettaData and it wasn't legal for Wander to be involved in any way with the Palisades Consortium. Besides, he was one of Max's closest friends.

Who else could have thought up the Palisades bid? Max didn't know Ted Hector, CEO of Palisades – was he brilliant? For that matter, what was Palisades doing in the deal at all? What did Ted Hector have against Luke Terry? And how did Mort know him?

At its heart, the Palisades bid was a mystery.

Max's fingers rapidly keyed letters into the phone and brought up the ASX feed to check ZettaData's share price. It was dropping rapidly – just below thirty-eight cents. In shock, Max hardly noticed the Junior Chorus filing off stage, seemingly endlessly, after performing five songs from across eleven centuries of the Western music canon, his chance to hear Sam come and gone. Now the Senior Chorus began their long march onto the stage. ZettaData's share price was being hammered by brokerage houses friendly to Coldstream – and all brokerage houses were friendly with Coldstream. The game was on: try and spook the ordinary shareholders into dumping their stock.

The prestige and clout of Palisades and Coldstream clearly worried investors, and with reason. But how they could force a deal through at three cents? He had a binding deal with Edgell, the only shareholder who could benefit, and as one of two strategic investors Edgell couldn't vote at the EGM. ANG had a shareholder agreement with Edgell, so the standard interpretation of the Corps Act forbade ANG from voting at the EGM, either. Only ordinary shareholders could vote; nobody could force them to vote for a deal that would destroy their own investments. Even after the lockdown had fully revealed the power of government to take previously unimaginable measures, it was unthinkable that the NSW or Federal government would ruin the small shareholders of ZettaData. And if they didn't, who could?

Max was confident he had the overwhelming support of the small shareholders, and their vote at the EGM would occur several weeks before the expiry of his exclusivity agreement.

It was obvious the Palisades bid targeted him too, by making a mockery of his campaign for fairness to small investors. His supporters like the Casners were now threatened with tens of millions of dollars in losses. Even though the Palisades bid appeared to have no chance of success, for the time being he and Terry were both being humiliated.

The Junior Orchestra and Choir were filing back onstage to join the Senior Orchestra and Choir. The timing of the Palisades announcement couldn't be a coincidence, either – it must have been deliberately released just before the Nightingale Concert. Its timing must have been Mort's idea – he would know Max would be at the concert to hear Sam. A nasty but clever stroke. Despite trying, Max had largely failed to watch Sam's performance. He had to hand it to Mort – he knew how to inflict pain.

Mort himself would be sitting quietly listening to the music – if he ever did listen to the music – relaxed and gloating – knowing he had Coldstream Holdings and Palisades' billions, and their investment banking teams at his back, while he and Ted Hector launched an attack simultaneously on both Mort's oldest, and his newest, enemies: Luke Terry and Max Ring. It was Mort's idea of a good time.

Max scanned the darkened audience. At last, down to the left and only a few rows back from the front of the auditorium he saw Mort, close enough to the stage to be lit by its light. Mort had just turned his head, and was looking back at Max. The music began and filled the theatre as Max and Mort locked eyes.

The prestige and power of Coldstream Holdings was continuing to deliver results for their client Palisades. ZettaData's shares were now at thirty-two cents, down twenty-four percent in an hour. Every decline made the Palisades bid seem that much less absurd – but the shares couldn't possibly drop to three cents.

The last piece of music was being performed by the combined junior and senior orchestras, and Sam was completely hidden somewhere deep within the crowded stage.

He wouldn't give Mort the satisfaction of appearing ruffled in the slightest. He had followed the breath through the shock of the initial skirmish and was safely and calmly on the other side. He was going to look happy and cheerful.

When the concert finally ended, Max clapped louder and longer than anybody else, and as the lights came on he stood up slowly in case Mort had any intention of catching up to him as the throngs of fathers filed out. Max had switched off his phone, and outside the theatre he chatted with several fathers as everyone else turned on their phones and checked their messages. Just as he expected, he started to be approached by fathers asking him about the Palisades bid. Max stayed relaxed and cheerful, telling everyone the same thing: it was fine, and he would be in contact with the company shortly.

As he waited for Sam to appear, Max noted a cluster of fathers standing around Mort, many of whom he knew well. Backing the big battalions, as usual.

'Daddy!'

'Sam, sweetie!' Max gave Sam a hug.

'What did you think?'

'It was lovely – one of the most memorable hours in years,' Max smiled. 'I just wish I had seen you better!'

Max walked Sam to her classroom and said goodbye, emphasising the normality of the situation by gently taking off her straw hat and giving her a kiss on the top of her head.

What he needed now was more information. He'd spent his career earning the right to access the best information in the market – it'd better be worth it now. He was going to see Richard Wander.

Chapter 47

Max's Porsche was still idling in the excruciatingly slow queue working its way down the long driveway of Nightingale to the exit through the gates on New South Head Road, but Richard's Executive Assistant Sharon Pinsent had already confirmed with a tone of calm hauteur that Richard would squeeze Max in between his afternoon meetings for a brief chat.

Max was now on his second-most-important call.

'Just one moment please, Mr Ring,' Luke Terry's EA was saying, and then the line went silent.

'Max.'

'I assume you've seen the announcement. We're both being made to look like fools.'

The line was silent.

'Who's the greatest fool?' Terry said drily. 'That's the question.'

'Anybody who accepts the Palisades offer.'

There was a calm silence on the line.

'It's pretty clear who Rupert Campbell considers the greatest fool,' Terry remarked.

'The greatest fool of all is the person who thinks they can frighten and intimidate the market—and voters—into thinking ANG's stake in ZettaData is worthless,' said Max.

'I couldn't give a shit what Mort Norton or anybody else at Palisades thinks,' said Terry. His voice was ice cold, but calm and considered. 'I'm not responsible to him or anybody else. I'm responsible to my shareholder minister and government, and my focus is – and will remain – the interests of the people of Australia.'

It was what Max expected. Terry proved himself at the beginning of his career with his fists and steel-toed boots, long before being offered responsibilities which revealed his first-class mind. ZettaData wasn't about flesh, blood or bone, it was only money at risk. Terry wasn't the typical outwardly aggressive, but secretly cowardly, investment banker or chief executive. He was a perfect ally in this stoush.

'This is a bizarre offer, Luke, but it's the work of bullies, not fools – one in particular. This shows Mort's desire to hit you and me as hard as he can – but he didn't put this proposal together, it's far too clever. I don't know Ted Hector of Palisades, but the proposal is the work of someone at the top of their game.'

Silence.

They didn't know each other well. Should he confide to Terry that he was beginning to suspect Richard Wander? Max had already been pilloried on Mighty Men in front of the nation and accused of everything from being a conspiracy theorist to an anti-vaxxer. Of course Terry was both informed and intelligent, and he would have known Max was being subjected to a propaganda barrage on the TV show. But Terry was also a politician and his decisions would depend on who his calculations indicated was the most powerful, and how closely their interests aligned with his.

Max decided to take a chance. 'Luke, the only guy with the brains to come up with the Palisades proposal is Richard Wander.'

'Impossible,' said Terry. 'He's advisor to ZettaData. Are you suggesting Wander would breach the Corps Act?'

'Campbell would be colluding with Wander, too,' said Max. 'I know it sounds crazy.'

'Accusing two of the top investment bankers in Australia of a grave breach of the Corps Act is pretty wild,' said Terry. 'Of course, my experience tells me anything is possible with capitalists.'

The idea that two of the top figures in the establishment were committing crimes to launch the Palisades bid sounded crazy.

'I must admit, against my theory, that I don't understand why two guys as prominent, and with as much to lose, as Campbell and Wander, would risk committing crimes over ZettaData?'

'I'm not going to talk out of school, but in board deliberations Richard has never said anything that indicates he is biased against your proposal,' said Terry. 'As far as I can tell he's been objective in his advice to directors.'

'Oh, I can tell you Wander's not happy about my bid,' said Max. 'Why, I don't know. And Campbell is already working with Mort, openly, in the Palisades Consortium. As you know, Mort is capable of anything . . . but Campbell and Wander? I have to admit, I don't see what motives they could possibly have. ZettaData isn't worth it.'

'I saw this morning that Norton & Ring filed suit against ANG,' said Max. Bob Henninger had sent him an email that morning with the news; it had seemed like a bombshell until the Palisades bid was announced.

Still, the idea that Mort was now suing ANG was almost unbelievable – except in the context of the Palisades announcement, and Max was sure the two events were somehow related.

'Yeah,' said Terry.

'I know as well as you do, Luke, there's no possible basis for a lawsuit by Norton & Ring against ANG,' Max said.

'Mort loves inflicting pain, it's what he's always done – and he's good at it,' Terry said.'

'I was Mort's partner, and I'll be happy to testify on ANG's behalf.'

'Thanks, mate.'

Finally, Max was out of the school gate but he was now stuck at the red light on Ocean Street. He heard Terry clear his throat. 'Let's divide up the work, Max. You focus on your deal, and I'll focus on the lawsuit.'

'Done,' said Max.

He slipped down Ocean and was racing up Greenoaks Avenue and across the top of Darling Point. Max felt good: he was shoulder to shoulder with Luke Terry and he had an exclusivity agreement with Todd Edgell. Whatever he was up to, Mort didn't have a chance.

Chapter 48

Max was only a couple blocks from Richard's office and hadn't given any thought yet about where to park. His former parking spot at Norton & Ring was, annoyingly, in a building only a block away – its loss one of Mort's petty victories along with the theft of his Mignano print. Let him have those cheap wins, Max thought, he was going to win ZettaData.

Max spotted a parking place on the street just a block from Wander's building, in a fifteen-minute parking zone. Max pulled into it, even though he'd be at Wander, Fleagle & Co. at least twice as long and the parking ticket would cost close to a thousand dollars.

Max set the brake and put the top up, thinking uneasily the Casners supported their son by saving much smaller amounts of money than the parking fine he was about to incur. But today, saving time was far more important than saving money – for everybody. Max hurried up the street and into the huge office tower, arriving only a minute or two later in the glamorous, faintly aromatic foyer of Wander, Fleagle & Co.

'Hello, Max,' said Sharon Pinsent, Wander's beautiful, chilly EA. 'Richard will have a quick chat with you just after he steps out of his current meeting.'

She glanced across the Wander, Fleagle & Co. reception area at a delegation of robed Middle Eastern men being shown into a conference room by two beautifully groomed and dressed employees. Stepping close, Sharon murmured in Max's ear, 'He's running late for his next meeting with these gentlemen.'

Max sat back on the Italian leather sofa. Continuous streams of elegant young people, many of them of East Asian and South Asian descent, appeared noiselessly from one door, crossed the foyer in all directions, and disappeared noiselessly through another door.

Another group of men emerged from a conference room with Wander walking in the very middle and spilled into the reception area. Max recognised the man with whom Wander was deep in conversation as managing director of one of the largest public companies in Australia, and he watched as Wander ceremoniously said goodbye to the departing group as if he were Doge of Venice.

As the men filed out to the lift bank, Wander stood perfectly erect with his hand raised slightly in farewell and when they disappeared he immediately pivoted and strode quickly towards Max.

He's very good, thought Max. Until then, Wander had given no sign of noticing him waiting.

'Maxie.'

'Richie.'

They shook hands and Wander glanced over his shoulder. 'I'm late for my meeting with a delegation from one of biggest sovereign wealth funds in the world,' he said quietly. 'But I saw the Palisades proposal – I'm here for you.'

Wander walked briskly with Max towards the door of yet another conference room, firmly drew Max by one arm inside, and closed it.

'Max – what the fuck is going on?'

'You mean the Palisades proposal?'

'We'll get to that – but I'm talking about all the crazy things you're saying.'

'What, the billionaire thing?'

Wander nodded. 'You're a social media phenomenon!'

'I can't control that – people just started following me.'

'Jesus Christ, Max – what do you think you're doing, saying all that shit in public?'

'Come on, Richard – you know how to make a billion dollars.'

Wander frowned. 'No, as a matter of fact, I can't say yet that I do know how – you certainly don't, either.'

'Monopolies, inside information, and special deals with government,' said Max.

'You've turned into such a shit-stirrer, Max – I don't know what's gotten into you.'

Not surprisingly, Wander was aggressively upholding the current order over which he ruled almost like King Pentheus in the Euripides play that was one of the sources for *TransGod*. Max wouldn't have been surprised if Wander's next sentence was going to be a threat to crucify him – but he was Dionysus speaking for what people really wanted. Wander had better watch out.

'Since you've raised the topic of shit, let's talk about the Palisades proposal,' Max shot back. 'It's a brilliant imitation of my bid – reads like a cynical joke – the way it pretends to help small shareholders while it actually crushes them. It's killing the stock price.'

'Maybe the stock price was already dead.'

'It was at forty-seven cents this morning!'

'I'm not a true believer.'

'It's also an attack on both Luke Terry and myself.'

'Come on, Max, you sound paranoid.'

Max held Wander's gaze. Wander wasn't used to that from other people. 'Am I, Richie?'

'I haven't looked at the Palisades bid closely,' Wander said, looking away, his thin lips pursed in his square jaw. 'I've been in meetings all morning.'

'Look at the proposal, Richie. You'll see in about two minutes what I'm talking about it. This is fucking Mortimer Norton looking for revenge.'

Wander shrugged. 'Could be. It is how he works.'

'The guy's a thug,' Max said. 'He's got no finesse.'

'Oh, I don't think you're giving Alexandra enough credit,' Wander said judiciously. 'She's had a huge effect on him, Max – shown him a new way of life, given him two young daughters.'

Max was having none of it. 'Richard, it was you who suggested I go meet with Mort when I returned from London. Our partnership was your idea.'

'Yes, and it was one of my better ideas,' said Wander coolly. 'It's worked out well for both of you.'

'Until it didn't.'

Wander shrugged. 'I always knew there was the potential for a personality conflict. But it took five years to be a problem.'

'Richie—Mort is a thug! He's a wife-beater! He was up to his neck in dealings with the mob in the Cross. People tell me they're afraid of being killed by him. Did you know all this when you put us together?'

Wander looked unblinkingly at Max. 'Mort is rough around the edges, but his bark is worse than his bite. Anybody in Sydney will take his call. You were his partner for five years—what do you think?'

Max had to admit that he'd had a similar view for years. Now he was no longer sure.

'You didn't by any chance structure the Palisades proposal for Mort, did you Richie?'

'I'm flattered, Max,' said Wander with his grim smile. 'Especially after all those nice things you said about it – but I won't dignify your insane suggestion by replying.'

'Let's be really honest, Richard: where did Palisades get the information to make their bid?'

Palisades was able to benefit, of course, from plagiarising major sections of Max's own bid document, but Max's read of the proposal confirmed Palisades had obtained access to extensive inside company information on ZettaData, not sourced from Max's bid because he hadn't included it in his own document. Richard was the obvious source of all this inside information.

'Max, I can't imagine what the two of us might accomplish by speculating about the resources available to a highly credentialed and resourced team like the one put together by Palisades-Coldstream-Norton & Ring, but I can only assume …' and Wander began a long, tedious, uncharacteristically banal description of basic investment banking practices. It was completely false, and Max could see from the amused gleam in Wander's eyes that he was perfectly aware of his own lies.

' … and of course there is always the possibility that relevant data from an already-existing technical engineering report might have been incorporated …' Wander droned on, carefully studying Max's expression.

It was a weird experience listening to Wander's monologue, as if the conversation was no longer about words at all.

It was a kind of seduction, like two lovers looking into each other's faces for something, and when they recognise it, their bodies are already aligned and leaning closer, they're savouring the shared awareness that their words no longer make any sense. The words have become sounds, delightful nonsense floating about the master logic of their desire for one another.

Max sensed Richard was extending an invitation, but he didn't understand what it might be. He felt hypnotised and disorientated.

Max shook himself, suddenly turned towards the door and reached for its handle. 'Ok, Richard, I needed to know if you were friend or foe. It's pretty clear now. We've known each other a long time and –'

Wander grabbed Max by the arm. 'Listen: I can get you an allocation in the Tunnel Consortium. Just let Palisades take over ZettaData. It's going to happen anyway.'

Max was stunned. 'The McConnochie Consortium?'

'Of course, the McConnochie Consortium.'

Wander had obviously been instructed by other key figures in the Who's Who of Sydney already in the McConnochie Consortium to make this offer to Max to get him to let go of ZettaData. Why was ZettaData so important?

'How much?' Max asked cautiously. Was he being offered a crumb or two? It would be an impressive gesture if Wander succeeded in prying loose five hundred thousand dollars or a million.

'Let's say ten bars.'

Max couldn't believe it – a first-tier allocation, indicating the others already in the consortium had agreed to be meaningfully scaled back to accommodate Max's participation. It certainly revealed the truth about how concerned the establishment figures gathered in the Consortium were becoming about ZettaData and his takeover offer.

Wander misunderstood his silence, a rare miscalculation revealing how anxious Wander was to close the deal with Max.

'It's the best investment of your career. You'll never sell, you know that. It'll just gush cash flow forever.'

Kairos.

Max was being offered the chance to become one of the ultimate insiders, anointed as one of the knights of Sydney's Round Table. If he let ZettaData go, and accepted the offer, he was about to become powerful, an influential insider, and very, very wealthy. He didn't need ZettaData.

Wander dropped his voice. 'And now that you and Ilona have signed your financial settlement, the entire position is for your account, alone.'

Max felt a nasty, sweet feeling of satisfaction arising inside him at the thought of the scale of the future profits she'd relinquished.

Wander was there for him.

'The McConnochie Consortium has set the toll for the tunnel at six dollars,' Max said. 'You know as well I do the tunnel toll should be more like four dollars fifty – that is, without paying off the politicians.'

Wander's face reddened.

' ... and if the banks truly had to compete to provide funding, and if McConnochie and the unions truly had to provide efficient construction services ...' Max plunged on, ' ... the toll would be closer to three dollars.'

Wander was silent, his eyes burning into Max's.

Max would have to go back to doing deals the way Wander did deals. 'Just because you can do something doesn't mean you should do it. It's not a victimless crime, Richard. People like us will make billions because everybody else in Sydney has to pay three dollars more than they should every time they go through the tunnel – average working people and young families, older retired people, and students – everybody – so that we get rich.'

'"As rigged as Captain Cook's ship" as I recall you writing in one of your famous Tweets,' sneered Wander. His complexion had returned to normal, and again his eyes sparkled with malicious amusement.

'That's exactly right, Richard.'

'Well, as far as I'm concerned, Max, you've just described a beautiful system. Lots of people pay a tiny amount of money with almost no effect on their own lives – which produces a very large – very positive – effect on my life. I think it's great! What could be better? That's capitalism.'

'It's not capitalism – it's plundering and pillaging. My ZettaData bid does the exact opposite. It gives ordinary people a fair deal. Thousands of people believed me and have invested alongside me, on exactly the same terms – just as I promised them. How can I give that up to become part of the McConnochie Consortium?'

The familiar hard smile appeared on Wander's lips and his eyes gleamed. 'Why not?'

Max sighed. A big part of him so wanted to do it.

'I can give you a couple days to think it over, Max.'

He and Wander were either going to become closer, or they were going to part ways. He felt anguish at the thought of losing Richard's friendship.

A sharp feeling of grief caught Max's breath. He had never imagined when he first saw the Palisades bid on his phone that morning that it represented a new flight path into an unknown future in which he would be enemies with Richard Wander.

He didn't have to catch this wave, he didn't have to release the arrow.

He could live a vastly wealthier and completely secure version of the life he had always known, with Richard Wander as his friend and closest ally.

Max shook his head. 'I can't do it.'

The conversation had turned out to be a collision with his fate.

'I don't understand,' said Wander severely.

He remembered Wander from their uni days, when they'd won the first and second medals in their year at the University of Sydney. Wander's smooth skin hadn't yet set into the grim resting face so intimidating to others. Back then his eyes were bright with intelligence and curiosity, and hadn't yet acquired the cold, contemptuous gleam with which Wander now sized up his prey.

'Because tens of thousands of people who invested after I announced my bid will lose their investments – the stock price is already down by almost a quarter. The very people who can't afford to lose money will get crushed.'

'Why do you care?'

A deep longing filled Max, an awareness of how much he not only admired but loved Richard Wander – and a palpable sense of what he himself was about to lose. Wander was born with warm blood and a heart sensitive to emotions. That was all gone now. Wander had deliberately chosen to harden himself and devolve into a reptilian predator.

'I can't do it.'

'How are you going to feel when your midlife crisis is over and you realise you kissed goodbye to a hundred million dollars+?'

'Richie, I'm going to take over ZettaData, I'm going to do it my way—and I'll never look back.'

'I'm going to treat that as your first reaction, not your final decision.'

'I never wanted it to work out this way,' Max said.

Wander nodded and glanced at his watch. 'I've been keeping a trillion dollars waiting, Max.'

Wander clearly couldn't believe he'd just rejected a hundred million dollars, but Wander couldn't see what he himself had lost, which was everything, as he pursued his insatiable desire for what he thought of as everything.

'Sure, Richard – of course.'

They shook hands.

'Max, we're old friends – all I can say is, I tried – I really did.' There seemed to be a hint of genuine sadness in Wander's voice.

Max walked out of the grand skyscraper, feeling light-headed. He felt crushed by regret. Breaking up with Mort months ago had been a huge relief, despite the shock of how it happened. The ending of their partnership finally brought some resolution, or the beginnings of resolution, to his conflicted feelings and regrets – not to mention about the inequitable sharing of partnership profits and his blighted dreams.

Even if Max was totally honest with himself and admitted there was probably some weird father-son dynamic between Mort and himself, an unacknowledged secret element in their relationship, he now realised how lucky he was that, when it all went wrong, he didn't end up going over a cliff like Mort's son Hugh.

But his feelings about Richard were more like those for Ilona. He loved Richard, despite all their mutual flaws and betrayals, mostly petty but many not. And although he was not convinced a break with Ilona was yet inevitable, their marriage was extremely precarious. Their future looked dark, at least as dark as the future of his relationship with Richard.

He had to admit the Palisades counterbid made Ilona's position seem more reasonable, almost prescient.

For all their flaws, these people represented three of the most important relationships in his life. He had lost Mort. Now Richard was lost, and it was increasingly likely he would lose Ilona.

Max felt very alone.

He strode quickly up Elizabeth Street – and stopped short.

Crumpled in the warm, late morning sunshine was a heap of metal waste. It was his beloved Porsche. The convertible top had been torn apart as if by a chainsaw and a foul-smelling mess covered its once-shiny surfaces and overflowed the cockpit: an unholy combination of construction debris and restaurant refuse, oil, petrol, and paint.

The Porsche had been crushed – no easy feat, designed as it was to withstand high speed crashes.

Max sprinted to his car.

Dozens of people, their faces stunned, were standing on the sidewalk looking at the wreckage.

Max double clicked the button on his keyfob, and like a faithful, dying dog, the taillights and one front light flashed. The remains of his beloved 911 looked like something half-digested by a Tyrannosaurus Rex – a bigger version of the kind of object that from time to time is found in the stomachs of captured great white sharks.

Several people turned to him with a kind of awed horror. An elegant, middle-aged woman, her face ashen, looked at him.

'This isn't –'

'Yeah, it was my car.'

Over the interior and exterior, there was burned wood, twisted pieces of metal, cascades of nails and screws, mounds of rotting, half-eaten food, blackened vegetables, and used sanitary napkins from restroom canisters.

Two people edged close to him and stood respectfully until he noticed them, like mourners uncertain what to say at a stranger's funeral. They told Max they had seen a truck with an industrial steel dumpster pull up next to his Porsche and start to unload it. The dumpster dropped repeatedly on the car, and when it was finally hauled up again, it ejected its contents onto the demolished chassis. Neither person knew – or would admit to knowing – the company's name that would have been painted on either the truck itself or the dumpster. The truck had completed its task and driven away.

Max was stunned, unable to say a word. His ZettaData bid had better be a meteor: dinosaurs dominated Sydney.

Chapter 49

'I 'll unleash the invisible on the visible! I'll hale those who don't believe in science through the streets by their hair ...'

Opening night.

'Standby LX 29, Sound 13, Flys 28,' Lawson's voice murmured.

Just out of sight beyond the curtain was the audience for *TransGod* and sitting amongst them in the darkness were Max and his wife, and her father with Alexandra. Peggy could hardly stifle her rising terror.

A live house never felt the same as an empty one to Peggy, perhaps because of the simple, tangible, differences: a theatre full of silent human beings was warmer than an empty one; their clothed bodies absorbed sound the way falling snow hushes a city. The mood of the audience almost always felt palpable, but this evening she was concentrating on the intense energy emanating from the two poles of Max and her father.

'– until they eat strange flesh like flesh-eating birds devouring baby turtles on hot sand!'

Peggy tried to stop imagining the tremendous tension between Max and her father by focusing on a total awareness of her environment. There was more carbon dioxide and less oxygen and a slightly more humid feel to the air; the smell was probably subtly distinct from the fabric and mineral dust and tired wood smell of an empty theatre. A live house was both exciting and comforting to Peggy, but tonight she was immune to the compelling charm of theatre.

Max couldn't know for sure, but he was convinced Mort was responsible for the destruction of his Porsche. Her father had no way to prove it, but perhaps he was beginning to suspect Max of being involved in the disappearance of Hugh's body. And right now, during the performance of the play, the Board of ZettaData was deciding whether to approve Max's bid or her father's Palisades bid.

Right on time, Claudia's left hand made darting movements in the gloom behind the proscenium and Peggy heard the faint *tink* of the handcuffs as Claudia grasped them in one hand and the huge pistol in the other.

'LX 29, Sound 13, and Flys 28 ... go.'

Terrible bird screeching tore the air of the theatre like an avalanche of broken glass.

'You've denied science! You're a disease vector! You say a virus sanctified you? You will die by a new virus!'

'LX 30, Sound 14 go,' intoned Lawson.

Max isn't taking dad's threat seriously!

Peggy felt sure the attack on the Porsche was a warning of worse to come, but Max had just shrugged of the possibility.

'Standby LX31, Flys 14.'

'... I'm responsible for maintaining order in this community ...'

Claudia and Peggy locked eyes. Claudia's cue was coming up. Since Max had told her they should stop seeing each other, Claudia had been focusing on her opening night entrance as her chance to dazzle Max and his wife. Peggy found Claudia's confidences excruciating because of her guilty intuition that she herself was responsible for Max's decision.

'LX 31, Flys 14, go,' said Lawson, quietly and clearly.

Red, auburn, and orange highlights flared up from the spotlights in the deep waves of hair on Joan Perrone's head. Opening night was proceeding like clockwork, the actors and crew performing exactly as they had in rehearsals. Normally, Peggy would find this deeply satisfying and reassuring, but tonight the passage of time, so predictably marked by the perfectly executed sequence of cues, was carrying her unwillingly, at an inexorable pace, to somewhere she did not want to go.

'LX 32, Sound 15, go.'

Peggy nodded to Claudia.

The first clicks of Claudia Bullivant's heels sounded like a time bomb. She stepped past Peggy into the shining light.

Chapter 50

'You've denied science! You're a disease vector! You say a virus sanctified you? You will die by a new virus!'

Ilona couldn't stay focused on the dreary play. She could hardly wait until the part she'd heard about when President Orange reveals himself to be wearing a leather bustier and thigh-high boots.

Her legs were stiff from sitting with her knees pressed together – and her stiletto heels didn't help either; her calf muscles felt like clenched fists. After the tuckshop conversation with Alexandra, the tension with Max had become almost unbearable as the premiere approached. Until then, she had been assuring him – and telling herself – she was just protecting herself and the girls in case something went wrong with his ZettaData deal.

The *TransGod* cast was small, and from checking out the Eden Street Theatre website there was only one obvious choice that corresponded to Alexandra's hint: Claudia Bullivant. In the photo she didn't even look that pretty – well, only just pretty – but the ambitious glint in her eyes spoiled her looks, as far as Ilona was concerned.

Slut.

How would she feel tonight when she saw her? The Stat Dec and financial agreement meant she was ninety-nine percent out the door of the marriage legally, and in her heart she was now past ninety percent out the door in reality as well, maybe more.

Suddenly, Claudia Bullivant appeared and walked across the stage, her golden curls flashing under the same spotlights where Joan Perrone's tresses smouldered.

Ilona tracked her progress, catching the way the shock of her heel strikes on the stage rippled through her body under the tightly fitted jacket and skirt. She always appreciated the finesse of another woman, and most of the time applauded it. The actress was a completely aware woman, offering herself as a sweet sacrifice to the audience. She could acknowledge that, entirely free of resentment, about her.

Claudia was pointing a pistol which looked huge in her little fingers, and Ilona suddenly realised she had almost been hypnotised by the sight of her hand – and immediately, with as much certainty as if Max had just leaned over and said it to her, she knew that dainty hand had touched parts of her husband's body it had no business touching.

'You're coming with me, sir,' said the actress. Five words!

'Oh, indeed I am!'

The little bitch thought she was entitled to her life – or at least to her husband – because she had blonde curls and her boobs bounced. Let's see how she looked after she'd had two girls of her own.

'Here's my wand, officer, it's for you,' said Dion, the god Dionysius in disguise.

Ilona watched, all appreciation utterly forgotten, hating Claudia, and silently pronounced her curse:

May you have a future without daughters – no children – or only boys!

That would serve her right.

'Use it wisely, often and well!' said Bill Atkinson, as he played Dion who with ominous docility allows Claudia to handcuff him and march him off stage.

The hush in the house was almost palpable as Claudia's heel clicks disappeared into silence – and only then did Ilona see the gruesome metal sculpture that was about the same size, and probably looked about the same as Max's old Porsche must have looked that week – a post-apocalyptic, nightmarish snare of twisted metal composed of tormented bird-like shapes which collectively manifested into the nastiest, most murderous, most desolately pitiless skull she had ever seen.

A shiver of fear instinctively ran down Ilona's spine, then she smiled – it looked like the coolest logo of all time.

Chapter 51

'You've denied science! You're a disease vector! You say a virus sanctified you? You will die by a new virus!'

Max surreptitiously checked the dim light of his phone to see if he'd received a text about the outcome of the board meeting. There had been no questions for him all day from ZettaData's company secretary, which was either a very good, or a very bad sign. Normally Ilona would have given him a gentle, reproachful slap on his hand, but she just glanced at him disdainfully and fixed her eyes on the stage.

As he watched the actor Bill Atkinson, playing Dion, insinuatingly respond to President Orange's interrogation, Max's eyes were drawn to Perrone's insatiable and indomitable earth mother Pandemia and the bright lights of the stage suddenly dimmed and spots shone on the skull flock descending above the three actors, projecting the shadow of the skull onto the backdrop behind them.

On stage President Orange, Pandemia and the mysterious Dion paused and turned towards a clicking sound. Claudia Bullivant appeared on stage as a Secret Service Agent, carrying handcuffs and a big pistol as she walked resolutely across the stage towards the little group at centre stage.

Max smiled affectionately at Claudia. He felt relieved and convinced that breaking off their affair was the right decision, but he was sorry he'd hurt her, although she'd taken it well: in fact, she'd anticipated him by telling him immediately how relieved she was that he had brought it up.

'I so agree,' she'd said. 'It's time, because I'm not happy waiting for you to stop by for sex, and even though we've had more meaningful times as well, I deserve a relationship that starts with meaning, not just stumbles into it once in a while.

'There's a flat in Surry Hills I plan to move to in the next two months, it makes more sense for me to live there than here in the CBD. We both knew this was temporary.'

Besides the peaceful ending of their relationship, many things seemed to be looking up for Claudia: the producer had told her a CAA agent would be in the audience tonight. Who knew? Maybe she would be on her way to LA before long ...

'You're coming with me, sir.'

The mellow, elegant aroma of Ilona's perfume rose to his nostrils. *She must be feeling warm*, he thought. Max glanced at Ilona but she was glaring at the stage.

Ilona shifted in her seat, ignoring him while she redeployed her long, slender limbs, re-crossing her legs at the ankles while staring fixedly at the stage. Max sighed quietly.

'Oh, indeed I am!'

Max watched as the shadow projected against the backdrop was gradually superceded by the appearance of a great metal skull made of bird-like ingots of twisted metal hovering above the President Orange, Pandemia and Dion.

The Zettadata board meeting had gone on all day long and was dragging on well into the evening. That couldn't be a good sign.

Wander would be using his position as financial advisor to the board for all it was worth to influence them in favour of the Palisades bid. It was obvious now that Mort and Wander had some kind of arrangement and were joined by Rupert Campbell with all the awesome market power of Coldstream Holdings. The board had approved his proposal the first time, which meant the independent directors Grimson and O'Toole had better judgement than Kent Logan had given them credit for. But now they would have to withstand the subtle threat that Campbell and Wander would blight their professional lives if they didn't vote for the Palisades bid. They depended on director's fees, consulting fees and the other benefits of being insiders, and Coldstream Holdings and Wander & Fleagle could swiftly eliminate their future prospects.

'Here's my wand, officer, it's for you. Use it wisely, often and well!'

Laughter rippled through the audience. Ilona, sitting rigidly beside him, was unmoved.

On the other hand, Luke Terry was on his side. As a likely future prime minister and a union man who despised the kind of manipulation and legalised fraud routinely practiced by Wander and Campbell, Terry was a power centre all on his own who could counter-balance Wander, and hopefully steady the chairman, O'Toole and Grimson. Because of his government indemnity Terry was also the only ZettaData Director who could act with total freedom without any fear of legal or financial consequences. Terry had to make sure ZettaData didn't become an election issue but as long as he didn't do something that would be held against him by Labor voters next year, he could do as he pleased.

As usual Mort was acting like he could also do as he pleased. The ruins of his Porsche made that clear. Peggy was deeply shaken by the crime, which was understandable given how much she, her brother and her mother had suffered from Mort. But it was hard to see wrecking his Porsche as anything other than Mort lashing out because he was going to lose by fair, legal means and hoped his dirty, ugly OG methods might intimidate Max into throwing away victory at the last minute.

It wasn't going to happen.

Still, with Wander guiding the discussion of the board, Campbell trying to intimidate the independent directors and Mort taking his gloves off this week, he could no longer be sure what was going on.

He wouldn't know whether he'd won until the chairman called him.

For that matter, Max hadn't been sure Ilona would actually get in the Lexus with him and go to the premiere, either, until the very last moment. Despite what she said about the Stat Dec and signing the financial settlement being a pure formality, in the last several days she was treating him as if she was actually weighing divorce.

Tonight might be our last public appearance as a married couple.

How did he feel about that? Max wasn't sure. On one hand, by breaking up with Claudia he felt much less guilty, rightly or wrongly, about his responsibility for the strains in their marriage. On the other hand, he couldn't lie to himself and say he wasn't attracted to Peggy, either: he knew he was. So he wasn't being a faithful husband to Ilona, either way.

Ilona's grievances had existed for years and seemed to be becoming more bitter, even though she knew nothing about Claudia or Peggy, and neither woman was a direct factor in their marriage now. If Ilona followed up the Stat Dec by pulling the trigger and destroying their marriage, in some ways it would be a solution. He would do everything possible to ensure Billie and Sammie felt loved and protected, and it might give Max a second chance at happiness. Divorces are expensive because they're worth what they cost.

In a sudden flare of blue-grey glare from the stagelights, Max's gaze fell on the program in his lap. He saw the photo of Peggy with a calm but serious smile and her biography as Assistant Stage Manager headed by her full professional name, Margaret Norton. She was so close – just out of sight behind the curtains.

Her father was a lot closer: Mort and Alexandra were seated only a row back and a few seats over from Max and Ilona. Max had been trying not to think about Mort's eyes boring into the back of his head: let him do his worst. As long as the board was with him, he didn't care anymore what Mort thought.

Dion now reappeared on stage and stalked to the centre where he was confronted by President Orange and a half dozen attendants, including the Secret Service Agent played by Claudia Bullivant.

President Orange exclaimed: 'How did you escape? Why aren't you in detention with your women?'

'Nothing but practicing complete belief can hold us,' snarled Dion. 'Your selfish choices have endangered the entire community!'

Pandemia appeared with an entourage of women, some capable of menstruating at one time or another, some who never had, and never would.

President Orange looked wildly at Dion and the women encircling him and his Secret Service detachment. 'There's been a misunderstanding!'

'You don't believe!' hissed Dion.

'I don't have to believe—I know!' said President Orange.

'I came out long ago. I discovered who I really am!

President Orange tore off his suit, revealing himself to be thoroughly trussed up in studded leather from his neck to his leather boots.

'I am a gay man!'

He had half-expected Peggy to counsel him to forgive Mort when he told her what happened to his Porsche. Peggy was convinced Mort was behind it, but her response was terror, which of course he immediately understood. Maybe it was time to buy a Tesla, anyway. Not because he was deluded into thinking electricity is clean, but because he admired Elon Musk. Besides, he'd been thinking about the fact that by attacking him, Mort had actually bestowed power on him. If anybody was going to forgive Mort, it would have to be him. He'd learned that much from Peggy about the importance of precision when it came to forgiveness: only the person who had been harmed has the power to forgive.

Back in the day, Cranbrook still required attendance at scripture class, and in the wake of his discovery of the Phil Garlick grave Max had complied with a feeling of indifferent hopelessness that far transcended the attitude of general reluctance exhibited by his mates, and in the actual discussions Max experienced a degree of boredom so intense it achieved an almost metaphysical quality.

'You think you've found absolution,' Dion retorted to President Orange. 'When I am the solution. Your vision fails! There is no "I am". We can be anything we want to be.'

But for that very reason he clearly remembered thinking how strange it was for Jesus to forgive people who hadn't done anything to him. Max had been bewildered, and even as a schoolboy he'd felt an uneasy sense of the presence of something eerie, when he'd heard these stories of Jesus forgiving people for things they hadn't done to him.

Maybe they were all crazy: Peggy, Tori and Jesus.

He was itching to text the corporate secretary and ask for an update, but he knew better. He could no longer text Wander: that channel of information was permanently ended.

The stage was a chaos of strobe lights as the actors danced wildly around the figures of President Orange, Pandemia and Dion.

'Don't you see a new race of women?' exclaimed Dion, sweeping his arm across the stage. 'Stronger, faster, bigger, and far more fabulous!'

Unlike the Nightingale Father's Concert, all he could do now was wait: for the decision of the board, and for intermission. Max tried to distract himself by focusing on the play.

'She is a woman,' cried Dion, pointing to Pandemia. 'I am a God!'

Chapter 52

Intermission. Ilona scanned the room. The image of Trevor Walker's ample, doughy body constrained by leather straps couldn't be unseen—but what hovered on her retinas was the black leather, metal-studded dog collar circling his throat. Time to control her feelings.

'What do you think?' Max smiled.

She wanted to kill him right there. She managed to crinkle her eyes into a smile, and was just able to say, indifferently, choking on her rage, 'I like it.' It was clear from Max's expression he didn't believe her, but she couldn't bring herself to care – not in the slightest.

It was show time – for real, not the fairy tale that had been just unfolding on the stage – the drama of real life.

I'm the star.

They stood up and began to work their way patiently down the row, and then up the aisle towards the passageway, Max resting his fingertips lightly on her bare shoulder.

Fucking hypocrite. Sleazeball. As long as Max kept his fingertips on her shoulder and put the dog collar around Claudia Bullivant's neck, she was meant to stay married to him – so he could feel important. *That's the deal, is it?*

'I'll get us champagne as soon as we get out of here,' Max murmured.

She was damned if she was going to live that way. She'd kick him out, move back with the girls into her newly renovated house, finished exactly the way she had always dreamed her home should look, and spend his money. It would arrive in nice, big fat deposits every month in her cheque account. The bright future ahead for herself, Sam and Billie.

Ilona knew she was being watched from all sides as the audience streamed up the aisles. She had learned to enjoy the glances, being studied by women and watched intently by men who were hopeful she would respond with an inviting look, men with agendas she didn't quite understand, like Richard Wander, whom she hadn't seen yet. Any icy pang shot down through her, just missing her heart and lodging deep inside her belly: tonight how many people already knew about Claudia Bullivant and were watching her, secretly amused, or – worse – pitying her?

She gritted her teeth behind a smile, swallowing hard to choke down the rising fury she felt about the position Max had put her in, humiliating her like this.

As the audience filed from their seats, Ilona absently associated dozens of faces with names, life stories, and the precise locations, in many cases, of their homes on streets she knew as well as she knew her own. In a sense these were her people. To hell with the boring, incomprehensible play itself—this was the main event, she and the audience were the real players, and she belonged, at last. It was only a few kilometres from the Eden Road Theatre, but in every important way she'd come a long way from Erskineville.

They climbed the stairs with the throng and made their way into the lobby, Ilona aware at every step of how she moved and was seen. Even as a teenager reading her mother's copies of *Women's Weekly*, Ilona's intuition told her the greatest actresses were not the stars of movies, television, and stage, but the women who made performances of their lives in the real world: who held their nerve, masked their sorrow or disgust, and concealed their true objectives while pursuing their goals persistently until they reached success. Women like Bianca McConnochie. Women like her.

'Oh, look, darling,' – how much that word cost her tonight! –'there are the Haddads,' Ilona said. Natalie Haddad was a formidable woman of great charm and power and she and her husband had just renovated their Federation mansion on the south side of Fitzwilliam Road just east of Parsley Road, down the slope from the Rings' temporary rental house. They only had Harbour views from the upper level but they were practically on the water and only a short walk from Parsley Beach – a location to die for. The two women's gazes fused in mid-air and they approached each other in a brief court processional, both sheathed in delicate fabrics, glistening with chic jewellery, their bodies snugly embraced by expensive and insubstantial undergarments.

'Darling!' cried Ilona.

'Darling, how are you!' exulted Natalie.

Max, who had stopped without her noticing and was checking his damn phone, began making his way through the crowd to her with a happy smile. As he arrived, he and Mark Haddad looked at each other with embarrassed expressions. Ilona noticed Max's face was flushed.

'Good news!' Max said.

'Yeah, mate?' Haddad responded indifferently.

'I just heard from the Chairman—the board's approved our bid!'

'You can have your allocation back.'

'Really?' said Max. Haddad was one of Max's first mates in the ZettaData deal; he'd told her Mark had put his hand up to invest a million, which Ilona had found immensely reassuring at the time.

'Yeah. I'm out.'

'I'd be very happy to take it back,' said Max. 'But it's a cert now—all we need is shareholder approval at the EGM, and you know that'll happen. Are you sure?'

Haddad leaned towards Max and said quietly, 'You can shove it where the sun don't shine.'

Max pulled back, and looked at Haddad in shock. 'Ok—your decision.'

Max looked around. 'I'll get some champers.'

'Not for us!' said Haddad but Max didn't seem to hear him.

So things aren't going so well for Max after all.

Ilona also pretended not to hear Mark, summoning her most benevolent and indulgent smile as she looked over her shoulder at Max as he turned and headed towards the bar. This was the evening, of all evenings, to keep up appearances.

She turned back to Natalie and Mark, and saw across the foyer that Richard Wander was standing with his wife. He turned deliberately at Ilona. Their eyes locked.

Richard's wife Poppy was chatting enthusiastically to somebody, oblivious to her husband. She was one of those women who looked clumsy in clothes. Sizing her up, Ilona surmised it was because her hips and especially her breasts were too voluptuous; they seemed to have their own volition and made Poppy's dress look like a sack. Ilona had never thought that much about Poppy before, but she reluctantly concluded Poppy might well be quite sensual looking and attractive when she was naked.

'So, how are things, Mark?' Ilona asked, glancing out the corner of her eye as Richard continued to watch her intently. She didn't pretend to follow the ins and outs of all the board meetings, AGMs, EGMs and the rest of the bizzo.

Although Poppy's figure didn't permit her to dress in a very becoming way, perhaps there was a little boy in Richard who needed the nurturing and comforting sort of maternal experience Poppy's big breasts and wide hips offered. Richard's eyes seemed to glitter as she held his gaze. Did he know about Max and Claudia?

'Couldn't be better with *us*,' said Haddad. 'How are *you* going? Max has been, um ... certainly marching to his own drum lately, hasn't he?'

'I have to trust Max knows what he's about,' said Ilona, aware that Mark's comment might have multiple meanings and choosing to assume it referred to Max's wretched deal. If she'd heard him correctly, Mark had just pulled the plug but she didn't want to know about it. It was Max's problem. Max's life.

She glanced reflectively into the middle distance, as if too smart to be duped by her husband, too strong to be affected by his professional failings. Almost magnetically, she found her glance drawn back to Richard, and allowed her eyes to rest confidently, challengingly, on him. For long seconds their eyes connected until, satisfied she had sent a message of imperturbable poise, Ilona looked away.

'You're bearing up so well, darling,' said Natalie sympathetically, bringing her focus back into their little group. 'You look stunning – I love your hair. Did you have it trimmed by Maurice?'

'Why, yes I did – I just have him trim the fringe, and keep the tips completely straight,' said Ilona. There was a sudden eruption of laughter and she glimpsed the Nortons talking animatedly in a big group, Mort's heavy, jowly head thrown back, leading the laughter. The photograph of Margaret Norton she had seen in the program showed a fine-boned young woman with large eyes. There was no resemblance between daughter and father.

Natalie drew Ilona close and murmured, 'Darling, you look gorgeous tonight. You're being so brave.'

'Thank you, darling,' Ilona murmured, hoping she meant Max's appearance on *Mighty Money* or his ZettaData bid, but willing to accept the implication Max was unfaithful as she inhaled Natalie's perfume. Over Natalie's shoulder Ilona's eyes again connected with Richard's, who gazed at her. *Perhaps he was confident enough now*, Ilona thought, ready to step up from the comforting solace of mummy to her sleek, glamorous, racing sloop body and the type of woman she represented.

Chapter 53

Max strutted through the crowd, and Mort smiled grimly to himself as he noted the cocky angle of Ring's head.

He thinks there are no fucking consequences in this world.

All the better for Ring to walk around with tickets on himself, but it was essential not to lose his temper. Ring could mouth off all he liked, but he was going to be as civil as could be. When Ring got what was coming, nobody must have any idea that he had any issue whatsoever with the fucker.

He had been planning to go much too easy on the fucker. With what was going to happen now, it was essential there wasn't any whiff of bad blood on his side.

Ring passed Richard Wander as he made his way to the bar. Mort saw him shake hands with Wander and Martin McConnochie. As usual, Martin looked like a chicken dressed in a very expensive suit, and he greeted Max with the expression of a man used to supplicants asking favours. Max said something that made Wander look up, find Mort in the crowd with his eyes, and raise both eyebrows.

Whatever it is, it'll have to wait.

Oh – ZettaData – those arseholes backed Ring.

It would be ok.

Ring's missus was standing by herself with the Haddads. Alexandra looked questioningly at him, reading his thoughts as they walked through the crowd.

'Yeah, let's go darling,' he said, steering Alexandra towards Ilona and the Haddads.

Mort glanced over his shoulder at McConnochie. Pussy-whipped piece of shit – his missus Bianca wore the pants in that house. And McConnochie had been too afraid Luke Terry would say "boo" to give him the slab he deserved in his Tunnel Consortium, until he took matters into his own hands and sorted things out with Luke. McConnochie was a good engineer but one day there'd be a reckoning for him, too.

'Yoo hoo!'

Alexandra waved gaily as they approached the Haddads and Ilona from behind. The Duchess was all blonde fringe and white teeth, lipstick delicately pink and her make-up as subtle as one of the Nolans on their walls. She had a healthy glow she might have acquired on safari. The Haddads turned on cue towards the Nortons and Ilona smiled at Alexandra.

He was still pissed off with Haddad. It was true Haddad agreed to relinquish his one million dollar commitment in Max's investment consortium – but he'd been jaw-boning Haddad for weeks to do that, who kept whinging about reducing his commitment to just two hundred and fifty thousand. He'd finally agreed to pull the plug completely – but pretty late in the day. It looked like Max had just got the word. He'd just now seen Haddad nodding as Max talked, and leaning in to tell him something on the QT – treating him like a player. Obviously, sucking Max's dick. Haddad needed a wake-up call.

He got it – now that Max was becoming a celebrity, Haddad thought he had to preserve their relationship. Playing both sides of the street. Well, that wasn't going to work.

'Good evening, darlings!' said Alexandra.

'Darling!' said Ilona as they kissed.

'Mort,' Haddad said cordially.

He moved closer to Haddad and with his hand barely extended, took Haddad's in his grip and began shaking it. 'Hello, Mark,' Mort said, their eyes closer than socially comfortable, but not blatantly so. Haddad's smile became a little rigid. Mort kept shaking his hand, held his own tight smile, looking into Mark's eyes, and let Haddad's hand spasm and flop around in his grip like a heart torn out of a sacrificial victim by a pagan priest.

At last, he let Haddad's hand go, kissed Natalie, and turned to Ilona, who was standing expectantly, looking at him with bright eyes.

'No bubbles?' Mort asked, allowing himself a mild indictment of Max, the only one he would permit himself in public this evening. He and Alexandra had their flutes of champagne.

'Good evening, Mort,' Ilona said, clearly expecting to be kissed. Birds sometimes need a change-up to keep them on their toes, still the chance to kiss Max's missus was too good to pass up. Mort leaned towards her and suddenly realised how much he'd rather stick his tongue in her ear instead – it was a gut thing, a truth like that. While he was at it – his dick would be even better.

The Duchess was standing right next to them, of course. Mort kissed Ilona on her satiny cheek, feeling her steady herself with elegant fingers, softer than Alexandra's, on his arm.

He shifted his head to kiss her on the other cheek, and up popped another thought. He glanced at Alexandra, and kissed Ilona's other soft, scented cheek thinking fervently how much he'd like his dick pressing against that cheek from inside.

'Pandemia reminds me of my favourite aunt!' Alexandra exclaimed. 'I just adore her!'

Mort glanced at her, but the Duchess didn't seem to take anything untoward from the two pecks on the cheek they'd just exchanged.

The Duchess liked to disconcert people at intermission by commenting on the performance, rather than swapping updates on renovations, children's private schools, frequent flyer miles totals, holidays, or business. Sydney society had learned to stay alert around Alexandra.

Ilona smiled nervously. 'I adore that skull but I'm not sure about all that bird screeching.'

Ring's missus was a nice piece of arse, no doubt about it.

'Isn't it clever?' said Natalie. 'It's really a work of art – I'd love to have that sculpture hanging in my foyer.'

'I loved the line about those poor darling little turtles skittering down the strand on their little webbed feet,' said Alexandra. 'I laughed so hard!'

Wander looked across the crowd at Mort, and cocked his head.

'Hello, everybody!' Ring walked up and handed champagnes around to Ilona and the Haddads. Nobody even pretended it wasn't tense. The men seemed to forget to shake hands until Mort extended his hand to Ring. Better play it to the hilt.

'How are you going, Mort?' Ring said, taking his hand.

'Really well, Max. How does it feel to be a television star?'

'Oh, I wouldn't say that,' said Ring.

'Mate – you could have your own show after this week,' Haddad chortled humourlessly, openly studying Max's reaction. 'Max Ring's Stock Tips!'

'Max Ring – Friend of the Friendless.' Mort had to play it cooler than that. 'Haha,' he added, as if he had said it with all the goodwill in the world.

'Well, at least I've got friends on the ZettaData Board,' said Ring. 'As I told Mark a few minutes ago.'

'Yeah?' said Mort, and looked into his eyes. He imagined making an incision along the hairline where he'd cut Ring's skin away, feeling the point of the knife grating his skull, before he ripped the skin down and off Ring's face.

The Haddads, The Duchess and Ilona all looked visibly uncomfortable behind their fixed smiles.

Mort smiled gently and shook his head. What would be the next part of Ring's body he ripped the skin off – the obvious one?

'You never know Max,' Mort said mildly. 'When you're on the hunt for great things you sometimes lose a harvest here and now.'

'You'd better hope so,' Max said. 'You look pretty empty-handed.'

Maxie, obviously elated with his victory, was being a total dick.

Ilona flushed red.

'Go ahead and skite all you want, Maxie, if it makes you feel better,' Mort heard himself say in the flattest voice possible. 'The market is just getting used to our bid. If the board didn't get it, that's their problem. We'll see how shareholders vote next week.'

'Yes, we certainly will,' said Ring, colouring. 'Don't be surprised if they feel the same way about you and your three cent bid Martin McConnochie does.'

Mort caught Alexandra looking at him uneasily, almost in alarm.

Ilona looked at Max, her cheeks and forehead fetchingly flushing a rose tint. 'What do you mean by that, Max?'

'Don't you remember darling? Martin declined to invite us into the Tunnel Consortium,' Max took a sip of his champagne. 'And Martin doesn't have anything against me.'

I'd love to shove that flute right down his throat, and take out a couple of his front teeth on the way in.

'I'm sure he doesn't Max. I just saw you stop and talk to Martin,' she said.

'Yep,' nodded Max.

'Discussing your favourite dog collars?'

'I beg your pardon?' said Ring.

Ilona's eyes darted around to the Haddads and the Nortons, checking to make sure everyone was listening to her.

'You know – the dog collar you put on Claudia Bullivant!'

Ring coloured to the roots of his hair. Even his ears turned pink. 'I ... I don't know what you're talking about,' he said.

Haha – The Duchess had been right. Mort cleared his throat and said nothing. Let the moment last as long as possible – excruciatingly, unendurably long.

The smug look had been smacked right off Ring's face. Good on Ilona.

'You didn't think I knew, did you, Max?'

Alexandra raised her eyebrows and she and Natalie exchanged glances.

Ilona looked around the group again as if she were rousing additional support, and then nodding at Max, she hissed, 'Do you want to put a dog collar around my neck?'

The chimes started, signalling the end of intermission.

'Ilona, darling –' Ring started to put his arm around Ilona's shoulders.

'Don't come near me!' she cried, twisting to escape him.

'Ilona dear, come with us, darling,' Alexandra said, stepping between Ilona and Max and steering her by the waist through the throng on their way back to their seats.

Haha – perfect! Mort followed Ilona and the Duchess and then looked around and scanned the foyer until he caught sight of Ring and watched his back disappear through the top doors at the back of the theatre, leading to the gallery. Let him stand among the cheap seats and contemplate his ruined life.

Inside the theatre Mort and Alexandra escorted Ilona to her seat, with Ring's empty seat beside her.

'Are you going to be all right, darling?'

Ilona nodded, defiantly, looking a little bereft.

'She'll be fine,' murmured Alexandra as they walked down the row behind.

'Haha,' said Mort, as they settled into their seats.

He stared at the stage curtain, watching the vertical shadows of its folds intensify as the lights dimmed. His mind was blank: the *aboulie* had completely vanished.

Chapter 54

M ax, standing against the back wall behind the last row of seats, released a long slow exhale, comforted by the ensuing sense of calm and the familiar theatre smell of a barn in summer. He'd lost both his seat next to Ilona in the VIP section and his welcome in the rental house in Vaucluse: both problems solved. It was ok—the play would be over soon and he hated the ugly, pretentious mansion. He might never again set foot in their real family home once it was renovated, either, but if it came to that, he didn't mind. He could live in Bondi.

Ilona's outburst was mortifying—but also baffling.

What the hell did she mean by dog collar and leash?

He'd always known it was a possibility Ilona might somehow find out, so he wasn't surprised she knew about Claudia. But a dog collar?

Despite himself, faint curling wisps of depression began to settle on Max and gradually became a dense, impenetrable fog. It was a certainty that Sam and Billie would hear about Claudia and the dog collar from their mother, as Ilona began an inevitable campaign to turn their daughters against him.

Once he was living in his own home and running ZettaData, even in the middle of a messy divorce, Max would do everything he possibly could to coax his daughters back into relationship with him.

His one consolation in this awful evening was that the board had voted to recommend his bid to shareholders at the EGM. He never imagined the *kairos* of ZettaData would reach completion at just the moment his marriage collapsed.

Almost reached completion.

The arrow he released when he confronted Mort at the AGM had been flying towards its target for months now, but wouldn't hit the bullseye until next week at the EGM when shareholders voted to approve his rights issue for ZettaData.

"Millions of my citizens are dying!"

"Because you're living a lie . . . "

"A lie? I came out decades ago!
I discovered who I really am!"

"There is no 'I am'.
There is no real!"

Playwright Reed Michaelis built *TransGod* on the ancient idea, dramatised by his sources in Aristophanes, Euripides and Tennessee Williams, that an epiphany – the appearance in this world of a god – is a moment fraught with great risk for the mortals who see the god. Sebastian Venable sees the great god of evolution in the Galapagos, but doesn't recognise that as a false poet it is he who is natural selection's next victim, and so he meets his fate of *sparagmos*. The comedies of Aristophanes functioned the way social media does today, cancelling the great and the famous in a chorus of mockery and contempt, and when Euripides responded to Aristophanes' cancel mob with his great play *The Bacchae*, his main character, King Pentheus, doesn't recognise Dionysius for who he is—his personal intersection with a terrible fate—and so he too meets his doom of *sparagmos*. Reed Michaelis had given his character President Orange all the arrogance of King Pentheus—and his fatal blindness to the fact he was talking with a god able to unleash terrible powers on him and his kingdom.

"You're not gay – that's a failed vision, yesterday's news—you're pansexual!"

Max smiled at the concealed pun: the libidinous god Pan was often depicted as part of the wild entourage of Dionysius. The Greek Australian Michaelis had nicely worked that into the dialogue.

"I can't believe that! I know who I am."

"You must believe—you don't have the courage to realise you're pansexual—we all are!
Everything is changing, everything is mutating into something new—that's evolution!
My worshipper Pandemia is proving it!"

Max watched broodingly as the prop that was the centrepiece of the production, the hideously fascinating skull flock, appeared and disappeared over the stage. He saw how the twisted ingots of the bird shapes expressed the way flawed individuals can coalesce into groups or parties so negatively organised they become a sign of death. The same process must also work in reverse: he had tried to transform himself, his investors and his supporters among the small shareholders, for all their collective flaws, into a group that generated new life.

What *was* the opposite of a sign of death hovering over Australia? What was the model capable of producing a just society for all Australians—a goal he and his little ad hoc group of supporters could work towards—and what did it look like?

The dramas of Aristophanes, Euripides and Tennessee Williams all agreed that the only choice the world offers is between a cruel, pitiless order or wild, chaotic, savage energy. Until he went to Byron Bay with Peggy, it was a vision Max thought science had proven to be true. Euripides' tragedy *The Bacchae* was the most famous play in the ancient world precisely because the Greeks and Romans saw in the tragedy a true description of their world.

Max suddenly realised Euripides had unknowingly scripted another famous epiphany far into the future beyond his own time. *The Bacchae* would have been well known to Pontius Pilate, who was a sophisticated Roman aristocrat. One night Pilate found himself interrogating a seemingly ordinary peasant just as King Pentheus interrogated Dionysius, who was seemingly an ordinary stranger. When did Pilate start to get nervous? Was it when he realised his prisoner's name was *Yeshua* which means "Saviour", so similar to *Eleutheroios*, which means "Saviour" and was one of the titles of Dionysius?

Did Pilate's hair stand up on his neck when his soldiers reported this Yeshua was accused of claiming to be a god? As Yeshua stood before him in chains, Pilate couldn't help[recalling all too clearly Dionysius had also submitted to the chains of King Pentheus initially. As Pilate began interrogating Yeshua in his dusty Praetorium he surely became aware of the Euripidean doom hovering over this potential epiphany, and realised with growing horror he might be playing the role of King Pentheus to a man who just might be a disguised Dionysus. The historical record clearly recounts Pilate's terror, his refusal to judge the stranger, the anxious warning from his wife, who too knew the tragedy by Euripides, to have nothing to do with the prisoner. What else could be the source of Pilate's famous desire to do anything other than impose the cruel order he represented on the mysterious disruptor who had seemingly arrived from nowhere?

As Pilate knew so well, Dionysus was capable of sudden ultra-violence. So Pilate gingerly proceeded step by reluctant step in case he was witnessing an improbable epiphany, a seemingly mundane *chronos* in which lurked a terrible *kairos*, even going so far to wash his hands publicly in front of the crowd to absolve himself of any guilt for Yeshua's fate until – much to his relief – the truth about the mundane reality of Yeshua was confirmed when he was thoroughly scourged, spat on and mocked with impunity by having a crown of thorns pressed down on his head, and finally marched to Golgotha where he was securely nailed to a cross and he died.

Max sat back in his seat and watched the final confrontation between President Orange and Dion.

"I love the world the way it is—I want to be who I always have been!"

"Then you won't be in this world much longer: too many have suffered and died because of your refusal to believe!"

"I refuse to believe!"

An agonised scream tore apart Max's thoughts like a curtain and reverberated through the theatre as President Orange ran across the stage pursued by dozens of women in costumes that looked like a cross between Grecian robes and Bondi silk shawls. Some women were powerful with wide shoulders, strong jaws, and long legs while others in the mob running across the stage looked lithe and elegant, and the costume swirled around the ample curves of others.

"I am your God!" cried Dion.

Max watched President Orange's fate unfold with growing horror – it was the terrible final scene. Amid President Orange's screams and the spine-shivering chorus of the women's savage cries, mixed with a hellish chorus of screeching birds, fountains of blood began spurting up through the writhing bodies of the attacking women. President Orange had disappeared beneath the tangle, but his screams shook the theatre, mingling with the raptor-like cries of the triumphant women.

Tennessee Williams imagined a fatherless world, created by a father's wealth but operated without a father's rules, and in Aristophanes and Euripides the fathers are deeply flawed: King Pentheus is a harsh tyrant and Mnesilochus is a cowardly sneak. Both fathers are lured into concealing their masculine natures by cross-dressing and then brutally attacked. A deranged mob of women murder King Pentheus by *sparagmos* and Mnesilochus is chased by a horde of angry women who shout:

> "We and our maidservants will punish her.
> Run and fetch coals and let's burn off her pubic hair in proper style,
> To teach her not to insult her own gender!"

Aristocratic Athenian women at the time of Aristophanes and Euripides obviously shared grooming habits with Ilona in modern Sydney.

The scene on stage was riveting: gobbets of bloody and quivering flesh, including identifiable parts like ears and fingers, began erupting from the seething heap of bodies and arced under the hot lights across the stage. The screams reached a truly distressing crescendo, and a pool of dark blood appeared at the perimeter of the heap of bodies and expanded in all directions across the stage as the victim was finally silent.

Max, like the rest of the audience, was deeply shaken.

Did *TransGod* mirror the modern world of Sydney in some way? Could it be possible? There certainly seemed to be a note of Aristophanes in what Sam had done to Trixie Norton on the sleepover months ago, but neither girl was brought up in a fatherless world. Or was the Eastern Suburbs itself a kind of a fatherless world in which men have distorted their own natures? Sydney is full of mothers who nourish their children with breast milk while instantiating language and Australian culture, but the women of Sydney also consider their political rights founded on the freedom to kill their unborn children.

'Thank you! Thank you! Thank you!'

Fifteen minutes of standing ovations, and a dozen curtain calls by the cast and a deafening storm of whistles and cries from the audience of "Author! Author!" had lured Reed Michaelis onto the stage where a spot light bathed him in iridescence.

Max noted even from the back of the theatre something about the aura of Euripedes' Dionysus: beautiful, golden-haired, gentle, and eerie – Reed was smiling faintly at the audience, his hands pressed together in a blessing.

'I just want to thank all of you tonight for being such a wonderful audience! This has been a great night for Australian women and the fight against hate, intolerance, ignorance and science-denial. Thank you! Love is love!'

Reed ran down the setting line blowing kisses to the audience and disappeared behind the curtains.

As the lights came up, Max stood by himself in the gloom at the very top and back, watching the audience pour like sand across the rows, up the aisles, and disappear out of the theatre as if it were an emptying hourglass.

As Max watched people talk quietly among themselves, or patiently wait for the flow of the crowd to provide space to take a step forward, he felt totally abandoned. The entertainment was over for them, and they were now thinking about the rest of their evening and lives. But his life would never be the same again, and neither would Ilona's or their daughters' lives.

He wasn't sure where Ilona might be – she had her own set of car keys, and Mort and Alexandra might also have offered her a ride in their Bentley and dropped her off at Hopetoun Avenue on their own way home.

He imagined Peggy moving around with the rest of the cast and crew somewhere behind the curtain, probably opening bottles of inexpensive sparkling wine to celebrate the wildly successful opening night.

Max left the theatre and walked to the spot where he'd parked Ilona's Lexus: it was gone. He walked up to Crown Street, caught an Uber and gave a Ramsgate Avenue address.

He had a small one bedroom flat on Ramsgate Avenue in Bondi. It was just a place to store his old books and extra surfboards, really. Once in a while, if he was tired after surfing he'd take a nap in the flat. He'd never taken a woman there.

The flat was located a block from the beach in a building of six units built in the 1960s, raised from the ground on concrete pillars that created a car park under the building and made it look like a brick fish tank. The attraction for Max was the large windows in his unit, which were almost floor to ceiling and provided excellent views of the beach. The building was full of light and air, and it was honestly ugly. He'd be living there for the foreseeable future.

He loved his Bondi flat; Max was tired of luxury.

Chapter 55

'**G**ood afternoon, Ilona Ring?'

'Yes,' said Ilona, looking into the eyes of a woman who was a blonde mirror of herself.

The woman offered Ilona her hand. 'I've heard so much about you. What a pleasure to meet you. I'm Sharon Pinsent, Richard's assistant.'

Ilona nodded, flattered and a little confused. Sharon seemed suspiciously friendly. She was all smiling hauteur, but rather than feeling intimidated, Ilona found herself approving of the other woman's beauty and her charisma. Ilona considered whether she herself measured up and tentatively decided she did.

Ilona followed Sharon obediently through the lush foyer of Wander, Fleagle & Co and down a long hallway filled with plants and art work.

'Please,' said Sharon, opening and holding a door for her.

Ilona thanked her and walked through, instantly dazzled by the views, the thick carpets, the artwork, the faint spicy aroma.

Richard Wander was at his desk, a fountain pen poised in his hand, a stack of documents in front of him, staring contemplatively at a span of computer screens. He looked up and smiled, then came around the desk.

The office almost pulsed with power and privilege, and Ilona couldn't help thinking of Richard's wife, sincere, heavy-boned and earnest – a startling contrast to this luxurious den of an apex predator.

'Ilona,' he said simply.

He stood up, sleek and purposeful, wearing a crisp white shirt, dark crimson tie, and a very dark blue suit with faint stripes. As he approached his presence was daunting, until she thought of him naked and curled up next to Poppy, nuzzling like a baby for the teat.

She smiled with amusement at the image, and Richard smiled in return as he gently kissed her on both cheeks, steadying her by briefly resting his fingertips on her shoulders.

'Coffee, tea, chai?' he asked.

Ilona shook her head. 'I have to pick up the girls soon.'

CBD traffic. She wasn't used to it – she almost never drove downtown – and she didn't want to have to make a bathroom stop in Richard's offices. She also didn't want to hold her bladder in the long line at Nightingale School and then wait until she got home to relieve herself. Despite her little game imagining Richard's mummy fetish, the offices of Wander, Fleagle were intensely more impressive than those of Norton & Ring and she felt a little overwhelmed.

'My macchiato, thank you,' Richard said to Sharon. 'Let's sit down.' He indicated a sofa upholstered in a honey and toast-coloured mix of wool and silk. It was elegant and inviting at the same time, sumptuously generous in every way.

Ilona had only visited Max once or twice at Norton & Ring, and there was always something uncomfortable about him in his offices, like a disgruntled lion in a zoo – while Richard moved completely at ease, more like a leopard on a savanna.

Ilona sank into one of the deep cushions. Richard sat next to her, crossed his legs, and placed his elbow on the back of the sofa as he turned to her.

'So, how's our Max?'

The proprietary 'our' seemed appropriate. Richard was one of her husband's best friends. Ilona felt emotion swelling inside and suddenly felt it was safe to share with Richard.

She smiled self-deprecatingly. 'I don't want to be that wife, already well on the way to becoming a member of the first wives' club, who has nothing good to say about her husband.'

'Ilona,' Wander said gently.

She didn't think he could do gentle – or was it only an expression of the secret little boy who needed to snuggle up to his mummy? Still, something about the way he said her name, especially combined with those formidable features, gave her a warm thrill. There was more than a hint in his voice of a real man.

'He's changed so much in the last few months, Richard.'

Wander nodded. 'Very true.'

Ilona rushed on. 'I almost feel like what happened between Max and Mort was a collision that started lots of other collisions – you know, like snooker – and Max has been careening ever since – wildly, all over the table.'

Richard raised his eyebrows and nodded, clearly in agreement with her. He sighed.

The door of Wander's office opened and Sharon appeared with his macchiato. As she looked at Ilona with her boss sitting together on the sofa, Ilona noticed an almost imperceptible hardening of her expression as she approached.

'Thank you, Sharon,' said Wander, hardly looking up.

But Sharon was looking down, intently, at Ilona, a cold, forbidding glint in her blue eyes.

'Do you know what, Richard? I think I *would* like a coffee.' Ilona looked at Sharon with a big, friendly smile. 'Can you make me a ristretto soy latte? *Thank* you, darling.'

She no longer feared the prospect of girl-on-girl emotional violence, not after everything she'd learned from Alexandra. Thanks to her advice, she was independently wealthy and here in the private office of Richard Wander. And Ms Sharon Pinsent wanted to have a go at her? *Challenge accepted!*

'He talks about shareholder rights,' Ilona heard herself rushing on. 'You know about those things, I don't. I can't tell if he's deluding himself, or he's half crazy. From the moment he signed that personal guarantee with the American hedge fund guy, I knew something had changed. And now he's ... ' She couldn't bring herself to speak too directly about Claudia Bullivant. 'He's becoming very unreliable, untruthful, in every area of his life.'

Richard shook his head. 'It happens all the time – but I didn't expect it to happen to Max.'

Perhaps he blamed her for not looking after Max, somehow.

Richard looked at her, his eyes warm in his severe face. 'Don't blame yourself, Ilona. It has all the marks of a midlife crisis. You see these things. You never know what triggers it. But it's about Max, not you.'

'Thank you,' Ilona said, lowering her eyes. Richard had seemed to read her mind. It was such a relief to be understood.

'The trouble is, Max is taking serious financial risks. You have a substantial family net worth, and arguably he's pretty much put it at risk.'

Ilona could feel her pulse pounding in her ears. 'But ... but, the Stat Dec?'

'Yes,' Richard nodded. 'I'm so glad Alexandra convinced you to take that step. It preserves your capital, but if Max gets sued personally, for example – and ZettaData is a public company and any number of shareholders or other parties might sue him for the actions he's currently taking, and if he loses these lawsuits – then you could well lose any income he's agreed to provide you. That's still a substantial exposure.'

Richard sipped his macchiato.

I should certainly say so! Max had committed to pay her and the girls close to four hundred thousand dollars a year. She felt a thrill of fear: there were so many damned ways things could go pear-shaped. Goddamnit.

'What would you recommend I do, Richard?'

His brown eyes were intense and totally focused on her. It had been years since Max looked at her that way; these days there was always something guarded or long-suffering in his glance. By contrast, now that they were sitting centimetres from one another, Richard was looking at her just as he had been doing for months from a distance at public events – just drinking her in.

'You have to consider your options,' he said softly.

He was making no attempt to disguise his attraction to her, which pleased her. On the other hand, she certainly hadn't gone to his office with the intention of seducing him. 'What *are* my options?' she said briskly.

'Oh, Ilona, you have many options.'

'Like what, for example?' She was enjoying his presence at such close quarters.

When did she have to pick up the girls?

'It really comes down to what you want out of life.'

'I don't know what you mean.'

She liked the idea of being able to toy with him. Personally, she felt totally objective.

'Ilona, you do.'

Did she know what she wanted? She knew Richard wanted her. Lately, she hadn't felt desired by anyone, except the young men in the petrol station who looked at her appreciatively when she paid. 'Um, Richard, my soy latte?'

Wander started, as if waking from a trance. In one lithe movement, he twisted around in order to reach a low table standing next to the sofa and pushed the intercom button. 'Shaz, can you bring that soy latte in please? Thanks.'

Ilona relaxed against the back of the sofa and crossed her legs, waiting with pleasant anticipation to be served by Sharon. She was surprised by the sense of power and purpose that filled her at having two people under her control.

'Would you like sugar?' Sharon asked through what Ilona discerned to be gritted teeth.

'No thanks, darls,' Ilona said with satisfaction. As Sharon left, she looked innocently at Richard while raising put the cup to her lips. She delicately sipped. Did icy Shaz dominate and humiliate him, while Poppy enveloped him in her mummy love? She saw Richard watch attentively as she ran the tip of her tongue across her top lip to ensure no foam remained. Did Richard abjectly prostrate himself before the women in his life, let them subjugate him – or was he actually a man?

'Good?' he said, his eyes on her lips.

Ilona nodded, thoroughly enjoying herself now.

'You can have anything you want in life,' he said.

She was intensely aware of his presence, their closeness.

'How?' she said carelessly. 'I feel as if I misplaced my life somewhere along the way. I don't know if I want it back.'

'Oh, you can't go back, Ilona, you have to go forward,' Richard said softly.

'And that's good—everything is fine.'

She felt his breath on her neck – and suddenly imagined Sharon Pinsent, just outside the closed door, stewing in her seat and counting every second that passed until Ilona left. She'd teach little Ms Pinsent a lesson – she was going to stay in her boss's office as long as she pleased.

Ilona put her hand on Richard's chest, feeling the full, soft cotton of his shirt under her palm and fingers, and gave him a little push. 'Do you have any specific strategies to recommend?'

'Of course I do,' he said.

It would be kind of fun, she thought, *to give Richard just a little taste of what he wanted – whatever it was*. If only because, somehow, afterwards Ms Pinsent would sense that the very last thing she wanted had, in fact, just transpired. It would be nice if Richard turned out to be a real man, too.

'Tell me something specific.' Ilona looked at Richard innocently, allowing the tip of her pink tongue to explore the right corner of her lips, as if seeking a few bubbles of errant foam from her soy latte.

Richard smiled, looking into her eyes with a triumphant gleam in his own. He reached for her nearest shoulder, and touching it with just a thumb and one finger, he caressed Ilona through her blouse until his fingers reached her neck and his fingertips touched her bare flesh, gently entangling in hair.

'Richard,' she said reproachfully, moving slightly. It was impossible to tell if it was the touch of a boy wanting his mummy, or a man filled with desire. Intentionally or not, she moved with more of a shimmy than a flinch.

'Can I be very specific?' he murmured.

'Of course,' she said, feeling a pleasant tingle going up and down her spine as he moved his fingertips through the hair at the base of her neck as if tracing letters of the alphabet.

'Specifically ...' he said.

Ilona realised she was swaying her hips slowly on the sofa. The shimmy had evolved.

He leaned towards her until his face was quite close.

Her perfect posture didn't change as she kept her neck erect and her face fully presented, not flinching or turning aside. She looked at him appraisingly, clinically.

Ilona parted her lips and for a moment allowed the tip of her tongue to appear pressed against her upper lip, as if trying to decide where to apply a piece of tape to the back of an envelope. Her tongue disappeared, her decision was made, and Ilona looked calmly into his eyes from two centimetres away.

'No,' she said.

He kissed her.

'No,' she murmured, her face slightly averted from his kiss.

'Not specific enough?' he asked, kissing her again, on the cheek, and she gently shook her head.

'No, Richard.'

'Mmm?' he said, and he kissed her delicately on the lips. 'I can be much more specific. I've wanted this for so long, Ilona.'

'That's very flattering, Richard,' she said as his arm circled her shoulder, and he began to gently draw her towards himself. She could feel her breast pressing against his strong chest. 'But I said "no".'

She shivered and raised her face to the ceiling, letting her head drop as she closed her eyes.

'You know what you want,' he said, letting his lips graze along her bared throat.

'No, Richard, stop,' she said, wondering how badly he wanted to do this. The thrill of her power washed through her, and she indulged herself by enjoying, but not quite trusting in it. She looked in his eyes.

He seemed hooked.

'Yes, I'll stop,' he said, smiling, and his gaze dropped to her lips. He leaned forward and kissed her again, letting his lips graze hers in the opposite direction this time. Her lower lip involuntarily pulsed against his, and she tasted the wetness of it.

'Stopping requires a state of transition,' he said, kissing her. She kissed him. 'When you stop properly, of course.' Another kiss. 'And it's important to stop properly.'

'Yes,' she said, exhaling. They weren't making sense any more, enjoying the shared awareness of it, the delicious complicity as their deeds began to overwhelm their words. 'Stopping is important.' Their lips touched again.

'Stopping is *so* important,' he murmured.

If Ms Pissy Pinsent opened the door and saw them, she'd see that it was her boss who was all over her, it wasn't Ilona coming on to Richard. Shazza would never get over that. Poor dear.

Richard kissed Ilona again and gathered her into his arms, and she could feel power underneath his gentleness. Her lips parted and joined his.

Ilona found herself thinking distractedly as they hurriedly opened and discarded their clothes, how ridiculous it was to be here, doing this.

This was her decisive answer to Max – she wasn't sitting in Double Bay with a girlfriend crying into her coffee, sitting around worrying what her husband might do next. And obviously this was a detour of some kind – but at last she was on the move.

'Wait ...' she murmured, trying to speak through their kisses.

'Wait for what?' he murmured, and kissed her fiercely. His hands were on her hips, gripping them softly but decisively, making her want to comply, and then sliding her underclothes down to her knees. She and Richard were now so far beyond the ability to make excuses if the door should open. What were the rules these days? Was this as bad as smoking in the office?

Richard was a risk taker – let him take risks!

She was now kneeling on the sofa, her breasts mashed against the luxurious cushions, her crossed arms resting on the back of the sofa, and her cheek pressed against the top of one of her hands. She wondered how he would touch her next.

So he wanted to fuck her? Fuck him!

She would never have let Max take her this way, of course, she would have worried about seeming subservient.

She felt one of his hands, soft but strong and knowing, gripping her inner right thigh and opening it more. Her knees spread wider on the sofa. His hand rose between her legs. They were way off script from her usual, highly specific, program for orgasm – but so what? How could Richard possibly know what she liked? She'd see what he had to offer.

Ilona looked wildly over her shoulder at him standing right behind her. It was a bit of a downer.

She would never have admitted this to Max, but years before when he was big, hot and eager for action, she thought he had a spectacular, beautiful cock. Even now, when her desire for it had waned considerably due to its ownership, Max's cock was still her standard, and by comparison Richard's erect penis seemed a little small, thin and precarious for her taste.

But, if anything, her momentary disillusionment committed Ilona even more to getting this done. 'Take me, baby,' she said, her voice low but distinct, resting her cheek against her hand.

Then she felt him taking her from behind, his hands on her hips as she slipped down onto him.

Crazy! She felt the pressure of him inside her as he rammed her down onto himself, heaving her up with each thrust, his other hand now on her taut belly pressing her into him, his knowing fingers between her legs. Oh god, how crazy!

Richard used what he had with considerable vigour, delivering an enthralling series of change-ups in rhythm, his thighs and hips working like truck pistons as he continuously shifted into different, low, slow gears.

It wasn't her fault how this worked out. It was insane. The whole thing had been totally Richard's idea.

'Oh – my – God,' Ilona panted, each word punctuated by one of Richard's thrusts. *This is crazy – crazy – crazy – crazy,* she thought. *What am I doing?*

Ilona let her head drop back, lifting her face to the ceiling and baring her throat, eyes closed to better absorb and savour every sensation. Besides Richard's powerful body Ilona felt the swaying tips of her hair brush her shoulders and the base of her neck.

Crazy, crazy, crazy ...

It was such an incredible relief, giving herself up to this man, and also giving up all the burden of being herself. Even though she was surrendering, at this moment that was exactly what she wanted, she wanted Richard to take it all away. He was a man, all right. If it was a surrender, it was a very sensual one – and temporary, of course.

Why the fuck not?

Richard was panting directly in her ear.

It felt great.

Fuck—yes!

Afterwards, they silently and efficiently put their clothes back on, and Ilona straight-ened her dress, patted down her hair, and checked the mirror to ensure her mascara hadn't smudged.

Richard gave her a last kiss and then, with an official air, opened the door of the office. He'd certainly proved to Ilona's satisfaction he was ready to step up.

Now they'd established that, she was ready to move on.

'Goodbye, Ilona,' he said. 'Ring me any time.'

As she passed Sharon Pinsent on the way out, Ilona leaned over. 'Thank you, darls,' she said, unable to keep the triumph from her eyes. On the surface Ilona was referring to the soy latte, but she said it as if thanking Sharon for personally administering the aphrodisiac. Which in a way she had done.

The only annoying moment, later that day, came when Ilona was driving to Nightin-gale and was trying to confide to Magda what had just happened with Richard. As the details unfolded Magda became shocked and increasingly indignant, and she kept interrupting Ilona with disapproving exclamations, and finally a crescendo of insulting comments about Richard's behaviour. At last Ilona simply broke off her account.

'Oh, Magda,' Ilona said dismissively, feeling contented and relaxed as she sat in the congested traffic of William Street on her way back to the Eastern Suburbs. 'What would *you* know?'

Chapter 56

Despite the heavy traffic, it was a beautiful morning on William Street as Max drove from the Eastern Suburbs to the Extraordinary General Meeting of ZettaData shareholders in the CBD. He pushed a button on his speed dial.

'Yeah, mate,' Luke Terry growled.

'Just checking everything's fine with your ministerial instructions for this morning?' Wander had cut Max off from information after he declined to withdraw his bid and accept an investment in the Tunnel Consortium. So what little he'd learned about Mort's lawsuit against ANG came from Luke Terry himself – and Terry wouldn't say much, except it was under control.

'It's sorted.'

Terry was asking Max to trust him. It wasn't easy. Terry had voted in favour of Max's proposal at the board meeting a few days ago, but then he was awaiting final instructions from his minister about how to vote at today's EGM as a shareholder.

'Sorted?' asked Max. He couldn't assume anything; he had to know more.

'I've been advised I have a couple options for how to act this morning.'

'Well, that doesn't build confidence. Can you just tell me, mate, which way you're going to vote?'

Terry had supported Max's bid consistently, and already confided he was likely to abstain from the shareholders vote that morning. They both knew the position suited Max. The most obvious interpretation of ANG's legal position under the Corps Act was that, as the other strategic investor in ZettaData, ANG was a related party to Edgell, and as a related party couldn't vote on Max's offer to acquire Edgell's securities in ZettaData.

'Let's just say that either way, Mort Norton and I are having a reckoning this morning,' said Terry.

That was what he was hoping to hear. 'It's been a long time coming,' said Max.

'That it has. At last we'll be square.'

Max was going to have his own reckoning with Mort.

Before he knew it, Max was on Elizabeth Street around the corner from the Royal Court Hotel. He parked in the fifteen-minute zone, daring Mort to destroy his car again, and walked to the hotel.

This time he sat in the front row, near the main aisle. With the two strategic shareholders unable to vote, the decision was right where it belonged, with the Casners and the other small shareholders.

Still, Max was uneasy. The ZettaData share price continued to wallow around twenty cents. There was certainly demand for shares as the good news about the board's unanimous decision flowed into the market, but steady selling by Coldstream and its allies in the market kept the air leaking out of the share price and preventing it from rising. By terrorising the market, however, Coldstream and its brokerage allies had actually concentrated the ownership of ZettaData common stock in the hands of Max's most determined supporters.

Max saw Susan and Hal Casner walk down an aisle and take a seat near the front. He headed over to them.

Hal smiled and gave Max a thumb's up.

'Are you feeling good?' Susan asked.

'Anything can happen at these things,' Max said, which was not actually true, but reflected his uneasiness. A surprise at a shareholder meeting was as likely as the Pope showing up to officiate at a bris. 'But I'm feeling as confident as possible before the vote.'

'Max, wherever she is, your mum is proud of you today,' said Susan, patting the back of Max's hand.

'I wish that were true,' Max said sadly. Even if his mother were still alive, he very much doubted that anything he did would make her proud; it never had.

'Oh, of course she is,' said Susan. 'Good luck, dear.'

Max smiled, hiding the momentary pang he felt. 'Good luck to all of us.'

Was his anxiety a real intuition or just meaningless jitters? It was impossible to know; he'd learned that once and for all diving with Peggy in Byron.

Max walked back to his seat, casually scanning the audience to find the major players. The Palisades / Coldstream Capital team appeared at the door and began filing through, a seemingly endless line led by Mort Norton and his fellow investor Ted Hector, followed by Rupert Campbell and more than a dozen members of their teams.

Something wasn't right. Why were they attending in force? The last thing Rupert Campbell, especially, would want to personally witness would be his clients and their teams being humiliated by the rejection of the Palisades bid in the shareholder vote.

The Board of ZettaData arrived and took their seats at the table on the stage. All looked calmly dignified – a total turnaround from their demeanour when he first saw them on stage at the AGM – as Chairman Luther Telford stood up and walked to the podium. Max looked around; still no sign of Wander. Mort and Ted Hector were only about ten rows back but, as he expected, they refused to let Max catch their eyes. There was something terribly wrong.

Max suddenly felt the awful weight of his responsibility. If Palisades was somehow to win this morning, the stock price would collapse to three cents, equal to their offer. Tens of thousands of shareholders who had supported Max and bought shares at levels up to forty plus cents would lose the last of their investments – tens of millions of dollars. But how could it possibly happen? It seemed as likely as a great white shark appearing on his dive with Peggy – possible, but wildly improbable. Given the stakes this morning, however, the overwhelming odds in his favour were turning out to be cold comfort.

'Good morning, ladies and gentlemen. It gives me great pleasure to welcome you all to the Extraordinary General Meeting of ZettaData shareholders. Thank you for coming. We've had a very eventful few months since we last gathered together in this fine venue. At the time, I had to inform you that despite the strong operating performance of your business out in the real world, it had been the duty of the board to initiate a capital raising to strengthen your company's balance sheet. I think it's fair to say that there are reasonable people who might have wondered whether your board had made the right decision, or whether any deal might be a good one. Certainly we all recall strongly-voiced objections made at that meeting, and dire predictions about the future of ZettaData.'

Telford smiled into the blinding lights as happy laughter swelled around the ballroom in waves of contentment and satisfaction. Max was having none of it. Wild thoughts skittered through his mind. Now that he and Ilona had executed the Stat Dec, what was left of their wealth was his. Could he reimburse shareholders for their losses if the vote went against him this morning? The damage would be far too much – what was left of his wealth would cover only a fraction of losses that big.

Max breathed, slowly and deliberately.

'Well, hindsight is twenty-twenty, and I am pleased to be able to put before you today not one, but two fully underwritten proposals,' Telford said. 'The proposal put forward by Max Ring and his consortium is recommended by your Board of Directors and by the Independent Expert appointed by your board to assist with the evaluation of the proposals. The other, the unsolicited offer made by Palisades Holdings, has been evaluated by your board and its advisors and judged to be not fair, and not reasonable. I'm sure you've had time by now to read the information we provided, even though we issued it after midnight on Friday night.' He chuckled deliberately into the microphone. 'I can assure you, your board had a good sleep-in on Saturday morning.'

A ripple of laughter drifted through the ballroom, as Max shifted restlessly in his seat. My god. He breathed slowly and deliberately to steady himself. He was close to panic – just as he had been when surfing that morning. And what would have happened if he had panicked then? He would have paddled in and missed meeting Peggy walking on the beach with Juanita. Thinking about the enormous losses shareholders would suffer wasn't helpful; he'd only spooked himself. The world was much bigger than just him and his fears. He'd face anything that might happen. The event is mind.

'Now that I hope everyone has had time to read and reflect on the various documents, I'll just move directly to the business of the meeting.

'May I have a show of hands please for all shareholders in favour of the proposal by the Ring Consortium?'

Max looked around to see almost the entire ballroom raise their hand, overwhelmingly supporting his proposal. His fears and doubts vanished. Evaporated without a trace. Max was deeply moved by their trust in him. He was surprised by how emotional he felt. Except for the births of Sam and Billy, he had never felt so good in his life.

'Well, I suppose that's very clear –'

'Chairman?'

Max suddenly seemed to see an eerie disembodied smile appear in the shadows of his mind, hovering like a Cheshire cat's.

Luke Terry was leaning into his microphone. 'Chairman, may I make a request as a director representing the shares owned by Australian Natural Gas?'

His voice carried to every corner of the ballroom. Telford looked around with surprise. 'Well, uh, yes you may, Mr Terry. What can I do for you?'

'I'd like to invoke the right to have the vote counted by poll, rather than a show of hands.'

Max tensed. It was a strange request. He and Luke had spoken less than an hour ago. Could it be he had instructions from his minister to formalise the vote count to provide political cover in case the other party tried to make an election issue out of the vote? It seemed only a remote possibility, but even strong governments could be afraid of their own shadows at election time.

For the next long, long hour, shareholders filed forward to the company secretary to identify themselves, confirm how many shares they owned, and how they wanted to vote those shares in relation to the Ring proposal. Max stood near the table hastily set up to take the votes. What had been the point of Terry's request? It was clear the vote was almost unanimously in favour of the Ring Consortium's proposal. As the last dozen or so shareholders stood in line to vote, Luke Terry handed Leonard Whyte, the Company Secretary, an envelope and nodded to him to open it. Max watched as Whyte examined the document inside. He looked at it again. He hurriedly scribbled onto the tally of votes and stood up and gave the tally and the document to Chairman Telford.

Telford's face turned bright red. He looked at Terry, whose face was expressionless, his arms crossed.

'Oh fuck,' Max said under his breath.

Telford walked unsteadily to the podium. 'Ladies and gentlemen, I have just been advised that ANG has decided to vote its shares in today's meeting. Because they control more shares than the rest of you combined, their vote will prevail. And it is my duty to inform you that ANG, along with a small number of the public shareholders, has voted against the Ring Consortium's proposal. Consequently, the proposal is defeated. ANG also advises they have agreed to sell their shares to Palisades at the price offered in their proposal.'

A lightning bolt flashed through Max's mind. Luke Terry had sold ANG's shares to Mort for three cents each? Terry had fucked him – and tens of thousands of small shareholders. Hundreds of million dollars in market value had just been destroyed.

Max was on his feet. 'Chairman! Chairman!'

Telford peered over the podium, trying to focus on Max, who wasn't even sure what he would ask Chairman Telford. Huge losses had been inflicted on his supporters – and Max himself would be reviled for leading them down the path to ruin. Coldstream Holdings, Mortimer Norton, Ted Hector—and Richard Wander—had won. Luke Terry's decision was incomprehensible.

Nobody was coming towards him with a microphone. Up on the platform, the company secretary rose and, maintaining a half-crouch as if staying below the trajectory of flying bullets, moved behind Telford and, standing up, murmured something in his ear.

Telford turned around and stooped to speak with his mouth close to the microphone. 'Ladies and gentleman, there being no other business before us today – this meeting is adjourned.'

'Chairman!'

The silence had taken on an almost physical presence in the ballroom. But now all kinds of exclamations, hoots, cries of outrage, and puzzled voices began to wash over Max and swirl around him, surrounding him as he stepped into the aisle and headed towards the front. Wander appeared from behind a curtain and walked out on the stage, up behind the chairman, and began talking in Telford's ear. Luke Terry had already collected his papers and was walking away from the table, without a glance backwards. The ZettaData directors were standing in little groups, talking in low tones, with stunned – even frightened – expressions on their faces.

Max rushed straight to the edge of the stage. Ormsby glanced down at him with the expression of a stunned mullet.

Max waved to Ormsby. 'Come here!' he said. Max planted both hands on the edge of the stage and in one bound was up on the stage.

Ormsby pulled himself away from the other directors and walked over to Max.

'Donald – what happened? I thought ANG couldn't vote? The Corps Act seems clear about Related Parties being excluded from the vote. I spoke to Luke this morning and he said he was going to have a reckoning with Mort.'

Ormsby looked grim. The ballroom was in an uproar, voices surging into a symphonic flow to action. It sounded like the start of a riot. Ormsby glanced from side to side. 'I'm not exactly sure. Terry just pointed at his dossier as he passed me on the way out and said that he had both a High Court ruling and a Special Counsel opinion.'

'A High Court ruling? You're fucking kidding me!'

'That's what he said.'

'What does the High Court have to do with this?'

Ormsby shrugged. 'I'm sorry, mate. That's all I know.'

Max felt like his head had been snap frozen. Mick Rosebery, Mort's mate, was a High Court Justice. He got it. It was dirty – but oh, so brilliant! The lawsuit between Norton & Ring and ANG was fake. Mort and Luke Terry must have made up, somehow, something that made it plausible for Norton & Ring to sue ANG. In public, they looked like they were having a major stoush in court – but Mick Rosebery would have approved a confidential settlement between Norton & Ring and ANG. The main item in the settlement agreement would be that ANG agreed to sell its ZettaData shares to the Palisades Consortium. That would make it look like ANG was forced to sell to Palisades, and Luke Terry would have the political cover he needed in the next election for helping out Mortimer Norton—who Terry's base absolutely hated because of his role in breaking the Green Bans decades ago. The lawsuit and the settlement were utterly dishonest, fraudulent, and a mockery of the legal system – but totally legal. Being a High Court Justice means never having to say you're sorry.

Mort and Ted Hector had delivered Max the biggest surprise of his life – but he didn't have to take it. He stepped briskly across the stage, walked to the podium, and tapped on the microphone. It was still working.

'Ladies and gentlemen, Ladies and gentlemen ...'

His voice reverberated through the ballroom, and people started looking up at him.

The crowd became silent. Below him Max saw Mort standing with Rupert Campbell and Ted Hector and their teams. All three men were smiling up at him now, as if watching him on a cross.

'Ladies and gentlemen, this isn't over! I'm going to take this to the Takeover Panel. I can assure you –'

The audio system was cut off.

Max stepped from behind the podium to the edge of the stage and called out. 'I can promise you I won't give up! What happened today is not right! I'm going to appeal!'

He'd find evidence to prove that the High Court ruling on the Norton & Ring lawsuit was a criminal conspiracy and present it to the Takeover Panel. It was his last chance to tell the truth.

The lights on the stage shut down and Max was bathed in darkness.

'I am not going to quit!'

Chapter 57

M ax could smell the ocean through his open window, but couldn't hear the sound of waves as he lay with his eyes closed. After the storm of the last few days, it must be completely flat. Lake Bondi. He had a noon meeting with the team of advisers he assembled yesterday afternoon after the EGM to work with him on the appeal to the Takeover Panel. He'd turned off his phone and computer before going to bed, and couldn't bear the thought of all the calls, messages and emails that awaited when he turned them on.

How to motivate himself to get out of bed? He'd been awake until three this morning, and now he felt paralysed. Everything had gone terribly, and it was hard to imagine his life ever getting better. It was so depressing Max found it hard to move.

Think of something good.

One thing.

One thing you're glad has happened.

Max opened his eyes and smiled. Ilona had been so eager to get the Stat Dec and financial settlement signed she'd agreed to great custody arrangements for Sam and Billie. He had been granted not just equal responsibility, but equal time, and she'd agreed they would live with Max during the summer holidays, even if he took them travelling overseas. That was only three weeks away.

Now he could get up. Max felt physically, not just mentally, beat up as he walked to the kitchen. He made coffee.

Plunger coffee.

He'd already spent time with Sam and Billie twice since he and Ilona split at opening night, and –

Coming from the balcony was a sudden burst of caterwauling and a cacophony of bird cries outside his living room window. A cat prowled along the balconies of the apartment building and had almost succeeded in catching a mina bird in her claws. The wounded bird was trying to escape: it sprang a few centimetres into the air and desperately flapped its wings – unable to fly – as four or five other mina birds dive-bombed the cat while it swiped at the hopping bird. Max opened the window and scooped up the cat. He walked to the next window, opened it, and reaching to the next balcony he put her down. She crouched where Max had set her down, blinking at him, stunned by her sudden change of fortune.

Max walked back and looked at the wounded bird, sitting hunched and motionless on his balcony. The other birds perched on the railing, gently encouraging the bird to fly away, but it flapped and fluttered, moved a centimetre or two, but couldn't succeed in lifting off.

After a minute or so the largest mina bird started a piercing cry similar to its battle cry during the attack on the cat. The cries of the other birds joined and became as piercing as the cry of their leader. Suddenly the big mina bird attacked the wounded bird, pecking at it. The wounded bird began to protest and feebly defend itself, shrieking weakly. Before Max could intervene, all the birds pounced on the back of the wounded bird or stood by its sides, pecking and clawing with talons and beaks that quickly reddened.

Max felt sick with regret, but it was too late.

The big mina stood by calmly and arrogantly as the rest of the birds continued to peck and claw until the injured bird listed on its side, breathing slowly and heavily. The leader then flew to the railing, looked about with a satisfied air, launched off the balcony and flew away, followed by the other birds.

Lots of species must do this sort of thing. It wasn't quite *sparagmos* – the chilling last scene of the play last week had made that very clear – but it was a bad, lonely, painful, frightening way to die.

I can't let the bird die alone.

He'd been unable to protect the bird—the brutal attack of the other birds was too fast and unexpected for Max to react in time—but at least he could provide the bird comfort in its last minutes. The crumpled little bird's eyes were closed, perhaps pecked out, but it was still breathing as it lay on the floor of the balcony where it had been left to die. Max gently rolled it into his hand, trying not to frighten the bird, and with his fingertips could feel it breathing.

Softly Max began to sing to the bird:

"Row, row, row your boat
Gently down the stream,
Merrily
Merrily
Merrily
Merrily
Life is but a dream."

How he wished it was.

Max felt the bird relax. It was probably dying, at least peacefully, its breathing rhythmic but very faint now.

Max put the little bird in a baseball cap and set it by the open window where it could die peacefully in the fresh air. That's how he would want to go.

He walked quietly back to the kitchen. By this time his coffee was stewed, so he made himself another one. He was going to take a quick shower and try to relax, and then brace himself and turn on his phone, read emails and texts, and—finally—check the internet to see what the media and analysts were saying this morning. He didn't want to know, but everybody else did and he had to face it.

Max checked the bird on his way to the bathroom. The bird had opened its eyes and was looking around. He took a quick shower and shaved.

It wasn't like he didn't know what was waiting for him when he turned on his phone. Yesterday the news services, analysts and social media erupted immediately after the EGM. Some commentary was genuinely shocked at ANG's decision, but led by Coldstream Holdings and Wander, Fleagle and their allies, a tidal wave of mockery, contempt, outrage and abuse had flowed like a tidal wave through his inbox, Twitter account, and through the early press and across social media. The emerging frame was that Max had front to even consider appealing to the Takeover Panel. Almost everybody who posted—and no doubt all the bots—dismissed his cause as ridiculous and Max himself as a Pied Piper for stupid people. The digital contempt and abuse swept him up and swirled him around for the rest of the day.

The hundreds of personal phone calls, emails and texts had been even more painful, many of them from supporters bewildered and shattered by their catastrophic losses. All he could do in return was tweet his determination to lodge an appeal and promise everyone he would keep them regularly updated.

After shaving, Max walked across the apartment to check on the bird.

The cap was empty except for a squeeze of white and black bird shit.

Max smiled.

The bird had flown away.

He had equal custody of his daughters plus summer holidays, and he had saved the wounded mina bird.

It was a start. Maybe enough of a start on which to begin building the rest of his life.

He'd work all afternoon and all night with his team, if that's what it took to produce the most powerful and compelling appeal, one that would be sure to persuade the Takeover Panel that the Corps Act was on Max's side and had been egregiously violated by the Palisades Consortium and Luke Terry's decision to cast a vote even though ANG was clearly a related party.

To hell with his phone.

Max put on his wetsuit and selected a board, the longest one he had, just in case he happened to find one tiny wave.

It was totally flat, so Max just lay flat on his board and paddled through the ocean from one end of Bondi to the other and back; at least it was exercise.

After a couple laps he sat up on his board only fifty metres away from the beach, where the big waves of earlier that week had pushed the sand banks in close to the beach. There was hardly a ripple this morning. Max could clearly see delicate scale patterns from a light summer breeze ruffling the water.

Hard to believe it was already the first of December, the day he'd expected to be the new owner of ZettaData. Unexpectedly, Max felt a surge of happiness, stronger than he felt when he realised the little bird had survived and flown away. A random moment of joy. Odd. Wondering why he'd inexplicably felt happy on the worst morning of his life, Max heard a voice on the breeze.

The faint sound of his name came across the water and he glanced over his shoulder.

Peggy was standing on the beach calling to him. Max raised his hand and heaved the nose of his board towards the beach as she waved, and dropping to his belly Max paddled to shore, gliding swiftly over the smooth water.

'Hey!' she called. 'I'm so glad to see you!'

Max stepped out of the water, and trotted up the beach. 'You're literally the only one on Earth who feels that way.'

Peggy met him just above the water line. He spiked the nose of his board in the sand and unzipped his wetsuit, pulling it down to his waist.

'Hey,' he said. 'What are you doing here?'

'As soon as I heard the news I thought I'd try and find you since you're not taking my calls,' she said.

'I'm not taking anybody's calls. My phone's not on.'

'Do you want to see my new ute?'

'Sure,' Max said.

Peggy led him up to the car park overlooking the beach and to an old white HiLux with a double cab.

'Like it?' She opened the passenger door.

'Yeah,' he said. 'I like the manual shift.'

'Hop in, I got us fish and chips.'

They sat in the ute together eating fish and chips wrapped in newspaper. She put her hand on his. 'Are you ok?'

'Not really. My lawyers tell me we should win the appeal, but I shouldn't have lost the vote in the first place. There's clearly a major alignment of forces against my owning ZettaData, but I can't be sure why, or what lengths they'll go in order to stop me.'

'Could it be as simple as dad wanting to buy it himself?'

'It could be,' Max shrugged. 'I'm also thinking about establishing a fund to pay back at least some of the losses suffered by ZettaData shareholders who backed me, but I'm afraid it would only be a drop in the bucket. The thing to do is win the appeal.'

Peggy turned and gave him her full attention. 'Max, it's easy for people to say you're crazy – it's easy for my father to say you're crazy – because you haven't accomplished anything, yet. But if you succeed, they may not like to believe what you've said, but they'll have to believe what you've achieved.'

'Thanks,' said Max, wiping his greasy fingers on the newspaper in his lap. 'That's the plan.'

'Don't let them discourage you, Max.'

'I'm doing my best.'

'You can do it,' and Peggy kissed him on the cheek.

Chapter 58

A warm, wet, salty breeze ruffled tufts of Mort's hair as he looked beyond Ted Hector at the pinks, purples and hazy glow of the harbour skimming by. For once Hector didn't look so fucking confident. He always wore pastel Polo shirts to signal he was important enough to dress informally, even post-Covid.

'Well, let's just say that Ring does win his appeal,' Hector said, leaning his meaty forearms on the rail of Mortimer Norton's thirty metre motor launch, *Saxon Princess*. 'What happens then?'

Llewellyn Reinough regarded Hector with the cool indifference lawyers acquire from careers profligately spending their clients' money.

'Well, Theodore, the Takeover Panel has various remedies available,' Reinough said with the relaxed manner of a perfectly healthy oncologist explaining the course of treatment to a cancer patient. 'But the most likely one if they were to agree with Ring's contentions, would be to nullify ANG's vote of its shares in favour of the Palisades proposal, and secondly, to nullify Palisades' agreement to acquire Todd Edgell's securities in ZettaData.'

'Holy Fuck – you mean overturn our deal and give the company to Max Ring?' demanded Hector, oblivious to the sight of the setting sun drenching Rose Bay, his brow furrowed in concentration as the golden lights of Cremorne and Neutral Bay spun behind him.

'In a word – yes.'

'But you wrote an opinion for both ANG and us, that said we're going to win!' Working with Coldstream Capital and the best and most expensive legal and tax advisers in Australia was all well and good – as long as it worked. But losing a high profile public takeover, especially because a risky strategy failed, would spell disaster for Hector. He didn't seem to be having fun any more.

'Yes, but to be precise, those are my opinions, not the judgement of the Takeover Panel,' Reinough said, relaxed pedant that he was.

'Thanks for nothing,' said Hector.

Rupert Campbell emerged from below deck, buckling his shorts. He was wearing a buttoned-up casual shirt, even uglier than it was expensive, the fabric straining against the deposits left by decades of sumptuous dinners. 'When are we picking up Richard?' Campbell asked.

'He's meeting us at the pier at McKell Park,' Mort said. He'd rather shit in his hands and clap than spend another five minutes listening to Teddy Hector whinge.

A young crewman in white shirt and shorts approached the little group with a tray of canapés. Behind him a young woman in a white apron carried a champagne bottle wrapped in a stiff linen towel.

The engines throbbed as the yacht motored towards the mysterious dark trees and sandstone parapets of McKell Park. A slim, dark figure stood with perfect poise awaiting their arrival.

Richard Wander came aboard looking relaxed and sleek in one of his ten thousand dollar suits. Mort glanced at Wander. 'You look like a real salt, mate.'

Wander pointed down to his loafers with their nubby crêpe soles. 'Bally,' he said briefly, indicating they were fine for wearing onboard.

'So – how do you like our chances, Richard?' Hector demanded.

'I'm here as advisor to the Board of ZettaData, at Rupert's invitation, and I have no professional view on the matter. I'm a neutral party,' Wander said, and smiled discreetly.

'But Richard—from what Lew here's saying, I could be up shit creek!'

'As a purely private, personal, subjective, off the record, indicative view,' Wander said quietly, 'I'd say Palisades' chances before the Takeover Panel are excellent.'

'I don't get it, Richard.' Hector's voice was urgent, almost quavering. 'I've read Ring's Application to Appeal, and Reinough's Special Council Opinions, and our position doesn't make any fucking sense. As a layman, it looks to me like it's Ring who's right, and we're the ones who are wrong.'

'Ah, yes – as a layman,' Wander's smile grew feline. 'I understand Llewellyn has already explained his conclusion?'

'Yeah – he did – and it contradicts the plain meaning of the Corps Act! Should we be going into damage control mode now – or wait until the Takeover Panel issues its opinion? I think we're totally fucked! Maybe it would be better to get ahead of it.'

The Opera House, lit up and glorious, whirled by in slow motion as the engines of the *Saxon Princess* throbbed.

'You just don't get it, do you?' Mort said, unable to bear it any longer. *Who needs a waste of space like Hector in this deal?* 'Those cunts on the Takeover Panel will call Max's appeal whatever we fucking tell them to call it. If we say it's blue cheese and stinking up the ASX, those cunts will rule that it's blue cheese and throw it out. Got it, dickhead?'

Reinough cleared his throat and looked disapproving. Mort knew he didn't like hearing talk like that – he'd been at many business dinners with Reinough while he pussy-footed around all evening as he billed three thousand an hour. But that's how shit really got done. Reinough just wanted to pretend he was above it all, when in fact it was how he had made his lucrative career: providing legal cover for dirty work.

'Is that right?' demanded Hector, looking around, alarmed and indignant.

Suddenly Mort was sick of this panicked punk and the rest of the candy-arsed cunts on his yacht, all of them – so tough and entitled on the outside, so soft and helpless when the first sign of trouble appeared. It was like they were all sitting around in their underwear again on Zoom calls. They wanted something – they should take it. Fuck all the dancing around on either side of the lines marked out by the Takeover Code and the Corps Law. This wasn't a fucking pandemic—it was about words on paper. Who gave a shit?

It was suddenly dusk, and except for the on-board lights that threw stark horizontal shadows, every face in the group had become indistinct. 'When did you say the appeal is being heard?' Mort asked.

'The conference with the panel is this Friday,' Rupert Campbell said.

'Why don't I arrange for Max to spend Friday and Saturday riding around in the boot of a car?' proposed Mort. 'When he gets out, he can make his apologies for not showing up at their precious fucking conference – and he might even decide to drop the appeal altogether.'

Hector looked at Mort. 'Haha, good one! I can think of a couple of other pricks I'd like to throw in the trunk with him. Especially if we lose.'

'We're not going to lose, Ted,' murmured Wander.

Reinough cleared his throat, again looking displeased.

There was a harsh clatter of the chains from the ship's anchors dropping over the side followed by two splashes, and then the engine was cut.

Campbell's eyes darted nervously in the sudden silence, reluctant to look at Mort and acknowledge he'd heard him. Very fucking scrupulous.

Wander shook his head. 'Mort, that's not funny. We have to go through the process and get the right outcome, and I'm confident Palisades will prevail with the Takeover Panel on the merits. Palisades has an exceptionally strong legal position.'

The boatswain approached respectfully in the darkness, lit from in back by the aft lights. 'Gentlemen, dinner is served.'

The men began to file across the deck, Hector and his advisory team putting the discussion behind them like a bad dream while Mort and Wander lingered in the comparative darkness on the prow.

'Mort, don't get impatient,' Wander said softly.

Mort grunted.

'We're almost there,' Wander urged.

He's not going to stop me.

'You're not going to do anything, are you?' Wander insisted.

Nobody needs to know.

'Why would I do anything?'

'Don't. Just don't.'

Mort looked at Wander, but it was too dark for either of them to see the other's face except as shifting shadows.

Wander put his hand on Mort's arm. 'Trust the process.'

Mort grunted again and started to walk away.

'Mate – promise you won't do anything,' Wander said.

'Lighten up, Richie – your idea of the three cent offer was the best laugh I've had in years – and it worked – and your secret weapon, the lawsuit with ANG, worked, too.' Mort winked at Wander. 'But the secret weapon is never the secret weapon.'

'Or it wouldn't be secret,' frowned Wander. 'Goddamn it, Mort – I'm running this deal. Everything is completely under control, and I want it to stay that way.'

'Ok, mate, so think of it this way. Maybe it's my turn to sprinkle a little fairy dust on this deal.'

'Promise me Max Ring shows up for the Takeover Panel on Friday.'

Mort put his hand on Wander's own shoulder and gave it a reassuring pat.

'I won't do anything that doesn't make our win better and Max's loss worse. Come on, *mate* – I had them crack open three different vintages of fuckin' Grange. Let's go show shit-for-brains what the world's best wine tastes like.'

Chapter 59

Max walked past the Art Gallery of New South Wales to the Domain parking garage to get his car and drive to his apartment in Bondi. Although it was still clear and sunny in the city, in the distance rainclouds were building up above the ocean off Vaucluse.

The conference with the Takeover Panel that afternoon had been ominous. They didn't ask him any questions about his appeal or the issues. The chairman had referred disapprovingly to Max's tweets about his appeal and repeatedly reminded him of his obligations not to seek to influence the outcome by using publicity and warned him he was willing to cite Max for contempt under Section 200 and subsection 190(1). Bob Henninger had just shaken his head as they left the conference. Without a word they sadly shook hands and said their goodbyes.

During the ZettaData takeover his bid truly came to life through the energy of social media, but now it looked like both he and his bid were being put to death by it. He was being subjected to digital *sparagmos*, and it was both agonising and intimidating, even though what he was accused of was almost entirely untrue, and even if the vicious tweets originated, not with actual Australians who had lost money in ZettaData shares, but from Russian trolls hired by PR advisors to the Palisades Consortium.

Max was sick of it all. He felt very little hope for his appeal, but regardless of the outcome, afterwards at least he would be able to disappear back into private life. If the Panel rejected his appeal, he would spend time developing a plan to help, as much as he could, those who would lose money if Palisades was able to forceably acquire their shares for three cents. That would take him through the summer. He'd have custody of Billie and Sam in a couple weeks, and apart from developing his plan to help investors, he'd give them his full attention. Maybe they'd get out of Australia and go skiing up north. He had already started picking them up from school and knew how painful it was for them to hear their father being called the greatest fool, the biggest loser, and worse. It was Billie who spoke for them both these days; perhaps Sam found it too painful to even ask the questions on her mind. One afternoon, Billie had said, 'Daddy, did lots of people lose money because of you?' There was no simple answer to that question, but Max had done his best – knowing as he dropped them off at the rental in Vaucluse that their mother would do her best to reinforce the misunderstandings he had just cleared up.

Max sighed. Peggy was planning to return to London in a few weeks, and he would have loved to take the girls to London, but it was far too early to introduce Peggy to them.

Clouds were building up in the east over the ocean, and even though the evening was warm and sunny they could blow in as night fell and affect the big Nightingale Gala at the Nortons. The Nightingale School Board had delivered a legal letter to him advising he was not welcome to attend as they deemed his presence to be a potential source of distress to the Norton family. Not that he had wanted to attend, but he was part of the Nightingale community and even before the Takeover Panel had ruled on his appeal, Mortimer Norton, who sat on the school board, was already successfully turning him into a pariah. What irony.

The lift descended towards the garage. Ilona would be attending, of course, in all her newly acquired glory as Alexandra's protégé and bestie. He'd offered to look after the girls but Ilona said no. Dropping off the girls was one thing, but she didn't want to actually see him right before the Gala, or any other time. Parking Level One. The doors opened.

Two men stared at Max.

In an instant Max knew something was wrong. He reached for the Door Close button.

Chapter 60

A sudden blast of music rolled over the Norton garden and reverberated around its walls. Mort knew the Duchess had been working on the Covid Charity Auction for months and it was important to her that everything went smoothly. It was 5.00 pm and the local noise restrictions had been lifted until midnight. What a shit fight that had been. He'd finally threatened the Weinsteins with excavating a new pool – six weeks of jack-hammering and bulldozers, guaranteed, during the day from 8 am to 4 pm – unless they dropped their objection to lifting noise restrictions for one fucking evening. Meddling fuckers – they were so pissie only because their daughters went to Ascham, not Nightingale.

Golden sunshine flooded everything from the west, but to the east big storm clouds mounted tens of thousands of metres in the air above the ocean, dazzling white and flesh-toned in the afternoon sunshine, but showing signs of inky purple along their underbellies.

'Weather's not that great,' Mort said. Low misty clouds from the east raced overhead.

'No,' said Kate, the event manager hired by Alexandra. 'They're not predicting rain, though.'

'Those clouds are fucking close, but maybe the wind will push them away, out to sea.' Mort glanced around at the restless palm fronds and the bobbing branches of the mature trees planted by Alexandra's vast landscaping team. The light gusts seemed to be coming from all directions – it was impossible to tell whether the wind would blow the storm away or over them.

He was looking forward to the evening in more ways than one. It didn't matter how Max was actually handling the pressure since he'd lost at the EGM. The PR firm Richard Wander retained made sure social media had come alive with vivid depictions of Max Ring going bonkers with wild hair and spiralling eyes, running ships into icebergs, hitting himself and pathetic stooges labelled shareholders with a big hammer. His personal favourite was the one that showed Max with his trousers around his ankles and his tongue hanging out as he buggered a sheep labelled 'ZD shareholder'. He'd thought of having that one made into a key ring – for his Bentley. It would remind him of Max Dickhead Ring and his demolished Nazi go-cart every time he went for a drive. Haha.

Mort walked along the pathway lined with rose bushes that looked like they'd been growing there thirty years instead of three as members of the catering and logistics crew walked purposefully past, nodding respectfully and bearing food, trays, hoses, electrical cables, and speakers. Hundreds of roses were already blooming, filling the air with fragrance. *Smells good*, he thought.

Philippine and Ukrainian boiler rooms had been hired to deluge Max's Twitter account and Facebook page with almost infinite variations on greatest fool, biggest loser, the obvious Mad Max, but as a skinny, weak torso, and fake messiah – with the face of Charlie Manson. His favourite of these was 'Max Ring: Zero', a line of zeroes running along the screen. Fucking brilliant. For a few thousand dollars a week an SEO firm made sure anybody googling Max was directed to these posts and images.

Up ahead Alexandra was surrounded by people. Her hair had been done that morning, her make-up was on, but she was still wearing casual clothes. From what little he could hear, Alexandra seemed to be giving them her final instructions for the evening. He turned to take a walk around the pool so he wouldn't interrupt.

It seemed to be working. Wander had told him several people who saw Max were unconsciously putting negative spins on what seemed to be quite harmless encounters. That was the power of a great story with momentum behind it. Just as the PR firm had assured him, people were now independently fuelling the startling gossip, and fresh content was popping up in searches and tweets everywhere. All just to soften up Ring's public profile, like a rotten banana in the hot sun, so that when he got what was coming, everybody in Sydney would feel it completed the tragic narrative of Ring's pathetic life.

It was the same PR firm that had coached him before the Palisades deal was announced to say nothing negative in public about Max – in fact, they had drafted several grudgingly respectful comments supposedly from himself, and made sure those comments were widely circulated. He had months of track record as a fucking financial statesman compared to the reckless dealmeister Max Ring. Most importantly, it had created growing distance between them. Except for a few brief losses of control from time to time – and fucking fair enough! – the public record was perfectly clear that he had no grudge, whatsoever, against Max Ring. The tone of his public statements might have been faintly sad, but they expressed no anger. Just a resigned dignity.

Which was good – because it wasn't fucking enough to just portray Max as handling all the disappointments, financial losses and stress increasingly badly. The ultimate point of it all was to guarantee the mother fucker really suffered.

'Hello, darling – you wanted to see me?'

He turned to see Alexandra walking quickly up the path towards him.

'I just wanted to make sure you're fine – not too stressed?'

Alexandra frowned. 'Well, there were some last minute issues – accidents just waiting to happen. I must admit I'm a little disappointed with Barry, he's normally so on it – but it's all fine, now. Barry and his team are great. I think we'll be able to handle anything that gets thrown at us this evening –' Alexandra looked up anxiously at the huge clouds floating overhead, '– unless the heavens really open up and deluge us.'

She kissed him. 'How are you, darling?'

That's when he made his fatal fucking mistake. His mind brimming with pleasant thoughts and images of all the mayhem he'd unleashed in Ring's life, he blurted the first thing that came to mind. 'Brilliant, darling – I was just laughing to myself about that GIF of Max buggering the sheep being one of the last things people see of him.'

'Oh, who knows what he'll get up to in future,' she said distractedly. She looked at him sharply. 'Mort, darling ... '

He couldn't help smiling. It was all she needed to see.

'No –'

He thought she would see reason. 'You don't want all that good work you did with his missus to go to waste, do you?'

To his astonishment, Alexandra turned pale. She stepped back. 'Mort – don't. I can't tell you how much I mean it.'

'Oh, sweetie,' he said, reaching out and putting his hand reassuringly on her shoulder. 'It's all going to be fine.'

'Mort – you can't.'

'Leave it to me, darling.'

Alexandra rolled her eyes and looked up at the sky, this time not seeming to see the clouds. 'Oh, god – on this night, of all nights – with the Gala about to begin. My dad didn't know when to stop, and that's how he lost everything, and I mean everything. Don't do this, Mort. We have such a beautiful life.'

'Darling, don't worry – you're just tense. Everything's going to be fine.'

Alexandra stepped up to him and held his face in both hands. 'Mortimer, my love, promise me you won't lay a finger on Max Ring. Don't have anything to do with him.' She stared into his eyes from centimetres away. 'Swear to me.'

He didn't blink. He held up his index finger and laughed, sounding genuinely amused and relaxed. 'Honey, I wouldn't piss on Ring if he were on fire. I swear to you, I won't lay a finger on him.'

'Ok,' she said, and kissed him earnestly. 'Thank you—you have no idea how much it means to me.'

He watched her walk hurriedly away to have one last look at the refrigeration units before putting on her gown and jewellery.

'Thanks, doll,' Mort said to a passing waitress as he reached for a glass of champagne. It was too bad jumping off the nearby cliffs at The Gap couldn't last for hours instead of a few seconds.

This was one evening the sound of the helicopters would be music to his ears.

Chapter 61

Max wasn't fast enough.

One of the men thrust a suit-coated forearm between the closing lift doors and jumped at Max, who hit the wall of the lift hard, but fought past the guy towards the doors. The opening was blocked by the other man, who grabbed Max by the throat and cuffed the side of his head with an open hand.

Max was breathing too hard to shout. He struggled as he was pulled out of the lift and towards a big black sedan.

'Get in,' said one of the men, wrenching open a door to the back seat.

'No –' Max puffed.

'Ok, dickhead,' said the man holding him from behind. Max was whirled around. He felt a hand on the back of his head. His face smashed into a concrete pillar. White bolts of lightning shot across his vision.

One man threw him down on the cement floor between two cars. Max tried to protect his head and face with his hands but the man's boot pounded against his head. The other attacker kicked Max in the groin and his neck stretched out, unprotected, in agony. While one grabbed Max by the collar and hauled him to his feet, the fabric taut against his windpipe, the other man got into the driver's seat. Max was dragged to the backseat of the car and shoved in.

The man got in beside him. 'No more fucking around.' The car backed up and began winding up the parking structure. Max was stunned, in pain, still conscious of the feeling of choking. The spinning of the car up the ramps made him dizzy and nauseated. Why is this happening? 'I'm going to throw up,' he said.

'You throw up in this car and I'll make you lick it up,' the man said.

'I can't, can't help it,' Max said.

'I'll take your mind off it,' said the man, reaching for the juncture of Max's neck and right shoulder. His fingers sought a nerve through the muscle tissues, pushing through

Max's suit and shirt. White hot pain exploded under the man's touch. Max cringed, trying to shy away, but was caught in a frozen moment of agony, the man's fingers relentlessly riding Max's spasming muscles.

Finally he let go. The car had emerged from the parking structure and was threading down William Street. Max could see people walk unconcernedly along the footpaths on either side.

Open the door, window.

The man put his hand between Max's legs, grabbing his testicles through the fabric of his trousers, and started to yank and squeeze. Max cried out but the man put his other hand around Max's throat, thumb on his Adam's apple, and squeezed so Max could make only choking gasps. It was agony between his legs.

The car stopped at a red light and the man let Max go as cars pulled up along side. 'Lie down, sister,' he said, grabbing Max by the throat and pulling him down below the line of the windows.

Malevolence radiated from the man like a furnace. Max could feel cruel joy, his exultant exercise of power. His body throbbed in pain, and his mind kept flickering, like a malfunctioning television, to snippets of inflicted agony. The fear was debilitating. He couldn't move. His limbs felt as if water were running in channels where his bones had been.

'Ok, sister, ready for another lesson –'

'No, no ...' Max tried to scream. But all he heard was rustling from his throat.

' – in doing what you're told?'

The man's hard grip circled Max's wrist and yanked his arm from underneath him.

'Here, I want you to see this,' the man said thickly.

Max felt disgusted by something in his voice, the sense he was listening to a stranger approaching sexual orgasm – like a pervert masturbating in a theatre. He saw the man's thick fingers in front of his face, holding his left hand, and then the man gripped his little finger like a piece of biscuit and pulled it back.

Max screamed. Just a few centimetres of tearing ligament and tissue and over-stressed bone, the horror of how his body was being abused added to the terrible pain. He cried out as the pain peaked. The burning continued, spreading up his hand and wrist as if his arm was on fire.

'Ok, sweetheart,' the man said, breathing hard. 'I'll let you enjoy the ride.'

Time slowed down into super slow motion, and Max experienced everything around him with a terrible clarity. The plastic back of the front seat next to his face reeked of petrochemicals. The odour of the cold dirt and pebbles on the floor of the car rose to him. Every slight bounce and sway as the car moved shot through his body in ripples of pain. He felt close to the hot tears of a child. The moments of torture seemed to merge into one unending moment of helplessness, suffering and humiliation. But now his mind cut and jumped raggedly to the worst surprises of each attack, replaying the details endlessly. He shivered uncontrollably in fear as cold rose from deep in his chest.

'All excited?' asked the man.

Max cringed and tried to control his shivering. What was going on? If they wanted money, why were they treating him like this? Did they want to break his will in order to get him to cooperate and make a video asking for a ransom?

Max took a deep breath, concentrated on it, and let it out. The pain was almost unbearable. But he could endure it for one breath. He breathed in again, concentrating on the way his lungs filled with air, and then slowly let it out. The pain was right there, gigantic, but he had survived for another breath. He breathed in again, slowly, concentrating on every sensation of his inhale. His mind started to calm, and jumped out of the loop of repeating, irrelevant thoughts.

He became aware of his situation, trying to avoid doing anything the man might notice. He tried to lie motionless. Worse than the pain, somehow, was the man's contempt, considering Max to be only a bundle of nerves and tissues to be twisted and compressed. He was being treated like a thing.

The breaths began to clear Max's mind. Soon Ilona would be at the Covid Charity Auction. It must be in full swing by now. The girls at home, being looked after by the babysitter. Peggy back up in Byron with her mum on the farm, either out in the fading light, or preparing dinner. Was she walking along the beach, thinking of their time together? Max felt a vast gulf separating them and opening wider and wider with each turn of the car's wheels. Would he ever see the girls or Peggy again?

He was probably going to die. He hadn't done himself any favours by trying to fight them off and get away, but the way they treated him was more ferocious than revenge for his resistance.

They were working for Mort.

There was no other explanation.

The way they smashed his face into the pillar guaranteed that Max would look dreadful in public for at least a week, depending on whether his nose was actually broken. His appearance and broken finger would be awkward for Mort if there was any plan for Max to reappear in public – or even to his family. The men seemed to have no concern for how his injuries might look afterwards. Probably because there was no afterwards. This wasn't a negotiation.

He thought of his daughters, their faces appearing vividly in mind, and he pitied them and himself. Billie and Sam couldn't possibly imagine him in this position, being treated like this. Peggy. She and Tori were so afraid. They knew what Mort was capable of doing. Once he just disappeared, they'd know they were almost certainly next on Mort's list of problems to solve. He'd probably been working all along on trying to find Hugh's body.

The man next to him grunted and shifted his feet. Max's shivering began to subside. His mind was becoming clear. He decided to keep shivering so the man next to him didn't detect any change. His fear was turning to anger.

The car climbed steadily, and then swayed through the unmistakable S curves of New South Head Road east of Double Bay – climbing towards Vaucluse. Strange. He would have expected to be taken west, maybe to a bikie hang out. Or to some industrial area in the Inner West or near the airport where there'd be an empty warehouse suitable for a loud conversation – and worse.

The car began the descent from the spine along Christison Park. He breathed in the old carpet and cold dirt smells of the back of the car, even with his head throbbing and his finger burning.

Mort lived in Vaucluse – but he would never risk everything by having him kidnapped, beaten up, and brought to his house. For what? Besides, the Nightingale Covid Gala was probably in full swing by now at the Norton mansion.

Maybe he was disoriented – in the brutality of his initial treatment maybe he hadn't noticed a turn-off, or had forgotten stretches of time that had actually passed? They had reached the bottom of the hill and Max glanced up, catching enough out of the corner of his eye to confirm they were threading their way through the hamlet of Watson's Bay, with its impoverished milk bars and chip shops in the midst of one of the wealthiest areas in Sydney. The car swung in a U-turn and Max felt the back and forth of the driver parking.

Mort. If Norton wanted him killed – a genuine shiver ran through his body – it must be at The Gap. They were going to fake his suicide.

The plan was obvious. Mort's place wasn't far away – only a few hundred metres – but that wasn't the point. They were going to throw him over the cliffs. That's why it didn't matter if his face was abraded, his nose and finger broken, and his testicles swollen – those injuries would be only part of the battering his body would endure after he was thrown over the cliffs and churned in the surf and boulders for hours. Fear mixed with a rush at the recognition his mind was working again. The surprises were over, even if his death might be only minutes away.

Hamartin

Max felt sudden clarity at the realisation he probably only had minutes to live. The first thing that appeared in his mind was the original meaning of the Greek word for "sin". *Hamartin* means to miss the mark, it refers specifically to an arrow not hitting the bullseye. That's all: not filth, or a stain, or sewage. Just missing the mark.

He'd always assumed this meant sin was a fairly innocuous concept—but now Max realised it was the other side of *kairos*. *Kairos* too is a metaphor based on an arrow being released, at just the right moment in the chaos of chronos, and flying through the air through a kind of special fateful tunnel until it unerringly hits its mark. Max had committed everything to the *kairos* of the ZettaData deal, not adjusting when first his oldest colleagues and friends, then his wife, and possibly his daughters, and then 90% of the Sydney establishment, had turned against him and finally become actively hostile. The truth was Mort's position was the popular one, not Max's. Even his death would be mourned by very few, if social media was any gauge.

Max had thought all these challenges and obstacles were part of his *kairos* and they would all work out: he was helping the Casners, influencing the Australian financial markets for the better—and getting close to Peggy. Now he was on the floor of a car and about to be murdered. He had missed the mark. The result was not *kairos*, it was *hamartin*.

Had he really sinned?

The man next to Max rummaged around in a cloth bag at his feet and pulled out a roll of grey duct tape.

'Can you breathe through your nose, sister?'

Max nodded. 'Yeah,' he managed. He didn't want to be hit.

'You better not be shittin' me, or you're going to suffocate. All that snivelin' you were doin' might a' blocked your nose.'

The driver said, 'He's got to have water in his lungs.'

'I know, I know,' said the man in the back seat with Max. He cut a short piece and taped it over Max's mouth and chin. Then he cut a longer piece and pressed it over the first one, so its ends reached both sides of Max's jaw and tucked under along his throat. This was a sign of Mort's power. It was pretty sloppy work to leave tape residue on his face and in his hair, but Mort had the pull to slow down any investigation that might happen. The first forty-eight hours are critical, and Mort, or his mate Mick, or one of his mates in the New South Wales police could probably delay an autopsy until almost all the physical evidence had deteriorated and disappeared. If his body washed out to sea, and showed up miles south on some beach in the Shire half-eaten by fish, these thugs could carve their initials in his skin tonight and it wouldn't matter.

'We gotta get it off, don't tape it all the way around his head,' the driver said.

'I know!' snapped his partner. He placed the back of his palm in front of Max's nostrils, which were flaring with the effort of breathing.

'He can breathe,' he announced. He pulled Max up by his collar, choking him, and as he was bent over, the man rapidly spun the duct tape around his wrists. It was as if the men were hardening themselves against any kindness, treating him like somebody who deserved punishment and death.

His loafers would be treacherously slippery on the cliffs. Better to be wearing just socks. Max stealthily rubbed his feet together and began to push off his loafers, disguising his movements with more shivers.

There would be no deal, no negotiation. They were going to kill him – it wasn't personal, just business. Max's shoulders had become far more flexible in the last few months from yoga, but he tried to lock them into a wide, rigid spread as the man taped his wrists, which he worked to keep as far apart as possible as the man wound the tape around the fabric of his coat sleeves. Fear again made his limbs feel watery, and he tried to summon the feeling of anger – he needed the energy. Mort Norton wasn't satisfied with getting ZettaData for himself, not satisfied with running Norton & Ring, it wasn't enough that his wife had turned Ilona against him and destroyed his marriage and his family – he was also having him murdered. Peggy would soon be back in her father's power. It was an awful thought, but none of it sparked the rage he wanted to feel coursing through his body. He felt weak. He tried to think of Ilona being told he had committed suicide, tried to feel indignant about Mort ruining his daughters' lives by forcing them to live with the belief their father had killed himself.

The engine switched off. Nothing happened. Darkness was falling.

A car drove by on the way back up the hill. Max wished he could be in the car, safe and warm, sitting upright, listening to the radio, and sitting next to Peggy.

'Ok,' said the driver. The locks inside the doors clicked, and he got out, closing his door quietly but firmly, and came around on the kerb side of the car. He opened the door and pulled Max up by his bound arms. Max was lifted backwards, and then he felt the kerb with one foot while kneeling on the seat with the other. The man who had been sitting next to him gripped the top of his head as if he was going to crush Max's skull and pushed him out of the car.

Chapter 62

'No, Max couldn't make it,' Ilona replied to Letchmi Narayan, the wife of Navneel Narayan. Letchmi didn't seem to know she and Max were separated.

Lovely people, the Narayans. They were totally out of the loop of Eastern Suburbs gossip despite being Nightingale parents. Just doctors. Compared to the crowd at the opening night of *Transgod* a couple weeks ago, they wouldn't have a clue what was going on in her personal life. For that matter, they might only know about the whole ZettaData drama from what they'd read in the papers and seen on the ABC.

'Oh, that's so sad!' said Letchmi, her honest eyes wide as she held an almost untouched, non-alcoholic drink.

'Well, these things happen,' said Ilona.

Ilona felt wonderful, her body smooth and firm like alabaster, but supple and alive. She had wowed Richard – he'd sent her a dozen texts from a burner phone since that afternoon. Every passing second she was trapped talking with the Narayans, she was squandering her amazingness. Her eyes skittered, surreptitiously searching for other conversation partners.

'Hello, darling!'

Ilona heard the friendly, familiar voice gladly, and turned to see Natalie Haddad and her husband Mark. They knew everything – it was such a relief. 'Hello, darling!' she exclaimed. She and the Haddads exchanged greetings, and then she introduced the Narayans, knowing they would drift away in only a few moments. Thank god.

'Oh darling, you look so glamorous,' said Natalie approvingly, taking in with one long glance Ilona's hair, her shining make-up and oiled skin, the ultra simple and outrageously expensive summer cocktail dress in a rare shade between aquamarine and teal that seemed to make her hair glow from within like polished mahogany, the delicate Gucci sandals laced around her ankles. At forty Ilona looked more beautiful than most women would ever look and she knew it.

Natalie stared into Ilona's eyes. She could sense what Natalie was thinking: with whom could she match Ilona tonight – who was the one suitably rich, powerful and available man that was her destiny?

Natalie squeezed Ilona's arm. 'Ooh – I could eat you!'

Ilona laughed easily, as she had learned from Alexandra. 'Oh, you're so sweet!' She savoured their shared, unspoken awareness, and was not surprised that she felt within herself only the faintest twinge of pity for Max. She was in, he was out. By choice – his repeated choices. She'd given him every chance.

'Can I offer you ladies more champagne?' Mark said, pivoting from the server whose tray he had just lightened by three flutes. Others were starting to gather around them and Ilona didn't notice when the Narayans disappeared into the crowd. The Trebuchets joined their group, and Ilona began to feel aglow with the tremendous energy circulating around and through her. The chatter was irrelevant; what mattered was the attention she felt, and the mutual regard. Although everybody had come in couples, of course, it wasn't as if many among the hundreds of couples here this evening hadn't undergone a few re-configurations. People who had been married to other people were now couples at the event, and of course new counterparts, both wives and husbands, were now joined until death or divorce did them part like so many family mansions, beach houses, country estates, or fourth, fifth and sixth homes being acquired and divested.

'Hey honey!' The thick, powerful shoulder and shaved head of Noah Timken appeared to the side of Lionel Trebuchet, and then his hairy wrist bearing a flute of champagne emerged along with the rest of him from behind the much taller ex-Prime Minister. He stood in front of Ilona smiling. The Double Bay property developer leaned forward, and Ilona struggled to avoid recoiling, affronted simultaneously by the inappropriately wet kiss applied in front of her ear and the way the gold braid hanging around his neck swung out from his silk shirt and grazed her right breast.

'I heard they chained up Mad Max for the night, hey?'

He'd obviously heard about the legal letter sent to Max by the Nightingale Board. 'Hello, Noah,' she smiled tightly.

Chains, dog collars – no doubt Noah would love to clip one of those on her – Ilona knew that his alliance with his current partner Tiffany, who was not the mother of his daughters, was shaky.

'How are the approvals looking for the hotel?' Lionel Trebuchet inquired, rescuing Ilona by distracting the developer with a question about his latest project in Darling Harbour.

Ilona let out a surreptitious sigh of relief and fingered a ginger and veal dumpling from the tray to her left. The beginning of the evening's endless round of prawns, foie gras, caviar, dumplings, and champagne.

Tra-dee-la lee la lee dee – We sing to thee Parthenope, Ilona secretly hummed in her mind. Mad Max. Not just Noah but everybody was calling him that now – or the greatest fool, or the biggest loser. The strange meta-Max hovering over the virtual world of Sydney for the last month felt somehow to Ilona like the full-blown growth spawned from the seed of the mysterious Pucci Instagram posted that fateful sleepover night six months ago. The Instagram image had sparked the meteoric rise of Trixie Norton's social fortunes, while it was hard to believe Max now had any chance of preventing the digital lynch mob that had formed around him from destroying his life.

'Oh, hello darling – what a marvellous night!' said Natalie. Ilona looked up to see Alexandra. Ilona started to smile but stopped short when she saw Alexandra's drawn face.

'Oh, hello, darling!' Ilona repeated mechanically, shocked into echolalia by the sight of Alexandra's strained expression. She wanted to ask Alexandra what was wrong but didn't want to seem untoward, clumsy.

'Is everything all right?' Alexandra asked, joining the women. 'Are you all enjoying yourselves?'

She was beautifully made up but her eyes skittered around the room. Her champagne flute seemed to teeter in rigid fingers. Alexandra almost seemed to be having a manic episode. Was she on Zoloft? So many were these days.

'Oh, it's so lovely!' Ilona said, trying to hide her concern. They'd spent the week together, preparing themselves for the Gala – and Alexandra had confided in her every detail of the enormously complicated planning required to bring together such a huge event. Ilona was shocked Alexandra wasn't presiding this evening as the triumphant, effortless society hostess.

'Wonderful!' said Alexandra and disappeared like a ghost into the crowd.

Ilona, the Haddads and the Trebuchets all looked at one another. Sylvia Trebuchet looked around at the little group, her candid glance seeming to extract a promise of confidentiality from each. 'We're all her closest friends . . . When someone behaves like Alexandra – assuming she's healthy and hasn't just had a cancer diagnosis, heaven forbid!

– it means she's having trouble with either men or money! Let's be extra sweet to her tonight . . .'

Chapter 63

His mouth taped, his hands bound together, Max emerged into night air saturated with sea salt and the scent of conifers. To his left a couple of hundred metres away he could see the warm, unobtainable lights of Doyle's, the iconic seafood restaurant on Watson's Bay. For a moment all he could hear was the sound of the wind rushing through the foliage around him, but then he heard a thunderous crash from The Gap as an unseen wave collided with the base of cliff in the darkness.

The wind caught the open door and slammed it shut into the frame. They were next to the driveway leading up to Artillery Station. The steel boom had been swung into place and locked, blocking the driveway. There was no function that night at the old colonial building, which meant less likelihood that drunken lovers would be wandering through the myrtle bushes looking for a place to have sex.

'Hey, he don't got his shoes,' Max's captor whispered.

'Who cares,' his partner said.

They pulled Max up the slope into the blackness under one of the conifers and behind a bottlebrush bush. The two stood listening for a full minute, and then the driver cautiously slipped ahead and motioned to his partner to follow. The man pulled Max out from underneath the tree and hurried him into the bushes.

Max's mind was racing. He was starting to feel the excitement of approaching battle. The bastards wanted to murder him by throwing him off The Gap – and they wanted it to look like suicide. Norton could either make him disappear without a trace, or make his death look like suicide. It was a compliment that Mort considered him still important and influential enough to have to murder with finesse.

But – as a practical matter – why The Gap? Christison Park, which they had already passed, had some good spots where these men could throw him over a cliff hundreds of metres high into the ocean. Zero chance of survival. But Christison is an open grassy area hundreds of metres wide, where Max's captors could possibly be seen carrying him or pulling him across those lawns by dozens of people living in the houses on Old South Head Road, or driving by, or walking their dogs. Max thought of the little metal plate in the fence that asked people to re-consider suicide and offered a telephone number for counselling. It was placed at the perfect location, inadvertently marking the best spot to leap from that section of the cliff – or to throw him over. Max shuddered at the thought of being dragged to it and heaved over the fence to the surf crashing against the rocks hundreds of metres below.

But The Gap was a risky place for Max's kidnappers, too, right next to Watson's Bay and the crowded pub next to Doyle's, not to mention Doyle's itself. On a balmy night like this, scores of people finished their eating and drinking by wandering to The Gap and looking at the moonlight reflections on the ocean below. A few dog walkers and joggers made their way along the cliff top path through Gap Park. But once it became dark, it became an intimidating place, with bottlebrush and dagger bushes crowding the path, and plenty of places for concealment.

Max knew three or four particular spots from which most suicides jumped from his days seacliffing with his mates as a teenager. A couple of them were very exposed to being seen by passers-by. He also remembered that the rock face below those spots tended to be full of fissures and cracks. As a teenager Max had climbed up all of them with his mates.

His captors began pulling Max up the slope. In addition to the bottlebrush and dagger bushes that blotted out the sky above their heads, their way was choked by rosemary, myrtle, and toothed daisy bushes. The branches and spiny leaves were invisible in the blackness, and tore at their faces as Max was pushed through the underbrush.

After several metres they stopped and shoved Max to the ground. A hard fist gripped his jacket's lapel and another pushed him back on his hands. He screamed through the tape as his body landed on his broken finger. They hunched in the brush and rolled to the ground. The men lay, completely concealed, close to the path. 'Quiet,' said a low voice, and Max received another blow that produced bright lights in his head.

Max forced himself to think this through. Tonight might cost him his life, but he had to ensure it would cost Mort, too. He had to do something to create doubt about the plausibility of his fake suicide, leave some kind of evidence that would be difficult – impossible – to suppress, by even a corrupt police investigation and Mort's mate Mick in the High Court. Broken branches wouldn't work. He couldn't get his watch off his wrist now, and besides it wouldn't mean anything, even if it were found. Exultant, drunken laughing carried on the gusty wind. The revellers seemed to be on the slope right below them. But there was no chance they could hear his muffled cries. Then car doors slammed in rapid succession, an engine started, and on a corkscrewing funnel of wind in the tossing ocean of air around them, he heard the sound of the car pulling away. Any possibility of help was gone.

His body itself was the best evidence. That was the reason they were going to fake his suicide in the first place. If staying alive tonight wasn't possible, than anything his flesh endured that testified to his desire to live, Max was willing to suffer – even if the odds were low the marks survived being eaten by the fishes and not examined for weeks. He'd gotten to the point where the last authentic gesture of integrity in his life might be to accept terrible agony in the hope of leaving unmistakable evidence that he had been violently murdered.

He sagged back on the edge of a sandstone slab. The edge was like a file, and Max began sliding his hands back and forth along it, hoping the sandstone was cutting the tape around his wrists more than it was cutting his skin – he tried to think of the pain as progress. His mind went to Sam and Billie, knowing they would be safe no matter what. As for Peggy and Tori, their situation was desperate as soon as Max was dead. Max knew exactly what would happen next – with him out of the way, Mort would make his move and do whatever it took to find out what happened to Hugh's body. Trying to escape to the UK wouldn't help Peggy. Max had to get out of this – he couldn't let Mort get his hands on Peggy.

The men rose and pulled Max to his feet. They climbed further, skirting the black bicycle spoke outlines of the bottlebrush bushes, but entangled in tenacious foliage, it was still too dark to see. Max's toes banged against sandstone shelves, stumps, and scree, and his trousers were being gradually torn to loose shreds around his bloodied legs by the bushes and shrubs grown brittle and unyielding in the ceaseless wind.

They scrambled in short bursts up the back slope to the left of the stairs and the main esplanade. Max guessed they were aiming to either hide in the bushes just on the other side of the wide shelf of rock above The Cove, or make their way to the path that ran above the main wall of The Gap.

The rough climb had stretched and loosened the tape around his wrists. He had been able to rub against the sandstone on several stops, not sparing his wrists or the palms of his hands. His wrists burned and he could feel the warm trickle of blood along his fingers, and Max was convinced he would be able to free his hands.

If his murder was going to look like suicide, Mort couldn't just have Max strangled and his body slipped into the sea at a lonely point of Botany Bay. Mort didn't own the entire New South Wales Police Force, he relied on the power of a few mates in key positions to suppress the truth, but they needed his help – the forensic evidence for murder couldn't be too clear. The sheer difficulty of getting an adult male, still alive, to the right part of The Gap without being detected had forced Max's captors to keep him conscious and semi-cooperating.

For a murderer, the main drawback with The Gap was the eroded sandstone cliffs only intermittently offered a long, sheer drop. In most places, the top of the cliffs are set back, so a body falling from the top of the cliff is likely to strike a shelf of sandstone only a few metres below the top. In most places, a person determined to commit suicide has to leap strongly out from the edge. As a result, there are few places that a simple shove could topple a person to their death in the waves breaking against the rocks at the base. Max had to rely on his memory of where those places were, and be alert as they approached one.

After half an hour of short bursts and pauses, Max and his captors lay in deep shadows. Silvery clouds moved at a stately pace in the dark sky. When he heard snatches of passers-by conversation from the path above, tossed like kites through the wind, Max felt a hard hand on his throat, ready to squeeze it closed. He flared his nostrils and his chest heaved as he struggled to breathe.

The cliffs at The Cove were only about twenty metres high, not guaranteed to kill in one fall, but a person crippled in the fall, even if still conscious, would drown in the rough water. The wide slab of sandstone was also a fairly safe place for two men to wrestle him over the side. Most of the cliff is fairly sheer, but the sandstone is very porous, almost pure silica suspended in a Triassic clay mousse; ancient seas had left it extensively fissured, cracked, and full of broken edges and shelves.

Along the right side of The Cove, Max remembered that several metres down there was just such a shelf, which would be connected to lower shelves where huge waves smashed into the cliffs and carried away great chunks of sandstone. Some of these shelves are formidable, but Max and his friends had not found them difficult to navigate years before. Of course they were young – and climbing in the daylight. On this dark night he was forty-three and had just suffered a severe beating.

A short protective wall one metre high runs along the path and blocks access to the shelf, but the wall is easy to climb, hardly more than a high step for an adult. Even if Max were unconscious, he knew it would not be difficult for these men to stand on either side of the low fence and lift him over it.

The path winds along The Cove, rising to the left up the main wall of The Gap. The main wall is totally sheer and curves away from the lip at the top like the outside of a teacup. There was one spot above the main cliff, Max remembered, where it would be possible to get across the fence and then hide in a clump of bottlebrush and rosemary until the coast was clear. There wasn't much room to manoeuvre, but the men could tear the duct tape off his hands, rip it off his mouth, and throw him over the cliff. That would mean a fatal fall of fifty metres, but it would be dangerous for his murderers, too, to get him over. It was totally black in that foliage and the footing wouldn't be good on the patch of disintegrating sandstone that thrust out above the main wall. If anyone heard him scream, his killers would have to take a longer escape route back down through the brush to where they had parked their car.

Max and his captors had come to rest behind a large clump of rosemary about twenty metres from the path, which at this point traced behind the wide shelf of rock above The Cove. It was only another ten metres to the spot on The Gap's main cliff where he felt sure they intended to throw him over.

They were now almost unprotected from the full force of the wind, which threaded the rosemary and roared all around them. The initial conditions of a storm had appeared with nightfall.

The men had pushed him down between them and lay, breathing deeply on either side of him. The sudden gusts of wind suppressed all other sound, but the sudden quiet in between the gusts was startling. Max heard a stone skittering down the sandstone shelf like a coin on glass. Then he heard the great boom of a massive wave breaking against the cliff. He shivered at the thought his body would be soon be bobbing in the cold water down there, sucked into those waves, and pulverised against rocks.

Maybe after his death some of his mates would risk pressuring the government into pursuing an actual investigation, not just go through the motions until the mystery was no longer being covered in the media. Max began to tear up. He wasn't sure anybody cared enough about him to stick their necks out. His daughters? Maybe when they were older, but then the trail would be cold.

Max sensed his last few minutes were passing right now. He didn't know whether the men intended to swing him over The Cove cliff directly in front of where they were lying or take him up to the clump of bottlebrush and myrtle on the other side of the fence above the main wall. They would be visible for thirty or forty seconds hauling his body across the shelf but once they made it to the other side of the fence and nestled into the foliage above the wall, they could disappear even as Max's body toppled to certain death fifty metres below. He heard another extended crashing and the sound of jets rising up and splattering against rock.

Max felt a thrill of adrenaline. All along he'd been wrong – it wasn't about the cliff, it was about the waves. The men didn't need a long drop from the cliff to kill him. All they had to do now was get him to the other side of the fence, cosh him to either stun him or make him unconscious – and then simply roll him over the side of the cliff – at the place almost directly in front of them, where the waves were biggest. Even if he was still alive when he landed in the cauldron at the base of The Gap, he'd be unconscious and certain to quickly drown – if he wasn't almost immediately pounded to death against the basalt boulders at the base of the sandstone cliffs. The blow at the base of his head would be indistinguishable from the other injuries he would suffer against the rocks below and his lungs would fill with water, which was essential for the police forensics team to find. Nobody would ever hear him scream, because by the time Max's mouth was untaped, he would be unconscious. Low risk, high plausibility: it was the plan.

He could see their heads tilted up looking at the sky. There had been several minutes of relatively clear sky, with only silvery wisps passing beneath the moon. Now a large cloud, its centre wide and black, was floating towards the moon. The men were waiting for this cloud to give them cover for the last rush across the path and over the fence.

The man's grip on him had been weakening through the effort of making it up the slope, and since Max had been unresisting the entire way, for the last several scrambles their hold had been more of a guiding hand on his jacket than the original restraint. His hands were now loose. They were about to strike – and they were focused on themselves – not him. Well, he had his own plan.

Max bolted up right between them, his arms swinging free.

He leaped directly through the rosemary, knees high. He remembered the first man's explosive speed from the parking structure and knew he had only three or four seconds to stay ahead.

'Hey!' came the angry cry behind him and instantly there was a crashing and snapping of rosemary right behind him.

Max ran across the sandstone in his stocking feet through the moaning wind. He had no hope of trying to run back down the slope to the street. He couldn't race them down the path, and he couldn't expect a chance dog walker to protect him from these men. He was going to go where they wouldn't dare to follow him. He ran directly towards the fence above The Cove.

Max stretched his leg straight out and hurdled the fence. With his mouth still taped he breathed lungfuls of salt air through his nose. His feet struck the rock on the other side and he bolted across the wide sandstone shelf towards the ocean. It was too black to see but he could feel the open air and the bowl of The Gap yawning around him.

Wind buffeted his ears. His eyes blurred with tears from the air rushing across them. He heard thudding behind him. He felt hard fingers just miss the collar of his shirt and scour his back – one of them had lunged, tried to crash tackle him, and missed – the same hand smacked his heel, almost bringing him down. Beneath the din of the wind and the surf Max heard a hard whump and a grunt as the man's body hit the sandstone behind him.

In the darkness twenty metres below, a flat shelf of rock washed by huge waves lay waiting for him like an iron frying pan that would shatter his body like an egg, pound his body against the cliffs, and then flush his remains out to the ocean as food for the fish. Max saw a sudden explosion of white foam in the blackness and heard the booming chaos of a wave boiling and skimming over the shelf as he focused on the right corner of the cliff.

Everything in front of him was black – just thousands of kilometres of ocean. The cloud had extinguished the moonlight. He only had a second or two to get his bearings before the men were on him. He looked over his right shoulder and saw the windows of Watson's Bay gleaming through wind-tossed bushes across the path, spitting faint gouts of light onto the stone outlines to his right. He thought he knew where he was – but he couldn't be sure. His heart in his mouth, Max scanned the perimeter of the cliff one more time, looking for a clue to where the next shelf might be, but there was only a shadow in the shadow.

He heard harsh, ragged breathing behind him. It was too late.

Hoping against hope the strange light didn't play tricks, Max jumped.

Chapter 64

'I never did like the Bennington, it's too green – who ever heard of a green donkey?' Trevor Levin said judiciously.

Ilona was feeling dispirited listening to Mort chatting with Levin about the four hundred thousand dollar Tim Bennington painting he and Alexandra had recently acquired for their living room wall. Levin was on the Board of the Reserve Bank, as well as about twenty other public company boards, in addition to his own family company. The Levin Foundation was one of the largest philanthropic organisations in the country.

'Yeah, well I was trying to cut costs,' Mort said. 'The Duchess wanted to buy a Sidney Nolan for that wall!'

Levin's eyes widened in surprise and then he and Mort shared a hearty laugh.

Levin smiled politely. 'Tim is a wonderful painter. I think he associates some spiritual qualities with various shades of green. I own several Arckuses myself. I may bid on this lot, as a matter of fact. It's certainly for a good cause.'

A few months ago, standing between Mortimer Norton and Trevor Levin, she would have been desperately trying to hold herself together, her teeth practically chattering.

Now Ilona focused on them as human beings, not on their reputations for power and wealth. She was no longer intimidated by the enormous sums they were talking about so casually. She understood the men were no different than five-year-olds in a sandbox showing each other their plastic shovels and buckets, each in the grip of mimetic attraction for what the other had. Mort himself seemed somewhat tame and almost conventional in this exalted social setting, which Ilona found quite appealing.

'Good luck,' said Mort.

'Thanks,' said Levin, moving off into the crowd.

'Another champers?' Mort asked, pointing at a passing tray.

'Yes, thank you,' Ilona said gratefully as she reached for the flute.

Mort seemed sated somehow, like a man who was exactly where he belonged. It surprised her that he exuded this confidence in a major social setting. Of course, he'd just won the ZettaData takeover, and his awesome Vaucluse property was the setting for a glittering event full of Sydney's elite. Ilona was surprised by how attractive Mortimer Norton could be.

'Mortie – what a shindig! Well done!' Mark Haddad appeared again from the crowd, and just had time to kiss Ilona's cheek and shake Mort's hand when they heard the announcement of the next lot being auctioned. 'Oops – it's Lot number 22, the rug.' Mark grinned. 'I'd better go find Nats and make sure we don't transfer too much charity from the family bank account to Nightingale School tonight!' He kissed Ilona on the cheek. 'Ciao, beautiful,' he breathed into her ear.

'See ya,' said Ilona, with a sparkling smile, aware that Mark Haddad's lips against her ear carried the faintest suggestion of a next step. It certainly wouldn't be marriage – his alliance to Natalie was set in concrete – and their dynasty was protected by a stronghold of numerous trusts stuffed with money and other assets. Even if she found Mark attractive, and she didn't, this was no time for her to be distracted by random dalliances. She needed to stay focused. Her next husband would be some man looking for his second, or third, wife. She'd better make sure she understood what he needed in order to feel important – and out-source it, if necessary.

Beyond the wall there was a low growling sound. Mort was startled and looked up. The low clouds hurrying past above them were lit from beneath by the lights of Vaucluse. He shrugged and looked at Ilona with a lopsided grin. 'Thought that was a helicopter.'

'Pretty sure it was a motorcycle,' said Ilona.

Mort looked at his watch.

Ilona glanced around: she hadn't seen Alexandra for forty-five minutes. She really should find her and ask her privately what was going on.

'Hello Mort, great party,' said Richard Wander, appearing with his wife Katrina, Poppy's real name, on his arm. Katrina's face lit up with a big smile to both Mort and Ilona, leading with her chin in a way that seemed simultaneously intimate, ingratiating, and totally insincere. Ilona felt her heart sink.

She allowed Richard to kiss her cheeks and then she and Katrina exchanged air kisses – Katrina leaned in and left her no choice – and Ilona stepped back, reeling from what felt like a horrid betrayal. She had just touched the flesh of a husband and wife who were joined together – and it was she who had introduced herself between them, and had now done so again – in an awfully immediate, tactile way.

'I'm guessing you'll break ten bars tonight,' said Wander coolly to Mort.

'You reckon?' Mort grunted. Ilona could tell he was trying to pretend he was indifferent to that staggering number. A ten million dollar haul for the Nightingale School Foundation would be well over three times the previous record amount raised.

'Isn't it all lovely?' Ilona asked Katrina nervously, scanning her expression for signs of what she might know. 'Alexandra has done such a marvellous job!'

'Oh, yes!' said Katrina, with the genuine warmth made possible by always taking people at face value.

'Yeah – I'm bidding on the Porsche Carrera that Peter Fitzgerald was driving when he beat Gricey,' said Wander. 'I'm buying it, whatever it takes – I reckon you'll bloody smash ten bars.'

'I'm a little concerned,' Ilona confided to Katrina, 'that Alexandra may have over-strained herself. She doesn't seem at all like her usual self.'

'Oh, really?' said Katrina. 'I spoke with her just a little while ago, and she seemed fine – you know, it's like being the bride at the wedding, you're at the centre of attention and so dazzled and distracted it just goes by in a blur.'

Ilona looked doubtful. Had she been dazzled on the day she married Max? But Katrina had a point, something about Alexandra's distraught state of mind did remind her of herself on her wedding day. But this evening was nothing like the portal to a bad marriage. What could be the matter with Alexandra?

'Haha,' Mort said. 'Nobody's ever beaten Phil Garlick in my book, and he was driving a super-charged Alvis. I don't know what it is with you guys and Porsches.'

'I'm just so proud of my girls,' said Katrina. 'They've been working so hard all year on their photography art project, and ...'

The Porsche reference was distasteful to Ilona; her own reaction surprised her. Then she recognised why: Mort and Richard were gloating. Now that these guys had eliminated Max from their lives and purged him from Sydney society, they were taking what they wanted from what was left. Mort had taken ZettaData. Wander had had Ilona herself – and now like Max, he wanted a Porsche, too. Right in front of Max's wife.

Ilona suddenly saw herself as just another luxury object in the eyes of these men, in a world where everything was available at a price.

'Sorry darling,' Ilona said, interrupting Katrina's chatter as gently as she could. She looked around. 'Has anyone seen the champagne lately?'

She'd come at a price only a few men in the world could possibly afford.

Chapter 65

Max lay flat on his back, momentarily stunned, looking at the black cliff above him against the deep grey skein of clouds just visible in weak moonlight. He had jumped from the right place onto a ledge about three metres down, but as he landed he slipped. The rock was impossibly hard and he let himself collapse like a rag doll to absorb the impact, cracking his head on the way down. Maybe it was the best outcome. He tried to feel grateful. He introduced his fingers cautiously into his hair at the back of his head, and his hair was wet. Perhaps it wasn't blood, everything was wet here from sea spray.

Max held his breath. The outline of the driver's head appeared above him, visible against the grey sky. He exhaled slowly, hoping he wasn't visible against the rock. The head disappeared.

He glanced down at himself. His skin and trousers, which hung on his legs in shreds, were dark, and so was his chest, but most of his white shirt was still tangled around his shoulders and arms, and it may have been as easy to see below as the clouds were above.

Moments before, he was tempted to just try to hide on the ledge, but now that plan was out. Perhaps he hadn't been seen, but he probably had been. The men might not jump – although perhaps they would – but they'd work their way around the cliff another way and come down to him. It wouldn't be easy, but they looked like guys up for the challenge. If they reached him on this ledge they could just smash his head against the rock until he was dead, or break his neck and push him into the waves.

He had to keep descending. He couldn't let them close in. They probably had knives or even guns. The fake suicide plan would fail if they had to use them, but murdering him was their main goal, and they would do what it took. Max reluctantly wedged his right foot into a fissure and groping for handholds on the wet rock in the total darkness, he made his way down through a set of shelves and ledges that descended almost like huge, primitive versions of the Spanish Steps to a point about five metres above the roaring waves.

He had two problems. The base of this part of the cliff jutted out into The Gap, meaning he could be seen from higher up. They might have torches, even tactical torches on their guns; he would, if he was a hired killer. His second problem was that his odds of survival in the heavy surf and huge rocks of The Gap was about the same as if the men spotlighted and shot him.

Max listened to the sinister hissing of the waves sliding across the rock bottom of the cauldron and the boom as they hit the base of the cliff just below. It was deafening from this distance.

Frozen with indecision, Max realised if he stayed on the cliff, time was against him. The men would work their way down, close in on him, and then kill him any way they could. If he wasn't immediately knocked unconscious and drowned, time was on his side: the tide was rising and flooding The Gap with more water, increasing the cushion above the rock. The waves were bigger and more powerful, but they had gentler shapes, and there would be more water depth to play with, a chance he could survive partly in the waves and partly under them.

He heard a scratching sound somewhere above him, and a handful of pebbles skittered down the cliff. The men were on their way down.

Another big set was coming in. He waited for another great wave to rush into the cauldron and boom against the cliff, hoping it had dissipated most of its energy, and then jumped.

The wave roared over his head, swirling him around and into the boulders at the base of the cliff. He didn't land too hard, but the water was as powerful as he had imagined – and he wasn't lucky with his timing. An inner surge still spiralling inside the wave like a steel spring caught Max and smashed him against the rocks like a hammer on an anvil.

Max was jammed against the boulders, sucked back out a few metres, picked up and then rammed against the cliff again, this time beneath the underside of shelves at the base of the cliff. He was held under water and against the rock for twenty or thirty seconds and it was terrifying.

He felt the current reverse, countless tendrils of water reaching out for his body. The withdrawing wave extracted him from underneath the shelf, and pounded him against the rocks as he tumbled away from where he had been wedged. He skidded for twenty or third metres, tossed helplessly in the tumult of water and stone, gasping for air – and then he was spun by more whitewater back towards the boulders heaped at the cliff's base. The sudden deluge of foam broke over him, heavy with water, and twisted his neck, his head snapping against the rocks. He blacked out for a millisecond, but the water was so cold he revived instantly.

Max's fingers clawed at slippery wet rocks. His left cheek, bruised and lacerated, pressed against a boulder and despite the pain, he tried to find grips for his knees and toes – anything to slow his slide back into the ocean, to help his numb fingers as he was sucked across the slimy curve towards the sea. He heard the roar of another wave and saw a huge dim wall of white foam in the darkness speeding towards him.

Years of surfing had taught him to stay soft and relaxed while tumbling head over heels in a wave pulling him in all directions. It wasn't that different from falling off a big wave and being tossed uncontrollably with his sharp, heavy surfboard spinning somewhere close to his body. Stay loose and soft to avoid being cut and pierced – or being knocked unconscious and drown.

Be soft, a drop in the water, a drop of water against rock – surrender to become invincible. If Max's body was hard like rock against the rocks, an edge against the edges, the hammer of the ocean would beat him against the anvil of the cliff and kill him. Yield so you can't be hit.

He had to calm down. Figure this out.

Here I am.

Max surrendered more completely, trying to breathe at every opportunity, not resisting, willing himself to be as pliable as the water. A huge wave flooded over him, tonnes of water lifting and smashing him against the boulders. He was almost washed up onto a rocky shelf at the base of the cliff, but as he slipped along, bouncing and scraping his agonised body against the rocks, Max realised he was too tired to climb out.

Max forced a powerful exhale and tried to let the air slip through his nostrils without water entering with it. He had to calm down. It wasn't that different than falling off a big wave and being tossed head over heels with his sharp, heavy surfboard in close proximity. He had to stay loose and soft. The rocks were bigger and just as hard, but they weren't as sharp as the nose of his board. He had to figure this out. Relax.

The cold water numbed the pain from the damage to his body. The water was helping him concentrate well enough to survive.

The roar of another wave. He could see the wall of white foam dimly mounting and rushing towards him. The only way to survive was to act like a drop of water, and hold his breath until the water released him.

Max was held under a long time, but he knew that ten seconds in extreme turbulence feels like a minute, and thirty seconds feels like five minutes. He had to remember his free dives with Peggy – as long as he didn't give in to the fear he would be able to hold his breath for well over two minutes.

He could see Peggy's face in the dark swirling wave. He remembered swimming behind and above her, her legs pumping and her green malachite bikini bottom tantalising him. Max almost laughed to himself – he was obviously still very much alive. He had quit when he was diving on the *Tassie*. He couldn't quit now.

When he was able to breathe again, he opened his eyes and looked up – and saw the silhouette of one of the men much closer than he expected, on a ledge about five metres above the water. The heavy clouds earlier that evening had thinned out to an overcast sky luminous with both moonlight and the reflected city light of Sydney. The man's outline was so clear against the clouds that Max recognised him as the one who had been in the back seat with him. He was pointing to something in the foam off to the left of where Max bobbed in the waves, watching him.

'Where?'

Max heard the harsh voice from somewhere above the man, but couldn't see him. The man looked up and pointed again, further in the wrong direction.

Max knew he himself was easy to see – his head and shoulders would be black against the white foam generated by the crashing of the waves against the cliffs. He had to get away. He dove under the water, and tried to breaststroke in the opposite direction. If only he could have hidden up against the base of the cliff, below and out of sight, but that would be subjecting himself to the full hammer and anvil treatment. It was like getting hit by a car under there – the breakers would kill him by pounding him to death against the boulders and the cliff. He would have to take his chances by staying out in the water as much as possible, away from the rocks, and below the surface as long as possible – hoping they didn't spot him when he came up for air.

Max could tell from the panicked way his tormentor had been calling up to his mate they were freaking out. They had botched their job and would have to face unknown consequences. Unless they risked their lives to jump into the water to try to drown him, how else could they finish the job? It wouldn't be easy to shoot him in the darkness.

The realisation that their options were almost as bad as his own gave Max hope. It was no longer simply captors and victim: the three of them were bound in a symmetry that was equally desperate for all of them. A thrill of grim glee coursed through his battered body.

Their sudden reversal of fortune, like the cat he pulled off the bird, amused him. He'd regained his desire and sense of humour: he had to figure some way out of the cauldron of The Gap.

He heard a low hissing and turned to see a monster wave send plumes of spray thirty metres into the air against both shoulders of The Gap and churn across the rocks towards him twice as high and heavy as a freight train that had jumped the railroad tracks and was skidding sideways, sweeping everything before it.

Chapter 66

M ort walked through the crowd, scanning for Alexandra. She seemed to have disappeared, impossible as it was to imagine. It was unlike her to miss even an instant of a party they were hosting – she was the consummate hostess and revelled in being at the very centre of everybody's attention.

Maybe his words to her late that afternoon still rang in her ears.

'Mort,' said a passing guest with a smile and a respectful nod. He didn't focus on the man's face. What he felt like was a cigarette, even though the Duchess hadn't seen him smoke in ten years – and this was no time to get her even more upset.

He stopped for a moment and somebody clapped him on the back. 'Great party, mate!' He turned to see Philip Allaway, normally somebody he loved to swap dirt with – Allaway knew some of the filthiest dirt in Sydney, and Mort was one of the few people he'd share his most putrid nuggets with. 'Cheers,' Mort said, raising his glass of champagne, and started walking again. He barely registered the startled expression on Allaway's gob.

The Duchess had surprised him – first, by understanding immediately the full significance of what he had said, and second by getting upset, seemingly almost distraught.

He should have anticipated how quick she was. Her father had been tangled up in some dark matters – not just the usual deaths from car accidents, drug overdoses, drunken falls from balconies in Monaco, vanished hookers. She loved her daddy, but she must have developed a sixth sense for how far over the line he and his mates were capable of straying. He was an idiot for slipping up. He knew her too well to be sloppy, but he was stunned by the way it upset her.

Mort started asking the catering staff where to find her. No matter how she was feeling, one thing he was absolutely certain about: The Duchess would go down with the ship – she might not be talking to the guests, but she'd be making damn sure the food and grog were flowing.

'She's just behind the tent, sir,' said the bar manager. Mort didn't like the apprehensive look on his face.

Alexandra was leaning against the heavy plastic wall of the white tent, clutching a glass that could be either water or straight vodka, her arms crossed, her head back and resting against the wall, her eyes closed.

Fuck.

'Honey,' he said quietly.

Alexandra started and opened her eyes wide.

He reached and tried to steady her, affectionately stroking her bare shoulder with his hand.

'Everyone's having a great time, precious – you've killed it! Pushed yourself too hard, hey?'

She surprised him by stepping into him, her arms still crossed, and pressed against his chest, almost like a little girl. He could smell her vodka.

'Mortie, darling, I'm hurting, but I'm ever so reluctant to tell you that. When you said what you did earlier this evening, you so reminded me of Daddy. I've had a lump in my throat all evening. I want to believe you – truly I do – but I have this sense of dread. I ... I don't think I can go through it all again. Truly I don't.'

'Oh, precious – you don't need to worry yourself,' Mort said, putting his arms around her and ceremoniously planting a kiss on her forehead.

She looked up at him, her eyes bleary with vodka, her pupils pinpoints from Xanax, but he could see the hope in them. 'Really, truly?'

'Of course, sweetie – everything is perfectly fine. Now enjoy your party. Everybody's asking for you.'

He led her out from around the side of the tent and back into the crowd. They walked up to a couple dozen people gathered around Martin and Bianca McConnochie, listening respectfully to Martin handicap his picks for the next election.

He kissed her and strolled away.

The Duchess would get over it. It would get a bit worse, of course, when Max's body was found. Still, she couldn't keep dragging around all her family baggage forever, for Christ's sake.

Mort looked around at the heaving crowd thronging his magnificent grounds. What's done is done.

Chapter 67

His only chance was to swim towards the wave and then dive as far down as he could, hoping it would pass over him.

Even the biggest waves only affect the water both on and below the surface for a metre or two – until they break.

He had to get as far away from the impact zone as possible.

The problem was that in some parts there was less than a metre of water, and in those shallow spots he'd get sucked right up into the wave and smashed against the cliff like an insect on a car's windscreen. The rising tide would help, but he had to hope that as he intersected with the wave, he was in a place that might have closer to two metres of depth – the absolute minimum he'd need for a wave this size.

He felt the adrenaline surge through his body and with the last of his strength Max swam desperately towards the huge wave, reaching it about thirty metres away, and as it towered above him, as black as the cliffs behind him, he dove, hoping for the best.

His dive ended abruptly and disappointing early. He was in, at most, less than two metres of water. His hands had slammed right against the rock floor. It was totally black underwater, but Max was sensitised from being in the water for the last hour, and realised he was in a spot that was broken up and full of cracks. He jammed his hands into the cracks, pulling his body down as flat as he could against the rock. His left forearm was halfway in a crack, his right foot had found another, and he flexed his foot, pushing his toes hard against the side of the crack as the wave surged above him and its currents started to suck on his body. Underwater rock climbing. Max clung to his holds desperately as the wave tried to peel him off the floor.

He just had to last ten or fifteen seconds before it passed over him. He felt the lift of the wave passing him—and as its terrible pull tightened on his body, every second felt like an eternity.

Then he detected the escalation cease, and a second later the pull of the wave slackened as it passed over him and towards the cliffs.

Max released his hold and popped his head into the air. He looked back to see the whole base of the cliff explode in what looked like millions of gigantic white peonies flying high into the air and being torn apart in a colossal, elemental *sparagmos*.

Seconds later a furious white tide of backwash caught him, burying him deep in its rip-tide, turning him over and over helplessly as it rushed him out to the ocean. He held his breath for so long his lungs felt like bags of needles, and even through the water sluicing past his ears and the roar of the surf, his pulse pounding in his ears was palpable. His hips, shoulders and head were slammed repeatedly against the shallow rocks as he rolled head over heels until he slammed his hip against the long rock edge of a submerged boulder just as the water spun him sideways. Max felt something pop and lost all feeling in his right leg.

He must have broken or dislocated his hip. His head popped back into the air, but now he knew the truth. The sea was going to win the contest. He was able to turn his head a couple of times and breathe, although all the froth and spray made it difficult.

You inhale a lungful of water—that's drowning.

Apparently a whole lungful of water isn't painful; it's a peaceful way to die. *You choke when your lungs are partially full, not when they're completely full.*

Max surrendered, allowing himself to be pulled out to the ocean without further fighting. He'd fought for as long as he could; there was no disgrace to being overpowered.

The current carried him into deeper water, and started to slow.

He was utterly rung out and exhausted, and now he knew he was going to die, Max felt peace. He had done his best. A whole lungful won't hurt. He could do it. Just relax and let it happen.

It was darker out here, wilder, lonely.

Here I am.

Max felt a change from underneath the water– a faint lift. It surprised him. The water flowing out of The Gap mingled with the waves sweeping in from the ocean. He was effortlessly buoyant and surrounded by foam like floating on soft champagne bubbles, the currents neutralising each other. Instead of dragging him and throwing him around, the water pressure was holding him up, with very little effort of his own.

Max was enveloped, embraced in a moving matrix of water and wind, the spray curling around his head, the currents of the sea seeming to nestle him as he bobbed in the centre of the boiling surf of The Gap, as if in the womb, the two forces of water cancelling each other out.

His lungs felt like they were bleeding or on fire. The next instant he felt his right hamstring and wondered if he could even float. It was getting cold, so cold.

Don't believe what you feel: it's not true.

Am I dying?

You are not dying.

In the eye of the storm of surf, he had been drawn unexpectedly into this one spot of peace. It was just like the pocket of a wave – a place where he fit perfectly.

The event is mind.

A roller washed over him without dragging him towards the cliff. Max wasn't sure, but thought he could see the men a couple of times silhouetted against different parts of the cliff. Max himself was just a tiny dark spot over a hundred metres out in the darkness and drifting further away. They'd never see him now.

The temperature of the water was no longer painful; in fact, it soothed his bruises. He was just rising and falling with the swell, not that different from sitting on a surfboard. The steady succession of inhales and exhales of briny air began to revive him, and the salt water caressed his body.

He stayed in the water as long as he could bear to, and in the gentler water found he could make his right leg slowly swirl around back and forth like a gondolier's oar, which meant that even with his hip dislocated, or whatever it was, he might be able to propel himself in one direction.

Max started to breaststroke cautiously towards the southern part of The Gap, where the cliffs are more broken up, kicking his right leg up and down in short, slow, painful strokes. Those sections hadn't been difficult to climb when he was a teenager, but he gave himself a fifty:fifty chance at best of making it up tonight in the condition he was in. Still, he might be able to climb up on the rock shelves, make his way up through the boulders and stones, and stay low enough through the bottlebrush and rosemary to get to the path. He'd have to crawl through the dagger bushes on his stomach and make his way up towards Signal Hill Reserve, just in case the men were still waiting and watching, which they probably were, but no matter what, he was on his way to shore.

Chapter 68

'Maxie's adorable,' said Juanita to Ilona. 'But so are you, darling – don't worry about having a bit of fun!'

Ilona smiled warily at Juanita. The heiress and chronicler of Sydney society through the pages of *The Waverley Gazette* was, she knew, a good friend of Mort's daughter Peggy. The fact she was here tonight proved she was not only socially indispensable but so socially adroit she had managed to stay on Mort and Alexandra's good side, despite her friendship with Peggy. That meant she could be on Ilona's good side, too. Very handy – as Ilona certainly wouldn't mind, now she was back on the market, being showcased in Juanita's social pages.

The crowd was beginning to filter out towards their cars. 'I think I'll chuff off home – I may have a look at the pictures my photographer took tonight,' Juanita said as she tucked her clutch under her arm. 'He showed me the most adorable one of the Wanders sitting together in the vintage Porsche!'

Ilona winced at the mention of Mrs. Richard Wander. 'These men love their Porsches, don't they ... '

'Don't worry, darling – I'll find one with you for the column – and if I see some good ones of you I can't print, I'll send them to your phone.'

'Thank you, darling,' said Ilona as they kissed goodbye. To be texted party out-takes by Juanita meant she'd arrived – post-Max – on an exalted new level of Sydney society.

Icy fingertips touched her shoulder from behind and Ilona almost jumped. She whirled to see Alexandra's face, anxious, drawn. 'Darling, are you all right?' exclaimed Ilona.

Alexandra's pupils were dilated. 'Is that gossip gone?'

'You mean Juanita?' asked Ilona. She'd never heard Alexandra speak cuttingly of Juanita. Was she out? Were Alexandra and Mort having some new problem with Peggy that involved Juanita? Was that what had been upsetting Alexandra this evening?

'Yes – she's been stalking me all night!' Alexandra said.

'Oh, she was just doing her job, darling,' Ilona said, eager to soothe Alexandra. 'You're the hostess, after all – and the Gala has been a gi-normous success!'

Alexandra looked around as if seeing her party for the first time, assessing its success only in its fading hour. The band was still playing quietly, and the clouds had lifted to reveal a starry night. Through the thinning crowd and the flourishing trees and shrubbery, Ilona and Alexandra could see the Trebuchets saying their farewells to Mort. The Levins were leaving with them.

'Don't go yet,' said Alexandra quietly, taking Ilona's arm. She clearly didn't intend to join Mort and help him farewell their most important guests.

'Well done, Morton. Cracker of an evening.' They heard Trebuchet's politician's baritone carrying across the distance. The old warhorse was slipping and getting Mortimer's name wrong.

Ilona followed as Alexandra skirted the clusters of remaining guests when possible and exchanged quick kisses when not. After a brief goodnight to the chairman of Sydney's premier auction house, who had donated his services for the evening and dropped the hammer on over twelve million dollars in bids, Alexandra looked at Ilona. 'Over four times the previous record,' she muttered with something like bitterness, as if the amount were only twelve thousand.

'Oh yes!' said Ilona. 'I had the loveliest conversations with Mort this evening, he kept listening in to the bidding and was just rapt over how well the auction was going!'

'Oh, *Mortie's* had the *most capital* evening,' said Alexandra.

'Darling, what is wrong with you?' said Ilona. 'The gala has been the biggest success ever! Your property looks gorgeous and everything was absolutely perfect – even the wind died down and the rain held off!' It was distressing to see Alexandra so agitated.

They stopped in a quiet place by a mature box hedge that Alexandra had ordered flown in from New Zealand and transplanted. Ilona faced Alexandra squarely and placed her hands on her friend's toned upper arms. 'Is there anything wrong?'

Alexandra looked at her with haunted eyes and took a deep breath. 'I want to believe everything is going to be ok. I want to believe Mortie. I ... I just have a premonition, a sensation, something terrible is about to happen.'

Chapter 69

'Billie! Sam! Billie!'

Max was still semi-conscious.

He heard a door creak and opened his eyes to see the acoustic tiles in the ceiling of his hospital room in St Vincent's. Max dimly remembered Juanita helping him limp into the emergency room leaving bloody footprints, naked except for the scarf Juanita had knotted around his hips.

When was that?

'I've already told you I didn't bring the girls, darling ...'

Max turned his head, groaning inadvertently in pain, as Ilona emerged from the bathroom in his private hospital room, still arranging strands of hair with one hand while patting her skirt into place with the other.

' ... because I didn't know when I got the phone call what had happened to you—attempted suicide, or – and I didn't want the girls traumatised.'

'Murder,' said Max, with great effort.

'I know, darling – that's what you said when I arrived,' Ilona said briskly, sitting on the worn vinyl armchair next to his bed and stroking – a bit roughly – strands of hair away from Max's forehead.

'Did ... they want ... to come?'

'No, darling,' cooed Ilona. 'They were too nervous.'

No way that was true of Sam: she would have been eager to see him in hospital – Sammie had even more balls than Alexandra Norton. It might be true of Billie ... no, it wouldn't be true of Billie, either, come to think of it.

Max's mind was clearing.

Ilona had no idea how well he knew his daughters: she was lying to him.

'They tried to kill me,' he said through thick lips. 'Two guys.'

Max closed his eyes again, distracted by vague fragmented memories of Juanita struggling to pull and push his bruised, cut, crippled and naked body into her car. She'd noticed him in the darkness lying in a gutter in Watson's Bay as she drove home from the Gala.

Max opened his eyes again.

'I'll ... be ... ok in time ... to take Sam and Billie,' he managed. 'Summer holidays.'

'Oh, Max, let's not –'

'I am taking them. I'll ... be ... fine.'

'Of course, darling. I'll prepare a menu plan for the girls for the entire six weeks – do stick to it.'

The tray beside his bed and the windowsill were laden with the bounty Ilona brought him: flowers from a Woollahra florist, a golden box of Italian chocolates, a stack of magazines, travel-sized containers of shaving cream, toothpaste, mouthwash, deodorant, shampoo, conditioner, and a razor and toothbrush. This was the first time Ilona had ever treated him with the thoughtfulness and attention to detail she habitually lavished on their daughters.

Ilona had also brought a bottle of champagne which was standing in an ice bucket next to her chair, and she'd had most of it. The untouched champagne in Max's glass was now almost flat.

Max turned away, moving his head slowly, painfully, and looked up again at the ceiling, staring at the tiles and their phalanxes of dots like high tech Aboriginal paintings. He wasn't on pain meds – he'd refused everything but local anaesthetic and paracetamol.

'Have you discovered anything up there?' asked Ilona.

'Not yet,' Max said.

Ilona tossed her hair and put on her sunglasses, lifting the frames until they rested just above her forehead in her hair. She gave Max a quick smile. 'Well, I must be going, darling,' she said.

'Ok,' said Max. The sooner the better. 'Thanks for all this.' He gestured painfully with one arm. 'It ... was ... sweet.'

'Of course, darling. Now, give me your hand.'

Max slowly presented his hand, palm up, on the blanket. His fingers were swollen, bruised, and rubbed raw, most of their nails torn and cracked, but the bones themselves had miraculously not been broken, except the finger deliberately snapped backwards by the man in the car. Max winced, but let Ilona take his hand in her own two hands. She looked directly into his eyes.

'Max, I believe you didn't try to kill yourself. I believe you didn't just slip on a walk in The Gap.' Ilona took a deep breath. 'I'm even prepared to believe there were two men who tried to kill you. Nobody saw them – at least nobody has come forward yet – but I'm willing to believe they were there, and they did this to you.'

'Ok,' said Max. She didn't believe him.

'So – why won't you have the hospital call the police?'

Max shook his head.

' – give them a statement and get the investigation started! Time is precious. Right now, dog walkers and joggers are wrecking any evidence that might still be there.'

'No point.'

'No point?'

'Mort. Mort did this,' Max gestured weakly to his wounded body with his free hand.

'Now, Max –'

'Who … ? Who else … would … want – me – killed?' he said the words slowly and painfully through his swollen, cut lips. 'Two men. Pros. Who else would –'

'I don't know, Max, I honestly don't. I don't know why you went to The Gap in the first place. I don't know why you would try to kill yourself. I don't know how you could slip and fall off the cliff. I don't know why two men would try to murder you, either. There's lots of things I don't know. All I know is, here you are lying in hospital, terribly injured.

'But the point is, if you believe Mort really did do this to you, say it on the record, and let the police do their work.'

Max shook his head and closed his eyes.

'Why, Max?'

Max opened his eyes. 'Nuh.'

'This is what I mean!' Ilona tossed her head in exasperation.

'No point,' Max said again.

Ilona's eyes filled with tears. 'Why Max? Because Mort controls everybody in the entire New South Wales Police Force – is that what you think?'

Max closed his eyes.

Ilona sat back down, leaned over, and kissed him on the forehead. 'Max, please, please, please – either call the police and give a statement – or stop the wild talk about Mort.'

'It's the truth.'

'Then give the police a statement, Max. Get an investigation started. That's why we have the police and the courts.'

'The truth won't make any difference.'

'You don't believe in our justice system?'

It amazed Max that Ilona could ask the question after the way ANG violated the Corps Act in the EGM and then the Tribunal found in favour of ANG and Palisades. She either hadn't understood what had happened – or didn't care.

'It's a legal system, not a justice system.'

'Max, you need rest. You've been through a terrible ordeal, but you need to know how crazy you sound this morning. Truly. I'm so glad I didn't bring the girls.'

'I'm not crazy.' He wasn't going to go through his reasoning all over again. Pointless.

'Max, I'm worried about you. I can just imagine what Sam and Billie would be thinking if they'd heard you raving about being murdered. You're exhausted and in pain. If you keep up this wild talk it'll be so embarrassing to the girls, as it is to me – and hurtful.'

'Know ... what ... hurts? This hurts,' Max said, gesturing to his bruised face and body.

If the two men had done their job properly, Mort's version of events would have been the only one. His own wife, sitting next to him in the hospital, so obviously wanted to believe – in advance – Mort's side of the story.

The motto of Cranbrook School is *Esse Quam Videre* – To Be, rather than to appear to Be. Whoever chose the motto didn't know Book Two of Plato's *Republic* very well – or he did know it, and had delusions Cranbrook would educate generations of moral heroes.

Plato described how the unjust man, who gaslights the public with appearances and only appears to be just, is treated with respect and chosen to be their leader. It is the unjust man who does business as he pleases, marries beautiful women, helps his friends and hurts his enemies, and – having gotten rich by being a corrupt predator – pays for magnificent sacrifices to the gods, and so is more loved by the gods themselves than the just man.

'Wild accusations are hurtful, too,' Ilona said reproachfully.

In contrast, Plato warned that it is the fate of the truly just man who actually practices goodness – not merely the appearance of goodness – to be scourged, tortured, bound, and at last crucified – and all because he should have preferred appearances to really being just. Max sighed. They hadn't crucified him yet: by the standards of Plato and his old school motto he'd gotten off lightly.

Euripides, an old man when Plato was born, was more practical. His advice in *The Bacchae* was 'to hold your hand victorious / over the heads of those you hate.'

Max picked at his bedclothes.

'Well, Max?'

Plato was right – there was no point in aspiring to be a just man. The world was full of appearances everybody treated as real – so they were real.

'Ilona?'

'Yes, Max?'

'I need more sleep. Give my love to Billie and Sammie.'

'Of course, Max!' Ilona leaned over and kissed his forehead, then stood up, picked up her Prada clutch, and tucked it under her arm.

Max closed his eyes and dozed, physically and emotionally spent, for how long he had no idea.

When he came to, the phone next to his bed was ringing. It was getting dark in his room, and he groped for the phone amidst the flowers and the chocolates until he reached the receiver.

'Hello, Mr Ring. This is Marilyn Wainwright from Mr Logan's office.'

'Yes, hello, Marilyn,' Max said.

'I hope you're recovering well. Mr Logan would like to see you as soon as you're discharged from hospital.'

Chapter 70

The ute careened down the steep slope of Hopetoun Avenue in Vaucluse, the suspension bucking like a brumby, Charlie at the wheel. Peggy tried to hold the mobile to her ear through the bumps and jolts. 'Go ahead, Mum – I already rang Dad, he knows I'm coming!'

'Did you tell him why?' asked Tori anxiously.

'Of course – because he tried to kill Max!' Tendrils of hair whirled around her, caught in the gusts from the open windows of the ute.

'But did you tell him – ?'

Her mother was afraid to suffer, and Peggy didn't blame her – her father had the sensitivity of an animal to the presence of fear in others.

'Not yet – but tell him what I'm bringing if you want to – I don't care!' Peggy lurched against Charlie as they descended, trying to catch her mum's words. 'Either way, he's going to find out really soon.'

'Oh, darling – you should at least prepare him!'

If her father was close to being a genius at anything, she knew it was his uncanny ability to discern the precise nature of the fear he instilled, and how to exploit it.

'We're almost there.' Peggy had felt she needed to ask her mother permission for what she was about to do, but now she was upset at how utterly cowed her mother was.

'There's no telling what he might do!' moaned Tori.

'Tell him, then!' Peggy felt her father's wild fury erupting inside her – a sensation her mother couldn't even comprehend – a primitive, savage exultation.

'Easy girl, you're so fierce,' murmured Charlie as he drove.

'Go –' said Tori, her breath audible through the phone. 'Handle him your way!'

'There!' Peggy said to Charlie, pointing with her arm. 'Take that left. Love you, Mum – don't be afraid!'

Charlie's two mates sat stoically behind them, their huge forms crammed into the narrow back seat, as Charlie downshifted to second gear and began to pick his way through the trucks lined up on either side of the street leading to the Norton mansion. The bump out was in full swing, with crews everywhere carrying dismantled audio gear, outdoor tent pylons, stage panels, tables, portable kitchens, and all the other temporary fixtures and equipment that had been required to stage the Nightingale Charity Gala. In the high sandstone wall surrounding the estate the gates were wide open, and crews streamed back and forth through them.

'Yeah, just drive right in,' said Peggy, nodding as the wheels of the ute crunched on the biscuity gravel in the driveway. 'There he is,' Peggy said.

Her father stood on the manicured lawn bordering the driveway, in suit trousers, a glowing white business shirt unbuttoned at the throat, and gleaming black shoes, squinting in the bright sunlight.

She knew he would be waiting for her outside. That was her style, too.

She opened the door and jumped out. 'Dad!'

He hadn't recognised her ute amongst the vast fleet of trucks, forklifts, cranes and utility vehicles, but when he saw Peggy his face closed like a fist and he turned and advanced to meet her.

'What did you do with Hugh, Margaret?'

Peggy stood directly in front of her father – deliberately within his reach. 'You tried to have Max killed!'

'Max who?'

'Max Ring!'

A mocking smile appeared on his face. 'What? What do you care about Max Ring?'

'He knows you're behind it, and I do, too!'

'Ring is just lucky he can swim,' Mort chuckled. 'It seems to be the only thing he can do right. He can't even top himself, by the look of it.'

'You've always been a murderer – you just fucked up this time.'

Charlie leaned in to Peggy. 'You're so fierce, girl, he's your father.'

'Goddamn you –' Mort took a step towards Peggy and reached for her arm. 'If Max Ring wants to jump from The Gap, what do you care?'

'Hey,' said Charlie, stepping forward. Charlie, George, and Bobby now flanked her protectively.

Peggy pushed her father's arm away.

'Jumped, my arse dad. You fucked up.'

'You're mad.'

'I'm not mad. – and unlike you, I didn't fuck up, did I? Do you know where Hugh's body is? I do.'

Mort's face darkened, and he breathed audibly. He forced himself to smile. 'If you think you're going to be protected by your Abo –'

'Don't say it!' Peggy said.

'Darling? Darling!' Alexandra was hurrying across the lawn. 'Oh Mort – Peggy, what's going on?'

She was wearing sunglasses and her usual beautiful clothes – a silk blouse, a pair of wheat linen trousers, and Gucci sandals. Mort put an arm around Alexandra's shoulders and looked coolly at Peggy. Alexandra looked up at Mort and then at Peggy, back and forth.

'You and your mother are so full of hate,' said Mort.

Peggy laughed bitterly.

'Look at her –' her father glanced for support at Alexandra, who crossed her arms, and then glared at Peggy. 'You're so full of hate.'

Peggy ignored him and addressed Alexandra. 'I'm so sorry you have to go through this, you're not related to us – my mum couldn't take it, either – not the special kind of hell we Nortons create around ourselves.'

Alexandra smiled weakly, putting her arm around Mort's waist. 'I'm … perfectly fine, darling. Your father is wonderful. What is this all about?'

Mort sneered and looked down at Alexandra. 'Margaret is here to tell me where Hugh's body can be found – but for some reason she's making crazy claims about Max.'

Alexandra started as if he had slapped her, and stepped away from him. 'Peggy, darling, what on earth is going on?'

Peggy looked at Mort. 'Wasn't Hugh's death awful enough, Dad? How could you try to kill Max – and who else has to die?'

'I don't know what you're talking about,' Mort said. In the blinding morning sunlight, his face was dark with blood. 'What have you done with Hugh?'

Alexandra pushed her sunglasses to the top of her head, and Peggy could see her eyes were wild.

Behind them car doors slammed with unusually harsh, urgent concussions. Peggy turned around to the sight of Bobby Allenhurst and two large men striding resolutely towards them across the lawn.

'Hey boss!'

Charlie and his mates faced the three approaching men but refused to move as Peggy turned back to see her father watching his men close in, a mixture of triumph and contempt on his face. Bobby stopped with the other two men on either side and drew back his suit coat to reveal a holstered gun.

'Want them cleared out, boss?'

'No!' cried Alexandra. 'Mort – don't let them do anything!'

Mort glanced around at the workers streaming in all directions. Bobby's gesture had been subtle but the moving teams returning from their vehicles were beginning to look curiously as they passed the group.

Peggy followed her father's gaze.

'You think you're so clever with your network of mates and stand-over men and bought judges,' she said. 'But I rang Uncle Kent on my way here, and before I could say anything he knew about it already –'

Peggy saw Bobby Allenhurst and the other two men shifting uneasily. 'Everybody is going to know, Dad.'

Alexandra took a step back, her face ashen.

'How long do you think it will be before the Trebuchets find out? Right now, it's still a few insiders, but what happens when more and more people know? What about your friends Mark Haddad and Trevor Levin?'

'Honey ... ' Alexandra said, faltering, a numb expression on her face. She took a step, reached out for Peggy's arm, and let her fingertips rest lightly on it.

Peggy pointed at Alexandra. 'I'll bet Alexandra knows, doesn't she?' she demanded.

'Darling ... you're talking nonsense,' said Alexandra faintly, as if pleading.

'How could you drag your wife into this, Dad? Did you think she would be able to live with herself if you killed Max? All your schemes and secrets are one thing, but murder?'

Peggy looked into Alexandra's stricken eyes and turned back to her father. 'Did you expect Alexandra to live with a secret like that for the rest of her life? Didn't you remember Alexandra sees the Ring girls every day? How could she face Billie and Samantha knowing you murdered their father? Do you think a normal person can live like that?'

'You're lying, Margaret – and I'd like to know how you know Max Ring. He's my former partner for a reason, and I don't want him anywhere near you.'

'Who do you think you're kidding, Dad?'

'Don't, don't ... ' Alexandra said faintly, covering her eyes with a hand. 'Please.'

'I want to see Hugh.'

'I don't care what you want,' Peggy said. 'Not anymore.'

'He's my son,' Mort said stonily.

'You're not going to bury him in that tomb.'

'I want him buried with me.'

'The dead are all equal, no matter how big you build our family tomb.'

'You'd better let me see him,' Mort said. 'This is your last chance.'

'Not unless you agree to what I want from you.'

Mort laughed shortly. 'Which is what?'

'Leave us alone – Mum, Max and me. Pay back Mum for her legal expenses. And we scatter Hugh's ashes on the waves.'

'No.'

Peggy shrugged. 'Ok – that makes it easy.'

'What?'

'We're going to get back in the ute right now, and we're driving home to Byron. But first, I'm going to stop by Uncle Kent's and tell him Max's side of what happened. Then I'm going to visit the Trebuchets in Woollahra – and I'll also see as many of our friends as possible. And while we're driving back to Byron, I'm going to call the media and the bloggers. You can't enforce libel laws in America, and I'll make sure the American bloggers know everything. Americans may not care about Aussies – but they love real crime stories and hearing about vicious bastards like you, Dad – and the Brits will pick it up, too. Good luck next time you're in Aspen or Knightsbridge. Do you think normal people could bear to shake the hand of a murderer? You may still stay out of jail – maybe – but you'll never see the inside of a boardroom again, Dad, not from Nightingale to ZettaData.'

Mort glared at her.

'Oh Dad, we're on the same side,' Peggy pleaded, desperate to break through to him. 'I don't want our family feared and loathed. Think of Alexandra and Trixie and Anastasia, if you don't care about Mum and me anymore.'

'You just threatened to smear us,' Mort glared.

'Oh – my *god* Mort. I can't bear this! Do something, honey!' cried Alexandra, clutching Mort's arm.

Peggy saw the wild look in her father's eyes. There was no hope of persuading him.

'Oh, just give it a rest, Alexandra! I'll take care of this,' Mort growled.

'Okay,' Peggy shrugged. 'Do what you want.' She looked uneasily at Alexandra, noticing she seemed distracted, jittery, and extremely restless.

'Agree to what Peggy wants! Anything! Are you mad?' Alexandra seemed to falter but she steadied herself and stared at Mort. 'You *have* to make this go away! Oh god, my god! ... Please ...'

Mort glared at her and grabbing her arm, he wrenched it. 'What's the matter with you? Relax! Margaret is acting as if there won't be any consequences for what she's threatening to do.' He glared at Peggy, a strange blank look in his eyes. 'First, she's going to tell me where Hugh's body is, and then she's not going to say a peep about any of this other horseshit.'

Mort nodded to Bobby. 'Take her, Bobby. Lock her up in the cottage. Get rid of these other arseholes.'

'Mort – are you mad? In front of all these people?' cried Alexandra.

Allenhurst stepped forward and reached for Peggy.

'No!' she cried, and stepped back.

The crews had been passing on all sides, once in a while looking curiously as the conversation got louder, but Peggy's voice and the sudden tension in the group was observed on all sides by passing workmen.

Charlie, George and their mate, also named Bobby, stepped forward. 'She's coming with us.'

Allenhurst turned to them and pulled his gun out of the holster. One of the other men did the same, and a wicked-looking cosh appeared in the hand of the third man. 'Get out,' Allenhurst said to Charlie.

Peggy gave Alexandra a piercing look. Was it possible she would really cooperate with Peggy's kidnapping, and whatever form of coercion, beating or torture her own father had in mind for her?

Alexandra seemed to come out of a trance. She twisted and grabbed Mort by both shoulders. 'No! No Mort – darling, don't do this!'

Mort's face twisting with rage, he swept his forearms under her arms, knocked them away, and planting his hands on her chest he shoved her so brutally Alexandra staggered back several steps and almost fell. 'Get the fuck away!'

Breathing heavily, he turned back to the group. 'Get the fuck off my property, before my boys put a pill in your arses to hurry you up.'

Charlie and his mates turned without a word and walked back to Peggy's ute. Charlie got in the driver's seat and slammed the door. Bobby got in the passenger's side and George climbed up and jumped on top of the tarpaulin on the ute's tray.

'Just as I thought!' called Allenhurst. 'You Abos are a bunch of cowards!'

'No, mate,' Charlie said, putting the ute into gear. 'We're going to collect the lot of ya'.

His head disappeared into the cab and the ute leaped in reverse towards the group. Allenhurst and his mate fired, hitting the rear window and the back of the tray as it careened in reverse towards them. Mort and Alexandra stood frozen for a second as the professionals scattered, diving out of the way. The ute screeched and started to swing to a stop. George jumped off the tarpaulin and landed on the other man with the gun. There was a muffled explosion.

Peggy suddenly reached for Allenhurst's gun arm and, clutching it like death, fell to her knees, pulling with all her strength and weight so he couldn't raise his gun.

'Don't shoot, Bobby!' Mort barked.

Allenhurst dragged Peggy on her knees through the grass as he struggled to free himself, but it was too late. He managed to throw her on her side, still holding on to his hand, disappearing as Charlie engulfed him. Peggy heard what sounded like Allenhurst's arm breaking as the two men hit the ground. Shakily, she stood up, just in time to see Alexandra hurrying back towards the house, something hectic and yet wilted about her movements. The crews had stopped and were staring. Half-a-dozen men were murmuring into their mobiles.

'What you are guys staring at?' Mort shouted. 'Get back to work – or fuck off!'

'Give us some straps?' Charlie asked a member of the packing crew, who gave him a handful. In a couple of minutes, Allenhurst and his two mates were lying on the grass, bound hand and foot in the straps. Allenhurst and one of the men were writhing, panting and groaning.

'He's bleeding,' said Peggy, pointing at the other man.

'He shot himself in the arm,' said George, who was holding the two guns. 'I patched him. He's lucky it wasn't worse. That one's arm is broke, too.'

Mort turned to Peggy, Charlie, George and their friend Bobby.

'Ok, Margaret, you win.'

'That's not good enough,' Peggy said.

Her father gestured at his men on the ground, at Peggy's friends. 'This is done. It doesn't change anything. I want to see Hugh. I'm not going to quit until I see him.'

'I knew you'd say that. But it'll be on my terms, not yours,' said Peggy. 'What are you willing to do to make it happen?'

'You can have your fucking funeral. You can scatter his ashes. I won't try to bury him in the tomb. I just want to see him.'

She studied his face warily. 'What about calling off your thugs?'

'Look at the useless fuckers,' said Mort.

'What about anybody else?'

'Yeah, yeah – done. You and Tori and Max are fine. And I'll pay her back.'

'You're not going to try anything?'

'I always keep a deal.'

'You and I can have a deal, Dad – but what Max does next is up to him. If he pursues you in the courts or the media, and I'm put on the witness stand or interviewed, I'll tell the truth. You have to understand that.'

Her father nodded. 'Ok. I'll handle Max Ring and his lawyers.'

'No violence. You mean it, Dad? It's really over?'

'Don't do it, Peggo,' said Charlie.

'I want to see my son,' Mort said heavily.

'Do we have a deal?' Peggy asked.

Mort nodded. 'We have a deal.'

'Where's your wife?' Peggy asked. 'I want her as a witness to our deal.'

Her father's forehead knitted into the familiar network of wrinkles – his old combative self. 'She'll be ok once she gets over the fucking vapours.'

'Ok, whatever,' Peggy said. She took out her mobile and thumbed to the camera.

Mort stepped closer, as if expecting her to show him something.

'I'm not going to show you a picture of where Hugh is,' said Peggy dismissively. 'I'm going to video you and me making our deal.' She gave the phone to Charlie.

'Now, Dad, stand here with me and repeat what you've just agreed,' Peggy commanded as Charlie raised the phone and filmed. When Mort was finished, she said, 'And in return I show you Hugh's body.'

'That's right,' said Mort.

'Ok, we have a contract,' Peggy said. She offered her hand to her father, who took it, and they shook hands. Peggy turned to Charlie, took back her phone, and watched the video to make sure he'd recorded the whole scene.

'Ok, Dad, you can see Hugh.' She nodded to Charlie.

Charlie raised his eyebrows and frowned. Again Peggy nodded.

Charlie turned and walked to the ute. He, George and Bobby opened the gate of the tray, jumped up and and removed the tarpaulin. A flood of water and ice cascaded down, pushing away the gravel in a widening circle and soaking Mort's men where they lay on the grass. An enormous heap of ice on the tray of the ute glittered in the sun.

Charlie and George reached into it and pulled the earth-stained coffin of Hugh Norton out of the ice, and eased it off the back of the ute with Bobby, standing on the ground, holding its end.

'Bring it here,' Peggy said.

Mort looked down silently at the wet coffin gleaming on the gravel in front of him. At last he said, 'Unscrew the lid.'

'Dad, you should brace yourself. He is in terrible shape.'

Mort was gazing at the coffin. 'If you think I'm afraid of the body of my own child, you don't know me very well.' He lifted his eyes to Charlie. 'Do it.'

Charlie took out a power screwdriver. Peggy stepped back as he rapidly removed the screws from the coffin lid.

There were sirens in the distance. Mort and Peggy exchanged glances. 'Max didn't get the chance last night, but there are plenty of people here who could have dialled triple zero.'

'It'll be fucking fine,' said Mort, putting his hand out to Charlie for the power screwdriver. He sank to his knees, breathing audibly through his mouth, and used its tip to pry off the lid.

Peggy gulped, stepped back another metre, and watched as her father kneeled before the coffin, gazing at what remained of Hugh.

He was still on his knees when a sudden, harsh report cracked through the air from the direction of the house. It was a gun shot.

Chapter 71

Logan had his face in his hands, elbows resting on his vast desk.

Mort had never seen him like that in his life.

' ... I had to make fuckin' calls – and in two cases follow-up calls, all over the New South Wales police, and then I had to ring the coroner's office directly, and I don't even want to tell you what a pain in the arse she decided to be. Plus there was one good quality iphone video, not Peggy's but one of the removalists who were standing there when you unleashed your boufheads on your own daughter – and I must have spent two hours talking to the networks and papers. Fuck – you know how to make a fuckin' mess. I've never seen anything this big.'

Logan looked bleakly at him.

It had been a very unpleasant half an hour with Logan already. Mort couldn't muster another word to say.

'I am sorry about Alexandra, mate,' said Logan, reaching for one of his cherry cigarillos. 'More than I can say. She was one of the best.' He lit up and squinted through the smoke at Mort. 'Well, that's that. Now, did I ever tell you about my cat, Periscope?'

'No, Kent,' Mort said reluctantly. He and Logan were no different in many respects – they both believed in always moving on as soon as possible. But it wasn't Logan's wife.

'Well, I used to like Periscope – about as much as you can like a cat – but he came down with this very unusual problem.'

Logan's eyebrows were drawn together in a deep double sine curve, his face red, and cigarillo smoke trickled up along the side of his nose.

'Periscope would stop pissing, and when he stopped pissing, he would fill up with his own piss until he was about twice his normal size. Understand?'

Norton nodded. He was struggling to follow the gist. He'd been in a daze since yesterday.

'Filled with his own bloody piss,' Logan visibly trembled with the effort to control himself. He stood up and loomed above his desk as if ready to spring across at Mort. 'Got it?'

'Bloody oath,' muttered Mort. He'd never actually experienced feeling like this before. Perhaps it was what grief felt like. If he'd ever known, he'd buried the feeling so deep it was completely novel to him now – and he wasn't actually certain what to call it.

'I had him taken in, and it turned out that he had a blockage in his dick – at the end of his dick – and the solution was to snip the end off. And so they did. And when they snipped the end of his dick off, all the piss came flooding out and he was ok.'

Logan threw the pen down on his desk and sat back in his chair.

'About two years later, it happened again. So I had them cut more of his dick off. And then, it happened again.' Logan took a long pull on his cigarillo, staring sightlessly at the blinds drawn across the windows of his office. 'So I had that fucking cat put down.'

Mort sat watchfully, saying nothing.

'Nobody likes a big, fat, sleek cat that keeps bloating up like a balloon with his own piss. People prefer a dead cat. Got it?'

Mort nodded.

'This is the last time, Mort, I'm going to fix your dick.'

Chapter 72

Marilyn Wainwright wasn't her usual inscrutable self as Max stepped off the lift and limped through Kent Logan's reception area one deliberate step at a time, slowly approaching her desk.

'Good morning, Max,' she said looking at him through her glasses with marked sympathy.

'G'day, Marilyn.'

He must look worse than he thought.

Her sharp eyes registered his loose linen shirt, drawstring linen trousers, and the sandals which revealed his bruised feet. 'My, you look like a guru without the beads and turban.'

'It's all about minimising skin contact,' he said. At least he could speak clearly again. 'Not even wearing grundies!' Max smiled, glad he could do that, too.

'TMI,' she said disapprovingly, with a rare, but sour, smile.

Max walked through the door to Logan's vast, magisterial inner sanctum.

Logan sat behind his desk, smoking a cigarillo. 'You're not looking your best, junior.'

Logan stood up and reached out to shake Max's hand.

'Have a seat, son,' said Logan.

Max sat down.

Logan leaned against the front of his desk, close to Max. 'Things got completely out of hand, Max. I probably should'na stayed so hands' off. But that's water under the bridge. What I was thinking, Max, is that we restructure the ZettaData acquisition and transfer control to you.' A blue jet of smoke launched towards the ceiling.

He looked at Max, his eyes kind. 'We'll have to pay an army of lawyers and accountants to get it done, and bring a couple brokerage houses into it, but we'll look after expenses –' Logan put a strong, gnarled finger on his own chest.

Max thought back to the sleek professionals sitting in the rows around Mort at the ZettaData AGM. As usual they were going to prosper in good times and bad times.

'There are issues with stamp duty, but I'll just get the Premier on the blower –'

Penance by rich guys. For Logan, it was the equivalent of flipping five cents to a homeless guy.

'And, in return, I forget all about this?' Max held up his left hand, his little finger in an aluminium splint. Slowly he stood up, Logan scrutinising every move he made.

Max began to fumble with the buttons of his shirt, slowly revealing the hectic pattern of bruises and bandages underneath, as well as the myriad healing scabs that covered his upper body. Logan grimaced as he looked at Max.

Max dropped the shirt on the seat and raised his arms to give them the fullest view. Unwillingly, Logan studied with reluctant fascination the mass of welts, lacerations and bruises that covered his upper body in a camouflage pattern of purple, green and yellow.

'More of the same below,' said Max. 'Not a chance I'm forgetting about any of this. I want Mortimer Norton in prison.'

'Ok, son,' Logan said at last. 'I get it.' He pushed himself away from the edge of his desk and stood fully upright, like a king reluctantly about to bring a council of war to a close. He passed Max, walked back around his huge desk, and slumped into his desk chair, reached out and lit a cigarillo, and began smoking, not looking at Max.

Max slipped back into his shirt.

'I can't say I'm surprised,' Logan said.

Max looked up and nodded.

'You realise, of course, your precious ZettaData shareholders are fucked,' said Logan.

'Oh, I thought Mort's deal was "fair and reasonable",' Max said bitterly. 'That's what the Takeover Panel ruled – and that's what the analysts and journalists in this town seem to think – or pretend they do. Besides, the deal's locked in. Stamp duty would kill any restructuring.'

'Well, that's true,' said Logan. 'But none of it matters, really – if you want the company. The only thing you can't change is the higher price Mortie agreed to pay Todd Edgell. That's only an extra bar and a half—three fifths of fuck all in the scheme of things. Everything else can be worked through. And if you don't do it, all those people you said you cared so much about will lose tens of millions of dollars they can't afford to.'

'Well, tell Mort to do something about it,' Max said. 'It's his company now.'

He knew Logan was right about the total annihilation of Casners and the rest of the small shareholders, but it wasn't his fault. He'd already done everything he could do, and almost gotten himself killed in the process. What more could anybody expect from him?

'I understand you've gone sour on the deal,' Logan said slowly. 'In that case, there's a place in the Tunnel deal for you. Martie McConnochie would love to include you. You can just take your allocation and go surfing for the rest of your life.'

Max sat back in his chair. 'Thanks – but no thanks, Kent. I don't want any part of that dirty deal, and I can go surfing while I'm petitioning to organise a Royal Commission,' he said. 'As far as I'm concerned, the deals can wait until Mortimer Norton is behind bars.'

But as Max said it, he realised he didn't mean it. As he said the words, he realised his hate for Mort was gone. He'd said it without realising he no longer wanted Mort to control his life in any way, including becoming part of his future through an investigation that might take years.

'Max, you couldn't even win your appeal before the Takeover Panel,' Logan said gently. 'What makes you think you'll succeed in calling a Royal Commission? You've been through a lot – it's shitty and it shouldn't have happened – but why waste another couple years of your life?'

Logan was right again, but Max was still angry.

'Maybe the answer will come to me sometime during the proceedings. I might even win this time, you never know. You don't own everybody, Kent.'

'Witty,' Logan pulled on his cigarillo. 'Very nice. But you've got your head up your arse. Do you want to help all those little shareholders like you once told me you did, or do you just plan to go tilt at another windmill?'

Max cleared his throat. 'Well, you know the terms I'll need on ZettaData.'

'Yeah,' said Logan. 'Except we can't change the price to Edgell.'

Max nodded. 'I know. And the only way to get this done in time is to get an emergency private tax ruling from the State Government.'

'Crouch'll be ok,' said Logan. He reflected for a moment, then he pushed the intercom. 'Marilyn, ring the Premier and tell him I want to come see him.'

'But there's one other deal that needs to get folded into this.'

'I'm glad you've reconsidered the Tunnel, son,' said Logan. 'That's sensible. I reckon after going through all this shit you're entitled to more dosh than you're ever going to squeeze out of ZettaData.'

'I'm talking about the deal Mort did with Peggy,' said Max. 'I've seen the video, but I want those terms documented by your lawyers, Kent. And I want you to sign as guarantor of Mort's performance.'

'I don't give guarantees,' said Logan.

'Then there's no deal,' said Max.

Logan took a reflective inhale on his cigarillo and looked at Mort. 'I think I can guarantee the deal this time,' he said.

'Ok,' said Max.

The buzzer sounded. 'The Premier can see you immediately,' said Marilyn Wainwright's voice. 'But he only has twenty minutes.'

'Thanks Marilyn,' said Logan. 'Right – let's go!'

Geoffrey 'Jeffers' Crouch was widely popular in the state for having parleyed humble origins as a fisherman's son from Mollymook into an emblematic career in politics. Max had never met him.

They quickly left the immediate environs of the Logan Holdings HQ with its massage parlours, illegal gambling dens, and third-rate coffee shops, and headed up the hill towards the Premier's office, just over five minutes away. That gave them fifteen minutes to close the deal.

The Premier's official functions take place in the State Parliament House, but the administrative heart of the State Government, including the Premier's office, looms above parliament from across Macquarie Street, and many floors above, in what is arguably the most prestigious business address in Sydney, part of the same complex in which the offices of Norton & Ring were located.

Crouch greeted Logan heartily and Logan introduced Max. There was no flash of recognition in Crouch's expression when he heard Max's name. If he'd been following the ZettaData saga or had been party to any of the dirty deals, the Premier gave no sign.

The men sat down and Crouch looked expectantly at Logan. He was surrounded by framed photographs of himself with luminaries from decades of Australian public life. A simple fisherman hadn't enjoyed a career like Geoffrey Crouch's since Jesus chose several of them to be disciples.

Logan gestured in the direction of Max. 'This gentleman and I have come up with a solution to ending the chronic problem over at ZettaData. You know it's been a fucking mess, and turned into a series of pissing matches, first between Mort Norton and Luke Terry and then between Norton, his American partner and this man here, Max Ring.'

Crouch looked worried. Anything involving Kent Logan, Mortimer Norton, and Luke Terry was a situation he wanted as little to do with as possible. 'This is the takeover that was appealed ... ?'

'Yeah,' Logan nodded, cutting off further discussion.

Crouch nodded uneasily at Max. 'Luke voted ANG's shares against it on a deed poll vote, right?'

'That's right, Jeffers,' said Logan.

Max watched Crouch look increasingly nervous. ANG was owned by the Australian Federal Government, but Luke Terry and most of his union faction were based in New South Wales and were major players in the state's politics. Crouch needed their support. It was clear he was desperately hoping Logan wasn't going to ask him to intervene in a factional quarrel within the union movement.

'I just got all the parties together and we've agreed an amicable outcome,' said Logan. 'It involves restructuring the existing bits and pieces of the deal and unwinding some of what's been done so far. There's only one problem.'

Crouch swallowed and nodded. The fingers of his right hand drummed apparently unconsciously on the desk blotter.

'Stamp duty,' intoned Logan. 'We can re-sort the puzzle pieces in a way that makes everybody happy, but it requires us to sell back some assets and generally move things around in a way that generates a lot of stamp duty. So we're here to ask you to get your people to give us a private ruling that eliminates all that extra tax and allows the ZettaData deal to go ahead as we've all just agreed to do.'

The relief on Crouch's face was obvious. 'Is that it? Of course, Kent! I'll brief the minister this afternoon and get him to task his bureaucrats and boffins with figuring out a solution – no worries.'

ZettaData was a go – in fifteen minutes.

Logan nodded and lit one of his cherry cigarillos, clearly settling in for a bit longer to chew the fat with Crouch.

'Is there anything else?' Crouch asked.

Logan looked at the Premier in surprise. 'No, not really. That was it.'

'Ok, well, that's fine,' Crouch said. 'I'm so glad I could help. I'm always here for you Kent, no problems – you know that ...' He hesitated. 'Kent, I'm afraid I have to sincerely apologise, but the Dalai Lama is in town. I'm meant to be across the street at Parliament House right now to welcome him to Sydney. I hope you don't mind – would it be ok if I excused myself?'

Logan's face was expressionless as he drew on his cigarillo.

'Kent, I'm sorry ...' Crouch stammered. He jumped from his seat and indicated his window. 'Look outside – you can see.'

Logan and Max stood up and walked to the window to see where the Premier was pointing. A red carpet had been rolled down the steps of Parliament House to the Macquarie Street gate. On the footpath a crowd of people and journalists stood waiting for the Dalai Lama to arrive and be greeted by the Premier.

'According to the rules of State protocol, His Holiness the Dalai Lama can't get out of the limousine until I'm there to greet him,' said Crouch. 'He has to keep driving around the block until I arrive to welcome him. He's already gone around twice.'

Logan walked back and sat down again. 'That's got nothing to do with me,' he said, putting his feet up on the coffee table.

Logan seemed to forget about the Premier welcoming the Dalai Lama. As the minutes went by, Logan smoked another cigarillo, told dirty jokes, and talked about the cricket. Crouch got redder and redder, squirming in his chair and gripping his knees, a fixed grin on his face. He darted glances back and forth at Max, the witness of his degradation.

Max watched the Premier squirm, thinking that Logan and Mortimer Norton both did it because they enjoyed it, it enforced discipline and kept the world working the way they wanted it to work. Only Max didn't see it that way, not any longer.

Logan started to take another cigarillo out of his battered gun-metal case, and it was clear he had settled in for at least half an hour in order to dismantle whatever might be left of Crouch's self-respect. Logan was showing both Max and Crouch he was one of the princes of this Earth, more important than the Dalai Lama. Max remembered that on one occasion, Stalin was informed the Pope disapproved of something he had done. Stalin replied, 'The Pope! And how many divisions does he have?'

Max had had enough.

'Jesus Christ, Kent!' said Max, interrupting Logan in the middle of one his jokes.

'Eh?' said Logan, cocking a surprised eye at Max.

'For Christ's sake, Kent – let Geoffrey go welcome the Dalai Lama!'

Logan looked coolly at Max. 'Says who, son?'

'Let the Dalai Lama get out of his limo, Kent,' said Max.

Logan gave Max his old dinosaur look for what seemed like a minute. At last, glancing away from Max to the Premier, Logan drawled, 'Well, I guess that's it,' and stood up.

Every line of Crouch's body expressed relief and humble gratitude as he said goodbye to his visitors. 'Cheers, mate,' he said, shaking Max's hand with extra vigour, unaware of the agony he was inflicting on Max, who strained every nerve to suppress any visible expression of his anguish. Logan turned on his heel and when he was a couple metres away, Crouch pulled Max close and murmured, 'Thank you so much, mate.'

Logan and Max went down the lift and Logan stared ahead wordlessly as the lift hurtled downward.

'You've got ZettaData now,' Logan said as they walked across the sumptuous foyer. 'Don't fuck it up.'

They stopped. Logan looked directly at him, and Max thought he saw something in that lined crust of a face he had never have expected to see, an obscure gleam hidden in the depths behind Logan's eyelids.

At his age, with his many health problems, Logan might die any day. Perhaps Logan envied Max the many decades he was still likely to live. Maybe it wasn't envy at all – the old man seemed to be sizing Max up clinically, marking him as just somebody else who would be around for a time and then, too, fall over, become still and cold, and disappear.

'See yez around,' Logan said, shoved one hand into the pocket of his suit, and turned on his heel. Max could hear Logan whistling to himself as he disappeared into the passing crowd on the sidewalk. Perhaps Max imagined it, but Logan seemed to be saying, 'This is all there is, son.' He suddenly thought of the word to describe the watery gleam he had seen in Logan's eyes.

Grief.

Chapter 73

'... our business is built upon very large numbers, because when the numbers of anything – atoms, grains of sand, stars, people – are big enough, they behave in predictable ways,' said Donald Ormsby. 'Large numbers connect the random chaos we experience as individuals with the order shaped by the laws of nature we see all around us ...'

Max smiled to himself. He'd invited the Casners on a special tour of ZettaData's main data processing facility with Ormsby.

It had taken just over a week – record time – but the ZettaData transaction had been sorted out and all its related branches agreed. Max bought the Palisades position in ZettaData and left common shareholders in the original position he had wanted to offer them. They were stuck with the high price paid to Edgell for his stake, but after he and Logan had received the special stamp duty ruling, Max knew he would be able to make the deal work.

Max, Ormsby, Hal and Sue Casner, and the technical crew wore white lab coats, anti-static booties over their shoes, and white hair nets as they moved through the operating heart of ZettaData with its eternal fluorescent light, cool temperature, and constant low humidity.

'If you don't mind me interrupting, Donald,' said Max.

'Go ahead, pardner,' said Ormsby. 'Ah been flappin' my jaws so long they ache.'

As Max turned to the Casners his right hip ached. 'What do you think, Hal and Sue? Wasn't this a good idea in the end?'

'I hope it's not too good an idea, Max,' Susan said mischievously. 'It might turn you into a billionaire – and then what would you do? You started out as such a nice man and you'd become a living, breathing policy failure!'

'I don't think there's any danger of that,' smiled Max.

Chapter 74

Max awoke before dawn on the morning of the funeral of Hugh Norton. He could hear the muted splash of small surf through the windows of his Bondi flat. It was the summer solstice. He listened to the silence, wondering what it would be like to hear the sound of Peggy's gentle breathing next to him. She was staying with Tori not far away in a hotel in Double Bay. For a community accustomed to the yearly dawn observance of ANZAC Day, mobilising for a funeral scheduled at dawn wasn't too onerous, and the Norton family was expecting a large crowd.

Max rose and dressed quickly in a white linen shirt and a pair of indigo jeans and left his apartment barefoot. He walked along Ramsgate Avenue in the darkness, listening to the sleepy songs of the earliest bronze wing pigeons and koels. No lovers lingered on apartment steps or against the sides of cars, no drunks were wandering home, and it was too early for dog walkers.

Max crossed Biddigal Reserve, where the air was slightly cooler and damp, making his way through deep shadows and the dim outlines of playground equipment. He descended the flights of stairs to the blackness of the beach, where the lamps along the esplanade cast the only light.

The crowd arriving shortly would include all his main opponents during the deal, along with many of their employees and allies, and Max knew he would soon be in the midst of many people who despised him and rejected everything he now stood for. Tens of thousands of people were grateful to him for the rescue of ZettaData, but for the most part they lived well to the north, west, and south of Bondi Beach.

He started walking across the sand towards South Bondi. After a hundred metres of gloom Max could discern the faint edges of small waves dimly reflecting the lights from town as they approached the beach.

Max felt wet sand under his feet and continued as the beach steepened until he reached the almost invisible waterline. Shadowy waves unfurled and washed his feet, nuzzling his ankles. The day he and Peggy first met on this beach the Bondi surf was much more powerful; Max remembered how it boomed during their conversation. The soft lapping sound in the darkness soothed him, and he watched spume appear in sudden white blossoms ahead.

Halfway down the beach, where it was darkest, Max stopped. He felt, more than saw, space yawning above him from horizon to horizon, and he looked up.

The heavy sea air of Bondi normally filters out most of the stars, but as Max stared up, he could see tens of thousands of lights. Arrayed above him were hosts and hosts of suns across millions of light years, august centres of energy in nebulae and galaxies unimaginably remote from one another, spiralling out in a sweep of incomprehensible mass and light and power. Ormsby's vision of order and harmony. According to Ormsby, the grander the order he was able to perceive, the bigger the meaning he could imagine. Max stared into the sky, awaiting insight, but there was no sign. No meaning appeared to Max in the darkness. Nothing. *Rien*.

He continued along the dark beach until he reached the boulders where Peggy and Juanita practiced their yoga what seemed like a lifetime ago, picking his way through the sand and the big rocks against the cliff face of South Bondi just visible in the street lights from Notts Avenue.

Standing unseen in the shadows of the cliff, Max saw the first arrivals for the funeral walking on the esplanade. The scattering of Hugh's ashes on the waves was intended to happen after daybreak. Max was too far away to recognise individuals, but they weren't walking dogs or jogging as they made their way slowly towards Bondi Pavilion. The purposeful walkers who would soon dominate the esplanade for the rest of the morning had yet to arrive.

Many of those attending the funeral would have seen *TransGod*, which was still running at Eden Street Theatre. Everybody in Sydney, it seemed, had seen it. Today's service would have been another relevant occasion for the spectacular main prop the reviewers and theatre-going public all loved so much, the flamboyant *memento mori*, reminder of death composed of metal birds. It was probably hovering in the consciousness of many of those arriving in the darkness at Bondi Beach.

Max turned and looked back up the beach. In the blackness, a line of indigo the width of a finger glowed along the horizon. The first light of the summer solstice. The skull flock had captured the imagination of Sydney, but what was the corresponding sign of life, the inspiring *memento vivere* – a reminder to live – and most importantly, a guide *how* to live?

Max watched as faint tones of sienna and umbre appeared in subtle layers above the line of deep blue light. Max turned away from the beginnings of dawn over the ocean and started walking resolutely across the dim sand towards the crowd. Hundreds of people, lit only by the lights from Bondi Pavilion and the lamps along the Esplanade, filtered down the ramps and stairs to the sand in front of the Pavilion.

Soon it became possible to make out shadows and silhouettes of people he knew. Directly in his path, on the perimeter of the crowd a few metres ahead, stood Richard Wander. He was in quiet conversation with several men Max didn't recognise in the dim light. Elegantly dressed in a black linen shirt and grey trousers, Wander smiled sardonically when he spotted Max emerging out of the gloom.

'Ah – gentlemen, allow me to present the bloke who resurrected ZettaData,' said Wander as Max walked up. 'Too bad he used his powers on a company that should have stayed dead.'

'We'll see, won't we, Richard?' said Max. The guy on Wander's left, Max recognised, was one of the Deputy Chairs of ASIC.

'Can we expect another demonstration of your power this morning?' Wander grinned.

The large bald man standing at Wander's other elbow chuckled appreciatively. He was Managing Director of one of the largest insurance companies in Australia.

'Max Ring.' Turning to Wander's friends he shook hands with the three men, recognising the name of the third man as that of a well-known Special Counsel.

Max and Wander sized each other up.

'Save your tricks for the next Norton funeral – it would be such a pity to revive the wrong one twice,' Wander said. 'Maybe just walk on water this morning.'

'Haha,' chortled the insurance man.

'See you around, Richard,' Max said.

He continued into the crowd, nodding and smiling on the rare occasions he was greeted, looking for Ilona and the girls, or Peggy and Tori.

As he made his way through the throngs of people, Max suddenly realised it was exactly Wander's jokes that proved Ilona wrong. At St Vincent's she had almost convinced him Mort's lies would prevail forever. But Wander's mocking comments proved he recognised, and simultaneously rejected, the truth. Wander was admitting what Max had accomplished. The storm of abuse for months on social media and in the press was also an ironic form of homage. The crown of thorns pressed down onto the head of their prisoner

Yeshua by the Roman soldiers tormenting him was both a torture and acknowledgement that Yeshua was widely considered a King.

Mockery is an incandescent filament illuminating the truth, a form of energy generated by the two poles of recognition and rejection. The Classical Greeks adorned the mathematical perfection of their temples by affixing their gods to the prosceniums. Using holes drilled unobtrusively into the hands and feet of the statues, the Greeks fastened them into place with pegs.

Pontius Pilate inadvertently produced the greatest epiphany of all time when he sentenced Yeshua to be nailed by his hands and feet to a cross in a parody of the way Greek gods were displayed on the Parthenon. An execution intended to maximise the humiliation and agony of its victim became a fusion of the Greek vision of gods in human form with a thousand years of mysterious Hebrew poetry prophesying the coming of a Holy One. The mocking display of the suffering body of Yeshua, hanging from a cross in a parody of the way Greek and Roman gods were affixed to temples, was elevated to a cosmic revelation of the God-man at the precise location where Heaven and Earth meet: on the vertical and horizontal axes of the eternal nexus of space and time.

There must have been over a thousand people on the sand, with more and more people descending the ramps and staircases as Max quickened his pace, now looking urgently for his daughters and Peggy. He passed Rupert Campbell without stopping while Campbell looked contemptuously at him from the middle of his group of hangers-on.

As Max moved away, he heard their voices behind him:

'Yeah – Max Ring.'

'Oh, *that's* the arsehole ...'

'The greatest fool ...'

'Haha.'

' ... of them all.'

'Lol!'

Max realised he didn't have any chance of winning Arjuna's way in the *Bhagavad-Gita* – not with these people, not this morning. The Eastern Suburbs elite didn't care about his position as CEO of ZettaData, and to Wander, Campbell and their friends what remained of his net worth was a mere heap of scraps, pathetic, utterly trivial. The detritus of a loser.

He was now in a part of the crowd where beautiful young people were everywhere, hundreds of young professionals working at the investment banks, funds managers, brokerage houses, law firms and banks owned or managed by Mort's allies. Max couldn't see them very well in the dim light, but he could smell their coffee. For the most part the young people seemed to be distracting themselves by joking quietly, preening or attending to their young children.

As he passed through their midst, Max started to hear murmured comments.

'That's Max Ring.'

'Who?'

'You know, the guy who –'

'Oh!'

Low laughter swelled from several sides.

The odour of cherry tobacco smoke wafted through the air and through an opening in the crowd Max saw Kent Logan, wearing a silk shirt, something he might sport playing poker in a Vegas casino. Logan stood with his wife, five or six of his adult children with their spouses and children, half-a-dozen of his mates, and two longtime bodyguards. The Logans and their entourage were here in force to honour the Nortons.

''lo, Max,' Logan said, squinting through the smoke.

'Hello, Kent.'

Logan didn't introduce Max, he just took him by the arm and walked him a few steps away from the rest. 'Listen, son, I've been thinking,' Logan said in a low voice. 'People don't invent their gods. Forget that hit play at the theatre—it's not right. What happens is, people murder someone – and then afterwards they deify their victim.'

'Ok,' said Max.

'That's your opportunity.'

'Thanks, Kent.'

'No worries, son.' Logan gave him a pat on the shoulder and Max moved on.

Making his way through the throng, Max came upon a contingent from Byron Bay, guessing from their sun-bleached hair, faded t-shirts, and boardie shorts, which was confirmed when Max spotted Charlie, George and Bobby. He hurried over and embraced each of them. There was no need for words.

At last, just beyond the heads and shoulders of the people in front of him, Max sensed who he'd been looking for, and in an instant somehow he already knew he'd find everybody together. Mort and Ilona stood with their daughters in the centre of a circle of people. Around them stood the Trebuchets, the Haddads, and the Levins. Tori stood on one side, cushioned from Mort by the family friends.

All eyes watched Max approach but he focused on the girls: Sam and the Norton girls looked numb, their faces blank, and Billie looked stricken.

Sam and Billie hadn't known Hugh, but were shocked and grief-stricken by the death of the seemingly indomitable Alexandra, whom they adored. Max had already spent hours consoling Sam and Billie, and also urging them to support Trixie and Anastasia.

'Oh, Billie,' Max said, sympathetically, and stretched out his arms.

Billie released her mother's and sister's hands and ran towards her father.

'Oh Daddy,' Billie wept as he picked her up and hugged her. 'It's all so awful!'

Max had heard plenty of conversations as he walked through the crowd about frequent flyer miles, private school fees, real estate, and the next election. The young Ring and Norton daughters were facing the tragedy directly – and with more honesty and maturity than most of the adults Max had passed.

'Yes, it is sad,' Max said. 'That's the truth.'

'It's death!' Billie buried her face in his neck. 'Death is so awful.'

'We're born to die,' grunted Mort.

Max closed his eyes and focused on Billie.

'It's just like falling asleep, darling,' said Ilona brightly. It sounded like a reminder, something she'd been telling the girls repeatedly.

Max hugged Billie, saying nothing.

'It's nothing to be afraid of, Alexandra – and Hugh – are fine,' Ilona continued. 'They're nowhere now. Nothing. They live in our hearts.'

Max opened his eyes and looked at the blank expressions of the other three girls. He felt Billie shifting in his arms, too. He gently brushed away the tears on Billie's cheeks, kissed her cheeks, and set her down on the sand. Only then did he notice Peggy had just arrived, and was standing a little behind her father and half-sisters.

'Billie dear, if I had to step in front of a bus to save you or Sammie, I'd do it,' Max said. He pointed to Mort and Ilona. 'I'm sure your mum would, too – and so would Mort, for Trixie and Anastasia. Death can't be such a terrible thing, if parents are willing to die for their children.'

'What about being dead?' Billie said, sniffling.

Max shrugged. 'I don't think fathers and mothers who die for their children end up in a bad place, so it must be ok to be dead. The worst thing is being separated from those we love, because we miss them so much.'

All four girls started to cry, it sounded like it might be with relief.

Ilona looked reproachfully at Max as Peggy stepped into the group.

'Peggy!' Trixie and Anastasia hugged Peggy and the Rings girls joined their hug. When the four girls released Peggy, Ilona and Mort reached out to their daughters, enfolding them in their arms. Max walked over, gave Peggy a hug, and kissed her cheeks.

'Hello, Ilona,' Max said quietly. Mort ignored them as they exchanged kisses.

Mort looked jowly and drawn. He seemed to have lost weight in the last couple weeks, and even his hair seemed thinner.

'Mort,' Max nodded.

Mort looked at him. 'Max,' he said at last.

'There must be three thousand people here,' said Trebuchet.

'Cor – you think so?' said Haddad.

Trebuchet nodded judiciously. As a former Prime Minister, he knew how to count crowds. 'I reckon,' he said.

'This is almost as big as ANZAC Day,' Haddad said as Mort straightened up. 'I hope you're permitted for that many people.'

Mort wore a crisp white shirt – the same colour as Max's but a hand-made cotton business shirt with long, pointed collar tips, grey worsted wool trousers, and hand-made English leather shoes. Still attempting to conform to Alexandra's taste. 'Nuh, we were expecting about five hundred people, and the permit allows a thousand – but so fucking what?'

Alexandra would, Max knew, have come up with something very different for Mort this morning – clothes and shoes that were elegant yet appropriate to wear to a beach ceremony.

'Exactly,' chuckled Trebuchet.

Ilona was wearing jodhpurs this morning – as Alexandra so often did – a light grey cashmere jumper and underneath Alexandra's trademark silk blouse with two buttons undone, and finally, sunglasses on the top of her head in preparation for the glare that would follow sunrise. She had her hand on Mort's shoulder.

Suddenly Max understood Mort and Ilona were on their way to becoming a couple.

If Ilona and Mort got together he'd have no choice but to fight for custody of their daughters. Max felt nauseated at the thought of ghastly joint Norton-Ring family occasions in the years ahead: Christmas, Australia Day, school concerts, graduations, weddings and, eventually, funerals.

'Let's go find your mum,' Max said to Peggy. It was now the luminous grey before sunrise and he could see Peggy's eyes clearly.

Tori had moved fifty metres away and was standing in a relatively empty patch of sand speaking with the celebrant, a handsome woman with short, iron-grey hair wearing a red Chinese jacket. The celebrant's team of twenty or so ushers stood in a circle listening to final instructions.

'It's time, my darling,' Tori said to Peggy. The ushers fanned out through the crowd asking people to begin moving in the pre-dawn dimness towards the ocean.

Max and Peggy crossed the beach together, holding hands. Peggy accepted many hurried kisses and sympathetic hands on her shoulders that slipped off as they walked by.

'Max, I heard what you said to the girls,' said Peggy. 'It's good for them to cry. They've been so shut down and that's how the road begins, the one I went down.'

Max smiled.

He could easily imagine a joyful life with Peggy – surfing, yoga – and possibly even children.

For the last twenty metres Max and Peggy made their way towards the water's edge through a dense tangle of people. At last they reached the ocean, their feet bathed in small, warm waves. Max and Peggy glanced over their shoulders as the crowd parted and Tori walked down the wet sand carrying the urn with Hugh's ashes, Mort beside her.

Two of Tori's friends from Byron carried a pole with a hot brazier glowing with coals. Two others walked behind the brazier, their arms full of white lotus flowers. The smell of hot metal from the brazier, full of glowing coals, mingled with the sea breeze. A luminous blue was mounting into the eastern sky.

Tori, Mort and their attending friends splashed quietly into the gentle, shadowy waves skimming up the sand, until they reached the southern end of the beach, close to where Peggy and Juanita performed yoga most mornings, and where Max had been standing in the darkness an hour ago. Max watched the clouds beginning to glow like alabaster, and the sky was pale yellow, peach, and subtle green.

Max suddenly knew what the *memento vivere* was – with its reminder not just to live, but how to live.

Yeshua was immobilised and utterly helpless, hardly able to move his limbs as he died, his hands and feet nailed to a cross. Max realised he didn't have to be a majority shareholder and CEO to make a difference in the lives of others and benefit his community. He could serve others in weakness, even in rejection. If he was true to who he was, appearances don't count. *Esse Quam Videri*—regardless of the cost.

The celebrant came forward and stood in front of the lead mourners between the vast crowd and the sea. She led the crowd in khirtan chanting as well as sacred Vedic funeral chants. She signalled for Tori and Mort to drop white petals onto the red coals in the brazier. Max watched as the petals floated down and blackened, shrivelling and twisting, lying flat and flaring up at random.

Sunrise was only minutes away.

The celebrant nodded to Tori and Mort, who held the urn with Hugh's ashes, but Max couldn't hear what she was saying and he felt himself being drawn away from the ceremony.

One of the most important people he had met on his quest for ZettaData was young Lachlan Casner, almost immobile as well as unable to speak, but with eyes full of peace and love. It was only his pride, Max realised, that had made him unwilling to serve others, except in certain ways. It was hard to accept, now that he was almost healthy again, and on his way back to wealth and influence, that he might be made perfect in weakness.

Emptiness is form, form is emptiness. The nothing that is. Everybody – no matter how old, sick, disabled or limited – has the power to help others.

The celebrant looked down at a paper she was holding and read something as the breeze ruffled her short, iron-grey hair.

'I am not there ...' she read. 'I do not sleep ... I am a thousand winds that blow –'

'I do not sleep ...'

'I am the diamond glints on snow ... I am the sunlight on ripened grain ...'

The words being recited seemed weak and insipid. A restatement of the obvious in poetry that compared poorly to Euripides.

The celebrant's words were snatched away on the breeze that stirs over the water just before sunrise, and Max could hear nothing else of the litany with which Hugh was being committed to sea and sky.

Instead, the words of the *Bhagavad-Gita* appeared vividly to him:

> As moths with exceeding speed pass into a
> lighted fire to perish,
> So pass the worlds with exceeding speed into
> Thy mouths to perish.

Thou devourest and lickest up all the worlds
around with flaming mouths;
filling the whole universe with radiance.
Grim glow Thy splendours, O Vishnu!

The worlds streaming into Vishnu's mouths were a host vaster than the zettas of stars in the universe. Max inhaled a long, deep breath and felt the fierce, pure truth becoming incandescent in him.

He looked up the beach and saw the sand glowing.

The celebrant beckoned Mort to step forward. Mort moved slowly, awkwardly, through the shallow water holding the urn with his son's ashes. Ilona stood on the beach holding his shoes. Mort hadn't rolled up his trousers before he walked into the quiet surf and soaked fabric clung to his legs.

Mort removed the top from the urn. A pearly light suffused the beach and after a few moments the breeze began to carry away Hugh's ashes in thin plumes.

The celebrant nodded to Tori and beckoned her to step forward. Tori bowed her head and remained motionless for a few moments and then stepped into the water. She raised her head, her cheeks wet with tears, and the celebrant beckoned again, smiling, saying something to her. The breeze strengthened and the brightening sky made every detail, every gesture, perfectly visible. Tori seemed surrounded by the glow from the horizon.

Tori raised the urn, tipping it into the breeze, and ashes streamed out over the water, whirling away in the wind. Tori gazed out, perhaps hoping to see one or two motes still dancing on the breeze. She turned and walked back through the water up to the crowd on the beach.

Max kissed Peggy on the nape of her neck. 'I'll be back soon,' he said and made his way through the crowd along the waterline.

People were walking, singly and in twos and threes, down the beach as Max walked north, and several joggers trotted through the wet sand.

Normally, the sight of relaxed people enjoying the beach was welcome. This morning, however, the people moving towards him looked like the dead making their way towards the next world. A middle-aged couple, victims in a car accident. A jogger in his early forties, felled by a heart attack, and like Max himself a few months ago, unable to shed his compulsion to compete as he trotted just a little faster than the other souls towards eternity.

Max's stride slowed almost to a halt as he was approached and then passed by the closest walkers. He noted the healthy colour of their skin and their vivid eyes. The sound of conversation and low laughter comforted him as he walked, all the variety of the David Jones fragrance counter wafting to him as they passed.

The sun was rising behind the sea, beneath great thunderclouds on the horizon, with an alarming increase in the intensity of light. Just as an inner glow seemed to have faded from the air, leaving the day to develop a uniform brightness bereft of mystery, the imminent appearance of the sun beneath the lordly clouds began to transform the sky.

Along the horizon, the tops of the thunderheads facing the point where the sun was about to rise flared into molten gold. A fan–like burst of rays shot tens of thousands of feet into the air, transfixing vapour floating above the thunderheads. A line of light insinuated above the sea and resolved into the arc of the sun. The great clouds reflected its light from their heights like ancient prophets whose words had suddenly been fulfilled in their inner meaning, and a great, turbulent blinding glory overcame Max's eyes as the sun rose above the sea.

When he could look up, Max stood staring at the sunrise, his mouth agape, his eyes wide. A long shining road had appeared in the sea between the risen sun and the spot where he stood on the beach. A wave carried the road's final length rushing up the sand and onto his feet, bathing them in the shimmering path to the sun. Max understood that every member of the funeral crowd, every human on the beach, every bird flying in the bright morning air, every dog and dog owner walking along the esplanade, would see their own dancing path of light – if they only looked. A great aching constricted his chest.

Max fell to his knees. He raised his hands, at first protectively against the sunshine and then, slowly, he turned his palms up as if to cup the shining abundance pouring onto them.

Here I am.

Max felt shaky, shakier than he'd ever felt in his life, even than when he'd crawled ashore at The Gap. He settled from his knees onto the wet sand, where he sat gazing at the sunlight play on the gleaming water. Waves soaked his jeans as he watched the dancing light on the ocean, but he didn't notice.

The shore breeze shifted out over the ocean like a breath.

'Max.'

He felt a hand on his shoulder and looked up at Peggy.

'What happened to you?'

Max's jeans were caked with sand, his linen shirt so wet it was mostly transparent. Dried salt spotted his face where sea foam had splashed the crown of his head. Max smiled and stood up, taking Peggy's hand, and they started across the beach.

A breeze surrounded Max and Peggy as they walked, drying the grains of sand on his jeans. As they crossed Bondi Beach, galaxies showered from Max with every step.

Acknowledgments

My undying gratitude for their decisive roles in the creation of *A Prince Among Men* and endless thanks to: Bryan Lourd; this is not the place to describe our life-long friendship but I'm a very different and far better person for being gifted by Bryan's friendship, and nothing like *A Prince Among Men* in its current form would ever have seen the light of day without Bryan; Dan Barnes, true friend through thick and thin during the tumultuous passages of our lives, generous, kind, wise, always caring and with nerves of steel; Zephyr Bloch-Jorgensen, trusted friend, brother, adviser, free diver and fellow traveller on the Quest; Bryan Skarlatos, a careful reader of early drafts, trusted counselor and an exceptionally generous friend, Jill Wran, first reader of *Prince*, wise and generous friend, lover of life, and deeply insightful and judicious literary expert; my brother Tony Dennison, lover of truth; Joyce Zaorski Flinn, friend and exceptionally careful and insightful reader of many drafts of *Prince*; Tony Sernack, friend, photographer and a man with the panache to straddle business and creative pursuits all his life; Arlene Tansey, friend and colleague, adviser and confidante; Aris Janigian, my friend and brother, a robust and inspiring example of a man leading the life of the mind and the life of action; my friend and editor David Groff, patient, insightful, gracious and tolerant; Tracy Van Dolder, my awesome cover designer and a talented writer in her own right and a wonderful and inspiring person, and my copy editor Debbie Watson, conscientious and understanding.

Special thanks to Susan Barnes, Elena Karabatos, Peggy Dwyer, Harriet Wran, Rick Holton, Lindsay Brdlick Viering, Peter Semmler, Anthony Marich, Andy Lukas, Lisa Stiepock, Michael O'Donovan and in gratitude for the lives of Saint Chin and Craig Chin.

Also By Chris Coffman

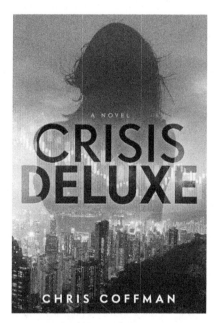

CRISIS DELUXE
AN AMAZON #1 RANKED NOVEL

Would you help millions if it cost you the woman you love?

An absorbing and sophisticated psychological novel set in the ceaseless action of global financial markets. Investment banker Alexander "Dusty" Street flies to Hong Kong for an emergency of global proportions. His mission: to calm Asian financial markets by completing a huge, troubled deal foundering in the early stages of a financial crisis. As he focuses on forging a deal, Dusty must also soothe his unhappy wife and children in New York.

Then the love of his life reappears in Hong Kong.

The beautiful Jaqueline Nin, whom Dusty hasn't seen in decades, is also married and now has a daughter. She and Dusty quickly confirm their original feelings, but seems at first like Dusty's dream come true presents him with the most painful dilemma of his life. In this entertaining and multi-layered novel, Dusty discovers for himself the meaning of true love. Dusty faces these complexities in a richly imagined Hong Kong just before the Communist takeover, and is forced to come to terms honestly with his past as he searches for a way to overcome the destructive forces engulfing his life, his career, and all of Asia in the worst financial crisis of a generation.

An absorbing, sophisticated literary novel this is both elegant and compulsively readable, *Crisis Deluxe* builds to a beautiful and unexpected climax.

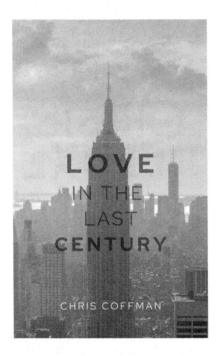

LOVE IN THE LAST CENTURY

The stories in this collection were written starting in the 1980s and through the late 1990s. They span the last part of the twentieth century from the late 1970s until just before the beginning of the new millennium. They could be called, following William Blake, songs of innocence and songs of experience.

The first story "Air and Angels" is about a group of young New Yorkers traveling in the Mediterranean who accidentally discover a nudist beach on the island of Corfu.

"Tropisms of an Imaginary Love" finds a young man attempting to deal with both his best friend's suicide and a powerful attraction to his beautiful girlfriend. "Breakfast at the Cosmic" follows an unusual New York friendship: two men meet every weekend for breakfast at a Greek diner in Manhattan as one man begins his rise to worldly glory. The story "Trading in Tender Parts" unfolds late one night in the East Village, during the years when it was still a very dangerous district in the New York, as a cynical and dispirited young man and a bold young woman negotiate who determines the way the night works out. "Mr. Jones and Me" is about a young banker and his powerful boss, a model for who the young man might become, in more ways than he wants to think about. "The Shock of Men" describes a reunion between a couple who try to understand the meaning of their mutual attraction in the context of each other's self-centered behavior. "When Most Away" follows a young man back to a meeting with the great love of his life, a relationship destroyed by his racist family, as he struggles with the psychological burden of his heritage. The eighth and last story "Lord of Hosts" ends the way the first story began, on a remote beach, as a late middle-aged couple from New York, contentedly married for decades, vacation on-shore of the Great Barrier Reef in Australia.

About the Author

Chris Coffman was born at West Point, New York and lived most of his life outside the United States until returning several years ago to live in Eastern Pennsylvania.

In addition to his novels, short stories and articles Chris worked for decades in Europe, the UK, the United States, Latin America, Asia and Australia as an investment banker and investor before founding Eden Road Wines, a highly-awarded wine company in Australia.

A Phi Beta Kappa, Magna cum Laude graduate of the University of Southern California, he attended Columbia University before beginning his financial career at Manufacturers Hanover Trust, which later merged with J.P. Morgan.

He now lives on a rural property just over an hour from New York City.

Made in the USA
Las Vegas, NV
01 September 2022

54547188R00256